THE FOREST CAVALIER

ROY FLANNAGAN *is the author of*

THE WHIPPING

AMBER SATYR

COUNTY COURT

The FOREST CAVALIER

A ROMANCE OF
AMERICA'S FIRST FRONTIER
AND OF
BACON'S REBELLION

by Roy Flannagan

SEARS READERS CLUB · CHICAGO

This is a special edition published exclusively for the members of SEARS READERS CLUB, P.O. Box 6570A, Chicago 80, Illinois. It was originally published by The Bobbs-Merrill Company, Inc.

To
PAT AND ROY, JR.

CONTENTS

I

Virginia Voyage

◈ 1

LAUNCELOT CLAYBORNE was a page of Catherine of Braganza, neglected queen of Charles II, when the misfortune of his uncle, Walter Clayborne, in 1665, took the lad far away to America. Lance's widowed father, Sir Mathew, at that time an equerry at Whitehall, was glad enough for an excuse to leave the perfumed atmosphere of the Stuart court.

Lance's education for two years had been in the hands of Queen Catherine's Portuguese monks and certain merry and secretly dissolute ladies in waiting. His father feared that the boy might become a popinjay with foreign manners. The monks disciplined the lad with a Moroccan leather strap, but they taught him too much Latin for the welfare of a Protestant scion, and the pretty ladies in waiting petted him too earnestly for the good of a boy who, on the threshold of adolescence, was becoming curious about the peculiarities of womanhood.

When Lance objected bitterly to his father's decision to make the long voyage across the western ocean, Sir Mathew explained that Walter Clayborne had been murdered in mysterious circumstances and that justice, no less than fortune, demanded their presence in Virginia. Sir Mathew was sole heir to Walter's rich property in the plantations.

"So find your stoutest boots, Sir Milksop," commanded his father. "We go whether you like it or not."

◈ 2

FOR years Walter Clayborne had written frequently to his soldier brother, and Sir Mathew, entirely dependent on the scanty bounty of an impoverished court, had frequently been tempted to leave London and join him.

11

Walter had done well in the dominion across the sea. A natural husbandman in spite of his gentle birth, he had acquired cleared land near Jamestown and had built a considerable fortune from tobacco, maize and cattle.

He prospered until one day he took under his roof a woman named Henrietta Hart, widow of a downriver farmer. Sir Mathew noticed a change in the tone of his correspondence after that and for the first time suffered forebodings over the future of his younger brother. It was strange for Walter, long a sturdy bachelor, to fall under any woman's spell. . . .

It had happened that Walter Clayborne needed a new housekeeper because fever had carried away old Dame Gaskins, whom he had brought from England ten years before. He made inquiry, therefore, and—not without difficulty, because women were not plentiful in the colony—he located the Hart woman.

There were tales about her. Gossips at Jamestown said that her elderly husband had died not from cypress fever but from too much nighttime exercise, but it was agreed that Henrietta Hart was a competent house manager. She soon proved it at Clayborne Castle.

Walter Clayborne called his brick H-shaped house on the bluff above Council Point a castle not in vanity but as a warning to the river pirates who not infrequently raided the farms along the James. He wanted the pirates to know that it was fortified so they would let him alone. He had mounted two swivel guns which covered his boat landing and could throw shot halfway across James River, and his house servants were trained to arms.

The manor smelled of rats, saddles and wet fur when Henrietta Hart moved in and put new life into the Clayborne servants. Shortly thereafter the place was as clean as the poop deck of a King's ship. Even the brass swivel guns on the tower of the palisado were polished brightly when Walter Clayborne returned from a trip to Jamestown.

Those guns caught the master's eye at once. He had expected the new housekeeper to make some progress against the rats and bedbugs. The repairs to the fireplace and hearth of the main hall were not out of the ordinary. The fresh sanding of the floors and a cleaning of the deerskin hangings at the windows were improvements of the usual kind. But the polishing of those guns was something that would have occurred to only one housekeeper in a thousand.

Walter called the woman in to commend her.

Henrietta Hart appeared in her working apron and cap. With her eyes downcast as though she expected a reproof she curtsied respectfully and stood trembling like a nervous pony.

"Mistress Hart," said Walter, "you deserve gold or land for the manner in which you have cleansed this Augean stable of mine. Your wages are not enough." He lifted a purse from the table and dropped it with a clink. "These doubloons or fifty acres?"

Henrietta looked up at him timidly. She had darkened her brows with charcoal, and she had used small touches of goose fat to separate her long eyelashes. In the glow of the fire her eyes were like jewels. Long since, Walter had lost all knowledge of cosmetic tricks. He observed only that this supposed drudge whom he had employed, this new housekeeper, was a beautiful young woman.

"I am content, sir," said Henrietta demurely. "Gold coin is scarce. Pray keep it. I need no gold, and I need no land if you will permit me to serve you here."

Walter was dumfounded.

"I am happy here, sir."

He rose and paced the hearth. He could not take his eyes from the woman. The hands folded at her waist were not those of a drudge. They were long and white and smooth. Above her lovely, swarthy, baffling face was clean, lustrously black hair just unruly enough to make charming curls around her neck. And there was shape to her. Beneath the formless apron he could see graceful lines.

"Gold it shall be, Mistress Hart," said Walter at last. "Ten Spanish doubloons a year in addition to your wages. And if you'll stay here, by God, I'll put you in my will!"

"Oh!" cried Henrietta. "Oh!" And she burst into tears. With great sobs of gratitude she fled from the room.

Not long thereafter Walter Clayborne again had occasion to observe that his housekeeper was a treasure. Cato, his body servant, was away that night, a sufferer from boils, and Henrietta came into Walter's room, charcoal pan in hand, to turn down the sheets and warm them.

He was already abed, reading his nightly chapter from Livy.

Showing shocked surprise and embarrassment at finding him in the chamber, she dropped the charcoal warmer on the hearth and started to flee.

"Henrietta!"

His sharp command made her freeze at the threshold like a startled hare. It was the first time he ever had used her given name.

Then, under his commanding eyes, like a linnet charmed by an adder, she glided slowly toward the great bed.

He took her hand gently and kissed it, back and palm. "You came to warm my bed, Henrietta," he said—and blew out the candle.

⌬ 3

THEREAFTER Henrietta Hart sang at her work and Walter Clayborne was a younger, gayer man. Clayborne Castle became a house of many parties and rich hospitality because of Henrietta's skill in managing the cooks.

The woman's charm increased. Her candor in reciting episodes of her drab life in London enhanced rather than diminished her attractiveness.

Born of an Irish actress, she had been reared in an impoverished nunnery near the Tower, she told him. At fifteen she ran away to become a kitchenmaid in the household of the Duke of Norfolk, and there she had been seduced by a jolly meat cook. Driven out by the man's not so jolly wife, she had become, in turn, the mistress of two students, a barrister, a leather merchant, a rich, stingy draper and a young nobleman from Languedoc who was in London with an ambassador from France. Her French lover, when he returned home, gave her a coach and four gray horses, the proceeds from which made her a lady for nearly a year.

"But I had a weakness, sir." Henrietta sighed with mock mournfulness. "I had a weakness for men. This time it was a lieutenant of the guards, a young baron who gambled away his substance—and mine. It was then that I got drunk. . . ."

She landed in a London gutter, as scrawny and as scrofulous as an alley cat.

Here the East End snatchers found her and sold her to a sea captain. The shipmaster brought her to Virginia and indentured her to a farmer, Roderick Hart.

Hart was a God-fearing, righteous widower who, had he known the ragged, feverish waif's history, would never have brought her into his household. To him she was at first but a cooking woman and a scullery hand. But soon Henrietta recovered from the voyage and began to bloom.

Old enough to be her father, Roderick Hart scourged his flesh by working fifteen hours a day among his black field hands. He read St. Paul until his eyes blurred. Sweating, cursing himself for his weakness, he prayed for hours on end for the power to resist the handsome witch who could cook a venison stew that tasted like pagan ambrosia. It was to no avail. Henrietta put him down one day in a maize field, and to salve his conscience he promptly discharged her indenture and married her.

"That's all," said Henrietta in her naïve confession to Walter Clayborne. "I was a model wife. I practiced none of my London tricks on Roderick. He died of the fever and left me his farm and three feather beds. It is on the river below Jamestown. I was planning to open a tavern there when you employed me."

"Your London tricks?" asked Walter.

Henrietta laughed. "I was a bad girl, Master Clayborne," she explained. "You would learn them perhaps?"

"Away with you!" Walter said, and to Henrietta's delight he blushed.

4

WALTER wrote Sir Mathew in detail of his new happiness.

You should come to Virginia, Mathew, and bring your fine boy. It is an enormous land. You could drop all England into the forest here and lose it like a pebble in a horse pond. The woods, indeed, are like a sea. To traverse them requires a special skill like that of a navigator. And like the western ocean, the forest is peopled with mysterious monsters whose nature no man has yet learned. There are lions as large as those of Numidia, bears so mighty that they can kill a pony with one blow, wolves more ferocious than those of the darkest portions of Germany. The beasts are more numerous and dangerous than are the savage inhabitants.

We hear dark tales of Whitehall, and it disturbs me that your fine son, my nephew, is being reared, motherless, by priests of the foreign Queen's company. You should bring him here, Mathew, where the air is free of evil. . . .

Free of evil indeed! Sir Mathew had snorted at this in view of Walter's admission that he had taken as his mistress an admitted fugitive from a London gutter. Mathew concluded at the time that there would soon be a serpent in his brother's Eden. And so it happened, as he was to learn later.

Sir Mathew's next communication from Virginia was a letter from Colonel Philip Ludwell informing him that Walter's body, thrust through with a tuck-sword, had been found behind the cobbler's cottage at Jamestown. Ludwell, a member of Governor William Berkeley's Council, advised Sir Mathew's presence without delay.

৶§ 5

KING CHARLES received Sir Mathew Clayborne in his bedchamber. The monarch, still in his yellow silk bedgown, was seated in a long French chair with a kitten in his lap.

"How now, old war horse!" said the King. "What brings you to me with such urgency?"

"A mission of justice, sire," Sir Mathew replied. "My brother Walter has been murdered in Virginia."

Charles sat up. The kitten ran, spitting, to hide beneath the bed. "Murdered!"

"Aye, sire. Permission is requested to visit Virginia and to investigate this matter."

"God Almighty, man. What do you expect to do?"

"Find the murderer, Your Majesty."

"But is there no law in that infernal land but that you should go out, sword in hand?"

"Furthermore," explained Sir Mathew, "I am my brother's sole heir, and he has extensive lands in the colony."

King Charles thumbed his chin as though reluctant to give consent. As a matter of fact the gay monarch was not sorry to see the old Cavalier depart. Such grim old soldiers reminded him of his martyred father and of the rough campaigns and long Scottish sermons that had preceded the Restoration. Charles had kept Sir Mathew at Whitehall in gratitude, but God knew he was the clumsiest courtier who ever bent a knee.

"I am losing too many of my old warriors," growled Charles. "But go if you must, Colonel Clayborne. Go with my blessing—and remember me."

Sir Mathew bowed over the jeweled hand extended by the King.

Within the month arrangements for the voyage had been made. Sir Mathew engaged passage on the *Saucy Mary,* Captain William Carver, master, purchased special provisions for their comfort and found a tutor for his son, one David Broome, a young Oxonian ex-parson.

Lance bade a heart-breaking farewell to the Queen and her ladies, made faces at the Portuguese monks as he received their blessings and reluctantly followed his straight-backed father.

~§ 6

BUT before the *Saucy Mary* cleared Fastnet Rock Lance had forgotten his sorrows and, clad in canvas breeks and smock from the captain's slop chest, he was well on the way to becoming a proper sailor.

Lance forever remembered many things about this voyage through the icebergs of the western ocean.

Daily his father had him at exercise with the foils, and daily there were two dull hours with David Broome, the tutor. Broome found the boy well schooled in Latin but weak in English and penmanship.

Lance liked his homesick tutor better than any of the Queen's monks, but for the time he was more interested in the sailors who worked the fat-bellied little ship. Captain Carver, a serious young man with many smile wrinkles around his eyes, was patient with the lad and taught him to box the compass and read the symbols on the charts.

Nick Jump, the quartermaster, also became a friend. After watching Sir Mathew and the boy at fence, Jump got out a shiny cutlass and showed them some sailor strokes, including the famous parry of the Duke of York.

Broome nagged at Lance for his too great familiarity with the crew. "On shipboard one should learn some seamanship as well as Euclid," Lance replied. "My father says that every Englishman should know his ropes."

Whereupon the tutor waved a ruler and vowed he would spank some knowledge through his pupil's buttocks. At this Lance, respectful of superior force, sat his threatened part down on the bench and picked up his book.

Lance also admired a fellow passenger on the Virginia voyage, Roger Kendall. The man had lived in Virginia since the first year of Cromwell's protectorate. His face seemed fleshless, and his skin was sallow from the fevers of the wilderness, but there was courage in his eyes. Kendall was accompanied by a bonded servant, Ned Peo, also a colonial of many years' experience. Peo wore leather clothing of strange cut, and he had many wild stories to tell of red Indians and the Dutch attacks on shipping in the James River.

The voyage was less interesting to Sir Mathew. He was a cavalryman and, unlike his former general, Prince Rupert, he hated oceans. And every league they logged toward Virginia made him more homesick for England. He had served fifteen years with Charles I, had fought Roundheads at Edge Hill, Nantwich, Marston Moor and Naseby. He had had six wounds of body and many more of soul before the Restoration brightened the skies of Britain.

Widowed by the Plague, the veteran had gamed away his estate in Kent. Thereafter, dependent on the King's bounty for a livelihood, he had chafed among the mincing sycophants at Whitehall and had looked with sad disfavor on the childish excesses of his pleasure-loving King. Still he loved England, every stick and stone of that green and lovely war-torn land.

Sir Mathew helped Captain Carver drill the crew against danger from the coastal pirates, played piquet with Roger Kendall and read the books he had brought along.

One night Sir Mathew had Kendall in to dinner in his cabin, and Lance heard them talk for hours about Virginia and Walter Clayborne. Kendall had known the younger Clayborne well, but he was hesitant to repeat gossip from the river plantations.

Sir Mathew was insistent. He wanted to know more of Walter's mistress, Henrietta Hart. "The woman was responsible, I suppose?" he asked.

"She is not a bad woman," Kendall insisted. "She is reckless perhaps. But she could never knowingly have betrayed your brother. She was devoted to Major Clayborne. So were we all."

"Who were his enemies?" Sir Mathew asked.

"I know of none," vowed Kendall.

"His friends?"

Kendall named a hundred, from Governor William Berkeley down. He could not suspect a single one, he said.

Sir Mathew frowned and then asked other questions about Virginia.

Clayborne Castle, said Kendall, was the stoutest house upriver from Jamestown and, unlike most colonial seats, it had many of the comforts of an English country place. There were thirty bondsmen, some of them Welsh metal workers who fabricated hinges and nails that Walter had sold at great profit to the settlers.

"Tobacco is currency in Virginia, sir," Kendall explained, "but so are nails. A long nail goes for a farthing. Small coins are so scarce I am taking back with me a keg of copper pieces from London."

Kendall warned Sir Mathew that the fevers and gripes suffered in Virginia were deadlier than the diseases of Flanders. He advised him to keep on hand a considerable store of Peruvian bark and to save some of his best brandy.

One day they saw a haze to westward. Captain Carver went aloft with his strongest glass. They were nearing the coast, he reported. Forty-eight hours later there was the glad cry: "Land ho!"

Lance ran to tell his father. He found him playing at dice with Roger Kendall in the roundhouse.

"Virginia!" cried the boy. "We can see Virginia!"

Sir Mathew took the ten-year-old on his knee and intently watched the board as Kendall, mindless of the news, clumsily made his cast. It was a two and one.

Sir Mathew smiled. "It is Peo, then?" he asked his opponent.

"Aye, sir. You have won."

"Will you play on?" asked Sir Mathew.

The planter sadly shook his head. "Alas!" he sighed. "Enough, sir. My tub of coins—and now Peo!"

Sir Mathew went out on the deck with Lance. "I've won Peo for you, son," he announced.

ᵉᶳ 7

To LANCE Virginia at first glance was naught but a limitless, awe-inspiring forest. Enormous trees, trees larger than the greatest oaks and yews of England, possessed the land on both banks of the James, and some of the trees waded far out into the stream as though anxious to capture water as well as land.

As the ship neared the shore the sailors shuddered and spoke of shipwrecked men who had been driven to insanity by the wolves, serpents and man-eating birds in the Virginia forest.

Peo scoffed at Nick Jump's fears. For those who knew the woods, he said, there was food, shelter and security as well as natural hazard there. And no man-eating birds had ever inhabited them.

"But there are serpents with rattles on their tails," insisted the quartermaster. "And there are beasts fiercer than the tigers of India."

"I know naught of your tigers," retorted Peo. "However, there are woodpeckers that make noise enough to scare a seaman witless."

Peo explained that horses and swords and cannon were of no use in the forest, and that Lance would have to learn to handle new weapons. He fetched from his chest a small French hatchet which, he said, was more useful than a sword in warfare against the red barbarians.

"Watch," he said, and flung the hatchet, spinning, along the deck. It stuck, blade deep, in the mizzen mast. Whereupon Nick Jump scolded the manservant as a vandal, but he looked on the lean Virginian with a new respect.

Lance had expected Jamestown to be a city like London and was amazed to find it nothing but a village among the tall pines of a little peninsula. As the *Saucy Mary* was warped into a berth beside the long wharf the town seemed a strange place indeed.

It had none of the neatness of England. Large houses sat beside dirty, unpainted huts. The fort was a great mud scar against the dark green of the forest, and part of its log foundations had already been washed away by the tide. Along the pier was a crowd of people as odd as the structures on the shore.

There were sunburned women in shapeless smocks and canvas aprons, men with long black beards who wore tight leather shirts and pantaloons, half-naked Negroes and befeathered Indians wrapped in fur mantles.

The women shouted to the busy sailors and laughed gaily at the quips which the seamen flung back at them. Half a dozen wenches fluttered aboard like butterflies as the ship was made fast, but Captain Carver had the girls herded aft until the men could be released from duty.

Roger Kendall escorted the Claybornes ashore and to Soane's tavern. Sir Mathew was clad in his finest silken coat and largest beaver hat, but Lance attracted more attention. He wore a suit the Queen had given him, a thing of orange velvet, with a white-plumed cap and red Moroccan top boots.

Lance walked as if he were still on shipboard because indeed the solid ground now seemed to be rolling like the *Saucy Mary*. It took the lad several hours to find his land legs.

Word came that Governor Berkeley would be pleased to receive Sir Mathew during the afternoon. Ned Peo, meanwhile, directed the unloading of the baggage and arranged for their departure upriver to Clayborne Castle on the morrow.

Sir Mathew took Lance to the Governor's house, and both were impressed by the courtly manners of Sir William Berkeley. With his blue eyes, high forehead, straight nose and almost womanly mouth this ruler of the Dominion of Virginia was extraordinarily handsome. He was plainly but richly dressed in blue velvet with a large coal-black wig.

"You are most welcome, Sir Mathew," said the Governor. "Are you comfortable at the inn?"

"Most comfortable, sir. We leave early on the morrow."

"You will find things at Clayborne Castle in good order," the Governor continued. "The steward, Abram Gale, is a jewel of great value. The crops are in, and there is little sickness this spring. I have sent a barge upriver to notify Gale of your arrival. He would have been here, but Carver brought the *Saucy Mary* in a week ahead of schedule. He took the northern route, I understand. He is a bold one, that Carver."

"It was a good voyage," Sir Mathew said. "We minded not the icebergs, and it was not unduly stormy."

They spoke briefly then of mutual acquaintances at court, and Sir Mathew took his leave.

Sir Mathew swore as they walked down the street to the tavern. "He did not mention your Uncle Walter's death," he growled. "Something is wrong with that icy-eyed old stallion. Next time we meet, I'll vow he will discuss that murder."

Sir Mathew decided to proceed to Clayborne Castle by land. He was sick of voyages. Accordingly Peo procured horses and, after dispatching the baggage upriver by boat, guided them along a trail that wound for a score of miles through the mighty forest to westward.

Lance never forgot that ride through the vine-hung pines, oaks and cypresses. The trees arched above them like the beams of a giant's abbey. The branches with their spring-fresh foliage almost obscured the sun so that there was a ghostly yellow light along the soft forest floor.

The boy glimpsed gray squirrels as they scampered up the great tree trunks, and once, as they journeyed past a marsh, they flushed a flock of turkeys—stupid-looking birds which flew like clumsy vultures and perched high on the branches of a dead pine with their necks thrust out like parsons reading prayers.

They passed an Indian town, long abandoned, its fields grown up in brush and weeds, its bark lodges crumbling. Peo told them of Totopotomoy, the friendly Indian chief who had led a hundred warriors westward with the expedition of Colonel Hill only to lose his life in battle with a horde of northern tribesmen nine years before.

"That was an ugly fight," the bondsman said. "Totopotomoy was killed, and so were many Englishmen. But the northern savages withdrew and have never been seen again."

Lance asked, "The Indian noblemen, Peo—what are they like?"

The manservant laughed. "There are no Indian earls and dukes," he said. "The fiercer fighters become war chiefs. Also there are wizards—we call them medicine men—who often have more influence than the chiefs. They wear false faces and make magic."

Sir Mathew inquired if there were any Christian Indians.

"Very few, sir," Peo replied. "Our parsons have labored with scant success. Indians have superstitions and fears, but they cannot understand a universal God. They have no laws or tithes or sermons. A tribe lives together in peace, and the barbarians treat one another kindly and generously. But they will rob and murder strangers any day in the week including Sunday, and they are as cruel to their enemies as Roundheads or Spaniards."

Did the Indian boys have tutors? Did they learn Latin and history? Could they use a sword?

Peo explained that Indian children had no books; they lived as they pleased and were but rarely punished by their elders. Lance marveled and vowed he would like to be an Indian.

The trail led them now to a broad savanna and, after riding through head-high marsh grass, they came to the Chickahominy River.

A horn was hanging on a post beside a small boat wharf, and Peo sounded a blast across the broad stream. In time a ferry came around a bend—a barge rowed by four wild-haired black men and commanded by a squat, bearded farmer who greeted Peo like a brother.

Horses and all, they boarded the craft and proceeded with the tide to a landing where stood a log tavern and stable shed. Here the ferryman's broad-shouldered wife served them sack, maize cakes and a salty meat pudding while the Negroes tended the horses.

Here also Abram Gale, the steward of Clayborne Castle, joined them. Gale resembled the planter Roger Kendall. He was a lean, feverish, sallow man—but his eyes were bright with joy at the arrival of Sir Mathew, and he was much pleased when he learned that Peo, Kendall's noted forester, was now a member of the household. He pounded Peo on the back until the manservant's eyes watered.

The remainder of the route was over marshy meadows that had been cleared of trees. Here and there they saw squat farmsteads in the distance and cattle sheds built of upright logs. Then beyond a creek which they forded without difficulty they came in sight of the James again and of the sharp bend around Council Point.

Abram Gale pulled up his mare and, smiling proudly at Sir Mathew, waved his hand toward the bluff above the Point. "There, sir!" he cried.

Among the oaks on the skyline stood Clayborne Castle. The house fitted the landscape as though it were part of the bluff. Even its log palisado seemed as natural as the trees which shaded the solid brick manor. It appeared small in the distance, but they could tell as they rode up the slope that it was a place of roomy proportions.

The house, indeed, was as large as any at Jamestown. Double-storied with the upper floor jutting out beyond the lower, and with the main-floor windows like arrow slots—too narrow to admit the body of a man—it was a castle in fact as well as name.

As they passed the heavy gate Negro houseboys ran to help them dismount. Other servants had gathered at the doorway. Abram Gale proudly presented them to the new master one by one—the house-keeper, fat Goody Lettice Ballard; the old butler, Henry Pettus; the cook, Black Candace, daughter of an Ethiopian; and the Negro house-boys, whose names were Cassius and Cato.

Inside was comfort of a type which was out of keeping with the military exterior. Though built only ten years ago, the place seemed old, but Walter Clayborne had held it firmly against pillage from land and river, and they found it furnished as luxuriously as the Governor's house.

The hallway was softened by Turkey carpets. The windows had hangings of native doeskin, and on the walls were painted leather shields. The great room of the east wing was the banquet hall, its shelves shining with copper tankards and cups of glass and silver, its fireplace of stone hung with pots and kettles. The western great room was the plantation's armory, and through the door they saw a rack of muskets and two brightly polished breastplates on the wall.

Goody Ballard showed them to their chambers, leading the way up the wide, strong staircase to the upper hall. The windows of the second floor were wider, and the leaded glass casements let in the sun on cleanly scrubbed paneling and floors. The chambers were furnished as simply as barrack rooms, but there were feather beds, tables of walnut wood and chests, some of which, they saw, were massive pieces in the Tudor style that had been brought from England.

Sir Mathew was surprised and pleased to find things so well arranged. "And I thought my brother lived like a barbarian," he mused. He tested the bed with his hand, which sank deep in the softness. "A fortune in feathers," he said. "We'll sleep well."

Sir Mathew spent two days at work on accounts with Gale. Most of the figures were in the steward's head. They balanced by every style of reckoning.

Walter, it seemed, had wasted effort on a few useless arts and crafts, but his lands had not been neglected. While taxes were high and the navigation laws had impaired the tobacco trade, their revenue was ample, and reserves to the credit of the estate were on deposit with several London merchants. Equipment, boats, outhouses were in excellent condition. There were men enough to cultivate new plantings.

Questioned carefully about his late master's death, Gale's honest face grew cloudy. "There was a woman here," he said hesitantly. "You know of her?"

"What of the woman?" Sir Mathew asked.

"She was very young and she had the beauty of a fallen angel, sir," Gale said. "She was kind to us all. We loved her because she helped us, and she attended the sick and performed all of her duties well. But . . ." Gale, after a long pause, repeated: "She had the beauty of a fallen angel."

"Where is she now?" Sir Mathew asked.

"I know not, sir. A month after Major Clayborne's death a black brigantine anchored offshore—and she went away."

Gale would say no more.

II
The Feud

LANCE CLAYBORNE remembered for the rest of his life how their sudden removal to America changed his father. In London Sir Mathew had been an aimless, awkward courtier, a veteran with a glorious past and no future. Here in Virginia, seeking the man responsible for the murder of his brother, the tough old Cavalier once again had a mission. There was a swagger in his walk, a fresh, fierce light in his eyes. He discarded his small sword and began to wear again a long military blade that he had carried in the days of the first Charles.

Soldierlike, he soon learned from Peo and from Abram Gale much of the geography of that colony of great distances, endless forests and bewildering water courses. Thereafter, he began a methodical search for the woman who, he was certain, held the key to the slaying of his brother.

Colonel Philip Ludwell, who had been Walter's close friend, was down with the ague at a new plantation on the York River when Sir Mathew sought him out.

Ludwell rose on an elbow and stared hard into Sir Mathew's intense eyes. "Look for Jesús Forke," Ludwell advised. "He has the woman. He knows how your brother died."

"Jesús Forke?"

"A merchant sailor," said Ludwell, the fever sweat beading his high sunburned forehead. "And go slowly, sir. Captain Forke is a favorite at Jamestown."

Ludwell, dizzy from his malady, would tell him little more.

"Was it a duel?" Sir Mathew asked.

Ludwell shook his head. "I think not, sir."

Sir Mathew repaired to Jamestown and, heeding Ludwell's advice, was discreet in his inquiries about the merchant seaman.

The man, now absent on a voyage to Barbados, was an influential

29

trader whose seat was near Lower Norfolk on the Atlantic coast. Forke, said Soane, the fat innkeeper, had been a frequent visitor to Clayborne Castle prior to Walter Clayborne's death.

Soane slyly hinted that there had been bad blood between Walter and the trader shortly before Walter's death, but the tavern keeper said nothing about the cause of possible ill will. The two men, he said, had been friendly for years, then suddenly seemed to become unfriendly. The reason? He did not know.

Henrietta Hart seemed to be virtually unknown to the gossips of the taverns.

Sir Mathew visited the Hart plantation seven miles downriver from Jamestown and found the stout house boarded up and deserted. He returned to Clayborne Castle, baffled and weary, to await the return of Forke from his voyage.

Sir Mathew's first disappointment was one of many that year and the next. Neighboring planters, all of whom paid him calls of courtesy, were exceedingly reticent about the case even when plied with Sir Mathew's best Madeira. It was plain that Captain Forke, whatever else he might be, had high connections at Jamestown and that it was not wise to talk evil about so close a friend of Sir William Berkeley.

The doughty Governor, it seemed, had changed. Once loved, he now was feared. Approaching old age, Sir William now had a warped love for power and for money. He was becoming rich from trade in beaver skins and through the sale by sundry agents of secret shipments of Orinoco tobacco seeds which somehow found their way out of the hostile Spanish colonies to southward. The contraband Spanish seed, planted in Virginia soil, yielded leaf of the highest quality, and so the tiny grains were worth a thousand times their weight in gold. One spoonful, properly used, could cover an acre with tobacco plants.

Sir Mathew was troubled by conditions at Jamestown, but he had other challenging difficulties also. That autumn he had his turn with Virginia chills and fever, the dreaded ague which afflicted most of the river plantations. And there was his energetic young son to worry him.

Lance, in fact, was beginning to forget his English manners to a point that caused his father concern and his tutor great distress. The boy found a tame wolf in the servants' quarters much more interesting than his history books. Jim Stag, a half-breed Indian, had taught him to shoot waterfowl and to trap foxes and white-tailed hares—occupations which seemed of much more consequence than lessons in Greek. And there was Peo, who took the lad into the forest at every opportunity to hunt venison for the table and to practice Indian lore.

Parson Broome used the rod, but with little effect. Lance took his beatings with indifference. He struggled to be obedient. He labored hard to maintain proper progress in his academic studies, but the fascinating wilderness around him remained his dominant interest.

That winter Lance discarded his red Flemish cloak for a wolfskin mantle which, when wet, stunk so abominably that Sir Mathew made him keep it in the saddle room. A Paspahegh squaw made him moccasins which he wore in place of his two-guinea boots. He was becoming an expert with an ash bow which Peo had helped him make.

At last Sir Mathew had to lecture Lance severely. "What manner of an English gentleman are you, anyway?" he asked. "Broome tells me you have become as wild as a Yorkshire highwayman."

Lance said nothing.

"Answer me, sirrah! Why these complaints? You are behind in Caesar. You have forgotten the succession of the English kings. In mathematics you are still an infant!"

"My sword wrist is strong," said Lance. "You said so yourself. And you have praised my horsemanship——"

"You evade the issue. What of your lessons?"

"I forget...."

Sir Mathew continued to frown, but in spite of himself he looked with inward pride on the boy in front of him. Lance had lost his small-boy's plumpness and was growing tough and tall. His face remained as handsome as his mother's, but the eyes had deepened and grown keen and alertly brilliant like a wild thing's. His sunburned skin glowed with health. Somehow the lad had escaped the swamp fevers.

The old knight started on a new tack. "Listen, my cock," he said slowly. "Listen seriously now, man to man. I have an enemy. *We* have an enemy—the slayer of your Uncle Walter. I want you to become a proper man so you can help me in this matter. Do you understand?"

Lance's eyes sparkled. "Aye, Father. I am ready."

"You'll never be ready until you are a proper man, a proper English gentleman."

"Yes, Father."

"So buckle down, my buck. Buckle down."

"Yes, Father."

"I want no more complaints from your tutor. Do you understand? You are no savage."

"Yes, Father."

So Lance returned to his books. He was puzzled somewhat by his father's flank attack. There seemed little connection between Caesar's Commentaries and the murder of his Uncle Walter. He could not understand why proficiency in history could have anything to do with the strange enigma his father was trying to solve. But his father had spoken, and thereafter Broome had less cause for sorrow.

Still Lance, for all his strained application to his lessons, continued also his special Virginia education. New scenes, weather wilder than he had ever experienced and mysteries of the forest blotted out his memories of Whitehall, Hampton Court and Windsor. The mosquitoes of Virginia were more bothersome than London lice. Peo's dialect was more expressive than monkish Latin. Panthers were much more fascinating than King Charles's Persian kittens.

The forest seemed to him like a great cathedral with its vast arches and its strange, ever-changing colors. Lance loved the music stirred by the wind among the leaves and through the tall columns of the timber. Pine music was different from oak music, but both merged in harmony with the songs of the insects and birds and other woodland sounds.

Peo dispelled his fears of the wild things by showing him the real dangers. The adder with the rattles on its tail was more to be feared than the slinking wolf. Beware of limbs and ledges from which a panther might make a surprise attack. In storms watch out for falling trees and sudden creek-bottom floods. And never, never attempt to shoot a she-bear when she had a cub with her.

Lance learned that most of the fears of the farmers were ill-founded. The howling of a wolf, terrifying as it was, could harm no one, nor could the wild screams of the forest cats or the deep calls of the great owls.

Peo at first was reticent about the Indians, and Lance had to ask

him many questions. Were they as treacherous as the farmers said
they were? Did they murder people? Where were the villages of
the red barbarians? How did they live? Jim Stag was an Indian and
yet he was like a white person, and so were the squaws at Jamestown—good-natured, quiet, doe-eyed folk like gypsies he had seen at
London fairs.

Then little by little Lance discovered that Peo secretly liked the
savages, that his ideas on Indians were as unorthodox as his comments
on the wild beasts all around them.

Indians were cleaner than English planters, Peo told him. Nor were
they more treacherous than the Spaniards or the Dutch. Yes, they
made war, but war to Indians was not just murder. They fought
neighboring tribesmen as English boys played games—to test their
manhood. Their towns were to the west. Someday, Peo said, he and
Lance would visit some of the Indian villages—which did not smell
so bad as Jamestown.

"You don't like Jamestown, Peo?" Lance asked.

Peo spat.

Lance laughed. "Neither does Father," he said.

"And why should he?" Peo snarled in his sharp colonial accent.
"His Gracious Excellency the Governor is pulling the wool over your
pa's eyes. The place is full of greedy thieves."

"How now, Peo?"

The manservant shrugged and lowered his voice. "Benjamin the
tinker was at Kendall's lower plantation yesterday. He said that half-
Spanish pirate Jesús Forke is anchored off Kickotan. Maybe you'd
better tell your pa."

Lance wasted no time in running to the house. He found his father
in the armory room mending the lock of a bellmouthed fowling piece.

When informed of the news the old knight laid down the gun and
stretched his lean arms. "Oho!" He cocked an eye at Lance and
added, "An enemy is good for a man, son. An enemy will keep a
man young. Let us hope that our enemy is on that ship. I shall ride
to Jamestown in the morning."

"May I go?" the boy asked.

Sir Mathew pondered a moment and nodded consent.

"May I take my pistol, Father?"

"Yes, boy, and I shall take my long sword."

Lance was too excited to enjoy his supper.

That evening at dusk there was a surprise. The horn sounded at the boat landing, and Lance and his father went to the gate to see a small barge pulling into the creek.

"A woman is aboard," said Lance.

"What!"

A swarm of servants was at the landing, and there were shouts of welcome to the new arrival. A moment later Lance and Sir Mathew saw a slim figure in black coming up the pathway, escorted by the chattering Negroes.

Sir Mathew stared and hastily adjusted the lace at his collar. "It is the woman," he said, half to himself. "The . . . woman."

ᴖᏸ 2

LANCE's first vivid impression of Henrietta Hart never left him. She was as Walter Clayborne had described her, except for a face that was distorted by a frown of the bitterest hatred. Her deep black eyes were wells of fury, nor did they light up when she introduced herself and curtsied respectfully in response to Sir Mathew's stiffly courteous bow.

Lance lighted the candles as their guest was seated by the hearth.

"You have sought me, sir?" she began. "I have been . . . away. I took the first opportunity to return to Clayborne Castle."

Sir Mathew nodded. His eyes were wary, like those of a swordsman facing an adversary.

Henrietta Hart sighed, her shoulders bowed as though she were very weary. There was no coquettishness about her, no challenge, as she said, "You look like Major Walter Clayborne, sir. I would have known you anywhere. And this fine young man, he is a Clayborne, too. Your son?"

"My son Lance, Mistress Hart."

Lance bowed. His father nodded a command, and Lance retired in silence—but no farther than the door.

His father and the young woman talked for hours.

She was as candid as a first cousin. And when she mentioned Captain Jesús Forke her lips dripped poison. "That half-Spanish spawn of hell! That lying papist pirate! That mincing, murderous, imitation gentleman!"

Sir Mathew calmed her with a glass of wine.

"He promised marriage and made me a fool again!" she snarled.

Her story came out like a flood. She had been happy and content as Walter Clayborne's housekeeper—and faithful. She had loved Sir Mathew's brother as had every soul who knew him well. Sir Mathew must believe her. With Walter Clayborne she had been good, and he too had been happy.

Then came the serpent to their Eden—Jesús Forke. He was but one of many frequent visitors to hospitable Clayborne Castle in those days.

The sea merchant was the most elegantly dressed man in the colony, a lean, tough person of sober mien but surprising gaiety of manner. His anecdotes of many long voyages made him favored company, and several planters had found business association with him of great profit. Somehow Forke could furnish items like Arras hangings and Turkey carpets to his friends free of port fees, and the utensils and cutlery he brought upstream in his sloop were furnished at half the price demanded by the Jamestown factors. There were choice household slaves to be had at Lower Norfolk, too.

With the lace at his collar, the jeweled rings on his fingers and the gold on the hilt of his sword Captain Forke had reminded Henrietta of the French nobleman who had given her the coach and four some years before in London.

As for Forke, his weakness was for wenches of every station. After one exposure to Henrietta's hot, merry eyes he began the chase, full tilt.

Though firmly loyal to Walter Clayborne, the woman, like everyone else, enjoyed the sea merchant's company. Neither in deed nor thought did she show the slightest disloyalty to Walter Clayborne. This only whetted the determination of her wooer, she said.

Forke, charm exhausted, tried gold, then a rare jewel which he called a sapphire of the stars, and garments that would have graced a queen. Henrietta, as graciously as she could, refused the flattering bait.

"Why must we two be lovers?" she asked Forke candidly. "You have a hundred women. Why have me?"

He could not answer such questions, but the devilment within him continued to seethe until one day he begged Henrietta earnestly to marry him. This naturally made the Irish beauty blink. It warmed her heart.

They were in the summerhouse on a knoll from which one could look over the broad reaches of both the James and the Chickahominy rivers. April had come up from the south all atwitter with bird songs from vast flocks of squawking geese and clouds of wood pigeons. The air smelled of fresh buds.

Captain Forke never had looked so youthful, so romantically impressive as on that day. His vest, brocaded in silver, was crossed by a velvet baldric that an earl might have envied. His coat, of bright-green silk, was the work of a master tailor who could have found employment with King Charles himself.

"I mean it, Henrietta!" said he in his deep voice with its trace of Latin accent. "You must believe me. I mean it!"

She decided that he did, and it caused her great confusion of soul. Why not? reflected Henrietta. Virginia was a great new land where such things happened. Among the widely scattered farmsteads many a loose woman had become a respected matron.

What of Walter Clayborne? To him she was—what she was. She never could marry such a man. Walter was a gentleman, Forke but a seafaring adventurer who could never be a gentleman. . . .

Could she be a proper wife? She wondered. She was barren; that would be a misfortune if she married. Forke would be absent at sea for months at a time. Sometimes he would take her, sometimes not. He would not have her on a slaving voyage. At home, manless, alone, could she behave herself?

Forke pressed her constantly for weeks. So subtle was his secretive courtship that for a time he turned her head.

Thereupon, with characteristic honesty, she discussed the matter with Walter Clayborne.

Walter flew into a tumultuous rage. "That greasy adder! That half-Spanish fop! That glob of stinking windrift from the southern ocean!"

Henrietta was horrified.

"I'd fight him if he were a gentleman!" roared Walter. "Marry you? He lies! He'd never marry you!"

She did not mention Forke again, and thereafter the romance went underground to be fed by impassioned love letters from the sailor.

At a meeting in Jamestown in May Walter Clayborne refused Forke's hand and looked at him with a contempt which even the Governor observed.

"What's wrong, Clayborne?" Berkeley whispered. "Why are you rude to my good friend Captain Forke?"

Walter shrugged off the question.

"No duel, Clayborne!" The Governor shook a warning finger. "No duel, you know!"

"Duel!" snorted Walter Clayborne. "Would I ever soil myself and fight a slug like that?"

His Excellency, badly shaken, sought a new pipe and a glass of wine.

Colonel Philip Ludwell and two others overheard Walter's words and were to remember them.

Two weeks later Walter Clayborne's body was found on the green behind the cobbler's cottage at Jamestown. He had been thrust through the heart with a tuck-sword.

There was much talk. Many people were questioned by the High Sheriff.

Jesús Forke said he had been at Lower Norfolk that night. No one knew of any other enemy of the respected planter.

Seconds of a duel were sought. Philip Ludwell, Walter Clayborne's confidant, knew of no duel. He told of Clayborne's remark at the Governor's house that he would never fight Jesús Forke.

"There was no duel," Ludwell said grimly. "Walter Clayborne either was murdered by that sea merchant—or on his orders."

Forke said nothing in denial of this accusation, nor did the High Sheriff act upon it.

Colonel Ludwell wrote Sir Mathew Clayborne by the next departing vessel.

Two months after Walter was buried among the pines at Clayborne Castle, Captain Forke brought his best vessel, his brigantine, upriver and took Henrietta Hart away with him.

"I had nowhere to go," Henrietta said. "I did not dream that

Forke had murdered Major Clayborne—then. Later, taunting me, he boasted of the deed. Nor was it a duel. A servant pinioned Major Clayborne's arms while Forke made his thrust."

"Where is this servant?" Sir Mathew asked grimly.

"He fell overboard on the voyage to Barbados," she said.

Sir Mathew paced the hearth while Henrietta sobbed and cursed.

"As Major Clayborne had predicted, sir, there was no marriage. He forced me as though I were a tavern slut—and laughed. I have been a prisoner for many months. He would not kill me. He enjoyed my spite. It pleased his cruel Spanish soul."

⮝ 3

SIR MATHEW, Lance and Peo rode to Jamestown the following day and stopped at Soane's tavern at noon.

To Sir Mathew's surprise, Soane expected him. "I have a message from His Excellency," said the landlord. "He requests your presence at his house without delay, sir."

Sir Mathew took Lance with him to his audience with the Governor.

Berkeley received them with the warmest cordiality. "You have been a stranger, Sir Mathew. I have been anxious to see you upon a matter of importance. And how are things at Clayborne Castle?"

"Very well, Your Excellency."

The Governor rubbed his small hands together. "For some time," he said, "I have anticipated an early vacancy upon my Council, Sir Mathew. My business with you was to ask if you would do us the honor—in event the vacancy develops—to . . ." He paused.

"I am greatly flattered, Your Excellency. I——"

"Then I may count on it? The appointment of course carries perquisites which, while of no great interest to a man of fortune, are, as you may know, not inconsiderable."

Berkeley's hands still rubbed together, and his blue eyes were now narrowed. Before Sir Mathew could say more he added, "And there is a man here in my study, a former friend of your brother Walter, whom I am anxious for you to meet." He turned toward the door. "Captain Forke, will you come in, please?"

Sir Mathew's back straightened as suddenly as if he had been thrust in the seat with a dagger. His eyes glittered. Lance noticed also that the veins in his neck began to stand out as though he were ready to explode.

But the old knight had been a courtier and a card player. With an effort which reddened his face he managed to control himself as his enemy, Jesús Forke, entered the room.

"Sir Mathew Clayborne, may I introduce Captain Jesús Forke of Lower Norfolk?" said Berkeley with a flourish of his hand.

Forke, smiling, bowed deeply. Sir Mathew did not bow. He stared at the seaman coolly as though memorizing every lineament of his long face. The man was immaculate in a blue coat brocaded with silver threads, and fluffy, spotless linen. He wore no sword.

Nor did Sir Mathew address this new acquaintance. Shifting his calm eyes to Sir William Berkeley, he said, "How very odd, sir. I came to town today to see the High Sheriff about this Captain Forke. It is my intention, sir, to swear out a warrant against him for the murder of my brother."

It was Berkeley's turn now to exercise self-control. He suppressed his astonishment, his hands still together. "Now, now, Sir Mathew!" he said. "There must be no trouble between you two good men."

"There will be no trouble, sir, if English law will take its course."

"But it's absurd, sir!"

"English law, Your Excellency?"

"Forke is no murderer, Clayborne."

"Then let the court decide it, Your Excellency." Sir Mathew added, "And as for the appointment to your Council, sir, please forget such a thing. I find myself unable to serve." He bowed to the Governor.

Sir William Berkeley stood open-mouthed as Sir Mathew, back stiff as a musket barrel, stalked out of his presence.

Lance followed his father, his back also very straight.

The Governor remained speechless. So did the elegant Captain Jesús Forke.

Sir Mathew could not find the High Sheriff that day, nor any magistrate or member of the General Court. Berkeley's messengers had found them first. A month passed before Sir Mathew was able to process his warrant. But there was no indictment found against Jesús Forke, despite the testimony of Henrietta Hart.

Even so, Captain Forke avoided Jamestown. His friend Sir William Berkeley advised him to take another voyage. The Governor had looked deep into Mathew Clayborne's eyes and had almost seen reflected there the Cavalier's own long, military sword. So had Captain Forke.

◄§ 4

THUS began a noted feud, the most celebrated of the extralegal conflicts that arose in the colony because of the arbitrary conduct of Sir William Berkeley and his sycophants.

As in the Clayborne case, Berkeley generally would try to win a man by discreet bribery. He had so done among most of the members of his Council and not a few planters in the House of Burgesses. These favored individuals were given lucrative appointments, certain exemptions from fees and tax levies, and government information that would help them in their tobacco trading. As for the men who would not play the Governor's game, some were ruined and others driven to far western plantations where they would be free to some extent from Berkeley's exactions.

Sir Mathew chose to remain at Clayborne Castle and fight, but he too acquired headright lands at the fall line of the James as a refuge if disaster should afflict his tidewater plantation near Jamestown.

Meanwhile with the precision of a general waging a military campaign Sir Mathew harassed Jesús Forke and Forke's friends wherever he found them; and they retaliated in kind. And between moves in this studied effort to keep the sea merchant out of Jamestown and the smaller ports the old Cavalier drilled his son like a dragoon recruit.

"It is you who will finish this affair," Sir Mathew said to Lance repeatedly when the boy was fifteen. "The years are crowding me, but your strength is growing as mine declines."

They practiced almost daily with their weapons until Lance, now nearly six feet tall, became adept at various sword tricks that his father had learned as one of Prince Rupert's peppery captains.

Peo, meanwhile, taught him wrestling and some of the arts of forest warfare which were a mystery to his father. He learned to use the knife and tomahawk and to load a fusil so it would throw an accurate ball.

To Lance it was a relief to escape his books and study weapons, but Roger Kendall and other neighboring planters were shocked at the lessons in violence that were being taught the young man. They feared Sir Mathew was turning the handsome lad into a brawling tavern knight.

Nevertheless, all was not bitterness. Sir Mathew seemed relieved at having established the identity of his brother's murderer. It gave him a clear objective.

He visited Forke's seat at Lower Norfolk by boat one day and, unrecognized among others who went there to trade in smuggled Spanish goods, he made a thorough reconnaissance.

Later, with Lance, Peo and three Welsh servants, he returned to the place, this time by a little-used land trail. Forke's agents were prepared to defend his factory from attack by sea—it was armed against marauding pirates—but not from a surprise movement by land. Sir Mathew and his men burned the warehouse and all its contents and withdrew unscathed.

This raid brought prompt retaliation. An armed sloop drifted upriver with the tide one night. Unable to elevate the deck guns sufficiently to throw shot into Clayborne Castle, the visitor blasted Sir Mathew's boathouse with twelve-pound balls until Abram Gale got his swivel guns into action on the castle's gate tower. It was a spectacular fight which caused much talk, because the firing, heard as far as Jamestown, spread rumors that Dutch raiders were on the river.

Forke's sloop soon withdrew, deck and rigging damaged and two men wounded.

The feud was pressed in other ways and at most unexpected times. Lance was with his father at the Goose Tavern in Middlesex one night when Sir Henry Chicheley, Lieutenant Governor under Berkeley, got full of ale and said a good word for Captain Jesús Forke.

Sir Mathew kicked two stools aside, hauled out his sword and sought to settle the argument then and there. And when Chicheley, shocked at this explosive action, refused to draw, Sir Mathew slapped his face with a heavy gauntlet. But Chicheley refused the challenge, pleading Governor Berkeley's edict against dueling. He offered Sir Mathew friendship.

Later in the year Forke hired bravos. There were many men with swords for sale, it seemed. And Sir Mathew, agile despite his sixty years, wounded three of them on as many occasions.

He throttled one man who, in the role of a highwayman, tried to unhorse him one day on the trail to Archer's Hope, and obtained from the hireling an admission that Forke was now offering a hundred guineas for another Clayborne funeral. Sir Mathew thereupon went to Jamestown and posted a notice on the pillory saying he would give "two farthings (only)" for Jesús Forke's ears. This caused laughter in the taverns which hurt Sir Mathew's enemy more than the defeats he suffered in the field.

Nor was Governor Berkeley amused. Cautious as he was against direct connection with the feud—he remembered that Mathew Clayborne had friends in the court of Charles II—Sir William nevertheless brought subtle pressures to bear on Clayborne Castle. Sir Mathew's port duties were increased above the usual rate, and other difficulties were raised to embarrass him.

But Jesús Forke remained away from Jamestown—to the great distress of Berkeley, the Council clique and other favored planters who had profited by collusion with the smuggler in past years. Forke showed great respect for Sir Mathew's resourcefulness—and steel.

For longer and longer periods the sea merchant took ship and disappeared, and the feud became dormant. But vigilance at Clayborne Castle was not relaxed, and Sir Mathew, who was winning friends among many who hated Governor Berkeley, rode restlessly among the eastern plantations, awaiting news.

III

The Forester

man's nose as well as his eyes and ears are always wa...
smell a thunderstorm and estimate its intensity. He could...
...by the odor emitted when the animal was frightene...

❧ 1

ONE of the most closely guarded secrets of Lance Clayborne's boyhood was his venturing into the deep forest with Ned Peo.
At that time in Virginia not one man in five hundred dared go two
miles inland from a river. The forest was a blank mystery. Untamed
Indians were demons to the average farmer. Sir Mathew's neighbors
would have been horrified had they known that his son had become a
woodsman.

But Lance, to his own amazement, discovered that land trails to the
west were in many cases much shorter than the water routes and that
good legs aided by knowledge of the forest could outspeed the fastest
barge between points on the winding streams.

To travel with Peo through the deep woods was to learn by example rather than by lecture. The man rarely offered advice or noted
a mistake unless it was his own, and Lance, by watching, learned
quickly.

Peo was a better hunter than Jim Stag, for he had none of the superstitions the half-breed Indian had acquired from his mother. Peo
used English common sense and English muscle in combination with
woodland skills.

Lance found in the forest challenges to his wits and strength that
excited his interest. Fear was the worst evil, the most difficult to
surmount in the forest—fear of becoming lost, fear of hunger, fear
of storm and flood, of darkness and mysterious noises and of prowling
outlaw Indians from the western hunting camps. The only antidote
for fear, he learned, was knowledge and everlasting alertness.

Peo never seemed to relax in the woods. He slept with one ear
open. Even when he ate he paused between chews to listen. The
man's nose as well as his eyes and ears always was busy. He could
smell a thunderstorm and estimate its intensity. He could follow a
deer by the odor emitted when the animal was frightened. In every
respect the bondsman was a better woodsman than any Indian Lance
ever knew—except the Chiskiack chief, Pipisko.

He met Pipisko one day when he was riding to the Middle Plantation Indian School to get some books for David Broome.

The young barbarian had been arrested by two farmers because he was not wearing the pass badge which all nontributary Indians were required to wear east of the Henrico county boundary. Resentful of the mauling which the two men had given him, the Indian was still resisting when Lance appeared around a bend in the trail. Proud of their capture, the two louts added additional kicks when they saw the well-dressed boy riding toward them.

"What has he done?" Lance inquired, dismounting beside the cold-eyed captive.

"No badge, your honor," said the farmer. "We're taking 'im to the Jamestown gaol because he's a western Injun and he ought to have the Governor's badge on him."

"I wouldn't beat a dog like that!" Lance said. "Leave off. Let him go!"

They flung the young savage to the ground. The Indian was back on his feet like a cat, his hands fumbling at his belt for weapons that were not there.

Lance turned to the Indian and, touching his arms, restrained him from a headlong attack on his tormentors.

Then, to his surprise, the half-naked lad spoke to him in good English. "I am Pipisko of the Chiskiacks," he said. "I am a student at the Indian School. I need no badge."

"Did you tell these men that?" Lance asked.

"I have said nothing to these hounds."

Lance had difficulty explaining the situation to the Indian's captors. They expected a reward from the Sheriff for this unregistered Indian. They protested his release, became angry and combative.

At fifteen Lance was deceptively slim, but the two farmers soon had reason to think that the young gentleman in the pretty velvet clothes and the big hat was made of spring wire and gunpowder. Lance knocked one of them semiconscious with a blow of his fist and within a second disabled the other with a hip throw.

Pipisko, meanwhile, proposed that both be choked to death and began actions to match his advice, so Lance had to buffet him on the chin also. Then, marveling that any young man's clenched hand could so resemble a stone-headed war club, the Indian obediently accompanied Lance to Middle Plantation.

He was, he said, a war chief of the Chiskiacks and a protégé of

Parson Black of the school. He had come to the school for three winters to learn the white man's customs.

He measured Lance with his intense eyes and added, "You would make a hunter. Have you a gun?"

"I have a gun," said Lance.

"A flint gun?" asked the envious Indian.

"Yes, with a fine Spanish barrel."

Pipisko sighed. "My thirty hunters have four Dutch wheel locks. Only one of them will shoot. So my people eat fish instead of flesh. It makes them weak."

"Does Parson Black feed you fish at the school?" Lance asked.

"Oh, no. We have beef and pork and venison." Pipisko slapped his bare chest. "I am not weak."

The aristocratic pride of the barbarian was warmly appealing to Lance. Thereafter, he visited him twice at Middle Plantation and had him frequently as his guest at Clayborne Castle. Lance, winking at the law, gave Pipisko a good flintlock, and they hunted together in the heavily wooded swamps of the upper Chickahominy.

At their tiny cooking fires Pipisko was much more voluble than Peo. And Lance began to understand the conflict present in this semi-civilized Indian.

"I think English," Pipisko explained. "It is no good for an Indian to think English."

"You are a Christian?"

"No. But otherwise I think English. I like guns. I like beef. I like salt. It is no good for an Indian."

"An Englishman cannot kill a bear with a hatchet as you did yesterday," Lance said.

"I can act Indian," admitted Pipisko.

"Why couldn't Parson Black convert you to the Christian faith?" Lance asked.

Pipisko searched for words awhile and answered, "An Englishman has one devil. The Indian has a hundred. I could not rid myself of all my devils."

"But what of the universal God?"

Pipisko sniffed. "Indians have no God, no gods, only devils."

"The white man has devils, too," Lance said and smiled. "Not like your devils, perhaps—but devils all the same."

"I know the devils you mean," Pipisko said. "I have seen them come in aching bones and running bowels and swollen toes. Even now one of your devils torments my people. You call it smallpox."

Lance could not meet the young brave's stark eyes.

"And another of your devils is rum, and another sermons. Do you know that I, Pipisko, can read and write the Beatitudes? I can count to a thousand. I have learned by rote many of the lessons of St. Paul. And yet my people die of smallpox and have only one gun among them."

There was a long silence. Finally Pipisko said, "I will move my tribe. I will teach them to be hunters."

"And I will help you," said Lance, and added, as he glimpsed the expression on the Indian's proud face, "You can teach me much, Pipisko. And if you would bear with me, I would like to know your people."

Pipisko's face relaxed. For a long time he gazed into the face of the white boy. Then slowly he said, "You have made me your friend. I will make you a brother."

⋙§ 2

THEREAFTER for three summers Lance and Peo visited Pipisko's people in the heavily forested fastnesses of the Rappahannock Valley. Sir Mathew objected at first, but since there was no fever in the uplands and Lance always returned heavier of bone and stronger of body, he became reconciled to these expeditions.

Pipisko's eager Chiskiack warriors learned to hunt with firearms and to make knives and beaver traps from strap iron. In return for these lessons in the white man's craft they taught Lance and Peo forest arts that no white man, not even the traders, had mastered.

Lance, although he never admitted it to his father or to any other easterner, soon began to admire the Chiskiacks. They were stronger and bolder than most Englishmen. In many respects they resembled, indeed, the heroes of Hellas and Troy about whom his tutor had discoursed at length during the winter months. Their code of conduct was almost identical with that of Homer's heroes. Lance knew Indians as sly as Ulysses, as impulsively brave as Hector, as stubborn as Ajax Telamon. He found the forest people friendly, merry, generous and loyal to their kind. They were cruel to their captives, but no more so than was the public executioner at Jamestown, who sometimes—under instructions from a court of Christian gentlemen—cut out a felon's guts and burned them in front of his still-living eyes.

Smallpox and measles had killed many of the Chiskiacks, but those who had survived these scourges were of a physical perfection to match that of Lance Clayborne. In the western hunting camps Lance never saw a sick Indian or a fat Indian or a crippled Indian. They never suffered from a running off of the bowels. Gout and rheumatism were unknown to them. Nor did their eyes redden or their teeth fall out. When they were wounded their hurts healed quickly and without mortification.

Lance soon learned to hold his own with Pipisko's wild young men. Thanks to English muscles, he wrestled well and he could outrun even the older warriors. His arrows, fletched English-style, were more accurate than Pipisko's.

Pipisko's summer hunts were largely journeys of exploration—searches for game to be taken later when the approach of cold weather strengthened the fur so it would bring good prices. The Chiskiacks, in small parties, ranged as far west as the blue mountains one summer to discover five rich beaver creeks and a small salt spring where deer were as thick as cattle in Devon.

Lance and Peo did not take their horses on these hunts, because there was insufficient forage in the deep woods to keep them healthy. The little Virginian ponies could survive on browse, like deer, but they could do but little work without grain. Maize was very scarce in the western woods—a food reserved for warriors.

❧ 3

ON THE trail Lance dressed like an Indian and thought like an Indian. Back in the noisy Chiskiack town at the end of a summer hunt, he would stretch his tough young muscles and think again like an Englishman.

Boyhood was passing. Another happy, challenging summer was over. He must return to the dull familiar people of his kind, go back to beef and mutton, to chairs and to feather beds, to small sword and baldric, lace and buttons. His father needed him to help supervise the harvesting of grain, the gelding of pigs and the curing of tobacco. His neighbors needed him to help work out the destiny of His Majesty's promising plantation, Virginia.

Free of fevers and of gripes, thanks to his weeks in the healthy western forest, Lance could do the work of three men during the busy autumn days. His father was pleased, his neighbors were envious. When winter came Clayborne Castle would be stuffed with rich provisions. Often the weather was as cold as that of Scotland.

·§ 4

SIR MATHEW suffered much during the season of cold weather. Not the least of his ills was his deep longing for England. Nostalgia assailed him front and flank.

He missed his wife. Alive, she had plagued him much. She had knocked the dice cup from his hand and scored him with a tongue sharper than a spit for bringing soldiers to their house, soldiers who smelled like saddles, drank heavily and hooked her Flemish carpets with their spurs. Nevertheless, she had been a comfort and a delight.

The old knight dreamed that her hands were on his cheek or smoothing his beard, which now bushed out untended. Again, when Lance was disobedient he thought he heard her gentle voice enforcing his authority. She had always done that, in spite of his choleric moods.

The dog barked, and Sir Mathew looked up, his daydream gone. . . .

His son had entered the room like a blast of frosty air. Lance's face was red from the cold river wind. Spray had frozen on his wolf-skin mantle, which he flung aside as he came to warm his hands at the hearth.

"We have the oysters, sir," Lance said to him, "and Peo snared a young goose for your Sunday's dinner. My Lady, but it's cold!"

Sir Mathew marveled at the bass voice of his son who such a short time before had been a baby in arms in Kent.

"You were a fool to risk the weather, lad. I——"

"Now, now," Lance said hurriedly. "We fetched a wondrous physic for you—oysters almost as large as platters. We have put a bushel of them in persimmon wine, and later we'll roast them. And, Father, there's smallpox in that Nottoway town upriver. Ten of the savages have died and many more are ill. They caught the infection from a Scottish peddler."

"Light the candles, lad. Smallpox, you say? It is well I have a lesser ill. But touches of gout are troublesome. We'll try the oysters for our supper."

Lance told him other news—a tale that Governor Berkeley was building a coach, the first one in Virginia; that a heavy snow had fallen at Martin's Hundred; and that one of Jonathan Minge's horses had been lost in quicksand near the Point.

And as they talked of local matters it seemed to Sir Mathew a lifetime since they had been in England. Still, Sir Mathew thought, he was an Englishman. Other settlers here were English. And he hoped in his heart that the colony itself was truly English. Already, in 1670, it was populated beyond the dreams of the hopeful adventurers who had planted it in 1607. Men died of fevers, but more men came in every vessel. And yet there were no more than a half-dozen villages in the whole colony. Virginia consisted of thousands of square miles of wooded wilderness, specked by an occasional plantation, cut deeply by bewilderingly crooked tidal inlets.

Sir Mathew's nostrils quivered. He beckoned to his son. "How many times," said he, "must I tell you to leave that stinking wolfskin in the hall?"

Lance took the mantle from the room and returned. His father inspected with a glowering frown his son's frost-chapped face, his bearskin doublet and broadcloth breeches stained with mud and salt spray.

"A veritable savage!" the knight declared. "Have you no pride left? A visitor would take you for a yeoman or one of these convict servants from Jamaica. Where is your sword belt?"

"I dress but to match the weather, sir. As for the sword, I cannot wear it in the canoe or in the forest, and the belt—that old one which has grown too small—I traded for a string of roanoke."

"For what?"

"Roanoke is shellwork, sir. The Indians use it for messages. See?"

In Lance's long-fingered hand was a multicolored web of beads. Flat, scarcely two inches wide, banded and starred, the strand was as smoothly flexible as a snake.

"Pagan trumpery!" his father said.

"A belt, sir," Lance declared, watching his father's face for any sign of real anger. Finding none, he declared boldly, "A Weyanoke sold it to me. He showed me others, but this was the best. See, this thing that looks something like a star stands for a moon, or month, and there above it—that curly thing—is a falling leaf. That means October in their writing; and here—this band stands for sorrow, and that little man there is supposed to be dead. The thing beside him is his clanmark, a fish called a sturgeon. It all means that the sturgeon clan of the Weyanokes lost a warrior in October."

The old knight could not disguise his interest. And in spite of himself he felt proud of this son who had made himself at home in the wild forest. But he straightened his back in time and glowered again. "Clean yourself for dinner, lad. The smell of you will dampen any appetite."

Dinner was served in the ancient manner at Clayborne Castle. In the west-wing room the entire household, with the exception of the black servants, assembled at a long oaken table on which was placed roast venison, meal cakes, boiled bacon and turkey stew, pease porridge and dried grapes, with pewter tankards of small beer and jars of red Henrico wine.

The room had fireplaces at each end, glowing with beds of hardwood coals which took the chill from the chamber. Fat candles in sconces on the walls warmly lighted the board.

The guests included Henrietta Hart, now the proprietress of a prosperous tavern on the river below Hog Island; the Claybornes' neighbor Roger Kendall; and his plump, merry sister-in-law Ann Short, who was not long out of England.

This lady sat on a hickory stool at the right hand of Sir Mathew, who was bundled in a robe against the draughts. Beside her, a constant prey to Mistress Short's mischievous eyes, sat the morose tutor David Broome. Opposite them Roger Kendall sat beside Henrietta Hart, whose face reflected great contentment at being included in such fine company. Lance, properly placed below his father's guests, contemplated the gathering and tried to forget his gnawing appetite.

Below them, on benches, were Goody Ballard, the housekeeper, pink of cheeks from her work at the spit; Abram Gale, the overseer, ready with his spoon of hollywood; Ned Peo; and a place for Henry Pettus, the old steward, who was at the other fireplace helping the black cook, Candace, roast the oysters.

Sir Mathew said blessings for the provisions. His brows came up and pleasure lighted his eyes as Candace placed the shellfish platter at his elbow. Within a minute all were eating in fine humor.

They talked of home affairs—of the quality of tobacco now cured and ready at the landing sheds; of a strange native ferret which the night before had killed half a dozen hens; of the threatening weather and the ice which floated in the Chickahominy.

Ann Short boasted of some woolen yarn she had made on a spinning wheel. "The yarn is for a quilt," she said. "We need some extra coverlets for these cold Virginia nights."

Henrietta sighed. "Alas, a husband is warmer than a bearskin robe." She winked at Ann and turned to David Broome. "As for you, Parson, you should know that a wife is warmer than a husband. Someday a bride will end your shivering."

The exiled clergyman sighed deeply. Ann Short laughed. Thereupon the parson bowed his head and laid aside his knife as though he had lost his appetite.

"The parson is a poet," Lance revealed. "A veritable Lovelace."

Broome picked up his tankard, and, face buried in it, concealed the wave of color that now suffused his cheeks. The parson did not mind the teasing. For all his confusion, it suited him to be the center of attention.

Lance pressed on. "He showed me a sonnet he had penned—about a maiden's nose. It was a round, upturned little beak . . . like Ann's!"

It was now Mistress Short's turn to blush. She did it prettily.

Roger Kendall came to her rescue by changing the subject. "Did you know, sir," he said, addressing Sir Mathew, "that a new Nathaniel Bacon has arrived in the colony? He is a Cambridge man, and they say he has considerable property. He has a seat at Curle's Neck and new headrights on the upper James. They say that Berkeley has invited him to join the Council."

"I hope he reflects carefully on that matter," Sir Mathew growled. "He may find his foot in a bear trap."

"He is a nephew of our present Nathaniel Bacon and, they say, the old man's heir," Kendall explained.

"I hear that Governor Berkeley is building the coach for his Culpeper bride," Lance remarked. "He has asked that we lend him Llewellyn, our smith, to help with the axles." Lance turned to his father. "I said it would be all right, sir."

Sir Mathew said nothing.

"Yes, she is still a bride," said Henrietta Hart. "And the old man grovels. Next he will want to build a road from here to Middle Plantation and pave it with marble cobbles."

When dinner was over Roger Kendall had a long conversation with David Broome. The upper Chickahominy parish needed a minister. There was a good glebe and a log church. There were other ministers available, but none so learned and few so well behaved as he. Would he be interested?

Broome's face turned very red and then white, in spite of the rosy firelight. "Could I be worthy?" he whispered. "Could I be worthy?"

Kendall patted him on the knee. "You are, my friend. For years you have been worthy. You have finished with the boy. You must now help us with others."

∽§ 5

THE Clayborne-Forke feud flared up fiercely, if briefly, during the spring of Lance's eighteenth birthday. Lance learned from sailors in Henrietta Hart's tavern that Forke was back in Virginia waters, based on Kickotan Creek twenty leagues east of Jamestown. The sailors added that the captain visited the Wain Wheel Tavern every evening. Henrietta warned Lance that Forke might have sent the sailors to lure him into a trap.

Weighing this information carefully, the Claybornes decided to act quickly. Lance and Peo started for Kickotan within an hour, determined to spring any trap that Captain Forke might be setting for his own defense or for the discomfiture of his enemies.

Thereupon occurred the fight which, not without some injustice, gave Lance Clayborne a reputation for adventurous violence second to no brawler in the colony. It was called the affair of the five swords.

The Wain Wheel Tavern, built on the water side of a massive tobacco wharf, was a forbidding sight at dusk when Lance and Peo approached. Unpainted, gray from the salt spray of a hundred squalls, its sign an almost spokeless wheel creaking on its chains like a gibbeted skeleton, the structure overhung the water of Kickotan Creek. The old building seemed to float on the dark waters.

Lance and Peo, after making sure that no boat was at the wharf and none of Captain Forke's bullies were in the place, entered the common room.

Watt Cary, the landlord, and his two broad-beamed Dutch wenches were at the fire, basting a saddle of mutton. Cary frowned when he recognized Lance and Peo, and the fluttering nervousness with which he sought to make them comfortable plainly indicated that he had expected other guests.

Peo went to the window and looked out over the broad creek. Lance took off his hat and gloves and stared hard at the now trembling landlord. The Dutch girls, after admiring glances at Clayborne's black wig and dove-colored doublet, scurried out of the room like chickens. That wig was worth two herring boats.

"You are expecting Captain Forke, I believe?" Lance said to Watt Cary.

The landlord started to shake his head.

Peo came over and took him by the throat. "You are?" Peo asked.

"In God's name!" cried the landlord.

"Speak out!" Peo commanded, shaking the man until his head flapped back and forth within an inch of the oak mantel.

Watt Cary, eyes popping from Peo's mighty grip, cried, "Yes!"

Lance now took his turn at the window and looked over the dusk-darkened water. Suddenly he pulled on his gloves and turned to Cary. "You will say nothing about our being here tonight. Do you understand?"

The landlord nodded. "Yes, yes!"

"You will see that those girls say nothing. Do you understand?" Lance's hand was on his sword.

"Yes, yes, your worship! They know no English."

Lance and Peo left the inn.

Peo scratched his head as they walked across the wharf to the stable yard. It was his way of asking his master what was next.

"We are early, as planned," said Lance. "But we must wait for our share of Master Cary's roast of mutton. I saw a boat on the creek."

"How many people?" Peo inquired.

"Five."

Peo whistled and fingered the French hatchet looped in his belt.

"This is another of Forke's moves," said Lance. "Take the horses, Peo, and hide them in the pines yonder. We'll stay in the bushes awhile and see what kind of terrors they may prepare for us."

The leather-clad servant grinned as he untied the horses and mounted.

Lance took off his beaver hat and cloak and walked into the high marsh grass beside the wharf, whence he could see the oncoming boat. The oarlocks were muffled—further evidence that a snare was being laid. Again Lance counted the silhouettes of five men. They wore cloaks. The man in the stern might be Jesús Forke.

Peo joined Lance in the shelter of the tall clumps of grass beside the road. Together they watched the boat disappear under the wharf.

The men climbed the ladder silently, paused on the wharf and examined the shadows. It was now almost completely dark. One of them peeped through the shutters of the inn before signaling the others to follow him inside.

Lance whispered to Peo. "I am sure they expect us. They will post a sentinel to warn them of our arrival. Be still, now." Mindless of his velvet doublet, Lance went belly down in the salty marsh grass beside his servant.

Two men came out of the inn and walked across the wharf and up the road past the stable yard. They took stations on either side of the road ten yards apart.

"Guards," whispered Lance in Peo's ear. "Take the one to starboard, Peo. Use the flat of your hatchet only, boy. Then tie him up with a strip from his cloak. I'll take number two. He is nearest, so I'll wait until you strike. The fools are watching the tavern lights. They will be half blinded."

Peo wriggled away into the darkness as slowly and quietly as a snake. Lance, loosening his belt, unhooked his sheathed sword and turned his belt around so the buckle would be at his back. Sword in his right hand, he crawled quietly through the grass toward the nearest cloaked shadow.

A sharp breeze was playing music in the tall pines, but neither stalker took any chances of being heard. It was ten long minutes before Lance, crouched behind his man, heard the clunk of Peo's hatchet and the thud of the falling sentinel.

An instant later the hilt of Lance's heavy military rapier struck the head of the other watchman.

They trussed and gagged the two guards thoroughly. Both men were bearded, after the Spanish style. Neither had the hard hands of a farmer or a seaman. Both had the heavy forearms and shoulders of practiced swordsmen.

Lance took their weapons and hid them beneath his cloak in the grass. "The odds have changed, Peo, my lad," he whispered.

"There still are three."

"And we must catch them with their feet under the table," Lance said.

They peered through the shutters of the inn, and Lance sighed with great satisfaction. Seated at the end of the table was his father's enemy, the sea merchant.

Forke was watching the spit. The glow from the hearth showed every feature of his swarthy face. A cutlass scar marked his left eyebrow, and there was a bullet mark across his chin. Otherwise, the countenance of this man, a known pirate and smuggler guilty of a score of felonies, resembled a solemn, devout separatist preacher. As Forke addressed his companions he nodded and gestured as though exhorting them to prayer.

Lance could not hear the conversation, but after a moment Captain Forke smiled. The smile completely changed the benign expression of his face. It split his jaws and showed his small, separated teeth. It was the grimace of a man in whom cruelty had long since taken the place of gaiety.

The lean sea merchant was elegantly dressed in dark velvet, with Flemish lace at his collar. Jewels glinted from his baldric buckle, and there was gold on the scabbard of the rapier that lay on the table before him.

His companions were more plainly clad. And, like the men outside, both were bearded like Spaniards. Unlike Forke, they had their swords at their sides, and their feet were under the table.

No pistols were in evidence. Lance remembered that Governor

Berkeley frowned on murder with firearms. Murder with the sword was different. Dueling was deplorable, but men who wore weapons presumably could defend themselves. Bodies found with sword wounds generally were adjudged to be those of incautious brawlers.

After one more reconnoitering glance through the shutters Lance slowly and silently unsheathed his long military rapier and leaned the scabbard against the wall. "Any more boats on the creek, Peo?" he whispered.

Peo shook his head.

"Listen, then," said Lance, his lips an inch from Peo's ear. "We attack without warning or parley. Disable. Do not kill. You will strike the man on the right. I will take the one on the left. Leave Forke to me, then. Do you understand?"

Peo nodded and drew his hatchet from his belt.

"Come on!"

Lance and Peo burst into the common room like a blast from a thunder squall. Peo shrilled a terrifying Chiskiack war whoop as he charged the table. He was the first to reach his mark—again with the flat of his heavy French hatchet.

Lance's first adversary managed to draw and go on guard, but, unbalanced by a leap backward from the low bench, the man went down at the second pass with Lance's sword through both his buttocks.

Captain Forke, startled though he was by the surprise assault, was ready by the time Lance could disengage his weapon.

The table collapsed. A bench was kicked aside. Lance waved away Peo and crossed swords with his father's enemy.

"The odds have changed, Captain Forke," said Lance.

"So you will murder me?" The pirate was panting, but he fenced well. He was, Lance observed, skilled with the edge, like most sailors. However, Forke did not slash furiously enough to expose his body to a thrust.

"Yes, Captain Forke, I shall kill you," said Lance.

"I have never harmed you, boy."

"You slew my Uncle Walter."

"In fair fight."

"That is a lie, Captain Forke."

Lance soon had the seaman sweating with play learned from his soldier father. His circle parry baffled Forke. His lunges at the throat harassed the sailor and forced him to use the point against his will. And eternally the boy jeered at his adversary. His talk was another soldier trick.

"It will be a belly wound, Captain Forke—low in the gut!"

Forke tried in vain to free his blade for a slash at the legs. Lance's point scraped his throat and brought flecks of red to the lace collar.

The sailor gave ground and tried to kick a stool toward his persistent foe. Lance's point flicked a button from Forke's brocaded sleeve.

"My father should be doing this, but he has the gout," said Lance. "He would have killed you in three passes, Captain Forke."

The sea merchant, now against the wall, received a light thrust in the thigh. He had to parry a furious assault which spun him sideways.

Peo shouted a warning. Forke's left hand had found a pewter tankard on the wall rack. He flung it clumsily at Lance's head.

Lance ducked the missile, but in this instant of diversion Captain Forke employed a new tactic. Before Lance could re-engage, the lean seaman dropped his sword and dove headfirst through the window.

There was a great splash. Lance started to follow his adversary, but Peo pulled him back.

They ran out on the wharf into the darkness. There was silence. Peo untied the boat, and they searched without result.

"No sailor can swim," said Peo. "The devil is drowned."

"That devil could swim as far as Maryland," Lance growled. "Smash the boat."

They went back to the tavern to help the Dutch wenches tend the buttock wounds of Lance's first adversary. They had to use chicken feathers for want of lint.

Next day Lance brought five swords home to Clayborne Castle.

Sir Mathew was astounded. The old soldier had much difficulty concealing his amazed pride in his son's achievement. "Bind the five swords into a sheaf and put them above the armory mantel," he directed. Then, turning to his tall son, he added, "Perhaps you'd better hang your own there, too, Lance. You may never have any further use for it."

"What do you mean, Father?" the lad asked.

Sir Mathew chuckled. "Who would fight you after this?"

Lance laughed nervously, fingering the hilt of his rapier.

"Yes, who?" his father said, staring into the flames of the hickory-log fire. "I suppose you must continue wearing it, Lance. It is the fashion. But before you draw it again, have good cause. You must not be a bully—ever. Keep in practice. Teach your sons that circle parry. But never, never use your sword unworthily."

Lance's bearded assailant whose bleeding buttocks had been patched with chicken feathers turned out to be one Cornet Gary, whose family was prominent in Accomack County, that nest of pirates over on the eastern shore. In pain and rage the man swore out a warrant charging the Clayborne boy with mayhem.

Lance was somewhat dismayed. He knew that his adventure had been an escape from assassins whom Forke had employed to murder him and his father. He marveled that Gary had the effrontery to swear out a warrant.

The County Sheriff visited Lance and with a flourish presented a summons. The boy rode off with the officer to see the nearest magistrate about the matter.

It was a lovely day and warm. The County Sheriff was convivial at first. They stopped at Hopkins' ordinary and drank some ale. Then two leagues farther on they stopped at another place, and Sheriff Barton, as before, drank two for one.

Lance Clayborne and the officer had been comradely enough for a while, but the ale soon made the Sheriff boastful. He proclaimed himself a mighty figure in the county and complained of his long ride to Council Point and lectured Lance on good manners. At last the young man protested against his uncalled-for insolence.

"I want no talk from you!" the Sheriff growled.

Lance reined in his horse and said, "I think you're drunk, my man. I want no talk from *you!*"

The Sheriff thereupon forgot himself entirely and, cursing, reached for one of the big pistols in his saddle holster.

The young man did not draw a weapon. He stood up in his stirrups, put one booted foot atop his saddle and with the other kicked the Sheriff from his horse. Lance dismounted, and as the officer rose and stooped to regain his fallen weapon he booted him roughly into the bog beside the road.

There, in terror at his youthful prisoner's unexpected strength, his mouth filled with muck, the Sheriff listened to a cursing which almost curled his hair.

Lance ended his reproof when, with further boyish recklessness, he tore up the summons and flung the fragments at the sputtering man. "Be thankful that I do not make you eat it, you son of a sow!" he concluded.

There were some who said that Lance disappeared that spring because he was afraid of the consequences of this assault on an officer of the Crown. This was not the case. He and Peo generally journeyed westward immediately after corn-planting time, the beginning of the fever season. This spring there were some western lands near Shoccoes to be inspected and a hunting tryst with Pipisko of the Chiskiacks.

Lance thought little of his encounter with Sheriff Barton. He had been no more lawless than many another Virginian.

⤙§ 6

As USUAL there was a great dance in the Chiskiack village when Lance and Peo arrived, and after that a ceremonial council, at which Lance delivered three pack-horse loads of gifts and the chief men recited the news of a year. Pipisko had lost two warriors to the Doegs, but he had captured two women and six trade guns. Their foes were hunting southward along the wide trail, he said, because the Doegs feared the Iroquois north of the Potomac.

Pipisko and his thirty fighting men were much amused by Ned Peo's stories of his master's recent difficulties. If Lance was half Indian, his servant seemed nine-tenths Chiskiack, so his chronicle was elaborately embellished with the stuff of legend.

"My master, Usack"—Lance was called this by the savages because he had seen a heron—*Usack*—in a watch-night dream three years before—"is a mighty warrior with the long knife used by Englishmen," said Peo. "The sword was a tongue of fire in his hand. It was quicker than a hungry snake, more deadly than a war hatchet!"

Expressionless faces watched Peo intently.

He held up his right hand, fingers outstretched. "And five enemies there were against him!" Peo modestly omitted his own part in the fray. "The wind from their swordplay whistled like a gale. And when steel met steel, sparks flew. Usack scorned the kill." Peo laughed. "But there will be one man who will not rest easily in his chair for several moons."

Thereupon Peo described the wound which Lance had inflicted on Cornet Gary. Pipisko smiled, but not the others. The warriors thought Lance should have killed his adversaries and chopped off their heads.

For weeks that summer Lance and Peo wandered with Pipisko and his young warriors along the ridges, returning at intervals to the village. There were signs of northern Indians to the east—a discarded Susquehannock moccasin, a broken Seneca arrow beside the trail. The foothills to the west and south showed no evidence of visitors. The beaver were tame out there. So were the bears and the deer.

It was sweet to rest in Pipisko's little town. Even a bark lodge was welcome after days in the open, exposed to blustery thunderstorms and the adders with rattles on their tails and panthers which lay in wait along oak limbs over the deer runs.

"Why do we do it, Peo?" Lance asked as he anointed a thorn ulcer with bear fat. "Why don't we remain at home and tend tobacco like other Englishmen?"

"Such journeys defeat the devil," Peo answered.

"How, my philosopher?"

"All men are in two parts," said Peo. "One part is devil, the other part human. In every young man the devil part is uppermost. When your father, Sir Mathew, was young he did not remain at home. He went awarring with Prince Rupert and King Charles. Since you live here in the colony, you must go ahelling among the Indians. You expend your devil's mood in the forests."

"But you, Peo. You are no longer a boy. Nor are you a bond servant any longer. Why should you come? Half those western acres near Shoccoes are yours, you know."

Peo frowned and shook his head. "Who am I to be rich, young master? Think you that I ever could hold that land against the Governor and his clique? Land means only trouble. I am just your hired servant, the son of a swineherd."

Lance snorted. "And a fool, Peo. This is Virginia, man, not Europe. Why should you not hold your land, be rich?"

Peo's sunburned face for a moment was sullenly cynical. "Be rich? It is not meant for sons of swineherds to be rich anywhere in this world. In these western counties there is a certain measure of freedom. The Governor cannot follow us out here. No sheriff ventures far from his courthouse. But to hold land, to gain wealth from it, is a different matter. Only the Governor and his Council can be wealthy men. Consider your father, now. He seeks to remain independent and to retain his property. But as sure as you and I are sitting here he will lose it if Governor Berkeley lives five years longer. The Governor will ruin him, just as he ruined Drummond and Lawrence and many another who refused to play at bowls and at chess with him and the fat men there at Jamestown. You are wise to take up western lands far from the plantations. You are very wise to learn with me the ways of the savages. They are better neighbors than those greedy men in the east."

Lance sighed. "But gentlemen are not supposed to live with savages."

"Yes, master," said Peo, staring into the fire. "Some young gentlemen had rather take their adventure from an alepot than smell fresh air. They will endure all manner of gripes and fever all summer instead of living as men should. Would you rather be a man—or a gentleman?"

"I can be both perhaps," said Lance, and smiled. "But let me be a savage awhile longer."

Peo's eyes flickered over his master's long body. "You are restless, for all your exercise. You take things too seriously." He paused. "Methinks you need a woman."

That summer Lance discovered that females belonged to a race as different from men as fox from wolf. The Indian girls were small-bodied, but in hungry times they could outendure the strongest man. They made pretense of coyness only to become, when the occasion suited their mood, as shameless as she-cats. They were filled with joy one day and, for no apparent reason, poisonously moody the next. All heaven could not make them love one man, but another, with some quirk of personality that no male could recognize, would set dozens of plump breasts glowing with the fires of hell.

The bold-faced Indian girls moved about in chattering flocks and beset a favored visitor like a horde of mischievous demons. They began to admire Lance Clayborne's thick hair, straight legs and strong, long-fingered hands, and passed candid comment on his now well-developed body, teasing, joking, dancing until, in spite of his self-control, he found himself at last burning with sensations which his tutor David Broome had told him proper Englishmen suppressed.

It did no good to threaten these persistent nymphs. They paid no attention to his rebuffs and curses. Unattached and, according to Indian reckoning, old enough to be a proper lover, he was a challenge to womanhood, and so they charmed at every opportunity, day or night. At last, in desperation, he had to make a choice.

Pipisko brought her to Lance one day, half dragging, half kicking her along.

"Her name is Miskee," said the chief. "Chattering Brook. She has a busy tongue."

Miskee was as softly lovely as an otter and as full of animal gaiety. Lance took her warm brown hand.

"You must beat her at least once every day," said Pipisko. "She is wild, this one. She is a Potomac girl—for you, my brother."

Lance understood. The captive girl Miskee was a gift, presented as simply as a new hatchet or belt. Lance must return the courtesy. He gave Pipisko his silver-chased pistol.

The warrior turned the weapon over in his brown hands. "It is well," he said, and ran his fingers over the barrel. Then he turned to go. "Do not forget to beat her!" he said, and left them alone.

Miskee immediately began to justify her name. She chattered. Within the month she taught him more about the Indian language than he had learned in three years hitherto.

There were words for making love that she used frequently—too frequently—but no word for love itself. She was completely an animal in this respect. There was a word for submissiveness, another for obedience, but none for tenderness.

She was prettier of face than many an English girl and as well formed as a nymph. A lively intelligence kept her black eyes alight, but except for her figure there was little in her that he could consider womanlike. She constantly reminded him of the difference between Indians and Europeans, between barbarism and the condition which he had been taught was civilization.

Most of the day she was kept busy at her normal duties by the older squaws. Miskee took her turn with a hoe in the village maize and squash patches. She cleaned, cured and bleached the summer deerskins, kept him well supplied with moccasins and learned to salt his stew properly. She also kept their bark lodge rainproof and reasonably free from vermin. But offduty she was gay and unrestrained.

She wished to swim in the creek among a dozen other naked Indians—and she wanted him to play there also. The girl constantly boasted of the physical perfection of her man, pointing to his various features as though he were a fine horse. And always she wanted—to the very limit of his fresh, not inconsiderable capacity—the pleasures of physical contact. In this she constantly embarrassed him in the presence of her merry companions.

The Indian boys and girls had none of the English notions about such things. They did not believe in sharing any pleasure in dark secrecy. In time he acquired some of the savage notions in this respect and shared in the fun.

Miskee smelled like hickory buds, and the skin over her firm muscles was a delight to touch. Many times Lance found himself wishing that he could hold her in his arms and caress her. But caresses were foreign, utterly out of place in the life of the barbarian girl. She could understand a cuff or a kick, but she got no delight whatever from a kiss.

It was this season with Miskee that the village was raided by a war party from the Doegs, a tribe from the north.

Nine Doeg warriors snaked into the village during the height of a furious thunderstorm, bent on stealing a pair of young Chiskiack squaws. So thick was the rain, so uproarious the thunder that the invaders were able to enter four lodges and bind the arms of their chosen captives before an alarm could be given.

Lance Clayborne shortly thereafter found himself in the thick of a melee the ferocity of which he was to remember for the remainder of his life.

The Doegs fought as a co-ordinated unit. Chiskiack warriors had to attack the raiding party one by one as the war cries called them into battle.

Blinded by the rain, Lance tangled with a slippery, paint-smeared giant about forty years old who unwisely held his knife backhanded. When the man's knife arm slithered from his grasp Lance ducked and smeared some sandy mud on his left palm. Then as the Doeg's blade nicked his shoulder the English boy secured a firmer hold and jerked his enemy forward.

Sliding in the muddy pathway from his own momentum as well as from Lance's pull, the savage lost balance, and Lance's longer, wider-bladed weapon reached its target. The Doeg's death cry and Lance's shout of triumph intermingled.

Pipisko was fighting at a door of his lodge. A man was down beside him from a hatchet blow. Another staggered past Lance holding both hands over his slashed abdomen. A Chiskiack at the corner of the council house was snapping a flintlock that was too soaked to fire.

Lance assailed Pipisko's immediate opponent from the flank as a tremendous lightning flash brightened the muddy scene. The Doeg dropped his knife and ran to the palisado. With fear and thunder goading him the warrior mounted the barrier like a squirrel and disappeared.

Pipisko's war cry marshaled ten warriors for a pursuit of the raiders, but the rain, heavier now than ever, ended the chase. Two Chiskiacks were killed and four of the enemy. The two captive squaws were recovered.

There was a feast of mourning the next day, followed by a dance of triumph in which Lance was awarded two tufted eagle feathers.

Miskee was more obedient and industrious after the thunder battle. Lance had slain one of the greatest Doeg war chiefs. He was now a proved man. She even learned at last to keep dog meat out of their pot. By then the approach of autumn was coloring the leaves of the black-gum trees.

Lance stretched his sun-browned arms. There was a bracelet of peake beads on his left wrist to protect it from the snap of a bowstring. On his shoulder near the scar from the Doeg's knife was his clanmark, a tattooed turtle. His torso and hips were bare, his legs encased in long, fringed semibreeks tied to his belt by rawhide strings. In the fold of his clout he bore his paint pouch. His elkhide belt had loops for knife and hatchet, and it was buckled behind his back. Chest, arms and face were smooth with bear fat pigmented with bloodroot and blue clay. Around his neck he wore a charm bag.

Traders had passed through and had not recognized him, nor would any Englishman unless he chose to identify himself. Peo was even more of a savage. His skin was of a deeper brown, and Peo was more artistic with his paint.

"We must start back to Council Point," Lance said.

"Yes, master. I had thought of that."

"Two days from now."

Peo went to round up the pack animals.

Lance summoned the girl. "Miskee!" In the Indian dialect he ordered, "Fetch me the doeskin leggings and my extra moccasins and matchcoat."

On most occasions Miskee chattered happily, but now she wailed until he motioned as if to kick her on the seat. Soon most of the younger women of the village joined in doleful chorus at the news. Pipisko hurried to propose that he remain until the moon of falling leaves and join the fire hunts in the uplands.

Lance shook his head. Sweet had been the time spent in the clean wilderness, but winter soon would be blowing in from the southwest. He had promised Ed Walker to help him with a new warehouse on Archer's Hope Creek. Then there was that matter with the Sheriff. He would have to pay a fine, perhaps. As for the affair with Cornet Gary, he would contest that case before the General Court if it were carried further. It surely was no crime to defend one's skin against a tavern brawler.

The Council Point plantation was a day's journey west of Jamestown, so there would be many tiresome visitors when cold weather came—dullard farmers, wandering peddlers and tinkers, new rich members of the Council trying to pose as gentlemen, officers traveling upriver to the Henrico garrison, shipmasters in from London offering stale goods left over from the markets of Lower Norfolk and Jamestown.

Any one of them could be a deadly enemy, a tool of that apostate pirate with a Spanish given name, Jesús Forke. For Lance could not believe that the wily merchant had met his end in the waters of Kickotan Creek. Someday he would reappear.

Lance sighed and stretched again. Oh, well, the feud meant some relief at home from boredom. Even the eastern plantations could be endurable with danger as a salt for his life there.

Ha! If the Governor's sycophants at Jamestown could see him now! In any event he would wear his pagan garments on the journey. They were superior to English clothes in the woods. Moccasins were silent on the leafy turf. Thorns that stripped the threads from English hose glanced harmlessly from the leg-length Indian leggings. His otter mantle was almost invisible in the woods.

Pipisko sat down beside him at the door of the lodge. The Indian's lean face was sorrowful.

"I hope to see you next year when the corn is ankle high," Lance said.

"I shall be glad, my brother."

"You will keep your young men off the wide trail from the north, Pipisko?"

"We shall remain here and range westward. We have a fine store of dried meat. We have the salt and ammunition which you brought us. Peo has repaired our guns and helped us make new traps. My people have become fat. The women are wailing at your departure. They make noise as though a warrior had died."

Lance smiled sadly, then said, "Miskee . . . You will care for her?"

"She will prosper from your gifts."

Lance again warned his friend against incursions in the direction of the wide trail, the great trail of many paths which already bore scouts from the Susquehannocks and other fierce tribes. If the Indians migrated southward, there would be border warfare. White men would shoot every Indian, including those who, like Pipisko, now wore a pass badge to the settlements.

"I shall avoid the wide trail," Pipisko promised.

Lance left his grain-starved horses with Tam MacFarlane, the factor at Shoccoes, and journeyed down the river on Colonel Hill's sloop.

Colonel Edward Hill, commander of the Henrico garrison, was a surly, tough man who, though wholly subservient to Governor Berkeley, hated to have his fifty men immobilized in the fort on the north bank of the river near Byrd's trading post. The Governor would not permit any movement by the garrison into the forest, and the men were growing stale from inactivity.

Colonel Hill was greatly interested in Lance's news that the Iroquois were active and that the Susquehannocks were being pressed southward. "It's almost time for another of those damned migrations," Hill growled. "The savages will move along the fall-line trail and shoot some pigs, and then there will be hell to pay."

The colonel was pessimistic also about affairs in the eastern counties. He said that a substantial anti-Berkeley faction had arisen among the farmers on account of new taxes. "I hope they do not inflict on me any of the eastern militia in case of trouble," Hill said. "The men are all full of fever by the time they reach the place of muster, and half of them don't know one end of a fusil from the other. However, if the northern Indians begin to raid, we will probably need every musketeer and pikeman we can find."

As the sloop, under a steady southwest breeze, passed Turkey Island, the elegantly dressed Colonel Hill unwittingly stared too hard at Lance's Indian garments.

Lance thereupon explained that they were the only clothes that he had with him, that his trip to the west had been one in which such habiliments were appropriate.

"No one could possibly recognize you unless you spoke," said Hill with a forced smile. "I did not mean to be rudely curious."

"Apologies are unnecessary, sir," Lance replied.

IV

The Masquerade

~§ 1

AT ARCHER'S HOPE wharf Lance, anxious to get home quickly, sent Peo over to a near-by plantation to borrow horses. He waited now, idly watching a crew of Negroes load tobacco.

The line of chanting black men rolled hogsheads from the wharf shed to a barge moored to the side of the shaky pier. A fat overseer, seated on a pile of bagged grain, looked on and occasionally shouted at the slaves in some heathen dialect.

Except for the loaders, the landing was deserted. The forest was pierced by the little muddy trail that led to the settlement a mile away. The vast trees crowded around the log warehouse as though jealous of this work of man and anxious to thrust it back into the black water. In the shadow of the pines the hurrying slaves seemed like insects.

As Lance leaned against a pier post he noticed other figures emerging from the woods beyond the storage house. It was a mounted party—gentlefolk, to judge by the quality of their horses and the color of their bonnets.

Among them was a graceful girl in a bright-blue riding coat seated on a gray that was much too big for her. The horse danced ahead of the little cavalcade.

The girl seemed strangely beautiful to Lance, who for months had seen only barbarians. Her hair, thickly braided and bound tightly, was as bright as new maize silk, and her eyes were large and merry.

The young man moved forward quickly to warn the rider away from the treacherous damp flooring of the wharf. Before he could block the way the big horse had leaped onto the slippery planks.

Lance reached for the bridle ring, one hand on the horse's shoulder, but by now the harm was done. The unfamiliar footing, the noise of his hoofs on the hollow boards, the odor of the sweating Negroes and the sight of Lance in his savage garments brought sudden terror to the animal.

Lance missed the bridle, then jumped sideways to the outer edge of the pier to block the way. The horse reared sharply and slipped on the moist planking.

The girl struggled clear of her sidesaddle and fell squarely across the young man's shoulder.

Lance teetered for a moment, trying to balance himself and to avoid the slipping, staggering horse. Still grasping the girl, he tumbled backward into the water.

Weeks in the wilderness had sharpened his wits. He sensed that the horse also would fall from the wharf. As they struck the water his last conscious act was to thrust the girl beneath him. The panic-stricken beast came down on top of them. . . .

Lance came to his senses beneath a pine tree on the shore. The girl was holding him with tenderness. He closed his eyes to let more of the fog clear from his brain.

A bump on his head was being bathed with cool water. He felt the sting of a cut somewhere on his bare shoulder. He moved slightly. There seemed to be no other hurts. She held him firmly and felt his right arm as though to see if it were broken.

"Keep still," she said. Then, addressing someone whom he could not see, she said: "He is coming to his senses now. I tell you he is not an Indian!"

"He wears an Indian's clothing. His upper body and his hips are bare. He wears those heathen diapers——"

"He is not a savage. He has a soft beard."

"Look at the clanmark on his shoulder——"

"Indians never behave as he did. An Indian would have let me break my neck. Savages do not rescue girls who fall from horses."

Lance sighed as though he were just awakening, then whispered, "You were not injured?"

The girl started. "Oh!"

"My thanks for rescuing me from the water," he said. "I am sorry I was so awkward."

"Hush now. You were hurt."

He moved again, and again she restrained him with strong hands at his shoulders.

"Savages never complain of little hurts," he said.

"You are not an Indian!" The girl turned to her companion. "Get me another gourd of water, Alice. He is coming to his senses."

Lance kept still awhile. The soft fingers of the girl were pleasant to his half-bearded face. Her warmth and soft loveliness had started his heart to beating rapidly. The fog that had blurred his vision began to clear.

She was the most handsome girl he had ever seen. The wide blue eyes, now compassionate, the fairness of her skin and her great rope of softly golden hair were like those of an angel in a painting he remembered.

She said, "If you had not shielded me just now, I would have lost my life."

"Why am I here?" he asked. "I think it is I who owe a life to you."

"Don't talk," she said. "You are injured. You have a frightful bump on your head. The water was not deep."

Her white teeth were nibbling at her lower lip, and her wide eyes were anxious. As she held him he realized with infinite comfort that for four long months he had been a stranger to English voices and the sweetness of English words. Not since his mother's death so many years ago had he felt the utter tenderness of an Englishwoman's hands.

Now, he reflected, if he were in the Indian town, he would be on his feet, deprecating with loud grunts his minor hurts. But it was pleasant to lie there with his head on the maiden's lap. He stirred weakly so that she pressed his shoulders down again and pouted at him.

"Must not move!" she commanded.

He smiled. "I like it here," he said.

Looking up at her lovely face, he remembered having seen it years before. Probably she was Ed Walker's sister Easter, who had been away in England. There was a hint of the London accent in her voice.

"They think you are an Indian," she said. "I know better. But for these heathen clothes, I'd think you were a gentleman."

"Why?"

"Because," she said. "You are impudent."

"Impudent?"

"Yes. You said you . . . you like it here."

"So would any man."

"See? Now you are gallant. If you had not risked your life to help me, I would be thoroughly ashamed."

"Please——"

"I would, indeed. No Christian ever wore a dress like this of yours. Why, it's barbaric!"

He started to sit up, but she thrust him down. "Keep still!"

"Where's my servant? Has he returned?"

"Yes. And now he has gone with the boys to fetch a litter."

"A litter—for me? Ho!"

"Who are you?" she asked.

"A wanderer. Who are you?" he asked. "Are you not Mistress Easter Walker?"

She looked down at him, wondering. "Why . . . yes. How did you know?"

"A sturgeon at the bottom of the creek informed me," he replied. "Now by your leave I shall arise."

He climbed to his feet a bit unsteadily because of his still swimming head and lifted her beside him. She looked up at him, surprised at his strength. Her head scarcely reached his shoulder.

His mantle had caught on a splinter in the piling and hung, still dry, above the water. He went over to the wharf and recovered it. Then, returning, he placed it around her shoulders.

She thanked him and said, "It smells like wood smoke. Is this an Indian cloak?"

"Yes," he said. "It's made of otterskin. Be careful now. Your clothing is still wet. This breeze is brisk. You may catch the ague."

She looked at him in almost frightened disapproval.

"But you," she said. "Why, you are half unclad. Your trousers . . ." She turned away.

"I see that you are not familiar with Indian clothing," he said. "The things are cut that way." Frowning, self-conscious, he had an impulse to flee.

Over on the wharf the fat overseer was laughing. Lance walked angrily toward him. The man got down from his pile of sacks and scurried aboard the barge. The line of Negroes halted. They laughed at the overseer's fright.

Lance's head, clear a moment ago, had now begun to ache from mortification. He faced the girl again.

"I'm sorry," she said, "I . . . I . . . you see I've been away in London so long. I've never seen the native dress on any except a native; I was . . . rude."

Her contrition heightened his embarrassment. To make matters worse, the girl's companion, accompanied by Peo and two young men, now came out of the pines. Peo had the horses, and to one he had rigged a drag litter made of poles and boughs.

"Here, take your cloak," she said.

He refused. As stolidly as an Indian he turned away. He decided that he would not look at her again. He signaled Peo, who was delighted to see him on his feet.

Lance drew his knife and cut away the brush litter so rapidly that he endangered the horse's skin. Then without a word he mounted and kicked the beast into a dead run.

Peo did not overtake him for quite a while. Lance cantered along in furious silence.

Finally he slowed to a walk. "Did they ask you who I was?" he asked.

"No, sir. We thought you had cracked your skull. I——"

"I'm glad she does not know my name," he said, half to himself. "My bare breech shocked the lady. She's not accustomed to the Indian garb." Then he cursed himself bitterly.

He was indeed hairy and half naked, but those long doeskin leggings tied to his belt with thongs were worth four horses, his otter matchcoat worth two more. What if his hips were bare? That was the fashion of the wilderness. Let her think he was a heathen, if she chose. She soon would learn better!

Then for a while he wondered why he was embarrassed. He swore again one of his father's most robust military oaths. Why should he care about her thoughts? Why should he bother himself about the opinion of a tender-fingered chit fresh from an English school—he who had known real women in the forest and had won three eagle feathers in the hunting camp of his adopted brother, Pipisko the Wary? If she were anything but an ignorant, unlettered foreigner, she would have recognized his clanmark and honored him.

Yet he felt his face flush beneath his growing beard. Her hands were soft. She had nursed him gently back to consciousness, mindless of her wetted garments. She had thought of him, not herself. She had bathed his bruised head and spoken to him anxiously, fearful of his life. She was strong as well as gentle, and as heavy-breasted as any Indian maid.

She had thanked him, but he had not had the grace to say farewell. She had thanked him, and he had been as rude as a savage.

Lance turned to Peo angrily. "Why did I run?" he asked.

In stolid gravity Peo replied, "Our Indian garments, sir, were cause enough. But young women have no business at that lonely landing."

Lance bit his lip. "Why do you lie to me?" he asked.

Peo frowned. "Is telling half the truth a lie, good master?"

"Yes. Tell all the truth. Why should I run away from a mud-soaked maiden even though I were wholly naked? Why?"

Peo thumbed his new-grown beard. On the road there had been no Indian girls to pluck their faces, so both had bushy growths. He cleared his throat, reached up and pulled a birch leaf from a bough that overhung the trail. "The woman is a witch," he said. "To every man some woman is a witch. She is yours, perhaps."

Lance laughed harshly. "I can almost believe it."

"I had a girl at Hatfield," Peo said sadly. "She was my witch. Memory of her pulled me all that distance back across the ocean with Master Kendall to find her married to a drover." He sighed again. "And yet, sir, I still remember my first sight of her."

"Never mind. You've told me of her many times."

"She——"

"Never mind." Lance breathed deeply of the autumn-scented air. He wondered if he would ever forget his first glimpses of the maiden of the wharf. Mounted, she had been as graceful as a queen, and he had seen her face through the dim haze of semiconsciousness. Steadily for minutes it had grown clearer and, as each feature had been revealed, more beautiful. Her lips were so perfectly formed that they would have seemed cold had they not trembled in solicitude for him; her eyes were deep and intelligent; a nose just pert enough; skin as delicate as dawn; body strong but rounded softly.

"I wonder if she'll remember me," he said aloud.

Peo shrugged. "Not again will she see you as muddy as you were today."

Lance frowned.

"Never mind, sir. Next time the lady will see you as an Englishman, a fashionable blade, begging your pardon, sir."

After pondering this idea with some satisfaction for a while, Lance finally changed the subject. "The County Sheriff, Peo—what was the scoundrel's name?"

"Barton, sir."

"Aye, Barton. Why did I kick him from his horse?"

"Did he not behave discourteously, sir?"

"Yes. And he was drunk, and when he reached for his pistol as though to threaten me I kicked him. That was it."

"Precisely, sir. Had I been there, I also would have kicked him."

"Was that a misdemeanor, Peo?"

"It was, sir. He was leading you to a magistrate to hold an inquiry because of that affair at the Wain Wheel when we fought the five blades."

"Yes, I recall. Well, that makes two misdemeanors, Peo. Before long I'll have to see the Governor and beg indulgence. My father will be in a rage, no doubt."

"He may have paid the fines."

"Not he. He might throw the Goodman Barton into the swamp again, but he would never pay my reckoning, nor would he see the Governor, either. He has little traffic with His Excellency, as you know."

Peo spat. "And many others likewise, sir. His Excellency is not the man he was when he led us into the woods in '56. That young wife of his, the Culpeper woman, has turned his mind toward riches, they say. And there hasn't been an election since 1662 unless he called one while we were away."

They rode in silence for a mile. Lance daydreamed again. He would have to ride to Tyndalls Point and find that tailor soon. He would show her that he could wear English clothes as well as any man. He would find her and prove to her he was not entirely savage.

◆§ 2

LANCE found his father, Sir Mathew, in better humor than he anticipated. A hailstorm which had ruined much tobacco in the county somehow had veered and spared the fields at Clayborne Castle.

The leaf had cured perfectly and but little had been spoiled in storage. The maize fields also had profited by this weather luck, the orchards had a bumper yield of fruit and two racing colts had turned out well under the careful hands of Gale, the overseer.

Four little bales of minkskins which Lance and Peo had brought downriver also cheered the old warrior. Times had been hard for years, and last winter's mink pelts were worth six shillings each.

Sir Mathew was surprised at Lance's report of peaceful Indians. Seamen had brought news of bloody trouble in the north colonies. King Philip's Wampanoags still were threatening the Massachusetts towns. Indians everywhere up north were restless. The price of fur accordingly had soared.

"Did our new men come?" Lance asked at dinner.

"Six survived the voyage," Sir Mathew said. "The grant of headright lands on their account has been made, so we can start planting upriver in the spring."

"Good."

"The scum of Plymouth," the old knight growled. "But they are likely, hardy brutes. Gale and Peo can manage them."

"I wish you could see that western acreage, Father," Lance said. "It's high and rolling land with many oaks. Soil is rich and deep where oak trees grow so large."

"Black oaks?"

"Yes—black oaks."

"Thick with Indian thieves, no doubt?"

"Peo and I can take care of them. The savages may slay a pig or two at times, but most of the thieving, I suspect, is done by wolves. The Indians have a healthy fear of the militia."

Lance told him about the Chiskiack hunting grounds among the hills above the Rappahannock River. Fur still was plentiful out there.

Sir Mathew growled, "So you have been living among those savages again?"

"For a while, sir."

"Have I not told you—?"

"If it were not for friendly Indians, we would not have found the western clearing we shall plant next season."

"Faugh. And you doubtless have had your fill of red-skinned wenches."

Lance smiled. "Indeed there is no lack of likely women."

"It's time you found a white girl, you hound! With your blood you could wed six thousand acres."

"Where?" Lance asked blandly.

"There are two widows. . . ."

"You'd have me marry two?"

"One is scarce twenty—the widowed Brantley girl. The other, Elizabeth Jives, is—well—is older—nearly twenty-six. Either would do. The elder widow has six thousand acres."

"I am barely twenty years old."

"That would suit either of them well. Besides, you could pass for twenty-five. You are bearded like an officer of the Horse Guards."

Lance smiled again. "We'll see, in good time. Perhaps it would be easier to take up more headrights in the west instead of marrying extra land. There is more room out there, but it's no place for sheltered widows, or simpering maidens either."

The boy flexed his lean fingers. "Ah, that is a country built for men! I've seen half a hundred deer at one salt lick, some close enough to knock down with a hatchet. Beaver swarm in every little valley. The dams built by the creatures have changed the course of many creeks. In some places a beaver pond fills up with dirt and leaves until the site becomes a marsh and finally a meadow. In these beaver meadows all the timber is so young that several acres can be cleared within a single season. This beaver-meadow land will grow maize stalks higher than my finger tips. The meadows are far richer than ordinary Indian clearings. You must go upriver with me soon and see our western quarter."

Sir Mathew's eyes were grave. This time he did not heed his son's new stories.

Lance paused, and said, "But I've not asked the news. Does all go well at the plantation?"

"Very well. Two bondsmen only died this month."

There was another pause, then Lance inquired, "His Excellency the Governor—is he still the youthful husband, or has he—?"

Sir Mathew snorted. "He is but a senile ass. I've seen him. He still nags at me for frightening his pirate friend away." Sir Mathew spat.

Lance scowled bitterly.

"I've seen the woman innkeeper again," Sir Mathew said. "She reports that Forke is alive and was last seen in Barbados in June. He has made two voyages in the slave trade, and doubtless he is richer than ever now."

Lance flexed his sinewy arms and smiled grimly. Sometimes he suspected that his father enjoyed his feud. It had given him an excuse to train his son to be a fighter, to make of Lance an instrument of steel. It was just as well. In Virginia a man needed a human enemy on whom to whet his wits against other formidable circumstances.

≈§ 3

GOVERNOR BERKELEY played no favorites at his autumn levee at his private estate, Green Spring, near Jamestown. Guests came from every eastern county to pay their respects and to celebrate with him the end of another planting season.

Punch was plentiful. Gossip flowed with rare abandon. Launcelot Clayborne heard some of it as he dismounted beyond the cedar hedge in the stable yard.

"—she swears he was a gentleman in Indian clothes," said one shrill woman's voice from the garden.

Another said, "Poor Easter."

Lance's ears burned as he moved to go away, yet before he reached the lantern light at the east-wing door he heard the high voice say again: "La! She is in a frightful state!"

Lance went into the hall. Easter—Easter Walker. What could they mean? A frightful state?

Absent-mindedly he left his cloak and hat in the hands of the Negro servant. The hallway was lighted by a hundred candles. His image in the great mirror startled him. He paused. At any rate he certainly was not a savage now.

His coat of mole-colored broadcloth had brocaded cuffs. Holland shirt and collar were as lacily immaculate. His silken waistcoat was cut with a flare above his gathered breeches with their gilded cords, and his baldric, on which was hung a dress sword which Charles II had given Sir Mathew, was embroidered in red arabesques. On his black shoes were Italian silver buckles in which were mounted a multitude of varicolored jewels.

This was not all. His long, well-shaped face, now smooth-shaven, was framed by a new coal-black periwig that would have been a credit to a duke. Lance had found it but three days before in the new stock of a ship from Liverpool.

His Continental clothes had changed his very posture. He no longer was a slouching forest runner. Once more he was the youth who years ago had been a cupbearer to Catherine of Braganza in Charles Stuart's court.

He straightened his baldric, pulled down his waistcoat and turned to enter the reception room. Blinking in the glitter of the candles, thinking still of the girl of the wharf at Archer's Hope, he suddenly stopped dead still.

She was standing with Ed Walker beside the fireplace screen! She was not ill at all, as he had feared. She was radiant.

He vowed again that there had never been a richer-bodied, more vivacious girl. Her eyes were as deep, her skin as pink, her hair as golden as he remembered, but, clad in a gown of purple patterned satin and alive with the excitement of gay company, she seemed too angelically fair to be human.

She glanced at him in candid curiosity, but she did not smile as her brother strode forward to greet the newcomer.

"Lance Clayborne! Where have you been, you rogue!"

Lance's words were inadequate because of his confusion, but as he was presented his bow was at least satisfactory, and as he raised his head dizzied by the touch of his lips to her firm, rose-scented hand he realized with dismay that she had not a spark of recognition in her eyes. There were now, on the other hand, plain, cold signs of disapproval.

Her first words were: "You are quite . . . famous, Master Clayborne." She had started to say "notorious."

Lance stepped back, blinking and fumbling at the ruffles of his cuffs. He was thoroughly shaken. Then he thought: why should she recognize him? Why should she be glad to see him? He was as unlike a certain muddied man in buckskin as a beast of a different species. On the wharf at Archer's Hope he had been a bewhiskered forest runner, a half-clad, bemired, bare-breeked lout in doeskin leggings. Here at the Governor's levee he was just one of two dozen glittering young cavaliers. His periwig made him seem older than his actual years. That alone could account for her failure to recognize him.

"I have heard many tales of you, Master Clayborne," she said, a chill in her voice discounting her politeness.

He flushed and found his voice. "You have been away in London far too long."

They traded a few words of small talk as fencers feel out their adversaries, she formal and aloof, he striving hopelessly for the faintest opportunity to stir a pleasant memory in her mind. He failed. To her he was another blade, a new admirer to be sharply discouraged at once lest he become obnoxious. She smiled at others in the gay party. To him she paid scarcely any attention whatever.

Ed Walker, full of gossip, wanted to know about his encounter with the Sheriff three months before. "How did you settle with him, Lance? They say you've been a—a fugitive."

Lance frowned ruefully and sought to change the subject, but the others in the circle seemed interested too, so he replied, "I did not know I was a runaway."

"The Sheriff said you were," Ed Walker teased. "He said you fled to Carolina with your five swords."

Exasperated, Lance turned to the girl. "The Sheriff was drunk and very rude, you see. I hope that you will not judge me by that circumstance."

She said nothing.

Ed Walker smiled. "I did not argue with him, Lance. I never argue with a very angry Sheriff."

Lance was anxious to protest, but now he noticed that the girl had other interests. Tom Hansford and another beau were at her elbow. It was plain she did not wish to talk of brawls.

Lance drew a deep breath, withdrew from the chattering circle. His new encounter with the girl had shaken him even more than the dramatic meeting at Archer's Hope. There was an aching sensation in the center of his body. He felt as though his heart had fallen down onto his hipbones and was slowly dying there. A chill began to tremble along his shoulder blades. He had to use his cambric handkerchief on his forehead. It suddenly had become wet. His feet seemed heavy.

It was only by conscious effort that he could keep his knees completely steady as he bowed to Lady Berkeley, to His Excellency and to the glittering members of the Royal Council of the colony.

Never in his life before had he been smitten to his very middle by one of the mischievous Cupid's darts. He had known passion, he had contemplated and appreciated beauty; but to the bewildering sensation that comes with awareness of a perfect personality of the other sex, and with an intermingling of tenderness, curiosity, desire, nostalgia, hopefulness and God knows what other elements of the spirit that can be stirred by a completely lovable woman, he was a total stranger.

The Governor and his lady were more gracious to him than he deserved in view of his reputation. They inquired of Sir Mathew's health, expressed regret that he had not been able to come and complimented Lance on the new grant of Henrico lands. He answered them; and as soon as he could politely withdraw he went to the terrace so that the river breeze could cool his head. There a butler offered him a pipe, which he accepted with relief.

Lance continued in the strange fog of new sensations. He had been thrown from horses. He had fought in murderous brawls, engaged in the tribal warfare of the Indians, fallen over a cliff on a foggy night, gone through a coastal hurricane that blew the very air out from his lungs. He even had struggled for his life on one occasion against a wounded she-bear. But never before, through sickness or through wounds, had he suffered such exciting pangs as now afflicted him.

His pipe went out. A man who was leaning on the other side of the pillar offered him some sparks from his. Lance thanked him, subsided once more into his aching reverie.

Women's voices chattered in the garden. There was music in the house, and dancing. In every group he seemed to hear her voice. He found himself breathing so deeply on the fragrant air that it increased his dizziness. His pipe went out again. He dropped the long clay tube to the brick flooring of the terrace.

Easter. She was named for a Saxon goddess. No wonder. Goddess of his ancestors, guardian of the portals of Valhalla, cousin of Aurora—one lovely pagan goddess whom English monks had never been able to exorcize. They had surrendered and had named a Christian festival in her honor. Easter . . .

For a moment his mind shifted to another pagan, and he rejected the idea that Easter ever could be like her. Miskee was a barbarian. The Indian girl had beauty, but she lacked one quality that Easter had in fullest measure. Miskee had no gentleness. She was a hot little beast of the forest—nothing else.

Again, he felt the soft hands of Easter Walker on his brow. . . .

4

THE man beside him had been speaking. Slowly Lance's consciousness absorbed the words.

"—a night which only Sir John Suckling might appreciate."

Lance straightened up. "I . . . I hadn't noticed," he said.

His companion stood relaxed against the oak column, and strangely Lance began to feel comfort in the presence of the man.

"I, too, am homesick," the stranger said quietly, as though he were talking to himself. "Virginia is a land of homesick people. I resent its wild beauty. It makes me realize that I am doomed to stay. It makes me feel that, should I return to England, I would be even more homesick there." He waved his pipe at the stars. "Look at that sky. No wonder Virginians rarely go back to Britain."

Lance had seldom concerned himself with such poetic reflections. He looked at the stranger curiously.

Without moving, as though in the course of the same soliloquy, the man said, "I am Nathaniel Bacon, the younger Nathaniel Bacon, Master Clayborne. Please pardon me for breaking into your mood, but I am full of punch—and when I'm full of punch I think aloud."

"Then we are . . . we are to be neighbors in Henrico!" Lance exclaimed.

"Yes, so I understand. I am opening a plantation at Shoccoes, near Byrd's."

Lance and Bacon shook hands.

Nathaniel Bacon had a lean, reflective face with deep-set eyes that in the darkness seemed to glow. Although he was dressed in the somewhat somber broadcloth garments of a barrister, he had the graceful body of an outdoor man. He was less than thirty years of age.

"Our new plantings are but a few miles apart," Lance said. "I passed through your clearing only ten days ago."

"Indeed? How is Dick Potts faring?"

"Very well, sir. I believe he'll make you a good man. He is a friend of my overseer. I have known him for several years."

"I'm glad they are friends," Nathaniel Bacon said. "Poor Potts has worried about his neighbors. That mark upon his hand, you know, has made him sensitive. He has made his peace with his former master, Allen. We have paid off the score, so Dick no longer is an outlaw, despite the brand on his palm."

Lance smiled. "That matters little," he said. "There are many, many fugitives from justice living west of Turkey Island, more than all the officers can ever bring to court."

"Yes, I know," said Bacon. "They are the Cossacks of our colony— buffers who protect us from pressure by the Indians. It will be interesting to join that company. I shall be too busy then to think of Cambridge, Fleet Street and the Inns of Court. How long have you been in Virginia, Master Clayborne?"

"Since '65, sir."

"Then you are not homesick?"

"No, no."

Bacon sighed with heartfelt envy and said, "Then you are lovesick, and that is infinitely worse. I'm sorry I brought up the subject."

Lance stiffened, but Bacon's soothing voice continued. "Infinitely worse. Two years ago when I returned to London from the grand tour I was stricken by a veritable cloud of arrows from Eros. I wrote verse for my Elizabeth. I lost my appetite for wine as well as food. I bayed the moon. I felt as though my heart were buried."

"I know!" said Lance so fervently that Bacon found it troublesome to keep from laughing.

For a time there was deep silence. Then Lance suddenly inquired, "You are a scholar, sir. Know you aught of Saxon mythology?"

Bacon, startled, thumbed his chin.

Lance pressed on. "Who was the Saxon goddess of springtime? Can you call her name?"

"Ostera, I believe. Ostera—we pronounce it Easter."

"Ah," said Lance. "Goddess of spring, Ostera."

"I think we need some punch," said Bacon.

Together they walked into the house.

For a time Lance forgot his distress of mind in his pleasure at the friendly sympathy of Nathaniel Bacon. Bacon had been in Virginia but one year. A graduate of St. Catharine's College, Cambridge, widely traveled, a former member of Gray's Inn, London, he had been much sought after for advice on affairs abroad. Sir William had placed him on the Council, which automatically gave him the title of colonel. His cousin, the elder Nathaniel Bacon, was also a member of the Council.

His principal plantation was at Curle's Neck on the James, but he had acquired other properties, including acreage near the Clayborne headright land at the fall line of the river. Energetic, beloved of his servants and his neighbors because of his good manners and his tolerant views, Bacon had made a good crop of tobacco his first season. He seemed destined to wealth and influence.

Lance admired the young man's slender, aristocratic body, his deep eyes with their warm wells of humor, and the proud posture that shamed some of the overdressed, newly rich gallants in the company at Green Spring.

"Virginia is making progress," Bacon remarked as they came into the glitter of the hall. "The Governor's brandy is superb."

A Negro brought them cups. Sir Henry Chicheley, Sir William's deputy, a tall and nervous man who wore a silver-colored wig, approached to greet them and ask the news from the James River country.

"We've never had a better crop, Sir Henry," Bacon said. "How did you manage in Middlesex?"

"Fine, fine," the knight replied. "Potatoes are the thing now, Bacon. Potatoes—the Peruvian roots."

"I've heard the things are as tasteless as acorn flour," Lance remarked.

"Nonsense, sir. Nonsense. Someday the crop will feed a hundred thousand people. Well salted, it is fine food for slaves—better than rice, much better than rice." Sir Henry buzzed off like a dragonfly.

William Drummond, lately returned from Albemarle, the newly expanded Carolina colony, was standing near the fire screen like a weary bull. Whenever a question was addressed to him the big Scot lowered his head and closed his eyes as though the query were a cannon ball.

As Bacon and Lance Clayborne spoke Drummond smiled. "Thank God," he said. "Come rescue me, young men of action. They ask me if there's gold in Carolina. They wonder why their shillings have not turned into crowns already! Damme! I tell you it's like any other country, except for its rebellious pirate population. Work is what it needs, not money, prayers and hope. No region can subsist on thievery alone—or hope. Virginia wasn't built on hope."

"Planted with hope," said Bacon. "Cropped by hard labor."

"You have it there, sir," Drummond answered. "Even proprietors must work hard in a land like this. Birds must be shooed away, insects plucked, the land kept free from weeds. In Carolina, as in Virginia, the birds are robbers, the caterpillars are Indians. As for the land, it is as good as the best up here, but no better. It is no Utopia." Drummond shook his head gloomily.

Sir William Berkeley was surrounded by members of the Council at the east end of the chamber. His Excellency, dressed in gray velvet and a powdered wig, was a princely figure among the others, none of whom were either as well tailored or as gracious. Daniel Parke was too thin for his blue coat and ruffles, and Councillor Corbin was too fat in clothing that he obviously wore but once a year. Robert Beverley, the Secretary, looked like a feverish hawk, and the two Ludwells, Philip and Thomas, were saturnine men, sallow from ague, who wore military-styled gold-brocaded surcoats.

Lady Berkeley, in purple silk which offset her baby-skin complexion, was as striking a figure among the ladies as Sir William was among the men. The low neck with its flaring collar of lace displayed her rich shoulders and a bust from which the gallants could not take their eyes for long. Her slashed sleeves had undersleeves of white, and her white cuffs were wired and starched to perfect shape. Lady Berkeley's shrewd eyes and straight, purposeful nose left much to be desired, but her face was softened by her blond hair, with its bobbed curls and the soft low knot which matched her incredibly fair skin.

Still somewhat of a stranger in the colony, Lady Berkeley reflected the grim pride of her family, the Culpepers, and the pretensions of the late Carolina governor, Samuel Stephens, her first husband. Except when she was chatting with Colonel Philip Ludwell, she seemed rather stiff, as though she realized that every woman in the room was examining her critically.

The costumes of none of the others remotely matched that of the Governor's lady. It seemed as though by design they had surrendered every hope of outdoing Dame Frances. Lance observed nevertheless that there were several better poised and considerably handsomer ladies who, unlike the Governor's wife, seemed to be thoroughly enjoying themselves. Some of the younger women were almost as playful as Indian wenches, and, he reflected, if they would cast off their stiff party clothing, they might be almost as handsome.

Outside the Governor's close circle were a number of planters in broadcloth as plain as Bacon's. They clustered near the window, obviously miserable in their starched shirts and, when they were off guard, just as obviously critical of the glittering Councillors and their ladies. They were out of place in Berkeley's courtly atmosphere with their muscle-bound movements and their heavy farmers' feet confined in slippers. Kendall was there, and Minge and Crews from upriver, together with several others whom Lance did not know. There were no ladies with them.

"My wife likes people," Nathaniel Bacon remarked. "She thinks parties are for pleasure, not politics, and so do I."

"I also," Lance said. "I have never seen any great enjoyment at one of these affairs. They are too stiff. . . . The Governor seems to be much older than he was last time I saw him."

"The populace is bothering him," Bacon said. "See those sour old stag hounds by the window? The populace, *hoi polloi,* has changed. Prices are too low. Duties are too high. The cost of the Culpeper proprietary irks our taxpayers. The western planters are nagging the Governor for a new Assembly. They are tired of Virginia's long Cavalier parliament. Poor fools, they think new laws will improve their situation. People expect too much of laws and of lawmakers. There is too much law. . . . Why don't you drink your punch? Hurry, man. I want you to meet Mistress Bacon. She is anxious to know her new neighbor."

Lance swallowed the contents of his cup and followed Bacon into the west chamber. It was full of ladies. There was much handclapping. A game of recitation was in progress.

Elizabeth Bacon saw them at once and came to pull them into the noisy circle. Like her husband, she was handsome and as well poised as a birch arrow. Her dress was of dark-red satin with a matching bodice that was trimmed in point lace, and her dark hair was confined in a pert Brussels cap. She stood out in the group like a merry queen.

Lance then saw Easter Walker. That young lady had only the briefest glance for him. His heart again fell down into his shoes. Throughout the progress of the game he became as awkward as a pigeon in a snare.

When his turn came to recite he tried to quote some lines from Sir John Suckling, but Bacon had to help him finish them:

> "But oh, she dances such a way!
> No sun upon an Easter-day
> Is half so fine a sight."

So they thrust him into the circle and made him kneel, so that he felt like an Indian captive waiting for the final stroke. If Easter Walker or anyone else noticed the use of her given name, there was no sign of it in the merry group.

He escaped at last to the garden, where he encountered Ann Brantley, a young widow who seemed overly glad to see him and much too anxious to push and pull him out of his dark mood. Lance did not know it, but she had stalked him like a hungry Diana since the moment of his arrival.

Squeezing his arm during their walk down the terrace steps she exclaimed: "Lordy, Lance, your arm is stronger than an ashwood sapling!"

He did not hear her. He was thinking of someone else.

"Was it Will Carver, the High Sheriff, whom you kicked into the swamp?"

"No," he replied, "it was Barton, the County Sheriff."

"Oh! Did the Governor say anything about it?"

He shook his head as patiently as he could. He was sick of the episode, and he still wondered why it had caused so much chatter.

"All the young men envy you, Lance," said Ann. "They too would like to kick sheriffs into swamps, but in these days there aren't many people who are so reckless."

He grunted and tried to turn back toward the house, but Ann wished to visit the spring, the incredible green fountain which had given Sir William's estate its name. They drank cool water which seemed to him much more palatable than the Governor's punch.

Ann Brantley stood very close to him, and Lance remembered that this was one of the young women whom his father had suggested he might marry. She owned eight hundred acres of cleared land on Queen's Creek.

Ann touched him with her fan. "You are not so wild as people say you are," she said. "But you should stay at home more, Lance. I have been dying to see you." She sighed. "You are one of the few people who make me feel like a girl. I forget the sorrows of widowhood when I am with you, Lance."

He grunted again, but with scant courtesy—and then immediately regretted his rudeness. He put his arm around the young widow as they walked back toward the house and gave her a friendly squeeze which, though he did not intend it to, nearly crushed her ribs. He could say nothing, however. Gallantry had died within him. His mind was full of the Walker girl.

They saw her through one of the narrow windows of the west room. She was standing by the mantel in vivacious conversation with Dame Drummond.

Ann Brantley noticed the intensity of his interest. "Did you hear about Easter?" she asked with a little jerk on his arm.

"Easter? Oh. What?"

Ann pulled him away from the window and said, "She is in love, they say."

"What? In love?"

"Last Wednesday she had quite an adventure down at Archer's Hope landing. Her horse became unmanageable. She was saved from a serious injury by a naked giant of a forester. She fell into the river, and she fell head over heels in love with him."

Ann Brantley did not know for many months what made Lance Clayborne's mood change so completely. The boy who had been as uncommunicative as an owl came to life as though she had doused him with cold water.

He turned to her, caught her completely by surprise and bussed her heartily. He told her that she was a charming princess, one of the most delightful women who had ever driven a man to drink. Back through the garden he walked her, holding her hand and kissing it at every step or so and throwing sighs to every point of the compass. Ann Brantley was quite dizzy when he took her back into the house.

ᴥᡲ 5

IT WAS not an accident, therefore, that brought Lance Clayborne to the neighborhood of Gull Cove, the Walker plantation, two weeks later. He was stubble-bearded as before—even fiercer of aspect than he had been that day at the creek landing, and he was dressed in the same dove-colored buckskins.

Had anyone seen him loitering in the long cedar-bordered lane between the house and the servants' quarters, there would have been some alarm. At times wild borderers caused trouble in this region north of Jamestown. But Lance Clayborne, as patient as a good hunter should be, took particular care to be seen only by her whom he sought.

It happened, then, that shortly after sunset on that perfect autumn day Easter Walker, riding down between the evergreens on her way back from the bedside of a female slave who was sick from the bite of a snake, reined in sharply with a little cry of amazement.

For lounging against a tree beside the lane, his mantle almost invisible against the brown vegetation of the field, was the forester of the wharf.

Her surprise and the note of joy in her exclamation somehow quieted Lance Clayborne's pulse. As he held up his hand in greeting he found himself strangely free of the embarrassment that had paralyzed him when, in another guise, he had encountered her at the Governor's levee.

She was off her pony almost before he could move forward to assist her. He kissed her hand with a grace that did not lighten her confusion.

In his deep voice he said slowly, "I hope my lady suffered no ill effects from her accident?"

"None," she said. "And you?"

He laughed. "No, no. Savages have hard heads."

"Savages? Are you a . . . savage, really?"

She looked up at him so earnestly that he gained further courage. He tied her horse to a juniper trunk and led her to a seat on the stile that crossed the rail fence to the tobacco field.

Thereupon he sank down in the shadows at her feet and in stolid silence began to contemplate the toes of his Chiskiack moccasins. There were many things he wished to say, but he waited for her to launch their conversation. He wanted to tell this pert blond young maiden that his woodland personality did not fear her; that now she was but a girl and he a man; she a woman, he a warrior.

"You ran away," she began with hesitation. "I wished to thank you. . . ."

He said nothing.

She began again, peering for a closer view of the face now shadowed by his thick fur cap. "I was frightfully rude to comment that day upon your . . . your western garments. I am genuinely sorry. Oh, I thought about it so often later. I am so glad that I can thank you now. You saved my life, you know."

He remained expressionless and silent.

The girl struggled on, her slim and lovely hands fluttering at her shawl and at stray fronds of yellow hair that the wind had torn from their bindings. "I inquired of everyone at the wharf," she went on, "but none of the people could tell me who you were or where you went. I wished to return your otterskin mantle—that lovely garment that smells of campfire smoke."

She paused then as though afraid to say more and stole another quick glance at the youth who was seated below her in the gloom. She could not tell him what she had dreamed, that she had thought of no one else for a score of days, that even the Governor's party had been dull because her fancy had been full of a strong-armed forester. She had hated herself for it, thought of all the awful tales of border men of their drinking and their fights; of their murderous cruelties; of the dirt and vermin in frontier cabins where whole families with their guests bedded together on the floor like pigs. This had not helped, for in her mind's eye there appeared always the clean-limbed tawny youth who by an act of selfless gallantry had saved her life. That otter cloak! She blushed to think of how she had held it beside her cheek at night until its wild fragrance had penetrated unforgettably into her heart and body. The cloak was at the house, but the woodland fragrance . . . This wild young man beside her . . .

She sighed. Her chin came up. She looked at him again in the dimming light. He was still as motionless as a hunting cat. Never in her life had she ever seen a human being so utterly still. Not even his eyelids moved.

What a fool she was! On a wave of warm blood came a violent self-scolding. She, Easter Walker, sitting like a dolt beside this fur-capped man, betrayed by a maiden's daydreams into believing that he was some entertaining Robin Hood. Faugh! She started to speak, but now she was exhausted by the pounding of her heart.

After what seemed an interminable time, his face still turned half away from her, he said, "The otter cloak is yours forever, my lady. And I did not come for thanks. I came to see if you really were a living person. The bruise on my head should have reminded me, but, though I cherished it, the bruise soon disappeared and left me wondering if I had imagined our adventure."

"Who are you?" she demanded angrily. Why had she expected such a pretty speech—and dreaded it?

"It does not matter," he said. "I am called Usack in Henrico, where I have a new planting on the edge of the Monacan country."

She started as though frightened by the terrifying frontier.

He said, "I'll go away. Please don't be afraid."

"I'm not!"

"Why are you trembling?"

She had not been conscious of it. "I'm *not* trembling."

"You are cold? I have another mantle here. This is of panther-skin."

"No, I'm not cold!" she said angrily.

There was a long period of silence.

Clayborne, hiding behind his hunter's immobility, was frightened, too, but not so much as she, so he maintained advantage. He marveled that this gentle girl should stand in awe of Indian manners. It was unbelievable that one who had been so poised, so self-possessed at Green Spring should shiver like a squaw here in the lane.

He did not now want her to recognize him as Lance Clayborne. It was strange how her deep eyes had been blinded. At the Governor's she had seen him only as one of many overdressed young Englishmen. Now . . .

She asked shyly, "What is that little bag around your neck?"

"Medicine," he said.

"What?"

"It was given me by the quickosough of the Chiskiacks."

"Oh."

"I mean the priest, the healer of the tribe."

"Oh!"

"I wear the bauble in the woods, just as I wear my paint pouch, knife and hatchet."

"The paint pouch? Is that thing there at your belt the pouch?"

"Yes."

She touched it timidly. "Is there magic in that too?"

"No. Just bear's tallow, powdered bloodroot, charcoal and a quill of pennyroyal essence."

"You paint your face?"

"Sometimes, and my body too. It is the custom in the west. The oil keeps the skin free from mosquitoes in the swamps while we are hunting. The paint and the fringes on our forest garments help make us almost invisible."

"You . . . fight?"

"Yes. It is not like the white man's fighting. Indians fight for sport."

Chilled, fascinated, she said, "But savages are vile. How could you hunt with Indians?"

"The deep-forest tribes are cleaner than English people."

"Oh, I did not know——"

"When their villages grow foul, Indians move. White men remain in their towns until their homes and their very souls rot to the ground. At every corner of Jamestown is a rum shop, in every alley there are thieves and bawds. In the forest there is cleanliness as well as beauty."

"Why, you talk like a pagan poet!"

"The woods make even children think," he said seriously. "One cannot talk back to the thunder or the wind, so men wonder and— talk to themselves."

"Oh!"

"My new planting," he said, "is on the very rim of the English world. Sometimes I wonder if I and my neighbors in the west are really English."

She smiled. "Since seeing you, I've wondered too, and yet . . ."

He said nothing.

At last, with difficulty, she finished. "And yet if all the men on the frontier are like the only one . . . I know . . . I believe I'd like the border well enough."

He was pleased, and yet he decried her pretty compliment. "Border men are as wild as savages. They do not go to church, for there is no religion except that dispensed by wandering separatist preachers. The men in the west have no spokesmen in the House of Burgesses because there has been no election for twelve years. Every home must be a fort like Clayborne Castle or the Allen house across the James."

"But there are regular forts."

"Hunh, they are no good. If the northern tribes should move again, war parties would pass between those posts and penetrate as far as Middlesex and Gloucester." He shrugged. "Indians will not fight at forts. They steal past them to plunder the farms that lie between."

"We rarely see wild Indians any more."

"I know. Therefore the east thinks little of them, but we out on the border often hear war rattles. They tell of danger from the north. Fifteen days' journey north there is King Philip, and even nearer is the empire of the Iroquois. They have Dutch muskets, so they have conquered many tribes. They are pressing other Indian nations down on us as they did in '56 when many white men were killed."

"You mean there may be war?"

He shrugged. "There is always danger of war out there."

"Would you . . . would you go to war?"

He looked up toward the northern sky. "Oh, yes. I must return soon to the border."

She frowned. "Before you go you'll . . . you'll come again to see me?"

He did not reply.

She took a deep breath, and, chin upon her hand, she looked up at the sunset-tinted clouds. There could be no reality in this encounter, she reflected. Surely this man beside her in the twilight was but a vision, one of the many which in the past had agitated her and delayed her errands, a dream such as all maidens have. Nevertheless, it could hardly be a vision, because she had touched the beaded charm bag at his throat and his paint pouch.

She turned.

The forester had disappeared!

Startled, she cried out. Her pony was cropping grass without concern. Up the twilight lane a cottontail hare cocked his ears and hopped into the scrub. A small owl passed silently overhead. She rose and whirled around as though he might have hidden behind her skirts, but the young man had gone.

Her foot touched something on the bottom step of the stile. Wondering, she picked it up.

It was the young woodsman's medicine bag. He had left it for her.

↤§ 6

WERE love affairs not normally adventures certain to distort minds and foster incredible fancies, Lance Clayborne's courtship of the Walker maid would seem only the figment of some imaginative minstrel. Surely no man had ever before confronted a maiden in two guises only to find himself in one eventually his rival in another. As a hairy forester he charmed the maid. As Launcelot Clayborne, Esquire, heir to Council Point Plantation, he made no unusual impression. The elegant young English gentleman at the Governor's levee was just another suitor. The wild Virginian with the Indian manners was an adored lover.

The gossips called Lance Clayborne the wildest man and Easter Walker most sought-after girl in all the colony. Both were mysterious figures—he because of his long isolation in his father's almost womanless forest stronghold, Clayborne Castle at Council Point, and she because for four years she had been away in London. Easter Walker had the gilt of England on her and with it the easy assurance of a person much older than eighteen. So graceful was her carriage that any planter's wife would have sacrificed a dozen hogs for half a dozen walking lessons from the girl.

Her posture was that of Diana. She had a voice with no colonial sharpness in it, although she had lost little of her Virginian accent. The girl could speak of new books and of court affairs and of French fashions. Withal she was so reticent that it required rude pumping to get the information from her.

Lance fitted no set pattern, or, rather, he fitted too many. At one time he was an ordinary farmer. At another he was an extremely elegant young gentleman in clothing fit for a Duke of Buckingham. Fastidious enough, he nevertheless took pride in his strong hands. He was skilled with tools as well as with weapons, and he was an excellent boatman. Nor did Lance scorn to use his legs. When the shortest distance to a given destination was unsuitable for horse or boat he walked there like a servant or a savage, even though the journey might require several days.

Lance believed himself a proper Englishman because he had been taught carefully by his father and his patient tutor Parson Broome. He rode well. He could shoot and fence and dance and make a proper bow. He had read the classics in the original—Caesar, Virgil, Horace, Homer and some of Euclid. *The Canterbury Tales* and Shakespeare's historical plays he knew, also the Bible and his prayer book and some of the lighter English poets.

Still it was not strange that he had acquired many traits foreign to his father and other Englishmen. To him venison was tastier than beef or mutton, and salt was the one precious condiment. The habits of panthers and wolves were more familiar to him than the wiles of self-seeking human beings. Experience in the wooded desert that was Virginia had swept away most of his childhood superstitions. He no longer feared the storms that made women run to their feather closets and cover their heads. Real Englishmen never could reconcile themselves completely to the sudden and violent changes of Virginia weather.

Lance at first enjoyed his masquerade with Easter Walker. As a forester he felt himself to be a full-grown man. He was as old as veteran warriors of the Indian towns. In his role as Sir Mathew Clayborne's heir he felt dependent on his father and sometimes rather ill at ease because he had had so little schooling and experience in Europe. Not so in his role as a borderer. In that he was as self-sufficient as a mountain lion.

Nor could Lance blame the girl for scorning a fop and giving adoring attention to a warrior. He preferred the familiar dangers of the west to the discomforting intrigue of the settlements. He endured the eastern plantations, but he loved the wild forests beyond the tide line of the four great rivers of Virginia. Out there the water was not poisonous, and men did not have to quench thirst with bitter ale.

Rough borderers were less dangerous than the tavern bullies of the water front. A man at least knew what the western renegades would do and how they would fight. They did not make plots and hire assassins.

After that brief meeting at Gull Cove, Lance, while in his normal dress, saw Easter only at a distance. He was afraid to destroy the spell. He sent the barge load of cedar poles he had promised Ed Walker and rode over one day to see the new warehouse which Walker was constructing on the creek, but he would not break bread or spend the night. He pretended he had other pressing business down the way. There among the busy carpenters his eyes strayed toward the house, and once he saw her two hundred paces off in the garden. She waved to them with her sun mask. Despite himself, despite the two hundred yards between them, Lance's heart jumped.

She gave only the casual greeting of a neighbor. It chilled and almost frightened him. If he were in buckskin, she would run down the path to meet him, but as Lance Clayborne he merited a distant signal only. He rode off despite Ed's urgent invitation to his board, galloped down the trail with a leaden pain under his Holland shirt. In daylight he was an ordinary boy. Only at dusk, disguised as a forester, was he, to her, a man.

Once again in the daylight, this time at Jamestown, he avoided her. A ship from Plymouth had come in, and he was there on business for his father. He forgot everything else when she appeared among the throng on the quay—and gave her scarce a glimpse of his new gray smallclothes as he fled.

This time Ed Walker was surprised. He chided his sister.

"That was Lance Clayborne," he remarked.

"Who?" she asked.

"Sir Mathew Clayborne's son. You met him at the Governor's levee a month ago."

"Oh, yes."

Ed thumbed his chin and said, "He ran away just now when he saw you. I wonder why."

She was surprised that he had directed the question straight at her. "Why should I know? Perhaps he's in your debt."

"He looked at you with burning eyes—and ran like a turkey. What have you done to him?"

Easter frowned. "I? I scarcely know the boy."

"It puzzles me," Ed said. "I thought that you would snare him as soon as you returned from London, but he seems afraid of you. Last week at Gull Cove he would not accompany me to the house to greet you, and here he fled as soon as you appeared. It is very queer. My eyes must deceive me. Can you be ugly after all? You don't look ugly, Easter. That dress is marvelous. Your figure isn't bad either. It has filled out very nicely."

"Nonsense! I have done nothing to your scapegrace friend, and if he's smitten, as you think, he has an awkward way of showing it. Most boys are glad to greet me at every opportunity."

"You haven't made a choice yet, Sis? It isn't Hansford?"

"It isn't . . . anyone."

Ed Walker thumbed his chin again. Easter had turned very pale, and then the color had come to her face in a red flood.

It isn't anyone. Easter Walker breathed the words again—but to herself. For she was thinking of a forester.

Thoughts of that forester came often now. They shamed her. She should dismiss such thoughts; she should dismiss the man who seemed part Indian, part Robin Hood. He might be clandestine evil; he was, perhaps, incarnate danger. He had bewitched her with his words, his otter cloak and his heathen medicine. He had given her daydreams that were things of fire and fury, that made her body burn and ache. He was so gentle, so calmly competent, so self-possessed—so utterly unlike the teasing, talkative young men of the eastern plantations. His eyes glowed in the dusk with magic light. His voice was deep as the echoes of a distant thunderstorm. Memory of him made her acutely conscious of her womanhood, afraid, ashamed, but still she yearned desperately for another glimpse of him.

She sighed. Her brother was forever mentioning her beaux. It would never do for him to know of this. No one must know. Let her father and her brother plan a match. Let them even talk of people like the glittering Clayborne boy. Let them talk of marriage as they pleased. She'd think of that tall forester. . . .

Not long afterward, again at dusk, he came to her. As naturally as though they had been lovers for an age she walked straight into his arms.

She called him by his Indian name—Usack, the heron. She scolded him, pried at his identity with questions which he smothered with his half-bearded lips, and she returned his kisses with a maiden ardor so fierce that he picked her up and sat her on the top step of the stile and scolded her.

"Stop!" he said. "We are not forest cats!"

It did not make her angry. She was grateful for the brusque rebuke that restored her self-control. She had heard women speak of passion, but never until then had she experienced it. It made her wish to melt, to draw this strong young man completely into her body. The tips of her breasts became points of fire. Like the otter cloak, this man smelled of wood smoke. It was a veritable witch's incense.

He sat down at the foot of the steps and took many deep breaths as he looked up at her. In a little while he said, "I have loved you since I first saw you at the landing. Before many moons I am going to take you away with me into the woods."

"Woods, Usack? What woods?"

He told her about the giant trees and the fountains in the western wilderness, of the salt licks and the deer and the animals no one in the eastern settlements had ever seen—wild cattle with enormous furry heads and fish without scales, small speckled salmon that were more delicious than shad, fat mountain partridges that called to one another by beating a tattoo on the ground with their stubby wings.

He spoke of the west as though he were reciting mystic verses. He seemed almost homesick for the wild places he described. She became jealous of his love for the wilderness.

"Then why did you come here, Usack?"

"Because of you," he replied.

"Surely there are girls in that magic country."

"There are no Saxon goddesses," he said. "There is no Ostera."

This put her into such trembling confusion that he rose like a shadow and took her hand.

"What do you know of Saxon goddesses?" she whispered. "What do wild borderers know of such things? I have heard that there is not a gentleman west of Turkey Island. I have . . . But you must tell me more, Usack. You must tell me who you are. This will not do. If my father or my brother knew that I was here in the dusk with you, they——"

"Hunh."

"If they knew you, they would love you, too, Usack."

Lance started to speak, but a memory checked him, memory of her chilling, indifferent disapproval at the Governor's reception. At Green Spring she had disliked Lance Clayborne. She had looked on him as did many others, as a brawling feudist and a fop.

"Usack? You will not tell me who you are? You even hide your face from me. Have you no other . . . costume, Usack? Where do you live, where do you sleep? You wear no shirt at all—just that Indian mantle. . . . Won't you say something? You have upset me so. You galloped away from me at the wharf. You ran away from me again the other night. Please say something, Usack. Won't you? . . . Usack, your arm is as muscular as the legs of my brother's racing ponies. I don't know why I like you. For the same reason, I suppose, that I love this naked land so much better than the teeming cities across the ocean. You are like this country, virile and serene. In London the bells drove me almost mad—the bells and the sound of wains and coaches on the cobbles every morning, and the cry of peddlers. In London people are not clean. In spite of the new buildings that were put up after the great fire, the town is dirty, Usack. I don't believe you'd like it there at all."

"You saw King Charles?" he asked.

"Yes, I saw the King twice. His memory of his early hardships has made him scandalously pleasure-loving, and they say that he knows little of Virginia. Otherwise he would not have renewed the large proprietaries that raised our taxes. He does not realize the novelty, the vastness of this colony. He asked me many questions about Virginia, but he did not listen, I am sure. It was but his way of being polite to a frightened provincial schoolgirl. He said my father must have many children to risk one on a voyage so distant. I told him that my father preferred to have his only daughter drown rather than grow up, unpolished, in a wilderness."

"Yet you admire Virginians," he said.

"Not all of them, Usack. I saw another man in buckskins at the fair ten days ago. His leggings were greasy, and his beard was down to here!"

There was a call from the house.

"I must go now, Usack. . . ."

He kissed her hand, said nothing.

"You'll come again?"

"Unless your father shoots me."

She frowned and said, "You shouldn't talk that way, Usack. You frighten me. When will you come again? Please take back your . . ." She handed him the little buckskin charm bag.

"You must keep it until I return," he said and handed it back to her.

"But I am afraid for you."

There was another call from the house.

"Good-by." She broke away from his embrace and waved to him happily as she ran up the pathway.

◄§ 7

ALAN WALKER, Easter's father, was a man of tremendous dignity, of unshakable opinions and very strict ideas as to all the more fashionable manners. He had come to Virginia in 1650, lean in purse but most industrious and gifted in the art of winning the good will of powerful men.

The foundation of his fortune was laid with tobacco during the days before the Navigation Acts squeezed so much of the profit from the magic herb. Subsequently he had improved his purse by breeding cattle on the grassy river islands and selling them to visiting shipmasters.

As was the case with many colonials who after relatively humble beginnings had accumulated substance and standing, Alan Walker's bearing was prouder than an earl's. When he strode down the streets of Jamestown or made his appearance at Middle Plantation, the village halfway between the James and the York, men turned and watched the stiff swing of his long gold-headed walking stick and looked with awe at his enormous silver buckles which caught the sun and shone on the skirts of his brocaded coat.

Easter Walker, like her homely brother Ed, had no such pretenses; otherwise she would have had no traffic with an unknown forester. Her sojourn in London had but strengthened her Virginian traits. Men's character she admired rather than their heredity.

Lance sighed. And as he spurred toward Clayborne Castle through the moon-shot darkness he dreamed of the beauty that this girl would bring to that outmoded fortress on the river.

Clayborne Castle smelled of leather and was overrun with mice. His father had little use for ordinary comforts. It suited him to live like a man in barracks and obtain much of his warmth from wine.

Soon, Lance reflected, there must be a house of brown brick on the acreage north of the river rapids in far Henrico. This girl would help him plan the house, arrange the cupboards and the closets as she liked, and have a special sewing room, and a bower in the garden.

Ha! Lance Clayborne wedded to Alan Walker's daughter! As he rode he smiled and clenched his fist. The most adventurous boy and the gentlest girl in the colony! That would cause talk.

His breath came quickly for a moment. What of it? He would have to marry someone unless an Indian foe outwitted him or Captain Jesús Forke returned and stabbed him in the back someday. All men married if they could.

Alan Walker would storm and sputter. He had sent the girl to London in the hope that she would find there a husband more suitable than any sunburned planter—had been disappointed when she returned, homesick for Virginia. Her marriage to a Clayborne might throw the pompous man into a fit; he was of the type who would want his daughter to marry more to his own advantage.

Sir Mathew Clayborne was not in favor with the Council or with the Governor, nor was the Clayborne scion. Lance's friendship with Henrietta Hart and her gay wenches had caused gossip. So had his long journeys through the western counties. To the quiet farmers of the parish he seemed old beyond his years and a dangerous, mysterious young man. They treated him with great politeness and talked behind his back as though he were a blood cousin to the devil. Law-abiding elder citizens spoke also about his failure to attend Sabbath services with regularity, even though he paid his church dues.

Fortunately, Lance reflected ruefully, they did not know of his visits to the Indian villages with Peo. If they had known of these they would have been even more horrified. In the east there was no understanding of such a life. Not even Sir Mathew condoned the pleasures of his summer days with his brother, Pipisko of the Chiskiacks, in country where bears wandered instead of pigs, where there were deer as large as horses and where men ate turkey breasts for bread.

Then there had been Miskee. His relationship with this subadolescent Indian girl could never be understood in the eastern parishes. Lance was a vigorous young man, and Miskee had met him halfway with the greatest delight, but there was nothing in their play that resembled even remotely the custom-ridden relationship of English couples. Indian girls could never be a part of English living. Miskee would be some warrior's faithful, hard-working—and badly bruised—squaw in a year or two. There was little doubt in his mind that she had already forgotten him. Life in the Indian village left no time for daydreams.

Nevertheless, his memories of Miskee would be treasured.

But as he rode, the vision of Easter Walker welled up into his eyes. The girl knew how to judge tapestries. She could speak of the latest fashions from Versailles, and once, when she playfully had fixed her hair in the French manner, she had awed and scandalized her more sedate friends. Her needlework was envied. The books she had brought from London were worn out by borrowers who had almost forgotten that books still were being printed in the world.

Lance knew that she was no tender lily. Her spirit was as daring as his own and her body was almost as strong. London had not changed the wild Virginian spirit and the tomboyish ways that had caused her father to send her out to London for an education among her English cousins. The gossips said she was a better archer and a better rider than her clumsy brother.

Lance kicked his mare into a canter. He would have to have this girl. He could not continue a foolish masquerade. Sooner or later she would discover that Lance Clayborne was not, as she believed, a senseless dandy.

Sir Mathew was awake when Lance returned. He was seated in the darkness by the southwest window, smoking to keep the insects from his face and staring up the river, which, starlit, looked like a mirror against the forest shadows.

"Ha, nighthawk!" cried the old Cavalier. "You've been to Henrietta's?"

"No, sir."

Sir Mathew sniffed. "Clad in your buckskins, eh? You are a savage!"

Lance sat down on a bench beside his father. "Yes, Father, but tomorrow I shall shave and become a credit to the tailor. I had some business that best were done in my western clothing, but at daybreak I shall squeeze my toes into my boots again and prove to you that western life has made my wrist almost as strong as yours. As for my legs, they are much stronger."

"Faugh! I've raised a clod, a woodchopper."

Lance laughed. "You have, sir, but we shall have great fortune when that plantation in the west is cleared."

"Have we not plenty here?"

"Our eastern lands grow poorer every year, and tobacco prices lower. Upriver is a nation, a separate kingdom where grain will grow and livestock fatten. The loam in those lands is bottomless. Maize grows twelve feet high year after year. And at night the air is fresh. The water—the fountain water is better than the best Madeira! I have never had the gripes out there."

Sir Mathew pounded his hand on the window sill. "I shall not run away," he said. "I shall stay in this scurvy colony here until—until——"

"Until you are harried into poverty by the Governor?"

The old knight's head jerked up. "What say you?"

Lance frowned. "You're not the only one who has incurred disfavor, Father. Look at Richard Lawrence, who now must keep a tavern to keep alive. Witness Drummond, former Governor in Albemarle, whose property is shrinking day by day. People are envying Byrd and Crews and all the others who are too far away to suffer Berkeley's levies."

"You talk like a rebel!"

Lance grunted. "Maybe I am, sir. In any event, I've come to think that Virginia is a dominion, not a Spanish province. We are supposed to be Englishmen, not serfs of a royal landlord. Here in the east no deed is sound, but upriver there are no governors, no greedy, fee-collecting favorites, no courts. We have savages, it's true, but the whims of savages can be divined in advance, and our arms can hold our property. I prefer savages to your dotard Governor and his Council. As for the yeomanry beyond the falls, they all say it's more pleasant to fall by Indian arrows than to be slowly starved to death."

Sir Mathew's fist slowly pounded the window sill again. "This land is rotten with rebellion," he growled. "You talk like one of Cromwell's Presbyterians! Were I the King or were I Berkeley——"

"You would be just, Father, and there would be no protest. Under you there would be no separate laws for rich and poor, the favored and the frowned upon. You would not be as grasping as a pirate."

"Indeed!"

"Yes, Father. I speak in all seriousness. From the distant border, where Governor Berkeley never goes any more, a man may see the dominion now in clear perspective. Once it was a feeble baby, but now it is full grown, a nation of proud people. It will not stand forever like a cow, to be milked by that gang of tax-free rogues who make up Berkeley's Council."

"Ha!"

"Call me rebel if you like, sir, but in the west we speak with candor. I think we've had a bellyful of Berkeley's injustice. Do you think this Captain Jesús Forke of ours is a rarity? Do you think that others have not suffered just as we have? I tell you, Father, there are other pirates just as guilty in Jamestown now. Have we brought him to justice? No—because he and all his kind have had protection!"

"Humpf!" Sir Mathew exclaimed.

❦ 8

NEXT day, shaved and clad in English garb, Lance rode to Gull Cove Plantation to challenge fate. Gone was the beard. He wore the finest wig and beaver hat any merchant ever had brought across the ocean. His linen was Holland, his vest was fit for a duke and his riding coat, befrogged with silver brocade, fitted his tall form as though he had been born with it on his shoulders. The Negroes at Gull Cove all came from the orchard to stare at this youth whose elegance was greater even than their vain master's.

For an hour Lance sat on the terrace and talked with Alan Walker. Edward was in the marsh with a new fowling piece, so the old man entertained his not altogether welcome visitor as best he could. Lance dared not ask immediately for a glimpse of Mistress Easter. He knew she was busy at her duties in the great house. He thought he heard her voice within instructing the butler and the maidservant.

The men smoked many pipes, spoke sadly of the low prices of tobacco, discussed the fishing boats out on the water, reviewed the latest news—now five months old—from England. But Lance heard hardly a word Alan Walker said. Whenever a footstep sounded his heart leaped, but she did not come out, nor would her father speak of her.

Would she, he wondered, know him this time as the forester? Were women's eyes as keen as people said? If she turned pale, he would know she recognized him. What if she were angry? His heart sank.

Scarce twenty hours before she had stood with him in the gloom of that lane out yonder, a path now lighted by the summer sun. He had held her hands, had felt her hair against his cheek, had breathed the perfume of her warm young body. Now . . . Why did she not receive a visitor? Surely as mistress of the widowed household she would greet a guest!

Lance's knees began to tremble.

Alan Walker was boasting of the squashes he had grown, each large as a ten-gallon pail. He reported proudly that he had bought a Berber stallion from a Jamaica trader because Spanish horses could stand the summer heat. How was Sir Mathew's gout?

Where was the confounded girl?

There was more talk. A Negro boy came along with a long-handled fan to drive away the flies. Another brought rum that had been cooled since morning in the well.

"The berries were plentiful this year," said Walker. "We have made twelve gallons of black cordial as medicine for the gripes."

Lance sought bravely to suppress his boredom and impatience. Surely Walker realized that he had come to call on Mistress Easter. Surely he would not sit there gabbling idly for another hour!

At the first pause in the steady stream of talk Lance launched an awkward hint. "I trust your daughter is well."

Alan Walker nodded casually and spoke about the rising price of salt.

Lance's wig was now uncomfortably hot, so were his boots. He tried again, this time more bluntly. "Your daughter, sir," he said. "Will she receive me?"

Walker cleared his throat and lowered his head with a frown of concentration. For several seconds he hesitated as though it were difficult to shift his train of thought from salt and powdered pork. At last he said, "My daughter, sir—harrumph—is indisposed. I am sure she is disappointed that she cannot appear."

Without thinking, Lance suddenly grew furious. His face flushed red. His hands moved as though to interrupt his host's harsh words. He started to rise, then checked himself as a cold flood of reason came.

Alan Walker continued, "She has been complaining of a touch of nerves, Master Clayborne. Perhaps it's ague. Perhaps it's just a bit of female vapors, don't you know."

Lance kept his tongue as he slowly won a minor battle with himself. This was a masquerade indeed! She would not see him as a suitor in his normal guise, although unknown to her he was her lover in another! She did not like him as Launcelot Clayborne, for all his property and promise in the colony. She would not even see him as a guest!

Walker pattered on, made matters worse. The girl, though very sweet, was full of London notions of late. She had been behaving willfully. If Master Clayborne would come again perhaps, he was sure she would be gracious as a Virginia hostess should.

Lance finally bowed himself away, frustrated, angry at himself and at the discourtesy of the girl. She cared nothing for the laws of hospitality. Faugh!

He spurred rapidly along the river bluff, beswearing himself for twenty kinds of fool, vowing that if fortune spared him another century of life he'd never show his face again at Walker's.

He cursed all foresters as dirty, drunken highwaymen, damned to perdition the treacherous doeskin garments he had worn the night before, called down maledictions on the chance that had brought him down to Archer's Hope that day, swore he'd never once again look twice at a maid, not even were she born a princess.

Was that cursed pain beneath his baldric—a love pang? He cursed again.

He was barbarian as well as Englishman. The girl was pure barbarian.

It was indeed a most unholy masquerade!

V

Ferment

⋙ 1

WHILE Lance Clayborne supped at Lawrence's Inn in Jamestown the saturnine innkeeper hovered over him to learn the news from the upland country.

Lawrence was an Oxford man. A failure as a planter, he had lost his mortgaged river lands five years before to a favorite of the Governor who challenged his title before the Berkeley-controlled General Court. Undaunted, he had won twice the yield of the richest farm by opening a tavern which soon became the favorite stopping place of visitors to Jamestown. Man and horse alike found Lawrence's a place of plenty and good taste. The host's gloominess was shot through with sharp wit. There were many who shared his discontent over the stealing of land and the exactions of the fee collectors of the Council.

The tavern glittered with brass and silver vessels and was fragrant with the odors of roasted meat and of wine and tobacco. There was a center board with benches at which the commonalty was entertained. For gentlemen there were booths around the walls with individual tables and straw-cushioned chairs.

Lance took a seat that faced the door and carved a rich slice from a leg of mutton which he surrounded with lentils, fresh from the garden, and a portion of hominy. He was hungry. For a time he barely heard the talk of Lawrence and nodded mechanically as if the innkeeper's questions answered themselves. Then, as food began to warm him, some of the agony of his mind departed.

He remembered his mission to the settlement. At every visit he asked the same question: "Lawrence, have you seen my enemy, the sea captain?"

"No, Lance, and there's no news of him," Lawrence replied.

Lance smiled. "Well, then, that chore is over. It is eleven years now since he killed my Uncle Walter and brought us to Virginia!"

Lawrence asked, "How goes it in the west?"

"As usual the west is fermenting like a vat of fox-grape wine," Lance said. "Byrd, Crews and MacFarlane sent their best regards to you. Good fur is scarce again. The hunters brought in less than two hundred weight of deer and beaver skins per head. Prices should be high in London this season."

"Did you go to the hills?"

"No, but Lederer was out again. He took a pack train of Mac-Farlane's out to the farthest mountains to bring back fur. Everywhere he found signs of northern Indian hunters. I went into the Stafford country for a while. The Chiskiacks and other friendly tribes are nervous. They expect a wave of enemies next year. The Dutch have armed the Iroquoian nations. The Senecas, of the Iroquois, are pushing the tribes of Pennsylvania and Maryland out of the northern hunting grounds."

Lawrence smiled wryly. "Aha, so the colony had best put its house in order, eh?"

"I'd say it were good policy. What's wrong now, Lawrence?"

The innkeeper's thin mouth snarled. "The same old trouble, my boy. The members of the Council find wealth; the common man starvation. If one beribboned, simpering robber goes back to London, a dozen take his place. The rich pay no more taxes than the poor. Members of the Council pay none at all and boast of it. The Governor——"

Lawrence looked over his shoulder. Two dark-skinned sailors at the center table were nodding over their ale mugs. He lowered his voice. "The Governor, woman-ridden now, is trying to grow rich. Lady Berkeley has hinted she may give him a son."

"Who credits such a tale?"

"It doesn't matter. Lady Berkeley, though a widow, is young enough to get a son, and—well, who would know the difference, save perhaps His Excellency? Never mind. After more than thirty years the man who once was devoted to the people is thinking about his property and little else. He is growing old and cruel, Lance. For God's sake do not antagonize him."

"I am not afraid of him."

"But he has many fears, my friend, and so is dangerous to everyone. He is older than he looks. He dreads men like you and Hansford who have grown up in Virginia. He even dreads Drummond and young Bacon because they are well educated and know the legal rights of Englishmen. The old fool wants a colony of peasants, not of gentlemen, a plantation of ignorant slaves."

Lance pushed aside the platter. "On the border we talk much of politics," he said. "There is dissatisfaction because there has been no

election for twelve years. A number of new plantings have no spokesmen in either House or Council and no protection from the colony."

"There is much unrest in the east, too," Lawrence said. "Men do
not mind being robbed a little, but beyond a certain point they cry
out. Not one out of four freemen has the right of suffrage. There
has been no audit of the public treasury for ten years. Notoriously
incompetent magistrates hold office only because they are rich or have
cousins on the Council. Bribery is common practice. There is no
regulation of the sale of rum, and even slaves get drunk, so women
are not safe within two leagues of any tavern. The law that supposedly bans trading with wild Indians is, as you know, a dead letter.
The Governor's factors laugh at the law."

"Has there not always been dissatisfaction?"

The innkeeper shrugged. "Not such as this." Lawrence scowled
again. "Once Berkeley was firm but fair. Now he is as grasping as
a Spaniard." His voice sank almost to a whisper. "First thing we
know there'll be a Cromwell in this land!"

Lance laughed. "Ohoo! You almost frighten me, good Lawrence!
You think it's bad as that?"

"It is no laughing matter, boy. Your own case, now . . ."

"What?" Lance's eyebrows went up.

"Yes, your own case, my friend. For two months the County
Sheriff has held a warrant for your arrest. He has boasted that he
will apprehend you, the son of a knight, by force and fine you like a
roost thief for resisting arrest."

"Barton?"

"The same—he who has been in office here so long. He whom
you, to the delight of the whole county, ducked in a swamp."

Lance smiled.

Lawrence peered toward the door. "It may not be a laughing matter," he warned. "By now he knows that you have returned to Clayborne Castle. Perhaps he has heard that you are here." Lawrence
looked toward the door again.

"You think I'd flee from that potbellied boar?"

"The boar has deputies—with cudgels—and a warrant, Lance. I
have seen the paper. It would be better if you'd submit, go to the
magistrate and settle that matter of the five swords."

Lance straightened his baldric on his shoulder, stretched, yawned and poured himself another cup of wine. "I shall do so at the first opportunity," he said. "It was worth the price, whatever it may be. Besides, a county warrant does not give an officer the right to insult a gentleman. He got his due. Who is the local magistrate now?"

"Alan Walker."

Lance started, upset his mug of wine. "He?"

"He has held the commission for three months."

Lance clenched his fist. "I saw him only two hours ago. He . . . But never mind."

The door opened. Lawrence, as though he had recognized the step of the stout man, rose hurriedly and, standing between Lance and the door, made shift to clean up the wine that Lance had spilled. For a moment the boy did not know that the Sheriff had come. Then he heard the deep, coarse voice.

"Damme, Lawrence! Where are ye, Lawrence?"

The innkeeper continued at his task, still shielding Lance from the newcomer and the two deputies who had followed him into the taproom.

But Lance thrust Lawrence aside and stood up. As he rose he moved his hat back from his eyes. "Why, Master Barton!" he exclaimed. "Well met!"

The Sheriff rocked on his heels in great surprise. His face turned white, then red. His hands fingered the air.

Lance leaned at ease against the wall. "You have more warrants, I'm informed," he said. "Soon, no doubt, I'll be called a highwayman or something worse. Speak, man."

Barton stepped back. "N-n-no, good Master Clayborne, I—I——"

The Sheriff's deputies also retreated. Only on rare occasions had they arrested gentlemen by force, and both had suffered many bruises.

"I've heard," said Lance, "you intend to have me by the ears and put me in the stocks; that you have awaited my return with joy so that your bravos here could make sport of me. Serve your warrant!"

The Sheriff's mood for violence had gone. He trembled before the catlike youth. His eyes dropped to Lance's long sword, whose hilt rested within two inches of the sun-browned fingers.

"No harm meant, sir!" he cried in a rush of words. "No, no, sir. No, sir! And the warrant has been withdrawn, sir. Cornet Gary has gone to England, sir!"

"Very well," said Lance.

Then as the frightened fat man started back toward the door he added, "Don't run, man. Have a drink now and tell Master Lawrence exactly what happened between us on that beautiful day at Haskins' bog. Step up, all three of you." Lance turned to the innkeeper. "Have the Sheriff and his men served, Master Lawrence."

Sheriff Barton did not enjoy his ale. And when all his efforts to talk failed Lance prompted him.

"Who said the first rude word on that ride to Walker's?" he asked.

"I did, sir. I was a bit in liquor, sir."

"Which of us was unarmed?"

"You, sir."

"And who reached for his pistol in a threatening manner?"

"I, sir. I didn't mean——"

"Never mind the drunken intentions. Who, then, was kicked from his horse into Haskins' bog?"

"I, sir."

"Well and good. The truth is out."

The seamen at the center table burst into laughter.

✑§ 2

FROM Lawrence's Lance rode down to Henrietta Hart's. He noticed that there was now a well-beaten path to her place from the main trail between Jamestown and Kickotan. Henrietta was prospering.

Men drank too much at Henrietta's. The woman and her two pretty servingmaids sometimes were robbed. More frequently they were rewarded richly by the lonely wanderers from abroad who were much pleased to find wine and woman flesh in such a place.

Generally, too, the inn had several guardians—men living on the bounty of the house until chance gave them berths on some outbound vessel. To many Henrietta Hart was mother, sister and banker. Seamen loved her flinty cynicism and her wild moods that shifted as suddenly as the weather.

Lance climbed the steep narrow stairway to her chamber, his scabbard rattling on each step.

"Praises be!" she cried as he opened the door. "Come in, you scapegrace staghound, you! Where have you been so long?"

She greeted him with a great flutter of linen and lace and embraced him until he lifted her up and dropped her back in place among the pillows of her big four-columned bed.

Lily and Mol, the wenches, ran in to greet him, too, and for a while the low-ceilinged chamber sounded like a cote of pigeons. Where had he been this time? How tall he'd grown! What news was there from the west? His father still was well? What a lovely vest and surcoat! And that baldric!

Lance sat on a chest with a mug of Henrietta's best sack, warmed by the pagan hospitable spirit of these people. They always made him feel like a noble knight.

Henrietta, who looked half her age with her rich black mop of hair in confusion around her swarthy face, chased her girls from the room before she answered his questions.

What of Jesús Forke? She vowed she'd heard nothing new about the wanderings of that infidel, except that he had touched at Charleston a twelvemonth before. Henrietta pursed her lips derisively when he told her of the false trail to Kickotan.

"All honor to you, boy," she said. "The pirate fears you, otherwise he would have returned long since to aid this robber Governor of ours. I tell you, now . . ."

The man now had four vessels, all of them marauders. A Cornishman who had sailed in one of them had told Henrietta that they preyed on Spanish slave ships at great profit. They rarely ventured north. But Forke, it seemed, longed for Jamestown and talked much of his past adventures as a favorite henchman of Berkeley.

Lance's fingers touched his sword hilt. "My father says it is good to have an enemy." He sighed. "Perhaps it is, but when one has no large ship to hunt him down, and if the villain will not come to sword's point, it is quite a bother."

He looked up. Henrietta, seated among her pillows like a cat, had drawn from concealment somewhere in the bed, a lean French dagger.

"Perhaps," she said, "I shall see him first."

Lance frowned. "That would not become you, Henrietta," he declared. "Leave him for us. That trinket——"

"It is no trinket, lad," she said. "A French whore at Tyndalls

Point gave it to me for a pot of Indian salve. The salve did her no good, but the blade is all right. I am saving it for Forke. You alone shall ever know I have it."

She shrugged her naked shoulders and calmly stowed the knife away in the ticking of the bedstead. "You don't know hate, Lance," she mused. "It takes a man and a woman to make hate. At first the man and woman stir up pleasure. Their life together is like a rich wine. I loved that scoundrel for a time, and if you should ask me why I could not tell you. Perhaps it was because, unlike most sailors, he had no awe of me. He treated me as though I were what I really was—a pleasure-seeking wench. So we had fun together with no pretenses. We were scandalously playful as though we together were the original discoverers of all the human joys."

Henrietta pounded a pillow thoughtfully with her fist.

"I finally built a life on it," she said slowly. "My husband was dead. Walter Clayborne was dead. I built a life on Jesús Forke. I was a fool. Damn his soul! Someday I'll cut off his head.

Lance laughed, and Henrietta's mood changed as though a dark cloud suddenly had cleared the sun. Rising from the confusion of pillows, she took him by the shoulders and looked deep into his eyes. "You've changed, boy!" she cried in amazed discovery. "You've grown up. You are so much older than you were last spring. What has happened in those woods?"

Lance blushed under her wide eyes until his sunburned face darkened like an Indian's.

Henrietta laughed. It was gay, challenging merriment. "I know," she said, chiding him. "I can see it in your eyes. There is knowledge there now—knowledge of how a woman is made, knowledge of the tree of life!" She took him in her arms, held his head against her warm throat. "A forest girl, you rogue?" she asked.

He nodded. And now, too abashed to discuss the matter, he put one knee on the high bed and returned her embrace.

Henrietta's bubbling mirth subsided in several deep breaths. And somehow her gown fell from both her shoulders, leaving her breasts bare to his kisses. Lance always had appreciated Henrietta's beautiful face and her wealth of well-kept black hair. Now as he saw a body that was even lovelier he groaned in ecstatic surprise.

She stopped him only long enough for her to kick free from her gown. And then it was a long moment before, with panted whispers, she was able to convince him that he should at least remove his sword belt and other things. Meanwhile she bolted the door and found a fresh bottle of wine.

Lance lingered four hours with this woman who had become young again. In that time he learned to laugh as they engaged in the old, old game which is played so often in naught but deadly seriousness.

"You need an English mistress," she said. "It never would do for you to measure women by some squatting forest nymph. It is so much fun to teach you, Lance!"

Lance sighed that it was most delightful, too, to learn. Her virtuosity opened his eyes and put new lights of wisdom in them. As for Henrietta, the young man's vigor soon had her gasping.

When he rode away he was happy if unsurfeited. The dark woman's wryly gay endearments had refreshed his soul and body. Galloping back to Council Point, he sang "Cavaliers of Scotland" at the top of his voice.

◄§ 3

A WEEK later at his Henrico farm far up the James, Lance wondered what the Walker girl would say if she could view his wild new plantation. Working eight slaves and six bondsmen who had arrived four months before, Peo had made some impression on the wilderness, but much labor lay ahead.

Forty acres of beaver meadow near the creek were clear and a hundred more of upland land were being burned over for the next year's crop. Trees, though long since girdled and dead, yielded but slowly. The oaks clung to the thick brown soil in spite of fire and ax.

Peo worked harder than his men. He watched their welfare as if they were children. His care was well rewarded. "It is much healthier in these uplands," he reported. "New arrivals downriver die, but here they fatten and soon recover from their homesickness."

One of the bondsmen was a smith, so the tools were in excellent condition.

Lance rode over every acre of his lands, measuring future fields with impatient eyes, examining the homesite he had chosen, crumbling the creek-bed clay between his fingers—clay that soon would be baked into bricks.

He noted that Peo had made satisfactory preparations for defense. Each of the English bondsmen he had trained to load and shoot. They had their weapons beside them always, whatever they were doing. The slaves he had armed with pikes and taught to stand in ranks on a moment's notice. Only two of these were shackled. The others were brown-skinned West Indies men who no longer were wild.

"We have few Indian visitors," Peo said. "We give no food, no presents. We allow none to stay here except young women."

"What of the upland Indians?" Lance asked.

Peo's face grew serious. "The tributary tribes are restless," he said. "They are not hunting to the north at all this year. Wampum bearers of the Susquehannocks have been in Virginia. One of MacFarlane's runners told me that they have been as far south as the Roanoke River and have had council with the Occaneechees. Pipisko is in the mountains with his little band. He is safe."

"Have the Susquehannocks moved their towns?"

Peo shrugged. "Not yet. The Doegs, who hold the falls of the Potomac, have become their friends. The Doegs sent war parties north this summer to help the Susquehannocks oppose the Iroquoian tribes. The Iroquois all have firearms."

Lance fingered the hatchet at his belt.

Suspended always above the heads of every inland planter was the menace of the savages. Tribes flowed back and forth through the forest like mists, and no one could guess their intentions. An accident to a hunting party could arouse a superstitious fear. A drought or a plague, war with a neighboring tribe, the kidnaping of a few girls, a flood or a freeze could send a swarm of Indians into a new territory, there to come in conflict with the struggling farmers of Virginia.

The savages presented only a minor problem to the organized militia of the eastern counties, but to the border farmers even the smallest war parties were dangerous. Each household had to protect itself until the county company could assemble and march.

Lance praised Peo for his progress and for the precautions he had taken. Few planters realized the peril that forever was hovering near them. Day in, day out, they would see no danger; so they became scornful of it and looked on the Indians as waifs of no more consequence than wandering bears. Not Peo. He had experienced the terror of 1656. He had heard much of the massacre of 1644, when savages had filtered through the frontier settlements begging food and brandy, behaving like spiritless tramps so none had suspected their intent. Then on a peaceful Sunday they had drawn their hatchets from beneath their mantles and killed two hundred Englishmen.

⊷§ 4

TAM MACFARLANE was the richest factor on the James and by far the boldest. His warehouse at Rocky Ridge near the falls was filled with skins each spring. His men were hard fugitives from the eastern settlements who rarely showed their faces when the guardship was upriver.

The Scot had learned four languages from the women he bought from distant tribes. He knew more of the lands beyond the freshes than any other man. Tam's small expeditions could travel more safely than a regiment of militia, for the savages desired to trade with them. Tam's men brought hatchets, powder, shot and cloth, fiery liquor for the festivals, and they took only skins in return. They did not want to plow the clearings and, like farmers, impose strict English law upon the forest people.

MacFarlane also dreaded farmers. They drove the Indians back, killed off game and reduced the profits of the fur trade. The bearded giant scorned husbandmen as superstitious weaklings, but he feared them, too. Large plantings were creeping up the river, and tremendous grants were being made to rich men who brought scores of slaves and servants with them to cut down the trees and plant grain and tobacco. The frontier was moving steadily westward.

The trader scowled, flung his pen down on his counting table and walked out on the porch. Before him, under the oaks, his half-breed children played an Indian game with rounded stones and hickory paddles. Beyond the compound at the wharf a barge was being loaded with cedar logs by singing Negroes. The Indian camp down on the flat, dirty, pig-ridden, sent up rank odors.

Tam surveyed his cluttered settlement with pride and pleasure. He would have no town like this if the farmers thrust him westward. There was little navigable water near the mountains. It would cost him an extra shilling per hundredweight to ship his furs by land and more than that to bring his goods from Jamestown. He would need extra hands to keep the trails open, horses by the score, much forage and grain.

For twenty years his trading post here at the falls had thrived. He was growing old. He could move his property without great loss. William Byrd had offered to buy him out, and yet . . .

Horsemen were coming up the trail from the ferry. Tam looked keenly for a moment at the cloud of dust. That might be Byrd now. The Scotsman cursed and peered again. Or maybe it was the new Bacon, a young man lately arrived from England who had a planting on the creek north of the river.

Young Nathaniel Bacon was a planter of an unfamiliar breed. Wealthy, powerful, he had a seat at Curle's Neck to the east and many servants. The Governor had admitted him to the Council. He deserved respect. Tam looked again.

It was the Clayborne boy, accompanied by a stranger—Bacon?

Tam wiped his mouth on his sleeve, reluctantly admitted to himself that they made a likely pair of bucks. Both rode gracefully. Clayborne was dressed from head to foot in doeskin, a lad with a body like an Indian's and a face that sometimes was as somber as a Quaker's and on other occasions was alight with Hell's mischief.

How did the boy know Bacon, the newcomer?

The two young men dismounted at the hitching rack beneath the oaks, and Tam walked out to meet them, his big voice booming welcome.

Clayborne presented his companion and Tam looked at young Bacon closely.

Here was a puzzling one indeed. Not yet thirty, Bacon had the self-possession of a graybeard and the alertness of a hawk. Deep-eyed and thoughtful, clad in a hunting habit of London make, Bacon radiated a subtle force that made the wild Scotsman's hair creep on his neck like the ruff of a wolf.

"My neighbors!" roared MacFarlane. "Welcome!"

Tam shouted to an Indian woman to fetch them ale, seated them on stools upon the porch, brought pipes of his best Orinoco and gave orders to a Negro groom for the refreshment of the horses.

"I've seen your new place, Master Bacon," said the Scot, "and that is a likely planting. Do you expect to build a house there soon?"

"Yes," Nathaniel Bacon replied. "We build this autumn."

Lance Clayborne added: "We seek your advice, Tam. We hear the Monacans to westward are rather restless."

MacFarlane pulled his beard for a moment, and replied: "Yes, sir. Very restless." He paused.

"Why?"

MacFarlane threw a suspicious glance at Clayborne, then said hurriedly: "You know as well as I do, Master Clayborne. You have heard about that nation of six-foot warriors, the Susquehannocks. It wouldn't surprise me if some of them had worked south and got into Master Bacon's clearing."

"Who said anything about Indians in the Bacon clearing, Tam?"

"Well . . ."

Lance smiled somewhat grimly. "I suspected you might know about it, Tam," he said. "That is why Master Bacon and I are here— that and because I wanted you to meet him and see the type of man he is. He has lost four brood sows. You say that Indians stole them, Tam?"

Tam MacFarlane's eyes dropped away from Lance's. "They could have taken them."

"But they did not, Tam, and you know it. I noticed on the trail that the man who stole Master Bacon's hogs wore Delaware moccasins. My guess is it was one of your men, perhaps that Irishman of yours who lives with the Delaware woman across the river."

"But it could have been a Delaware."

"This far south? The thief was a slew-footed man, Tam. Did you ever see a slew-footed Delaware?"

The big Scot now was decidedly unhappy. Lance waited and watched the new perspiration break out on his face.

At last Lance turned to Bacon, who had listened to the dialogue without expression. "I don't think you will lose any more hogs, Master Bacon," he said. "I think some of Tam's friends failed to realize that we could identify Delaware moccasins. They took you for a newcomer. Was that it, Tam?"

The Scot did not reply.

Lance smiled now to break the tension and clapped MacFarlane on the shoulder. "You are a heavy-handed rascal! Four hogs. You aren't as tough as you once were, Tam. Once you would have burned down all of Master Bacon's slave quarters and, perhaps, cut the throat of a couple of his servants." Lance turned to Bacon again. "Tam is gloomy. He is afraid that farmers are going to ruin his fur trade. He has scared more farmers in his time than all the Indians in these forests have."

"But we shall not harm his fur trade," Bacon protested.

"No? You will fence your planting, won't you? Your cattle and horses will eat marsh pasturage on which the deer now are feeding, won't they? You will dig pudding stone for iron out of your creeks and break the beaver dams. Your plowmen will frighten away the wolves and foxes and raccoons, won't they?"

"But I'll use only a little land," Bacon said.

"When you succeed, though, other farmers will come. They will swarm all along the river and chase the fur deep into the woods. Tam is right. We shall ruin his trading post in time. Fur and farmers just do not mix, do they, Tam?"

"We will buy goods from this post. That should compensate him for his loss from furs," Bacon protested.

"Nothing will do that," Lance said. "Tam is a fur trader. He is not a merchant like Byrd. He belongs to a different breed."

MacFarlane had picked up a softwood stick and was whittling it idly with his big knife. This Clayborne cub! Tam could not help admiring the boy in spite of himself. Men had complained before of hog stealing but not like this. They had whined and talked of going to court. To court in upper Henrico! They had threatened to tell the Governor, although they knew that MacFarlane was the Governor's agent. Not Clayborne. That boy knew the border country.

"You must curb your heathen foresters, Tam," Lance said. "Please be good enough to tell them that Master Bacon now is a neighbor of mine, that his cause is my cause and that I am, like you, a hairy, heathen forester." Lance paused a moment. "And please remember this for yourself, Tam. If Master Bacon's planting is raided again by any except real Pennsylvania Indians, that Delaware squaw is going to be a widow. Will you explain that to your Irish hog thief?"

Tam nodded phlegmatically and whittled away on his stick.

Lance had finished his talk.

Thereafter they all forgot the matter and were friendly. Bacon marveled at MacFarlane's failure to take offense; since he was a barrister not long out of London, he was shocked both at Lance Clayborne's candid talk of retaliatory violence and of Tam MacFarlane's simple acceptance of the threat. That was one law out here at least, it seemed. A man defended his own. In London if a stripling of twenty had stood up against a powerful trader like Tam MacFarlane and in effect had charged him with thievery and threatened violence, the gesture would have seemed rashly absurd. Tam had taken it as a matter of course.

MacFarlane now invited them to eat and drink. A squaw brought in pitchers of milk, squares of maize cake and, much to the amusement of them all, a small roasted pig.

Tam told them stories of the farther mountains, where there was a spring from which hot water flowed winter and summer, and a cavern that was supposed to be filled with diamonds, but because it was haunted by Shawnee witchwomen, had never been explored. He asked Lance if he were inclined to pay a visit to the cavern.

Lance shook his head.

"I am a farmer now, Tam. I am done with chasing gold and jewels and listening to tall stories brought back by your hunters. I am going to start digging my substance out of the ground like an honest man."

Tam grunted sadly and turned to Bacon. "What has got into the boy? Is he really going to be a farmer?"

Bacon smiled. Tam laid aside the platter.

"The lad always has been skeptical," Tam said. "He is the only man on this border who does not let his imagination run away with him as soon as he says farewell to chimney smoke. He sees straight, talks straight and shoots straight. I don't know anything about your stolen pigs, Master Bacon, but if Lance says my Irishman stole them, I'd wager ten to one he did, and if Lance had come to me and told me that I stole them or had them stolen, I'd be sure that I'd been walking in my sleep."

Lance smiled and retorted: "Tam can pull your leg and make you like it, Master Bacon."

When they took their departure Tam tried to persuade Bacon to accept a bale of deerskins as indemnity for the stolen hogs, but on whispered advice from Lance, Bacon refused. They shook hands cordially with the trader.

Tam, as he waved to them, nodded toward Lance Clayborne and shook his head ruefully.

This parting gesture remained in Bacon's mind as they rode homeward. "I am afraid this affair will cost you your friendship with MacFarlane," he said.

Lance laughed. "Not at all, sir. At that, I would not value the scoundrel's good will at the worth of even a single hog. Tam is a businessman, Master Bacon. He cannot afford to be angry with me or with anyone else who might be useful to him, and he never will be the friend of anyone who is not tangibly useful. He would cut his grandmother's throat for an extra shilling. You will not have more trouble from him. As for me, by next summer he will be offering me a large fee to guide one of his trading parties to the salt marshes, or to look at that diamond cave. He has been to the farther mountains, but none of his men know the passes, so he always tries to employ Lederer or me. Lederer is out at the salt marshes now."

Lance explained that deerskins no less than beaver pelts figured in MacFarlane's trade and that their principal source was the salt lick seventy leagues to westward.

"He owns the beaver trade," Lance said, "but since beaver is the Governor's monopoly Tam's profit is small. He depends on deerskins for his fortune."

"He works for Sir William?"

"Yes. He is owned soul and body by the Governor."

"Did you know that Sir William has seated me on his Council?"

"Yes. The Governor also, in one sense, is party to the theft of your hogs."

"You believe that?" Bacon asked.

"Of course. The Governor's policy is to check settlement at the freshes of the river, to keep farmers out of the fur country above the tidewater so the Indian hunters can bring him beaver. He wants agricultural settlement diverted southward to the Carolina plantations in which he has a heavy interest. He is one of the proprietors of Albemarle, you know."

"I learn something new from you every hour, Lance," Bacon said.

They ferried the river on one of Byrd's barges and rode slowly eastward toward Curle's Neck.

The young lawyer was very thoughtful for a while. At last he spurred closely beside Lance and said: "The Governor will not look kindly on your new plantings?"

"I am sure he will not," Lance replied. "The less we say of them in Jamestown the better. But we must be firm with anyone who attempts to harass our people. My overseer, Peo, is under instructions to run down and kill anyone, savage or white man, who molests our stock. It would be well to give the same order to your man Dickon Potts. It is futile to ask any redress from the Henrico garrison. Colonel Edward Hill, the commander, is the Governor's man. He sits in his little fort on the riverbank and does nothing except collect wild stories to tell His Excellency."

"Suppose real Indians raid us? There is much talk about the threat from the Maryland Indians, those Susquehannocks."

"Potts as well as Peo will know enemy Indians in a moment," Lance said.

He explained that if hostile tribes flowed southward, it would offer a task for the militia rather than for the little garrison under Colonel Hill.

"There are some stout men in the border companies," he continued. "The old Covenanter, Thomas Mathews, has a clearing up near the Potomac. The half-caste Catholic from Maryland, Giles Brent, has settled with a considerable group of farmers on Aquia Creek, south of the Mathews place; and there are a number of other men with western plantings—Joseph Ingram, a former professional soldier, Crews, Wilsford, Walkett, Page, Milner, Turner, Cheeseman, Whaley and others. MacFarlane's crew has harried them all, but they have remained. They will be ready even if MacFarlane stirs up the Susquehannocks."

Bacon was rather shocked at this suggestion. "You mean that, Lance?"

"It is a possibility, Master Bacon. All you have to do is look at the situation from the point of view of the fur traders. They do not have to ask the Indians to make trouble for the border farmers. All they have to do is to persuade the savages to come south. Trouble then would be inevitable. The Indians will steal stock on their march.

It is much easier to shoot a hog than it is to bag a deer. The farmers thereupon will move out and kill some Indians. That will start a blood feud and mean the death of several farmers. The militia then will assemble, and there you will have another little Indian war."

"How strong are these Susquehannocks?"

"They have at least two hundred warriors."

"A paltry force."

Lance shook his head. "No, no, a large one. Indians do not fight as we do. They move rapidly in small parties. Two hundred warriors, unchecked, could devastate four counties in a week."

"Surely . . ."

"They are as slippery as eels. Someday I'll teach you how to fight against a war party. You will need to know that when you have built your new farmstead."

At Curle's fork, where the trail to New Kent turned north, Lance Clayborne pulled up his horse, and said farewell. Bacon urged him to ride on to the Neck and spend the night, but the young man shook his head.

"I must get on to West's Point," he said, "I must get home soon."

⤙§ 5

LANCE CLAYBORNE often had journeyed alone. Normally he preferred it, because it was safer. But now as he rode northward he missed the companionship of Nathaniel Bacon. The man had said little, yet he had a rich understanding, and, unlike most settlers fresh from England, he was interested in the colony as it really was. With apt questions Bacon had drawn information from the simplest circumstances.

Lance had taken new heart from the quiet neighbor whose very silence seemed weighted with good judgment. So long had the boy encountered only the wild border people that his acquaintance with Bacon gave his spirit a strange restfulness. For years his father's hatred of Captain Jesús Forke had hung over his household like one of the poisonous river fogs. It had kept Sir Mathew away from the gaming table and the bottle and his son away from friends of his own kind.

The boy now rode over wooded hills like folds of a fat giant's paunch which made the trail treacherous. Indians could creep along these wooded ridges and through the tangled gullies and reach the settlements unseen.

The only way to fight them between the Pamunkey and the James was to march against their villages and thereby force the warriors to stay at home on the defensive. Such expeditions were costly, and sometimes they came to grief. Colonel Hill's command in 1656 had been beaten. The Indians destroyed five white farmers for every warrior killed.

Unlike most planters of that time Lance knew the Indians too well to hate them. During hunts with the Chiskiacks, he had learned the sign language and had acquired a working knowledge of Algonquian, the language of the eastern Virginia tribes. An eighteen-year-old Potomac widow had sewn his doeskin hunting shirt and the handsome leggings and moccasins which Bacon envied. Miskee, the girl of the Chiskiacks, had made his summer cap of squirrelskin and the broad belt from which his French hatchet hung.

As he rode Lance remembered the awe which he had felt when as a child he had first seen virgin woodland. He did not wonder that so many settlers retained their fear of it as long as they lived. Most farmers were like the cattle that they tended. Their eyes always were on the land. They could not see the glory of the forest. The husbandmen hated trees because they shaded the soil.

Lance spurred forward rapidly. On the morrow he would sail down the broad York on Captain Roger Jones's ketch to see the Walker girl. This time, he vowed, he would not be dumb; he would tell her who he was and why he worshipped her. He would strip off his disguise and stand before her as a worthy suitor. If need be he would flee with her at the risk of Colonel Walker's wrath and Edward's friendship. He would . . .

He had promised her he would come before moonrise; that this time he would take back his medicine. His hand touched the spot upon his neck where hung the Indian charm which she had touched.

As he cantered onward through the forest, he heard disturbing sounds. At West's Point to the northeast drums were beating. Approaching the ferry landing, Lance heard plainly the exciting rattle-thud-thud. As he rode into the settlement half an hour later, men were assembling at the customhouse.

"Hey ranger," one of the troopers called. "Welcome!"

Dismounting at the tavern, Lance went inside for news. He found Captain Joseph Ingram, shaggy as a wolf, laboring over his muster roll.

⤳ 6

"THANK God," Ingram said, "You must have dropped from Heaven, Clayborne. Are you going east?"

"Yes," Lance said.

"I want you to take a message to Governor Berkeley. I cannot spare a man."

"What's wrong?"

"Hell to pay. Get yourself something to eat, and I'll tell you the tale."

Lance sat down at the table and ordered a fowl and a mug of wine from the landlord. Ingram pushed aside his papers and ran his hands through his long hair while he collected his thoughts.

This militia captain, Ingram, had fought under a different name during the English civil war, but Lance knew him as a careful, conscientious borderer who, while he growled at every military obligation, loved his war hatchet far better than his tobacco hoe. It was said that a dozen of Ingram's New Kent militia were worth a company of any other officer's because he trained them well and made them like it. His farmer-soldiers were able to fight Indian-fashion.

Ingram finally spoke. "I have just come back from Potomac country," he said. "A man up there in Stafford County named Thomas Hen and one of his servants were knocked in the head two weeks ago by some Indian hog stealers. Hen lived long enough to identify the Indians as Doegs. Giles Brent, a Catholic half-breed on Aquia Creek, and George Mason took some men out to punish the Doegs. They found the Indians in two lodges and surrounded them while they were asleep. Then Brent started shooting, and when it was over they found out that they had killed not only Doegs but a dozen Susquehannock warriors and squaws. It means all kinds of trouble with the Susquehannocks. Some of them are already south of the Potomac. That's why we are getting ready here. I want you to tell the Governor about this situation. Inform him that the Susquehannocks, who want to come south anyhow, have taken the episode as an excuse for coming into Virginia. I expect the main body of the tribe to cross the river at the first freeze. They will raid until they have satisfied the blood feud started by Brent's attack. At last reports they had at least three hundred young warriors."

Lance whistled.

Ingram added: "War is certain. There are enough Susquehannock warriors to wreck every plantation from here to Occaneechee Island."

Lance frowned. "Can you let me have a fresh horse?"

"I'll have to spare you one," Ingram replied.

"I'll go at once to Jamestown," Lance said. "I'll not go by boat."

He ate his food with scant relish. Ahead was another large-scale Indian migration, a muster of the militia, many farmers knocked on the head and mutilated by raiders, dozens of border plantations abandoned. It was a grim picture.

Ingram raised his head. "I have sent messages to all the outlying plantations, but not many of the dumb fools will heed the warning. They will look for Indians for a couple of days, and if none appear they will become careless. Please tell the Governor that his forts are no good against a threat like this. He must have mobile forces to root out the Indian camps."

Lance directed the landlord to provision him for his journey and to include two gallon measures of maize for his horse. Half an hour later he was on the trail to Jamestown.

ᵉᔧ 7

EASTER WALKER never had felt a flutter of her heart until she encountered the courteous frontiersman at Archer's Hope landing. Past eighteen and mature of body she had attracted many a hopeful beau. None had stirred her to anything except neighborly interest. Neither Tom Hansford nor John Lee fitted any of her dreams for the future. Even Arthur Allen, the widower supposedly skilled in methods of attracting women, was just another visitor.

She had changed. Her father no longer complained because she neglected proper supervision of the servants. The old house at Gull Cove was clean as a new shilling. All the provisions for winter were stored. The feather beds and the quilts were in good repair. Kettles had been mended and the knives all sharpened by the tinker. Ample firewood had been cut and stacked by the Negro boys. Hogs that had been penned for the winter slaughter were fat.

Alan Walker spent most of his time at his countinghouse over at Middle Plantation. Her brother, Edward, was forever hunting water-fowl in the marshes. Leathery Aunt Lucy, her father's sister, helped about the house, mainly with womanly chores. Easter had taken over most of the management of the home plantation, and, since the servants loved her, the task was not difficult. On some of the soft autumn days she had too much time for dreams.

The leather-clad man who had held her in his arms and kissed her had given her delight beyond anything she ever had imagined, but the situation had frightened her. She recalled one day years before when she had been out on the river with her brother. A summer squall had come up suddenly and had engulfed them in a torrent of sound and lightning and rain and high waves. She felt just as she had that day when she and Edward struggled for their lives under that storm. She was being swept along, blind and helpless.

It was, Easter realized, an indiscreet and highly hazardous situation. The man seemed more than half barbarian. He wore the costume of a savage. He was as alert as a wild animal and as quiet. Certainly he was no ordinary farmer.

Who could he be? He was not a new arrival. His speech was that of a Virginian. No recent settler could be familiar with the distant western forests. Whole families had been swallowed up in the remote wooded desert at the head of the rivers. It was a way to escape debt, tithes, taxes and judgments for criminal offenses. For all she knew the tall man in leather was a robber.

She could not help it. Usack. Whenever she whispered the name it made her heart almost choke her. Usack, a veritable physical incarnation of fascinating, beautiful, mysterious, dangerous Virginia— and she loved him.

She tried to make her father talk about some of the western families. He knew the Milners and the Walketts and Pages, among others. He referred to them in suspicion and disgust as "those people"— meaning those who were out of favor with the Governor and, therefore, out of fashion and out of fortune. They lived from hand to mouth like peasants. Their houses were built out of logs. They were forever sending petitions to the Council and the House of Burgesses. They were nobodies.

Easter remarked: "I have heard there is no ague out there and the water is wholesome."

"How about wolves?" her father said sarcastically. "What of the Indians? They are more poisonous than the worst water in Jamestown. There is plenty of Indian trouble right now. Captain Roger Jones has told the Governor that they have started murdering people on the upper Potomac."

"A war?"

"A threat of war always prevails out there. It is worse than Tartary."

Easter fell silent. Perhaps that was why Usack had not returned. She shivered.

Usack did not return for days which seemed to her like years.

◆§ 8

AT JAMESTOWN there was little thought of Indians. A ship had landed with long due woolens, linen, kitchenware, tools and gewgaws. Much of the cargo was purchased before it could reach the warehouse.

The news from England was grasped as eagerly as laces and furbelows. Charles II now had fourteen acknowledged children. Nell Gwyn still reigned a favorite concubine in spite of all the others. The Duchess of Portsmouth, the Catholic mistress, had contracted the Italian disease. His Grace, the Duke of Buckingham, was writing plays. The court was prosperous. The French king still was paying a large pension to Charles Stuart.

The Governor, Sir William Berkeley, growled for several days over his dispatches. The Governor's young wife, Lady Frances, tried out her new dresses on Colonel Philip Ludwell as she read him letters filled with highly spiced gossip from Whitehall.

At a wedding feast the King had become roaring drunk and had tried to break into a bedchamber filled with maids of honor. . . .

Colonel Ludwell was not amused. Lady Berkeley was forever teasing him with recitals of amorous adventure and putting him off as though he were a child trying to reach the high shelf of a honey closet.

"You are not human, my lady!" he complained petulantly.

"But you, yourself, Philip, always have said that women do not belong to the human race."

Lady Frances laughed and flung the strip of arras on which she was working across both their laps and, beneath it, touched his hand.

Ludwell sat still and gave her slim fingers an answering squeeze. They made her like a sparkling girl, these flirtations in the sewing room. She was a coldly clever woman behind her glitter, and she no longer was a girl, but she liked to feel and to look like one.

"Where is your heart?" he asked. "If it is there covered with that lovely Flemish lace, is it quiet, or is it racing like mine?"

"Faugh! You have no heart, Philip."

"Here, feel."

But she withdrew her hand and again took up her large embroidery needle. "We must stop this childishness," she said.

He protested. "The King, then, is childish? The Duke of York is childish? The whole court is childish?"

"Yes, silly one. They play at being rakes, as farmers drink too much wine in order to forget their troubles."

He sighed deeply. "Then I shall acquire some troubles," he said. "Then possibly you will take pity and let me teach you the——"

"Hush, Philip!"

"Teach you the——"

"Hush, I said! You must not talk of such things. I am not one of your strumpets."

Ludwell leaned back and groaned.

This scion of the Cottingtons, this widower who was cleverest of all her courtiers, made Frances Berkeley dream of a happiness which life hitherto had denied her. In this land of muscle-bound woodchoppers his was the most gallant voice.

He was the wealthiest man in Virginia, owner of three houses at Jamestown and developer of three large eastern plantations. He never wasted time in chasing whores or threw away money in speculative voyages or wild trading ventures.

She was convinced that Ludwell was waiting for her, biding the hours until Berkeley's death. He wanted no immature maiden as his second wife. She could manage his household as could no other woman in the colony. And marriage with her would ally him to the great clan of the Culpepers. It might make him a royal governor.

There would be joy as well as strength and power in Philip Ludwell, she reflected. Blushing, then, she remembered that she had promised William Berkeley a son. Perhaps Ludwell...

ॐ 9

WHEN Lance arrived in Jamestown he found the Governor in an evil mood. Seated at his magnificently carved desk Sir William was fretting with the rings on his long plump fingers when Lance made his entrance. He welcomed the young man civilly enough, but at the news he bore, Berkeley flew into a sputtering rage.

Lance stood quietly until the Governor found his voice to vow that he would hang both Brent and Mason.

"By what authority did those people march?" he asked, and fell to pacing the room.

Lance attempted to explain. It was, he said, a routine punitive expedition of a small detachment of volunteer farmers. Such counter raids were common all along the border. It was plain that Berkeley fully realized the seriousness of the slaying of the Susquehannock warriors. The Governor's fingers fluttered, and he pulled at the lace at his throat.

"A full-scale Indian war!" he cried. "A war because of stolen hogs! I have a horde of rebels on my hands!"

"There was murder, sir," Lance said. "The Indians committed murder."

"Murder, yes, but by Doeg warriors, not Susquehannocks. Those Pennsylvania Indians aren't fisheaters. They are giants, man. They are giants and they fight. This thing means war!"

The Governor wrung his hands and muttered, half to himself. "The fools. The thrice-compounded fools! Not one of them knows what an Indian war can mean. Fool farmers! Children!"

He turned and thrust a jeweled finger out at Lance. "Think you, my friend, that you know anything about an Indian war, you who have played at war by chasing hen-roost raiders? Faugh! One Indian can slay a dozen farmers. A hundred Indians can cost this colony a hundred thousand pounds!"

Lance did not reply. He wondered if the Governor's choler had anything to do with the gossip which had surrounded his wife and Philip Ludwell. But no. Sir William's mood seemed entirely the result of Lance's bad news.

At last the old man calmed down, but he continued to think aloud. "They will realize in time what they have done," he said. "They will miss a crop, two crops, perhaps. That will impress the grubbing fools! They will understand when they have to leave their border shacks and come east for food and protection."

Berkeley spat into the fireplace. "Brent! That half-breed renegade! He had a purpose in this! So did Mason. Farmers, both of them. They'd like to see the fur trade ruined. This trouble means a general muster, Clayborne."

ꝫ 10

IT DID mean a muster. The only calm spot in Jamestown was Lady Berkeley's sewing room.

"William will wage another campaign," she said to Philip Ludwell. "No," he said.

"It is his nature to go in spite of his years, Philip."

"I know. But now you are here. He will not go."

She smiled. "Nor shall you," she declared. "The western men started this affair. Let them do the work. I shall advise him to use John Washington. Washington has his eyes on some western lands. Let him go."

"Allerton has higher rank."

"Let Allerton go, too. It will sober him for a while."

Ludwell shrugged. "So be it, my lady. And if the affair ends in a clutter, blame me not, please. There has been hell to pay in New England, you know. It has been a costly war up there. The Indians have learned something about strategy, and a great number now have firearms. Canonchet——"

"Oh, bother the Indians, Philip. You haven't even noticed my French perfume."

He sighed. "But I have, dearest, and to the detriment of my soul."

"Foolish one!"

"You need no bottled scent, love. You have reduced me to——"

"Now, Philip, none of your lewd gallantries, now."

"Yes, I supposed it would be futile to voice things that you know so well."

She leaned over and tapped his wrist with her fan. "Why do you say there will be a clutter, Philip?"

"A campaign will mean trouble in the east as well as difficulty in the forest," he said. "There are people here at Jamestown who will say that Sir William deliberately has started trouble with the Susquehannocks in order to unite the eastern plantations; further that he is playing politics with Maryland."

"Oh, there is always talk."

"Yes, I know. And in the west the farmers will say he is siding with the Indians in order to protect his fur trade. The fact is, of course, he is planning to hold back the northern savages so the war will not affect the Occaneechees to the south. It is with the Occaneechees that Sir William's traders do business."

"MacFarlane is agent for the Appomattox country. Have you ever seen him, Philip?"

"Oh, yes. And I would not trust him as far as I could kick him."

"What a bull he is! They say he has twenty wives."

"And I have none."

She laughed.

≈§ 11

LANCE came impatiently to the cedar-bordered lane and repeated the owl cry at intervals. For hours, it seemed, he waited. When she came his heart beat so furiously that for minutes he could not speak.

Easter Walker touched him as though to see if he really were alive, scolded him for his long absence, then trembled when, in halting sentences that bristled with pagan Indian terms, he told her of his adventure in the north.

"Oh, Usack, I am afraid for you!"

He squared his shoulders with a warrior's pride.

"Must you go again?"

"Yes," he replied.

"And then?"

"I shall come back here for you."

She drew away from him. "What did you say?"

"I'll come for you. You will help me build my house at the falls of the James."

"No! No!" She was fearful.

He took her hands. "I know you will because . . ."

"Usack, I don't even know who you are!"

"Oh, yes, you do, my angel. You know that I'm a man who cannot sleep for thinking of you, that you're a woman who——"

She laughed nervously. "Who also has trouble sleeping sometimes, Usack."

He caught her in his arms and held her, unresisting. His breath went from his body. He seemed to float in the air. Then the touch of lips shivered through him and through her.

He forgot his frontier manners, murmured endearments taught him by his long-dead mother, kissed her eyes, and hair and the soft warm spot behind her ear.

"Oh, Easter, darling . . ."

But now she thrust him firmly back. "No, my . . . my dear one, no . . ."

"Easter——"

"No. I must not, cannot. I'm afraid, Usack!"

"You? Afraid! Ha, ha! You are afraid of nothing, Easter Walker. You might hate, perhaps, but you'll never fear me or anyone alive. Not even the secrets of your heart and body frighten you."

For a while she did not speak. Then she said: "Myself I do fear sometimes, Usack. And I fear war. You must go. My brother may have to go. If anything should happen to you, Usack, I would die. I know."

"You will help plan our house near the falls?" he whispered.

She put her fingers across his lips. "I said no such thing!"

"I'll build a new sloop to take you up the river. We shall have a vessel as fine as Cleopatra's barge."

"But there are Indian troubles, Usack," she said. "Frances Berkeley told me just the other day that it is almost time for another Indian war."

He laughed and kissed her at the quivering corner of her lips. "Indians? They are children, Easter. With my men we could live happily in the middle of an Indian war. We will not be sheep, like ordinary farmers. Besides, the Governor will hold them back just as he has done in years past."

They said nothing for a while and then she asked: "Who are you, Usack?"

He smiled and kissed her. For a moment it was on his lips to admit that he was Lance Clayborne, but the sweetness of the moment checked him. It would not do. If he confessed his little masquerade, she would be angry. He would have to leave her and go westward at once. It would not do to leave her angry at him.

Gently he released her, stopped to pick up his fusil from the stile. "I cannot tell you, dearest," he said. "I must play my game a little longer."

Then like an owl which speeds noiselessly through the dusk he disappeared.

VI

Border Campaign

◄§ 1

CERTAIN that all the warlike Susquehannocks would move south at the first opportunity, Sir William Berkeley acted with vigor. The best trained bands of the counties were alerted at once, and before the end of the day orders dispatching them to the Potomac line were on the way. If a show of force could hold the main body of the savages north of the Potomac, war might yet be prevented.

A trusted messenger was sent by boat to the Governor of Maryland with a suggestion that Maryland border forces rendezvous with the Virginia column at the Potomac falls. Ships hurriedly loaded with provisions were dispatched up the rivers to intercept the marching columns and assist them at the crossings.

As Lance rode westward he passed many small bodies of militia moving to join the expedition. Officers trained their rugged levies on the march. Some of the troopers never had ridden before, some of the foot soldiers never had learned to fire a musket; but the men seemed willing enough, thankful of opportunity to taste high adventure. They sang rude songs and joked about their blistered feet and bruised backsides.

Couriers returning from the north all told the same story now. The Indian raids had ceased, the Susquehannock war parties had withdrawn across the river into Maryland. Men who had fled their farms after the first onslaught were returning to complete their harvest. Governor Berkeley had ordered those not in the militia levies to assemble at the river crossings and draw subsistence from the common store, but they disregarded him. Home ties were stronger than the threat of war.

The new soldiers marched on doggedly. They learned additional trail lore every day. The weak and sickly were left behind at scattered farmhouses. The others grew muscular and so lean that their garments no longer fitted them, and they had to punch fresh holes in their belts.

The little army of militia spoke almost every dialect of England and the Isles. Lance saw former seafarers from Devon, Essex farmers, tall yeomen from the Midlands, red-haired Scots, and wizened Irish boys out of Dublin. Some of the officers were young blades excited at their first call to an active campaign. Others were old Indian fighters who paid scant heed to drill and trained their comrades to run about from tree to tree in pairs so one would have his fusil ready while the other could reload or change his flint. A few were veterans of Cromwell's army who growled mightily at the lack of discipline in the scattered columns and preached of hell-fire and brimstone.

Lance found Nathaniel Bacon riding with the Henrico levies as an aide to Colonel Hill. For a time they rode together. Bacon's eyes twinkled with excitement as he watched the column filing through the trees.

"They are likely pagans!" he exclaimed.

"That oldster a pagan?" Lance pointed to a grizzled graybeard whose nose had been mutilated by a sword cut. The man was reading a Psalter as he rode.

"Yes, those old Ironsides are barbaric like the rest. Look at that chin! He would like nothing better than to roast a heathen Indian. The depths of hell he worships, but he has no regard whatever for the uplands of Paradise."

They watched a company of Gloucester men go by, lean farmers with faces yellow from long bouts with the ague.

Bacon shook his head. "I do not know what they are," said he, "but this I do know: they are from England, but they are not Englishmen. Not one."

Lance looked up curiously. "You have noticed that?"

"Yes, Lance. These men are more than Englishmen. Look at their eyes. You do not see eyes like that in London or Plymouth. They have a new kind of pride and hope in them. In England a man works in the narrow channel of his class—works like an animal under a yoke, without hope. Here in Virginia men work with boundless opportunity right within their reach. There are no class barriers, no limits to their ambition, no fetters of custom, no princes."

Bacon squared his shoulders. "Already I feel the liberty of this land," he said. "Soon freedom will be marked on my face just as it is on the faces of these marching men."

Puzzled by Bacon's reflections and vaguely disturbed, Lance spurred after him.

For a long time the slim scholar was silent, but his alert eyes continued to sparkle.

Inexperienced on campaign, Bacon was as ill-equipped and awkward as any, but he soon became a favorite among the men. He joked with them about discomforts of the trail, swore that every wasp in twenty leagues had made him a blood brother, that poison ivy had been planted by Mother Nature for the chastening of his soul.

He made light of misfortunes with a brutal candor that the men enjoyed, but when two incautious troopers mired themselves in quicksand at the Pamunkey crossing his ingenuity saved their lives. Unlike some of the other officers, he did not hesitate to wet his boots and labor with his hands. Inspired by his example, the command gathered grape vines and worked together until the unfortunates were extricated.

In camp he taught them songs which horrified the Puritans among them but caused great glee—gay ditties he had learned at Cambridge or had picked up in his travels on the Continent. The men made up new verses as they marched.

On the second day Lance Clayborne reluctantly bade farewell to Bacon and other friends in the marching levies and rode over to Colonel Allerton's plantation in Westmoreland.

He found Allerton at his Potomac landing, directing the loading of his sloop with forage. He was a bluff, red-faced man, whose feats among the fleshpots of the colony were notorious, but a person of high spirit and keen intelligence. Exiled son of a Massachusetts Bay settler who had come over in the *Mayflower* in 1620, Allerton was widely traveled and one of the wealthiest planters of Virginia. His beard was trimmed to a sharp point beneath his flaring mustaches. His bearing was erect and resolute. Sword scars marked his left temple and forehead.

He read Berkeley's letter, frowned, but as Lance watched his expression changed. Eyes half closed, a wry smile on his lips, he looked up. "My thanks, lad," he said. "Do you know the contents of these instructions?"

Lance shook his head.

"You ride with us?"

"I join the Henrico rangers on the trail when I have your permission to go."

Allerton rose from the great bundle of cut maize on which he had sat down to read the dispatches and waved his hand. "You will stay with me while the men are gathering. I wish to talk to you about those Susquehannock beggars. I hear they're wilder than King Philip's band up in New England. Who is their war chief?"

"A man the traders call Bloom," Lance answered. "Many of his young men are armed with muskets."

"Hunh. They will be willing enough to talk peace when they see our force."

Lance was surprised. "Peace, sir? They have slain more than a dozen white men in the past three weeks."

Allerton pursed his rakishly bearded lips. "Yes, lad, but is not the object of war to win peace?"

"I know, sir, but——"

"I see. You young bloods would have us exterminate every Indian in Virginia. Possibly it is a worthy aim, though like ridding Chesapeake Bay of herring it is—well—difficult."

"They are not so numerous as herring, sir."

"Yes, but far more slippery and troublesome to catch."

A dull weight settled over Lance Clayborne's heart. Here was the commander of an expedition, a keen and able man by reputation, who before he marched seemed to be willing to admit defeat. Lance wondered about Governor Berkeley's orders. Could Berkeley have instructed Allerton to stand still and make peace, to give the Susquehannocks safe conduct on their southward march?

Colonel Allerton spoke again. "Do you think we could pin them down, destroy them?"

"No, sir, but we could find their camps and one by one root them out. We have western Henrico men who can follow the dimmest trails. We could pursue their bands one by one until they are scattered and exhausted."

"I see. What if they enfort themselves like Dutchmen?"

"We could take the fort."

"Ha! Let's hope so, lad, for messages from Maryland indicate that these tall tribesmen from the north are not ordinary Indians. I have been told that Maryland is calling up a thousand men—which means they'll get two hundred, I suppose. How many are there in the Virginia column now?"

"Full three hundred, sir, half horse, half foot."

Allerton asked many questions about the companies Lance had encountered on the march. As some of the officers were named Allerton pulled his beard with a skeptical smile.

"The militia are unpracticed, sir," Lance said. "Some yet do not know how to load a musket. A few are London men, newly arrived."

Allerton laughed. The big planter's mirth rasped like a file. The slaves who were passing fodder along the wharf turned in alarm, then hurriedly resumed their labor. Allerton laughed again and began to tear to pieces the letters from the Governor. Bit by bit he fed the fragments to the southern breeze until the last scrap had fluttered out over the water.

◆§ 2

LANCE spent two days at Allerton's sprawling luxurious plantation house. Then, at the head of sixty Westmoreland cavaliers, he and Allerton rode northwestward to the Potomac to join John Washington and the little army.

Washington, an impulsive, handsome Potomac planter, who was as tall as any Susquehannock, lived close to the border and had been exposed to Indian raids. Veteran of several punitive expeditions, he knew enough of leadership to be irked by the Governor's order which decreed joint command. When Allerton informed him of the plan Washington growled like an angry bear.

"Devil's blood, Allerton! Doesn't the old man trust either of us? We are given joint responsibility."

Allerton's hands went up in a rueful gesture. Washington took out a coin and rolled it over his thumb.

"Shall I toss it, Allerton? This is a lucky groat."

Allerton shook his head. The question of command, he said, could be resolved by the agreement of a council of officers. To this Washington finally acceded and the county officers were summoned.

It was decided that Allerton, the senior in rank, should command the foot, and Washington the two troops of horse.

Within a week the column ferried the Potomac on herring boats, joined the Maryland militia; and, guided by a party of friendly Piscatawa tribesmen, the little force moved into the fastnesses.

꿏 3

LANCE CLAYBORNE'S memories of the campaign in Maryland later were to be blurred by other events, but he realized at the time that this was an extraordinary affair. Here was the first occasion in which trained bands of two separate and often hostile American colonies had assembled for the common defense.

Despite differences in religion and in political policy between the two colonies, despite frequent previous threats of war over boundaries, despite competition in tobacco culture and trade, and despite the strangeness of Maryland customs, farmers were farmers in Maryland as well as in Virginia—and farmers hated Indians everywhere.

There was not a fur trader among either the Virginia or the Maryland militia. All these men hated skin buyers as well as Indians.

Pennsylvania Quakers were in the Maryland column and fugitives from New York and New England—religious fugitives—but farmers all. Their common bond was love of land, fierce interest in their property and the public safety. The campaign, what with intrigue behind the scenes, a divided command, too great a number of awkward, untrained men with weapons in their hands, did not seem promising. But it was momentous.

Blood was drawn the first day—white blood. A Gloucester trooper died from an arrow launched from a laurel clump. Thereafter for two weeks the expedition was surrounded by red hornets who stung at every opportunity.

Strong detachments of trained rangers were sent forward to reinforce the Piscatawa scouts, but many days passed before they located the nest of the buzzing savages in the swamps of the Potomac. Washington then urged Allerton to bring up his foot troops as rapidly as possible.

Washington assembled the cavalry in a solid force and led them beyond the Indian camp, pretending that he had failed to find it. On

the following day the cavalry closed in around the deep swamp. Not
an Indian had been seen all day. After dismounting the soldiers
worked their way through the tangle of underbrush and grapevines
to the clearing.

Here once again they learned that Susquehannocks were not ordinary savages. They had fortified two acres as skillfully as Continental
sappers. The position was out of cannon range of the river and its
guardship. Ditched on four sides, walled by upright green pine palisades set very close together, with the top screened by branches, the
Indian camp was formidable and the barbarians were ready. The first
trooper who blundered within range received an arrow in his kneecap.
The savages almost caught the man before he could crawl to safety.

By nightfall, when Allerton's foot troops arrived, the cavalry had
wasted many pounds of powder and shot to no avail. The screaming
Susquehannocks threw rude jokes as well as arrows at them, called
them women, and with their turtle-shell rattles kept every man awake
and anxious until long after the next day had dawned.

A company of Marylanders, angered beyond control, flung themselves against the ditch at daybreak and lost four men. Throughout
the day the dead lay like pincushions in the black water, unavenged
except for a single red-skinned boy whose bold curiosity on the parapet cost him his life.

Lance Clayborne had never before seen Indians who, generally,
were so disciplined and alert. At Allerton's request he and a party of
Henrico rangers scouted the fort all day. He estimated that there were
at least two hundred warriors within and half as many women, many
of them fighters as able as the men.

A collection of arrows showed that Doegs and Delawares were with
the Susquehannocks.

Allerton rubbed his gnarled hands together thoughtfully and retired to his tent.

John Washington assembled Ingram and other veteran Indian fighters to discuss the situation. It was agreed that cannon were needed.
A pack train was sent to the riverbank for a boat gun, but, inadequately
guarded, the party was waylaid before it reached the Potomac and was
forced, fighting, to return empty-handed.

There was fever in the camp. The men were restless not only from
illness but also from lack of sleep. The Indians' war songs kept them

awake. Smudge fires failed to control the swarms of mosquitoes that preyed on white flesh until men were frantic.

By day the chief men among the savages taunted the militiamen and displayed frightful trophies or recent raids on the settlements, the arms and legs and hair of children and of women. At night the Indians would slip from the fort and raid the horse lines. Washington doubled the guard but with scant effect. The enemy killed and butchered horses beneath the guards' noses; they slipped past and killed sleeping soldiers. Before the siege was a week old ten men had died, and the flesh of a dozen horses had gone to feed the savages.

Washington submitted plans for a mass assault, but his co-commander shook his head. "We have them pinned down, John. Why sacrifice more men?"

Frowning, Washington waved his hand impatiently. "Have them? This camp is like a hogsty. The Indians are better disciplined than we are. If we don't fight now, we had best go home."

"Nonsense, John. They will bring peace belts to us tomorrow, I am sure."

No peace belts came. Within their log enclosure the Indians danced and sang nerve-tingling war songs.

Lance Clayborne and a band from western Henrico were directed to patrol the area north of the lines. As he expected, all of the Indian hunting camps for twenty miles were deserted. Except for the strong force within the fort the Susquehannocks had scattered. The tribesmen outside the fort operated in small mobile war parties which struck suddenly and then fled no one knew where.

Every pack train from the near-by Potomac landings required a heavy guard. The Indians by some mysterious instinct seemed to know whenever provisions were on the trail. Men moving southward from the fort were not disturbed, but nearly every column that marched to reinforce the besiegers was harassed somewhere en route.

Nathaniel Bacon frequently accompanied Clayborne on outpost duty. The English barrister had become thin and hard of muscle. His London clothing was in tatters except for his great beaver hat with its cocked brim and jaunty feather. His sword and pistols were well kept.

Beyond the confines of the camp Bacon stretched his arms and sighed in great relief. "I wonder," said he, "if there are as many lice at every siege?"

Lance smiled and said, "You'll have to find a squaw to pluck them."

Bacon scratched himself reflectively. "Is that the way you do it? But I referred also to human lice."

"I thought you admired these Virginians," Lance said wryly.

"I do, but some Englishmen who are their officers I cannot admire. Nor, I believe, can you or any other man. Allerton is indecisive. Washington is too reckless. Half the officers won commissions because of birth or acreage—not merit. I say, a few more campaigns like this and the militia will be decimated. Why do we stay here anyway? We are accomplishing nothing."

Lance leaned down from the saddle and examined dim footmarks on the leafy sod before he replied: "The savages must be held here. If we permit this big band to escape, the Susquehannocks will ravage the whole colony. We are fortunate that we have placed so many of them under siege."

Bacon frowned. "Siege!" he cried. "I thought we came here to destroy them!"

"We did."

"Yes?" Bacon's brows came up. "You're sure we came to destroy them?"

For a moment Lance felt a strange twinge below his heart. Bacon's tone was cynical past belief. "You mean . . ."

Bacon's eyes hardened. "I mean that this campaign is a farce, my lad, and the men will know it soon enough. I mean . . . I mean that Berkeley does not want these savages destroyed. I'd wager my cloak against a rabbitskin that the Governor is parleying with their chief men behind our backs. He talks to them of the future beaver trade. Allerton is obeying orders, Lance, and trying to hold them here— nothing else. That is why we have not overrun that pile of sticks long since."

A great disquiet chilled Lance's shoulder blades. Bacon laughed at the young man's rueful face and said slowly, "I see some colonial policy in this expedition, Lance. I read a great deal about it in London before I ventured to Virginia. The idea is to permit only a few men to benefit from the American plantations. What wealth there is must be funneled through a small group that is bound firmly to the present ministry at Whitehall. It is the Spanish system—the only system that they know—because England is inexperienced with colonies. So what happens? A handful of men become rich, the remainder must become docile drones. These latter may not by any means become prosperous because if they do, they make trouble and expense for the Crown. Every penny spent on a little local border war like this is considered a penny wasted. The important thing is to preserve the fur trade, not the safety of the border farmers. The only reason this expedition was started was because the Governor wished to check the savages lest they annoy the eastern farms. He cares nothing for the western farms. He wants them abandoned because they interfere with the fur monopoly."

"You must have been talking with Minge and Crews," Lance said reflectively.

"I have. And I see it clearly now."

"But I want to live in the west. It is healthier, and the land is better. . . ."

"So do I. So do many people. There is real wealth in the lands above the tide. But to live out here we must procure a change in policy. Virginia somehow must get away from the Spanish system. We must prove to the Crown that we are English yeomen, not Spanish slaves; that we are productive farmers and citizens of the Crown rather than a mob of bondservants exploiting a single plantation. The King doesn't know this country. He sees only fur and tobacco. We somehow must make him see that this land is a part of England."

"But you said yourself, Master Bacon, that these men out here are not English any more," Lance protested. "If they are not English, what are they?"

"I wonder." Bacon stared into the forest. "Whatever they are, they have the rights of Englishmen."

◆§ 4

ACCUSTOMED to existence in the wilderness, Lance Clayborne minded the discomforts and the hazards of the siege less than most, but, like the other officers, he was hard put to keep the men in his detachment well fed and in fighting trim. Long days passed without sight or sound of savages. They would remain so still behind their barricade that the pickets wondered if they had fled, and only learned better beneath a sudden flight of arrows. The untrained militiamen befouled their camp. Flies deprived them of rest by day while mosquitoes kept them awake at night.

The troops grumbled because the Governor sent such scant supplies. They cursed the Marylanders and their gray-garbed priests, who, said they, brought the camp ill luck. Also the men talked much of politics.

A new Assembly should be called. The little army should be reinforced and furnished with cannon. Fair taxes should be levied so the expenses of this Indian war would fall on all alike. Colonel Allerton and his staff on an inspection tour one night encountered in the Henrico camp a mock trial in which the "Governor," a soldier in a wig made of rope ends, was in the witness box. A tall, blond farmer was examining the defendant.

"Your Gracious Excellency!" he sneered. "We have taken the liberty of indicting and haling you before the bar for certain high crimes, felonies and misdemeanors which strangely have developed in your old age much to the dismay of the common men who depend upon you for guidance, protection and prosperity."

"Hear, hear!"

"We indict you, Excellency, for sending us second-hand ships' biscuit in which there are not enough weevils to sustain our strength. . . ."

Colonel Allerton smiled. As long as the men made jokes about their rations, conditions at least were normal. He started to turn away, but the words which followed the outburst of laughter checked him.

"We indict you also, Most Sacred Excellency, for building forts behind our backs when you should be reinforcing our front. We ask that you answer charges of failing to support this expedition. Finally, sir, or perhaps we should say *sire* in view of your recent pretensions to royal estate, we charge that for some time past you have shown every inclination to value beaverskins higher than the hides of farmers!"

The speaker paused. He had caught sight of Colonel Allerton and the other officers at the rim of the circle. Abashed only for a moment, he continued, "In consequence, therefore, Most Benign Excellency, we have deliberated and found you guilty as charged. Accordingly we sentence you to one month's servitude in the siege camp on the Potomac, during which you will starve, itch, sweat and freeze; secondly, that during aforesaid period you will walk three leagues in Colonel Allerton's most uncomfortable boots and listen to at least ten of his speeches on the gallantry of Virginian yeomen; finally, should you survive the above tortures, it is decreed by this rump court that you proceed without delay to London there to explain, if so you can, the recent maladministration of this colony and take the consequences at the hands of our good King Charles."

There were jeering cheers and laughter.

In early December, near the northeastern corner of the Indian fort at a post partly cut off from the camp by the winding creek, seven sentinels from the Surry company forgot their vigilance and played at dice. Indians slipped from the works, slew them all and took their horses.

The disaster shook the camp. Some of the companies openly talked of mutiny. Even Allerton was aroused. He called a council.

Lance Clayborne attended as an aide of Colonel Crews. Crews, a rawboned squire whose body seemed much too large for his head, was bitterly angry at the inactivity at headquarters. He had fought Indians for twenty years and could not understand it.

"This fort is like the hog the devil sheared!" he roared. "It yields more noise than wool."

There was nervous laughter. The unit commanders, who gathered in the glade before Allerton's log hut, all were excited. Ingram and Bacon were there. Peter Ashton, one of the most debonaire captains of the colony, was ragged now, his hair unkempt, his beard a towsled thicket. Moore Fauntleroy, from Gloucester, scarce could walk from ague. Francis Gray wore a sword with six inches of tip showing through its brush-battered scabbard. To one side the Marylanders huddled. Major Trueman, the senior officer, wore his best cloak. Giles Brent sat at his elbow. The meeting was a stormy one.

Crews asked Allerton why he did not attack the fort. "My men are ready!" he declared. "Why should we rot and die inactive?"

Ingram proposed a ruse. Let the English force be weeded out like Gideon's band, he said. Let all save the best and strongest fighters be sent home with bugles blowing. Thereupon a picked war party would surprise the Indians as they emerged from their fort.

Allerton shook his head firmly.

Crews spoke up. "Then, perhaps, the commander will give his reasons?"

Allerton bristled. "I am in command, sir!" he said.

"We speak in open council, Colonel Allerton. You summoned us to hear our thoughts. Think you the Indians don't realize our sad condition? First thing we know they will sally out and surprise us again. We must fight or go home. I say attack!"

There was a roar of assent from the circle. "Attack! Attack!"

Allerton started to speak and was cried down.

"Attack!"

Flushed of face, his lips pursed angrily, Allerton by his silence gave assent.

The officers began to leave the circle before he could dismiss them formally. Eyes were alight. Captain Peter Ashton threw up his hat and cheered as he ran to join his command.

At daybreak all was confusion in the camp. A heavy fog descended. Companies missed their way, became intermingled. A keg of powder that was opened to supply the Maryland men was found to be defective, and it was necessary to recharge a hundred muskets. Efforts to keep the preparations secret failed utterly as the poorly disciplined men shouted to one another to keep up their courage.

The sun had been up for a full hour before the columns could be formed.

Lance Clayborne was with the two commanders at the highest point in the clearing. Washington was as impatient as a cock pheasant. He walked up and down, chopping at the dogwood bushes with his sword, muttering to himself. "Two hundred warriors, full four hundred English, and we fumble around in the swamp like drunken seamen!"

Allerton sat on a fallen tree trunk, scowling and scratching himself. The drummer beside him, an old man who once had beaten the tocsin for Monk's infantry, watched his face anxiously for the signal.

The Maryland men still were not in position.

Clayborne who was watching the Indian barricade suddenly exclaimed, "Look!"

A tall savage had pulled himself up among the tree branches at the top of the palisade and was holding up his hand in a sign of peace.

A shot was fired, but the Indian did not move. His arm remained upraised. He was signaling to Major Trueman, the commander of the Maryland line.

"It's Oneota, a war chief of the Doegs," Lance said. "He is willing to parley."

Allerton shouted a command. The firing was suspended.

"We'd best go around and see what he wants," Lance suggested.

"Ha! He wants peace," Allerton said.

"I'm not so sure, sir. He thinks that we should want peace, because he has slain those seven troopers. We'd better get around there quickly. Those Stafford rangers might kill him. He must pass them to reach the Maryland commander."

Allerton asked John Washington to remain at the observation post. He buckled on his sword.

The tall Indian now had leaped down, outside the barricade. He was followed by four others, all of whom held up their right hands. They were fully painted, their ruffed heads bright with feathers. None had a weapon.

Allerton, scrambling through the swamp, panted triumphantly, "We have 'em. They want a parley."

Lance Clayborne was not so optimistic. He feared that the savages, because of the loss they had inflicted the day before, were far from being in a mood to surrender. Also he was afraid that the militiamen might lose their tempers when confronted by the arrogant barbarians.

They heard loud shouts in the forest ahead and hurried faster.

As they reached the lines of the Stafford County men, Lance Clayborne's heart went down to his boots. The Indian ambassadors were there, but all five of them were dead. A ring of excited militiamen stood around. The men were wiping their hatchets on tufts of grass.

Young Lieutenant Hunt, commander of the company, leaned against a tree, eyes wet with angry tears.

The soldiers fell back as Allerton approached. For a moment he looked at the sprawled, bloody corpses.

Hunt stiffened and saluted. "The men," he gasped. "The men——"

A trooper came up and kicked Oneota's body. Hunt flew at him, struck him with the flat of his broken sword, threw him on his back into the muck.

"Five men," Lance Clayborne said. "All of them war chiefs, and one of them a Wyandot."

Allerton's mouth was open, his face a pallid mask. "My God!" he cried, "These men have murdered ambassadors!"

Hunt tried to explain. The Doeg, Oneota, had killed the brother of his sergeant during a raid two months before. The sergeant had lost his head. The men swarmed around the Indians, cut them down before he could gain control.

Allerton, pale and shaken, gave the order to attack.

◄§ 5

DRUMS sounded and the rolling notes of the charge came from four sides of the enclosure. A furious fire opened.

Lance ran to join Crews, Bacon and the Henricans. The militia were emerging from the forest in a ragged line.

There was a cloud of arrows from the fort. A rattle of musketry rose also as the savages expended ammunition they previously had hoarded. At three points Indian missiles checked the rush. On the higher ground Washington's dismounted troopers, each third man carrying faggots to bridge the swampy ditch, reached the barricade. Reloading, they fired between the palisades and with their hatchets strove to make a breach. Thereupon, a swarm of yelling Indians leaped over the barrier and closed with them, war clubs swinging. Lance Clayborne beat one down with his musket butt; Bacon pulled another from Washington's prostrate, cursing form. None of the savages who sallied out escaped. Yet their sacrifice saved the fort. The weakened point was reinforced.

Arrows loosed from above began to hiss among the troopers. They withdrew in disorder.

Shrill screams of rage and triumph now came from the Indians. "Where are our ambassadors?" a shrill voice cried in English. "Where are our cockarouses!"

There was another sally as though the savages were beside themselves with rage. Washington had to use his reserves to prevent the maddened mass from breaking through his line. At that, the Indians won through to the horses and filled three of them with arrows.

Major Trueman, of the Maryland militia, called on Allerton and Washington the following morning. "We are fighting without honor," he declared, "Nor have we hope, food, or horses. Half my men have voted to march for home and are on the way. I am leading the remainder now to join them."

Allerton protested but without success. Washington sat and said nothing.

Despite the loss of their young war chiefs, the Indians operated with even greater cunning. They concentrated now on the remaining horses. Scarcely a day passed but that the number of half-starved mounts decreased. Washington withdrew the horse line farther back into the forest, but this did no good. The savages slipped through and, in the dawn mist, loosed arrows and stabbed sentinels until only the boldest men would stand guard.

Allerton became embittered, desperate. The men who had slain the cockarouses deserted before they could be punished. Lieutenant Hunt died of fever. It now was whispered that the Stafford militiamen had killed the chiefs deliberately to force the Governor to fight the Indians to extermination. Allerton credited this report. His mood became so furious that none of his officers dared approach him without his bidding. Allerton then went down, fever-ridden. Washington lost so many horses that now it would be impossible to pursue the savages even if they broke and fled.

For days the Indian rattles were still, but the savages were alert, as patrols discovered to their sorrow. Nor did the Indians waste away from lack of food. They thrived on stolen horseflesh.

Suspicious because of the savages' silence the white scouts watched carefully. Then came the final catastrophe of the campaign.

In the mist just before dawn one morning bright lights flared up suddenly inside the palisade. The sentinels cried out, and the militiamen investing the fort awoke suddenly and grabbed their weapons. A dozen Indian bark huts were ablaze.

Without waiting to assemble in formation the Virginians rushed toward the fort.

Bloom, the Susquehannock war chief, had foreseen just such an eventuality. In the bright light of the flames twenty warriors charged the position of the James City County company. With their hatchets they killed ten men, and through the wide breach in the line the whole garrison of the fort moved out and into the swampy forest.

The Indians were two miles away and safe from pursuit before John Washington was able to assemble his excited, demoralized force.

⇜§ 6

ONCE more Lance Clayborne brought bad news to Jamestown. Moving night and day overland he arrived forty hours ahead of the first stragglers from the border force.

The town was busy with the last fruits of a scant harvest. There was a line of oxcarts, each loaded with hogsheads, before Drummond's warehouse. A ship was tied up to the pier. Four others waited in the reach. The hitching rack at Lawrence's tavern had scarce room for one more mount. The wharf was crowded with farmers who, huddled in their cloaks against the west wind, stolidly watched the tobacco they had grown with so much pains hoisted into the hold of the *Pride of Plymouth,* a fat three-master.

On the beach before the Council House Sir Henry Chicheley was drilling a troop of horse. Very precise and elegant was the company with its evolutions. Rupert himself might have been proud of them. The young gentlemen wore gray-broadcloth coats, jackboots and wide-brimmed beaver hats, each with its sea-eagle feather. Their swords flashed brightly.

Waiting for the Governor to have his breakfast cup, Lance watched them with a bitter frown. Allerton and John Washington had been inept enough at forest warfare, but if Chicheley were sent against the savages three hundred men instead of fifty would be killed.

The cavalrymen paid no attention to the travel-worn young man in leather. Lance was patient. Dreading Sir William's stormy temper, he was happy at an opportunity to rest, with his back to the porch post, his eyes half closed in the sun's glare.

Shortly came the familiar roar, and the Governor came stamping from the house. He was in high good humor, but when he saw Lance Clayborne standing at salute beside the steps he stopped, frowned and peered as though someone had dashed cold water in his face. "You here!" he cried.

"With news for your ear alone, sir."

With a groan Sir William ushered the messenger into the house. He dismissed a servant, who was attending the log fire in the audience room, seated Lance on a bench, and, braced upon his aging legs, waited by the hearth.

This time he listened in silence, his long nervous fingers laced together.

Lance reported briefly. The militia were withdrawing south of the Potomac. Allerton, sick, had returned home. John Washington would keep the wide trail from the north closed if supplied with food, horses, grain and extra blankets for two hundred men. The Indians were to the west somewhere. They had suffered little. A large-scale war had come to Virginia soil.

Berkeley's fingers shook. A new migration of savages southward . . . fur trade destroyed . . . ten thousand pounds already spent in futile effort . . . more bills to pay . . . more taxes to collect from grumbling farmers . . .

The Governor spat a sharp oath. "I have the most murderous subjects ever to afflict a royal magistrate," he cried. "Those insane fools along the border *want* a war. Too wild to fight properly in ranks, they slay Indian ambassadors by treachery! They have earned the scorn of every decent man from Florida to the Hudson River!"

Lance Clayborne knew better than to argue.

Berkeley continued. "What troops have I, what money? I gave Allerton militia enough to overawe and check the Indians. What did he do? Lost five per cent killed, and twice that many sick or wounded and earned the savage's contempt! Where are others to be found?"

The Governor paced up and down again. "You, Lieutenant Clayborne! You bewhiskered panther! What would you do?"

"I cannot presume to advise Your Excellency."

"On my command?"

"Well, sir, a ranger force might be formed—a small band of footmen well supplied with powder. It could be kept in the field until every Indian hunting camp is burned. Some of the men who stayed with Washington are tough. Sustain them all winter, and they will drive the Indians to New Amsterdam."

Berkeley's lips curled. "How sustain them? Think they I'm made of gold?"

Lance did not reply. In spite of himself he sensed that the Governor was not altogether surprised at the failure of the campaign; further, that he was not nearly so displeased as he pretended to be. As he looked up again Berkeley's eyes bored into him.

"What think you, lad?" the Governor now said in a softer, almost wheedling tone. "You know the situation. We've repaired the forts. What more can those misguided farmers want?"

Lance spoke slowly. "Security only, sir. They will fight to guard their property, but without powder and ball they cannot move into the forest. The Council and the burgesses must give them ammunition, or the Indians soon will be at Tyndalls Point. The Susquehannocks have snowshoes like the Iroquois. They make war in winter, sir."

"They could reach Tyndalls Point?"

"Yes, sir. Already they have filtered through the line of frontier posts. I passed two burning farmhouses four leagues east of the Rappahannock fort."

The Governor's hands clenched. He picked up a pipe from the mantel and let it fall.

Lance rose to his feet. "By your leave, sir, I shall retire."

Berkeley waved his hand. "Yes, yes. Go now, and report to me tomorrow. My thanks for your speed, bird of ill omen!"

Lance bowed and left the chamber.

ᴥ§ 7

LANCE went over to Lawrence's Inn there to be surrounded at once by a group of anxious elders of the town. He sat in a corner of the hearth and wearily answered a rapid stream of questions. The latest roll of the dead he had been forbidden to disclose. Enough bad news already had come south. He sought to put on the guise of optimism, but in his face they read the gloom.

William Drummond, his gray eyes bloodshot, swept aside the questioners and faced the tired boy. "You'll tell us little, eh? Well, we shall tell you much, young man. Those men who have left their bones in Maryland have died in vain. You must tell their ghosts there in the swamps that Berkeley will make peace no matter what the Indians do. Yes, tell them that!"

Lance opened his eyes and took another draught from his tankard of hot wine.

Drummond, more than half drunk, lowered his head and raged on. "Yes, tell them the truth, Lance Clayborne! Tell them that the Governor let that expedition fall to pieces. Tell them that you've lost half a hundred men, three hundred horses. Tell them that young Nash is dead, that Walter Eanes is dead, that many families in the colony have lost a son, a father or a cousin. Tell them that the expedition failed while Berkeley secretly and treacherously sought peace. Yes, peace with bloody red wolves. Tell them that he seeks peace and beaverskins, that the banner of the colony now should be one of Berkeley's beaverskins!"

Lance was shocked by the bitterness of the man who once had been Berkeley's unsuccessful deputy in Carolina. He blinked and took another sip of wine to clear his tired brain.

Drummond spat. His rugged face was scarlet in the fire light. "I don't blame them for killing the savage ambassadors!" he cried. "They were Allerton's men—those Indians. They were operating behind John Washington's back!"

Lance, light-headed from fatigue, overwarmed by the wine, tried to conceal his thoughts with scant success. In spite of himself his own doubts about the expedition's leadership were reflected in his face.

Drummond was savagely angry and so was Lawrence. The grim affair north of the Potomac was simple enough to them. Allerton, the turn-coat separatist, had played the Governor's fur-trading game, had sought peace with the Indian leaders. The militia had foiled him by killing savage ambassadors. Only then had he ordered his fever-weakened, almost powderless force to attack. Allerton, the tool of Berkeley, was a traitor. Berkeley had become a traitor to guard his beaverskins.

In the storm Lance attempted to shake the weariness from his buzzing head.

Tom Hansford elbowed to his side. "How can the Governor profit when the Indians are making war?" he asked.

"Yes, how?" Drummond mocked. "How? I'll tell you how, my friend. I'll tell you that the savages do not war upon Sir William. They have raised their war clubs against the border farmers, not the traders, and they fight the militia with the powder they gain in a clandestine trade with Berkeley's agents!"

For a while Lance felt himself rocked upon wild waves of argument. His head began to ache. A jug fell from the mantel with a smash, prodded by Drummond's nervous cane. A bench was overturned. More men crowded into the already suffocating taproom.

"He has taxed us blind to build a chain of useless forts," said Lawrence. "What Indian ever paid attention to a fort? They will sneak in on us like dogfish through a sturgeon net. The Governor must chase those red-skinned beasts, root out their villages and drive them back beyond the mountains!"

"We must demand a new Assembly!" someone cried. "To hell with beaverskins! Down with the traitor traders!"

There was a cheer.

"We must circulate a new petition!"

Without a restraining voice they railed against the Governor and Council, vowed the Indian war would be finished in spite of the beaver merchants. For once the easterners were in full sympathy with the border men. Blood had sealed a bond between them.

Lance Clayborne slept twelve hours in Lawrence's best bed, awoke, and dozed again, this time to dream that the war was over, the colony at peace and he the happy husband of the Walker girl.

What a bed! His body felt as though he were floating in the air. For the first time in four months that tough body was entirely secure. There were no Indians at Jamestown—yet. There were twenty thousand farmers between him and the hatchets of the Susquehannock giants. Most of the farmers were like sheep, for no one had taught them how to resist the raiders; but even if the Indians could overwhelm John Washington's band of rangers, it would take them many days to penetrate in force to Jamestown.

It was strange that he should think of peace, he who had been weaned on a sword and trained as an instrument of strife and had spent much of his time seeking a family enemy. The Walker girl, perhaps, had made him weak, the girl and dreams of that rich new farm near Shoccoes in the west.

With peace he could sleep often in a bed with love to soothe his violent moods. Then by day he could labor and grow rich from the produce of his big plantation. Together he and the girl could explore the river coves, wander through the pines on which the wind played rich tunes and entertain a horde of gay friends at the end of every harvest season.

A great clattering belowstairs roused him from his reverie. Colonel Nathaniel Bacon, sleek, rheumatic, had come to ask news of his relative. There was a great bustle among the scullions and horse boys, because the rich old Councillor was free with copper coins. Lawrence ordered Canary for his guest.

Lance rose, pulled on his garments and went down to the common room. The elder Bacon's eyes blinked as he examined the man in stained buckskins. "You are the Clayborne lad?"

Lance bowed.

"Nathaniel Bacon, the younger—you know him?"

"I have that honor, sir."

"Is he—is he—?"

"He is by now, I expect, safe at his home on Curle's Neck, sir." The old man cleared his throat, fumbled with his ivory-headed cane.

Lance added: "Men would never want a finer comrade in the forest, sir. He alone was worth two companies of troops."

"Hummmm. I see. A headstrong, willful boy, too. Eh?"

"No, a thoughtful and courageous man, sir."

The Councillor blinked again and looked sideways through his little eyes. "Indeed?"

"The most respected planter on the border," Lance said.

Bacon ordered meat and made Lance sit beside him while they broke their fast. As they dined Lance examined the older man with care. Here was one of Berkeley's favorites, one of the men whose greed had bled the colony for years. Like the Governor he was cool and shrewd, but there were lines on his fat jowls and forehead— marks of anxiety. Though not yet fifty he seemed much older in spite of the youthful cut of his velvet coat and the liberal seams of his breeches that disguised his growing paunch. He resembled his young cousin not at all.

"You say that Nat came from the campaign with credit then?"

"With more credit than many another officer," Lance replied. "He led the men who saved the day in the last fight at the Indian fort. The militia made a furious attack. Bacon is without fear, and all love him for his kindness and generosity."

The Councillor chuckled with great satisfaction and thumbed the fold of flesh beneath his chin. "Glad I am to hear it. Damme! I've had worries about that boy. He has strange notions in his mind. When last I saw him he was prating of the grievances of certain of the up-river runagates."

Lance sensed now that the older Bacon had something on his mind, perhaps a message to his young cousin. They lighted their pipes while the serving boys piled new logs on the fire.

At last the Councillor said, "Do you think, my lad, that the war now will subside?"

Lance shook his head.

"The killing will continue through the winter?"

"I fear it will, sir."

"No, no. It must not!"

"The season will be perhaps a total loss so far as skins are concerned," Lance said, not without a touch of malicious pleasure. "Most of the western tobacco has spoiled in the fields. Back in the forest the treaty Indians have had to flee from their hunting lodges before the wave of Susquehannocks. They say the Marylanders may have peace, but that is because the Susquehannock war parties are leaving the Potomac country and moving south."

Bacon pounded his fist on his knee. "We must have peace somehow."

"We can have it only at the price of war. The Governor must give us extra lead and powder from the guardships, organize a stronger frontier force, find the Indians and fight them again."

"Why, good lad? Why? Isn't it to our advantage to seek peace?"

"Only at the cost of many dead farmers, sir. The Susquehannocks swore they would kill ten whites for every chief murdered on the Potomac flats. Their five ambassadors, you know, were cut down in cold blood. Like Scythians, the savages declared a blood feud. Would you give them fifty settlers' lives in exchange for five of theirs?"

"Maryland gave them a reward. Why can't we buy them off?"

"Already they have taken some of the payment of their choice. It is blood this time. Stronger war parties are coming southward. With every murder the border men are more anxious for revenge."

"But, my dear boy . . ."

"Things have gone too far," Lance said. "The Indians have ways of torture that would make a Spaniard envious, sir. The border men will fight them now no matter how much His Excellency, the Governor, might wish to pay for peace. What would you say, sir, if your nephew died with burning splinters in his eyeballs? You would arm yourself for vengeance. There are many western families with such scores to settle."

Bacon pondered, his fat fists clenched. "I think," he said, "that we must call a new Assembly."

"It would be a wise move, sir."

Bacon arose. "Tell them, then, that Berkeley shall call a new election; that we of the east this winter will meet the western men in a new Assembly here and decide about this war."

"Yes, sir."

"And be sure you tell my cousin that. He has battered me with letters until my eyes are red. Remind him, lad, that he, too, is a member of the Council." Bacon started to go, paused and returned to the table. "Tell him also, Master Clayborne, that the tax plan which he professes to favor will cost him five thousand extra pounds of Orinoco."

The Councillor gave him the letters. He departed in a chair borne by four Negroes.

Shortly thereafter a slave came from the Council House with a message bidding Lance to the Governor's presence.

Sir William greeted him courteously, seated him beside the fire in his inner chamber with a tankard at his elbow and pipes ready filled in the rack beside his chair.

The Governor put on much pretense of boldness, but Lance sensed tension in his manner. He asked many questions. Lance explained, with the candor of the camp, the troubles of the expedition; how they had waited in vain for ammunition, food and for new troops to replace those wasted by fever and wounds; how the Indians, well trained in warfare by Dutch renegades, had fought with discipline and skill.

Berkeley's face was pale. "And our men disregarded the Indian flag of truce!"

"I saw no flag, sir. Oneota gave the sign of peace. Perhaps the men from Stafford did not know the sign."

The Governor's lip curled almost savagely. "You think so, Clayborne?" he asked. "You think that men from that wild border region do not know the Indian gestures? Are you a rebel, too, that you would seek to justify that deed?"

Lance stiffened. His right hand moved nervously as though he willingly would have risen to resent such bitter language.

Berkeley ironically held up his arm in the Indian sign of peace. "Keep calm, my gamecock," he commanded.

"I do not defend those murderers," Lance said hotly. "No more frightful crime was ever committed in this colony. Yet, sir, the Indians were incautious and arrogant. One of them was recognized as the murderer of a border family. They gave the officers of our force no time to provide them with a guard against blood enemies among the militia."

Berkeley tapped his long fingers on his chair arm. His eyes narrowed as he scanned Lance's still indignant face. "You believe this killing was not premeditated, Clayborne? Do you really believe this tale you bring to me?"

Gripping himself firmly, the young man did not reply.

Berkeley's brows came up. "Then I'll assume you do, despite a wisdom that is beyond your years. And I shall tell you this, knowing well your loyalty to the Crown and colony: those murders were the acts of traitors, Clayborne, traitors who would commit this land to a costly war. It was planned by rebels who were unwilling to have peace. It was a deliberate act of treachery to your commander, Allerton, and me. Allerton should have prevented it but his men got out of hand. I shall hang the slayers of those Indians! They have prolonged this war."

The Governor rose and paced up and down the hearth a moment, throwing explosive words over his shoulder as he strode. "Tell Washington I am mustering new forces under Chicheley. Tell them there'll be a winter campaign of defense. Tell them to keep a screen of rangers on the wide trail from Maryland and maintain contact with the river forts. Tell Washington to warn all the seventy-one plantations and to look for the crossing of the Indians with the first big freeze on the Potomac River." He paused.

"Shall I tell them also, sir, that there will be an election in the spring?"

Berkeley stopped as though arrested by a bullet. "What? Who told you such a thing?"

"I understood from Councillor Bacon that this is being contemplated."

Berkeley's pink cheeks turned pale. "Nonsense!" he roared. "You'll hold your tongue regarding such a thing! You understand? No such action has been taken."

"Yes, sir."

"You will return to the Potomac crossing, Clayborne. These letters here will give sole command to Washington until Chicheley joins him. Allerton will remain at home. Here, lad." Sir William handed him a packet of dispatches wrapped in oiled linen.

Lance rose and, with a salute, took his leave.

⋖ 8

THAT evening in the lane at Gull Cove the young man waited with impatience. Twice he gave the owl call. Anxiously he watched the brightly lighted house afraid that Easter Walker might be away from home.

Perhaps it might be well that he did not see her. Long days upon the trail would pass more quickly if his memory of her beauty could be dimmed. Warriors should not have women on their minds. Months might pass before his return. Evil days were ahead, days of uncertainty and unrest, days of violence. Perhaps he was a fool to stand here waiting like a lovesick hawk. This adventure was fantastic anyway. It was beyond the credibility even of a minstrel. Perhaps the Walker girl by now had found her senses. Perhaps she realized the danger of secret meetings with a leather-stockinged stranger whose real name she did not yet suspect. The maiden was a fool, and so was he. For a moment he had an impulse to depart; and then he realized he could not, that he would stay there in the lane until cock-crow unless he saw the girl. The Governor's dispatches—plague on the Governor's dispatches! Indian war—the war could wait. He could not endure another day unless he heard her voice.

There was a rustle at the stile that made his heart leap. A second later she was in his arms. She, a fragrant bundle, whispered delightfully, "Oh, Usack, I thought you'd never come. You are bad to wait so long. Bad . . . bad. It's been so long, Usack."

He could not speak for many minutes.

"Where have you been?" she asked. "I feared an Indian girl had taken you, or that you'd been killed in that awful border war; and no one knows you, Usack. I have inquired. I have asked for the handsomest frontiersman in Virginia of every stranger who comes past. I've made myself a laughingstock for love of you. My friends think that I am crazy. They believe that I love a phantom, but I know better."

She clasped his sinewy arms and then drew back. "What is this thing on your belt?"

"That is a war hatchet."

"Oh."

They sat down on the stile, and Lance tried to breathe away the choked sensation in his throat.

"I'm so happy to see you, Usack," she declared. "It was foolish to think you would not return to me. I am sorry I thought such things. I am glad I prayed that the Indians would not kill you. My prayers, you see, were answered."

"Never fear," he said. "No Indian will kill me. I think of you and shoot straighter than a bee can fly."

Her fingers touched his square, half-bearded chin and smoothed his hair. Then her fingers went to her throat, and she unfastened a chain. "Here, Usack, is your medicine. You must take it now. I have been frightened terribly for fear you'd come to harm."

She tied the little buckskin pouch around his neck. It was warm and fragrant.

He said, "It's doubly powerful now, I know, because you've worn it. Perhaps I shall be needing it in this next long march of mine."

"Long march?" she cried. "Oh, Usack, don't leave me. Father

says that there's rebellion in the air which is more serious than the Indian war, that we will have trouble in the spring. We need you here to guard us."

Lance started to mention his talk with Berkeley, then caught himself.

He held her tightly.

"You could never frighten me, Usack. There are other men who do, men like . . ."

"Who?" he asked.

"Men like Arthur Allen or Launcelot Clayborne. My brother thinks that Lance Clayborne wants to add me to his list of broken-hearted girls. I met him at the Governor's last levee. Do you know him, Usack?"

He drew back to keep his suddenly pounding heart from betraying him.

"Ann Brantley's head is completely turned," she added. "She says he is older than his years and quite a romantic cavalier. Have you met him, Usack?"

He nodded.

"Edwards says I should not let Ann Brantley get him, Usack. He says that I could have him if I choose."

When he made no reply she was pleased and added: "They say Lance Clayborne is courtly, shrewd and rich, Usack. Some believe him a careless roysterer; others believe that he is as cold and pitiless as a mountain Scot, because of his family feud with a sea merchant. But I scarcely know him, Usack. Edward is always talking about the man, but I have almost forgotten how he looked at the Governor's party, other than that he was quite a dandy there in the candlelight. The Governor envied him his wonderful black wig and Sir Henry Chicheley wanted to rob him of his jeweled buckles."

She moved closer to him as though to say: *Can't you see I am teasing you?*

He remained silent. His vanity rather than his jealousy pained him. For a moment he was out of his western character entirely, and the spell there in the lane was broken. He remembered every moment of his misery at the Governor's reception. She, it seemed, remembered his wig and buckles, nothing else.

She continued: "I suppose all girls must marry someone, Usack, and I think that girls who can find a husband they can love are most fortunate. I could never love a tavern knight who consorts with abandoned women, kicks law officers into swamps, wages a feud and wastes fifty guineas on a wig and half as much again on Italian buckles. Can't you see that?"

"You did not see the man beneath the clothing?" he asked coldly.

"I supposed that beneath such garments there could not be much of a man, Usack."

"And you have been at court?"

"I saw no genuine, honest men at court."

She was beginning to become disturbed at his tone. For the thousandth time she wondered, painfully, who this man Usack could be. Long since she had sensed that he was a gentleman, that he was the scion of one of the better families of the colony. But she knew all the gentle families, and he fitted none. Nor could he be a new arrival. He had demonstrated too complete a familiarity with affairs in Virginia. Who? Who? She knew better now than to ask a direct question.

"Is Lance Clayborne a friend of yours, Usack?"

"This man you have described, this dandy, is not my friend," he growled. "However the real Clayborne is a friend of sorts, so I can forgive him his tailor and his buckles. I can forgive him also the reputation which the gossips have given him. Like other young men he is a thoughtless fool at times, but I have seen him as a warrior."

"You frighten me, Usack! You talk so strangely!"

He also now was frightened. For a moment he had lost completely his forester's identity, had become Lance Clayborne. This would never do. He changed the subject.

≈§ 9

AT CLAYBORNE CASTLE next morning Sir Mathew spoke of war. Lance, in the rush of preparing for his journey, spoke of Easter Walker and of marriage.

"I need a wife," he said. "She will do."

"You are a fool!" his father cried, but he was not ill-pleased.

"Make any terms you can," Lance said. "I want the girl, not Alan Walker's gold."

"You are stark mad!"

"It matters little. Unless you present the matter and Alan Walker gives consent, I shall steal her on my return and be married by a separatist preacher in the wilderness."

"God forbid!"

Lance picked up his fusil and his belt arms. "You ride with Chicheley, Father?"

"Yes."

"But you'll see Alan Walker before the muster?"

"Yes," his father growled.

A quick embrace and Lance was galloping westward on his mission.

Time was short. He had delayed his ride ten hours for his visit with the girl. He would have to make it up. He had picked Prince, the strongest horse at Clayborne Castle.

The weather thickened at every mile. A freezing December mist stiffened every twig and made of it a vicious club to bar his progress. Twice he had to stop and beat away the ice which formed on his cloak and cap. He failed to keep the priming of his fusil dry; and this annoyed him, because everywhere beyond the Henrico boundary were signs of Indians—a broken cooking pot made of red clay, the feather of a grouse, a mountain bird, a faint footprint which had a Susquehannock seam-mark on the instep.

He was absorbed all day in problems of the trail and in obtaining from his valiant horse as many miles as possible. It was the second day before he realized that he had made a grievous error there at Clayborne Castle.

Blood of Beelzebub! He drew rein.

The perspiration seemed to freeze along his spine. He turned and started to go back. His heart became a block of ice. But it was too late to turn back. By now his father had called on Alan Walker.

His father had asked her hand for him, the Clayborne boy. His father knew nothing of Usack and the masquerade!

He groaned, hunched forward in his saddle, sick of soul; then he laughed with feverish irony. What a dolt he was! He had made the worst misstep conceivable.

What would happen now? She would hate him for this business. When she discovered his identity she would think his father's visit was a test of her faithfulness!

He groaned.

Her fidelity to Usack, the forester—he had not thought of this before. Suppose she weakened and agreed to wed the Clayborne boy? Suppose, when she was confronted with the hard, cold facts, expediency conquered love, and she took the wealthy dandy and forswore her forester? What then?

The nightmare of these moments haunted Lance for many days. Who was he, anyway, or what? Usack, the wild Virginia heron, or the Clayborne boy? Was he a Virginian or an Englishman? If he were both could she love one and hate the other? Hell's fuel! She would hate both forever, and he could not blame her for it!

A noisy flight of crows brought him to his senses. He pulled out from the trail and walked his mount to a knoll off to the right. Here, holding the beast's nose lest he snort or whinny, he waited.

Now that the leaves were gone from the trees, he could see five hundred yards. More crows flew from their covert ahead of him and circled noisily. A deer crashed past at full speed.

Indians! He saw the single-feathered headdress of a warrior above a holly clump two hundred yards away. Others followed, single file, coursing steadily at a trot. A war party. Susquehannocks. . . .

Lance tightened his hand over the horse's nose.

They would cut his trail—find where he had detoured—follow for a time, perhaps, to see if they could get within arrow range.

What were Susquehannocks doing so far south? Had the rangers been swept aside? He looked again. Now he could count twenty of the red marauders. A large party.

Lance's heart thumped noisily as the column passed. Holding his breath as though to quiet his pulse, he watched now for the scouts in the rear. He waited anxiously for three minutes. By now the foremost Indians had seen the fresh tracks of his horse and were waiting for the main body. He looked again. There was the rear guard, three alert young men.

He picked up his fusil, mounted and walked his horse forward. Then, behind a dense clump of aspen trees, he drew rein, turned and circled through some big pines to a point within easy range of his back trail. Here he loaded an extra charge of deer shot into his fusil, reprimed the pan, and, sitting motionless in the saddle, waited.

The war party, he believed, would follow his track in order to learn his mission, and, if possible, to check him with a long-range arrow shot. They might think that he was some wandering farmer whom they could surprise by a stealthy approach before he could take advantage of his horse's speed.

Ten minutes passed. Lance opened and closed the fingers of his right hand to relieve the stiffness of his fingers which had gripped the musket lock too tightly.

There was an almost imperceptible movement beside a cedar bush ahead. A lean warrior rose cautiously, examined the cleared space across which the horse's trail passed, turned and beckoned. Two others followed, and another—tall, sleek men with their faces striped with black war paint. Their weapons were ready. Suddenly they stopped, turned toward him. The foremost warrior quickly raised his bow. Lance fired at a range of less than thirty yards.

He spurred away and looked back. The Indian was floundering on the ground. The others had taken cover. Lance dismounted briefly to reload, this time with ball, and galloped on his way.

The Governor would not hear of this. Couriers were not supposed to stop and fight. There would be wailing, however, in one lodge of the Susquehannocks. The members of that war party would think twice before they ventured off the trail again to shoot a messenger.

Twice he had to detour to avoid encounter with other southbound bands of savages. Sometimes his horse would warn him, at other times distant birds. He did not consciously read the signs of the forest, but he was so accustomed to evidences of peril that when it threatened he seemed to feel a change in the air around him.

At Ebenezer Ward's abandoned plantation on the Po River he found the bodies of two Negroes, mutilated after the fashion of the northern tribes. He hoped that the saturnine farmer had seen the remains of his slaves. It would make him more careful in the future.

Lance cursed bitterly as he spurred on his weary horse. There seemed to be no way to teach the average settler to guard himself against attack except to show him the results of an Indian raid. He would believe then, become very much enraged and send petitions to the Council.

If all could only forget that they were not in England, refuse to permit long periods of security to lull their fears, the savages soon would leave the country.

Then Lance recalled the talk of treachery in the Maryland campaign. Had Allerton really desired to take that fort? Or had he, under orders of the Governor, merely sought to hold the savages pending Berkeley's parleys for a peaceful settlement? Certainly John Washington had been no party to such a scheme—but Allerton? That shrewd son of a Plymouth separatist, that Puritan exile, had rejected every plan that had held promise of success.

The young man pulled his mantle closer about his shoulders, shivering at the thought. Treachery. He recalled the rotting, arrow-pierced corpses in the fosse, the savages' captives who had died so slowly and so noisily, the wounded whose noses were cut off before they could be rescued from the Indian women. Berkeley knew what Indian warfare was. It seemed unthinkable that the Governor would take sides with the traders. Yet the evidence was strong. The Governor was growing old. He wished to gain a fortune in beaverskins and to earn an earldom before he died.

Once Berkeley had valued the border men, because, like the Cossacks on the rim of Muscovy, they absorbed the first shock of barbarian attacks and guarded the eastern settlements from destruction. Now, with his wealth at stake, he saw them as troublemakers only.

Lance cursed roundly the ill fortune now gathering in the colony. A year before he would have welcomed strife as a relief from boredom. It was different now. There was a girl whom he must have, come strife or peace. There was a home to be built.

At best it would take him weeks to mend his case with Easter Walker. She was proud. Her very soul would seethe. She had scorned the dandy, but now she would hate as bitterly the forester who had fooled her.

Again he asked himself: Who was he? Was he one of the wild border men or was he a soldier of King Charles? Was he Usack the Heron of the western marches, or was he the proper heir to Clayborne Castle? Was he Virginian or Englishman?

⌘§ 10

LANCE found Washington at the Potomac fort. Ingram was with him, and Crews of Henrico, with half a hundred frostbitten rangers who now huddled with the garrison at fires in the cluttered muster yard.

Washington held the packet of dispatches for a moment as though they were hot and then, beckoning to Clayborne, retired into the bark-walled hut that served as headquarters.

There beside a hickory fire he read the Governor's instructions, mumbling to himself the while and stamping impatiently with one enormous, booted foot.

"Thanks, Clayborne," he said at last. "Pull up a stool and dry your feet. Good. Be careful. Not too much heat at first or you'll have chilblains to your knees and ruin your leather. There."

Washington sat down and flung the Governor's letter upon the burning logs. He took his scabbard and with the tip touched the blazing paper so that all of it was consumed.

"We feared you'd had a mishap, Lance," he said. "At least four war parties have won past us since mid-month. They were Susque-hannocks. Their main body is north of the river six miles west. There is broken ice on the river now. If there is a freeze they will cross no matter what we try to do to stop them." The tall militiaman stared thoughtfully into the fire and continued, "Did you encounter them?"

"I collided with one band," Lance said.

"What?"

"No harm was done, sir. I showed them my horse's heels. I counted twenty of them. There are nineteen left."

"Good. Good. How did you leave Jamestown?"

"There was some warlike preparations, Colonel. Sir Henry had his troopers at drill."

"But the Governor said nothing of . . ."

Lance smiled wryly. "I hardly think Sir Henry Chicheley's command will venture westward, sir. At Lawrence's no one had any hope that his force would ever march. They said the Governor paraded troops to quiet criticism."

Washington frowned and rubbed his bearded chin. "I see."

"Naturally there is discontent. Many a family lost a son or brother in that sad affair up north of the river. They do not understand why we failed in that campaign."

"Nor do I," said Washington.

Lance pulled off his moccasins and rubbed his chilled feet.

Washington was silent for a while, poking at the coals with his scabbard. At last he looked up. "Clayborne, you are Indian-wise beyond your years. What would you do if you were in command at this outpost?"

Lance pondered a moment, his eyes upon the now blackened letter. "I hesitate to advise you, sir. . . ."

"Nonsense, boy. What would you do? You are familiar with the situation. A certain hog was stolen, two men knocked on the head who sought to interfere, a punitive expedition and the murder of two lodges full of men, women and children because of Brent's error. Then we marched and, what with conflicting orders, lack of discipline and shortage of supplies, were beaten. So here we are, a handful now, trying to stop a southward tide of savages that probably will keep flowing no matter what we do."

"Aren't there still other factors, sir?" Lance asked, staring at the ashes of the Governor's letter.

Washington frowned. "Perhaps it's best we do not mention them. Nevertheless all of us should see the Governor's side of this dispute. In 1656 a similar wave of northern tribesmen passed through here. They defeated a column of militia, but in time the migration passed on without doing much further damage. His Excellency doubtless thinks that this one, too, will pass."

"What if the Susquehannocks pick Virginia hunting grounds and decide to stay?"

"They never would do that. This is the most populous of all the colonies."

Lance said: "That would mean more glory for Bloom, the principal Susquehannock war chief. They are not trader Indians, the Susquehannocks. They are fighters, better fighters than any except our choicest men. If I were in command, sir, I'd select a small mobile force and strike their camps. They will cross in scattered bands."

When Washington did not reply immediately Lance clenched his fists and added: "Damn it, sir, the Indians are not better men than we are! Although our militia companies have gone stale we have men in them who are good warriors. Bacon and Ingram are worth a hundred savages. Crews, Fauntleroy and Bland are each better than a hundred. I tell you, sir, these men will fight no matter what the Governor says. They will make their own resources if the Governor denies them supplies. They will not abandon their plantations permanently without a fight."

Washington's chin set firmly. A deep, stubborn wrinkle marked his forehead. "The Governor does not believe that any Indians would be foolish enough to pause in the presence of a line of river forts. His strategy is to maintain a firm defense and wait the passage of the new migration."

Lance frowned.

Washington held up a long forefinger. "So there you have it, boy. The border farmers want to march and root out the Indians no matter what the cost in men and money. The Governor believes that it will be cheaper to hold the line and wait. We cannot form a mobile force. We will have to obey his orders."

Lance flushed. It seemed almost as though John Washington with his calm cynicism were taunting him—Washington, the hard-bitten planter who had tried with all his might to defeat the savages only to be frustrated at every turn. But Washington had asked him seriously what he would do.

With nerves raw from weariness and exasperation, Lance growled an oath.

"Perhaps the Governor," Lance cried sarcastically, "might do better than build forts. Let him pick fifty border farmers by lot, chain them neck to crop and turn them over to the war chief of the Susquehannocks. Let him then say to these farmers, 'My friends, patience! You are the price of peace. All the Indians will do is roast you slowly and eat your tongues before you die.' "

Washington frowned.

"That would be more merciful than trusting to those forts," Lance said bitterly.

Without moving, save to poke the fire once more with the tip of his battered scabbard, Washington stared down into the coals. "You, too, Clayborne?" he said. "You rebellious, too—the son of a courtier who was knighted for valor on an English battlefield?"

"I am no rebel," Lance reported sullenly. "Is it not the right of any Englishman to criticize a public policy? This wild land is ours as well as Berkeley's."

Washington sighed. "This land has, indeed, a strange effect on men."

"So do beaverskins," Lance said.

"Hush, lad!" Washington climbed to his feet and closed the door. "You are repeating dangerous gossip."

"I wish it were no more than idle talk, sir. But I have lived among the treaty Indians——"

"What?"

"I have spent months among the treaty Indians, living as a savage. The Potomacs have Dutch muskets. So have the Doegs and Piscatawas. The Monacans and the Occaneechees in the south and their allies the Nottoways, Tutelos and Saponi have English muskets, sold to them by Governor Berkeley's fur traders. All these tribes and more besides will join the Susquehannocks unless we march against the northerners. You know this as well as I do. All the border agents of the clique at Jamestown now trade in powder, ball and muskets with the wild tribes. There is quick wealth in beaverskins, and beaver is the Governor's monopoly."

"Hush, lad."

"I am telling you nothing that you do not know already, sir. It is common talk."

"I'll order you some ribs of venison and you'll feel better."

Washington went to the door and gave instructions to one of the sentinels.

Lance pushed back his hair. For a while there was silence. His host flung fresh logs on the fire. The room brightened as the hickory flamed up.

"You have a plantation near Shoccoes, Lance?"

"Yes, sir."

"I see. You, too, wish at last to settle down. There is a girl?"

Lance made no reply to this although the blood rose to his ear tips until they burned.

"I see. Well, keep calm, boy. The better people of the colony must stand with Berkeley. We must somehow help put down this wild talk. It's doing no one any benefit and threatening harm to all. It can do no good to force the Governor's hand. Soon he will see the situation as it is and, doubtless, give redress. Virginia must not have a civil war."

◄§ 11

"VIRGINIA must not have a civil war," William Berkeley told his nervous Councillors at Jamestown.

But a tornado of protest was gathering. There was a cabal in every tavern. Farmers no longer took off their hats when gentlemen rode past them. Sir Henry Chicheley's young cavaliers encountered scornful rudeness on the streets. Men began to protest the fees charged them for port services, for deeds and for marriage licenses, and employed clerks to check the proceedings of the House of Burgesses. Beggar Indians all fled from the town after two such had been killed by drunken rowdies.

William Carver, the High Sheriff, resigned. Some said he was in sympathy with the masterless men who raged against the Governor. County Sheriff Barton employed a larger posse and armed his men with pistols as well as with hangers and cudgels. At Middle Plantation and Kickotan as well as at Jamestown carpenters were employed to build more stocks and pillories to handle the growing swarm of petty malefactors. A new gallows was erected on the road to Green Spring and decorated with a lean highwayman who, in his final speech, called Berkeley a poor imitation of Charles I and predicted that he, too, might encounter an executioner.

The Governor employed agents to discover the sources of the widespread sedition. They brought blood-stirring reports. They said that every farmer in six eastern counties was at one with the western men who were insisting on a new Assembly. Nervously the agents reported, with as much diplomacy as they could, that the Governor had lost every vestige of his once great popularity. There was a secret printing press in Warwick County which was publishing violently rebellious lampoons that men distributed at night.

The Governor believed that Richard Lawrence was a leader of the disaffected clique at Jamestown, but all of his efforts failed to produce any proof of this. He also suspected Drummond, his embittered former agent in Carolina.

Determined to kill the snake of rebellion, he could do no more than nip small segments and throw them in jail. He could not find the head of the snake because at that time it had a dozen heads.

⋙ 12

LANCE rested two days at Washington's Potomac fort before he rode south to join Peo at the new plantation. His hairy overseer was ready for fight or flight. His log hut was fortified and moated on three sides, the servants well supplied with ball and powder and on guard.

Peo listened with a long face as Lance described the terror along the northern border and told him that the raiders soon would strike the James River farms.

"We must hide our gear, Peo," Lance said. "And we must take the men to Clayborne Castle. There will be no crop west of Turkey Island this year."

Peo smote his work-roughened hands together angrily.

"Thirty plantations already have been abandoned."

"Is the Governor coming west?" Peo enquired.

Lance shook his head.

Peo laid down his pipe. "Then he'll have rebellion on his hands, sir."

"What!"

Peo frowned. "I know, sir. I know the temper of the farmers. Even honest traders like Colonel Byrd are now disturbed. He has had to send his wife eastward to safety. So has Master Bacon. As for the men south of the river, they say the Governor should be impeached for leaving them exposed. Not since Cromwell's time have I heard so much sedition. Nor can I blame them when I think that we, too, will have to flee and leave our land untended. The Governor has forgotten . . . Cromwell."

"It seems so."

Peo now lowered his voice so that the servants at the door could not hear him. "A meeting will be held at Jordan's Point Wednesday of next week, sir. Colonel Crews left word here for you to come at any cost. There is talk of a new petition to the Governor and—should he not heed it—a letter to the King himself."

"Are you sure, Peo?"

"Yes, sir. The Charles City County men called the meeting. Colonel Crews says they are openly rebellious, and something must be done to give them wise direction. He spoke of Bacon as a likely leader."

"But Bacon . . ."

Peo smiled slyly. "Yes, sir. Bacon is a newcomer, yet he learned much on the Potomac. Moreover, Bacon is on the Council. His influence is greater than that of any farmer on the border."

"I see. There must be politics as well as war."

"Perhaps they always will be allies—politics and war."

Lance rose to his feet and walked to the narrow, oak-barred window of the lodge. At the far edge of the clearing he saw a man standing watch. It was one of the new bondsmen, but he handled his musket well and kept himself concealed beside a giant stump. Then the sentinel's body tensed as though he'd heard a sound.

"Look, Peo. That outer guard . . ."

As Peo ran to his side Lance at the window saw the sentinel raise his musket to his shoulder. There was a puff of smoke. The man peered into the forest's edge a moment, pulled ramrod and started to reload. After another look the man lowered the barrel of his piece, drew a hatchet from his belt and retreated, running toward the house.

Lance and Peo, fusils in hand, were out of the house in a moment, moving to aid the fleeing watchman. As he ran Peo shouted to warn the other servants.

The Indians already? Lance swore viciously as he examined the priming of his weapon.

The savages did not pursue the sentinel. The man reached the footbridge safely and stood there trembling with excitement. "Four of them!" he cried. "There's black paint on their faces—war paint!"

By now the other men had mustered, arms in hand. The foot-bridge was drawn in. Extra bars were dropped across the stockade gate. The forest, forty yards away, was still.

Lance grounded his weapon.

"I'll have to warn Bacon," he said. "They'll reach his place by morning."

Lance did not waste a moment. Taking the best horse at the planta-tion, he rode eastward as darkness fell. He reached the main trail from Byrd's trading post without encountering sign of hostile savages. Thereafter, depending on the speed of his horse and the reluctance of the Indians to fight at night, he followed the narrow pathway for three hours. On two occasions as he topped the long ridges between the Chickahominy and the James he saw small fires to the north. Once he smelled smoke and made a wide detour which cost precious minutes, but by midnight he had reached the plantation gate at Curle's Neck.

A surly farmer wearing a rusty Spanish helmet challenged him. "Stand back."

Lance's tired horse shied at the lantern light.

"Stand back or ye'll be shot where ye are," the sentinel warned.

"Don't you know a savage would not ride a horse?" Lance cried. "Open the gate."

"Indians ride broomsticks for all I know," the guard replied. "Stand fast."

The man lifted the cow horn at the pillar of the gate and sounded a mournful blast. Bacon personally answered the summons.

He greeted Lance with delighted surprise. Together they rode over to the house.

"I see you already have been warned," Lance said.

Bacon swore grimly. "Yes, and with a vengeance. They have killed my overseer and one of his men. I have just returned from Jamestown. Look."

On the cottage porch covered with deerskins was a still form.

"Dick Potts?" Lance asked.

"Yes, Potts. They overwhelmed him. These are not Virginia In-dians, Lance. The savages are Susquehannocks."

By the firelight of the main room Lance noticed that Bacon was bitterly angry. His hands trembled as he tried to control the violence of his feelings.

They sat in silence for a moment.

Lance finally said, "I came to warn you, sir. I'm sorry I was too late to save old Dick."

"They caught Potts and a servant in the field near the river. I don't knew why they did not burn the tenant house. The woman escaped."

"Blood feud," Lance explained. "They are slaying only able-bodied men in payment for their cockarouses. Bloom has sworn to kill fifty white men. Then he will send a peace message to Berkeley."

Bacon's face turned redder than the glow from the fire. "Peace now?" he cried.

Lance looked up. "Will you ride to Jordan's Point?"

"Yes!" Bacon answered fervently.

A serving man brought food and wine.

"Thirty plantations have been abandoned," Lance remarked. "They cannot be defended one by one, for the savages have penetrated deeply. We must form a mobile force, follow them and break up their camps."

"What of the Governor?" Bacon asked.

"He is relying on his forts," Lance said.

"Aye, forts!" Bacon retorted, his fists clenched till the knuckles whitened. "Forts! Trying to keep back a savage flood with little posts at intervals of fifty miles. Faugh!"

Bacon rose and standing at the mantel filled a pipe. In the firelight his eyes blazed feverishly. He sat down again, long-stemmed pipe unlighted, stretched out his booted legs and stared into the fire.

"Lance, I don't care what the Governor does," he said. "These border settlers will have to act. They must march against the savages again whether or not Berkeley furnishes money and munitions. We cannot wait. It is now a choice of life or death. If we cannot find powder, we will have to fight with axes. But fight we must."

Lance put down his cup. "There seems nothing else to do," Lance said.

He told Bacon of Peo's report, how the whole colony now talked sedition, how men even mentioned Cromwell.

"It is not sedition that is the issue," Bacon said. "It is the public safety. It is not rebellion to protect one's life and property when the Governor cannot or will not do it." He raised his head.

"Lance, we have the material for a tremendous nation hidden in these forests. Regardless of Berkeley and his beaver merchants, the King will thank us for defending it."

⊸§ 13

MERCHANTS HOPE PLANTATION south of the James on Jordan's Point looked like an army camp. Farmers from fifty miles around had come by boat, on horseback, and afoot, streaming from the most remote plantations on the border. Some had their families— refugees from the abandoned farms to northward—others, like Lance Clayborne and Nathaniel Bacon, had servants with them and were ready to march against the hostile raiders.

William Byrd and Crews were there. William West, John Turner, Dominick Rice, John Bagwell, and many other leading planters from south of the river were present. There were men, too, from West's Point and from the Rappahannock highlands. Colonel Thomas Goodrich had escaped with only the clothing on his back, and Peter Gordon, another northerner, suffered from an arrow wound.

They greeted the new arrivals, Bacon and Clayborne, with enthusiasm. Crews led them to the house where deputies from six counties were assembled.

The portly Colonel Byrd was very serious. He rapped on the table with his sword hilt and a silent ring of stern-faced men formed around him.

Lance stood at the outer edge of the circle, watching the bearded faces of these county leaders. All were angry and uncertain. Some of them drew back from Byrd as though they distrusted him. Byrd started to speak, only to be halted by fiery Henry Isham.

"Wait, Byrd," Isham said and turned to Bacon. "We are glad to see you, sir," he said. "We are in disagreement. We have disputed all morning long. You, being the only member of the royal Council in this gathering, may bring this group to order."

"What word has come from Jamestown?" Bacon asked.

"None," said Isham.

"You have sent appeals?"

"Every boat that has gone downriver for a month has taken an appeal to Berkeley. Meanwhile, the Indians have reached the freshes of the James."

"Yes," said Bacon. "They murdered two of my men yesterday afternoon."

The news caused a flurry in the circle. Bacon's face grew pale as he told of the raid.

Isham's hand was at his sword. "We must march," he said. "We can reinforce Washington's band and hold the main body north of the Potomac if we strike quickly. When the river freezes they will be over on us in a swarm unless we block the trail southward."

William Byrd spoke up. "Act without orders or authority of the Governor?" he asked. "The rangers on the Potomac are starving I hear."

Isham half drew his blade and thrust it back into its scabbard with a bang. "Yes, without authority!" he cried. "How can we wait?"

There was a cry of approval. The Rappahannock planter, Goodrich, said, "We cannot wait."

William West, a lean graybeard in buckskins, growled an oath and roared, "If we wait, our farms go up in smoke. Snow will not stop those Susquehannocks."

Crews explained to Bacon that the Charles City men had taken powder from the guardship off the point and distributed it. Tam MacFarlane's whole supply of lead had been requisitioned and even now was being molded into bullets. MacFarlane himself and all his men had fled. Crews whispered that the whole group here at Jordan's Point was desperate.

Byrd elbowed to the table, his plump face sullen. "This is rebellion," he said in a low voice to Bacon. "My counsel is unheeded. Maybe, sir, you can lead them back to wisdom. If I know Berkeley, he will froth when he hears of this convention. Speak to them, Bacon, calm them. We cannot launch a campaign without authority from the Governor and the Council."

Bacon's face was pale. "Why not?" he asked. "My overseer was killed yesterday. All of us will be killed unless we act in concert. This whole border will be devastated, if we sit here and wait for the tides from Jamestown." His voice had slowly risen.

"Hear, hear!" cried William West. "Listen to the cock from Cambridge!"

"Hear, hear!" cried other voices.

Bacon moved to the table. There was a hush.

Addressing Colonel Byrd first, Bacon said, "I cannot agree with my friend and neighbor that action in defense of the western plantations would constitute rebellion against His Majesty's authority. There is no law that forbids a man to defend his home. Speaking as a barrister and as a planter newly come into Virginia, I say I'd do the same thing if we were in England. I say further, as a member of the Council of this dominion, that there is no law to tie our hands and leave us to the mercy of these savage warriors. God and human nature bid us fight. I am confident the Governor in good time will arm us with authority and place at our disposal for this war the full equipment of the colony. Meanwhile, from our present resources we must send bands out to hold the savages in check. Quickly, too, we must form a striking force to find the Susquehannock camps and destroy them. This business cannot wait. I suggest that we elect Colonel Byrd to lead this expedition, and inform His Excellency of what we do."

There was a roar.

Bacon turned to Byrd. "Will you serve, Colonel?"

Byrd's eyes dropped. He shook his head.

William West began to laugh harshly. "Ho! Ho!" he cried. "I see that some of us fear the Governor more than the Indians."

"A good thing," Byrd retorted. "It's well some of us should fear authority. It's well enough to help the soldiers at the fort, it's well enough to guard this camp with all its refugees, but it's contrary to the law and the rulings of the Council for any one of us to lead an expedition without commission from His Excellency."

"What of Tam MacFarlane?" a sarcastic voice cried from the circle. "Let's find him. Let's have a beaver merchant lead us."

This caused wild, sarcastic laughter.

West walked up to Bacon and laid a heavy hand on his shoulder. "We'd rather have you, cock of Cambridge. You fear neither Indians nor Governor."

West now addressed the circle.

"Let's have Bacon!" he exclaimed. "He owns no beaver pelts. He is a planter, not a penny-pinching factor, and he is a member of the Council. On the Potomac he was a bonny fighter. Let's have Bacon!"

"Bacon! Bacon!" There were cries from all parts of the circle.

Colonel Byrd was smiling cynically. Crews stood with his head down, fingers in his belt.

Isham exclaimed, "Take command, then, Bacon! End this confusion. Organize the camp. Let us distribute what supplies we have and get to work."

Bacon called the whole band of volunteers to council about a big campfire that night. Three hundred men crowded about the blaze. A great silence fell as their young leader moved quickly into the circle and held up his hand.

Parson Deeds from Windmill Point offered the invocation, a prayer that Providence might arm the band with determination.

Bacon thereupon stood for a moment, looking into the eyes in which reflection from the firelight glittered. In a scant minute—a minute that seemed an hour because of the dead quiet—every man felt the keen inspection.

Then Bacon began to speak. "I see a mob of men," he said in a low voice. "I see, however, a few who wisely brought their arms with them. Hereafter every person in this camp must bear his arms at every moment and have a weapon at his elbow when he sleeps. You understand? I want guns brought to council. I want them brought to mess—everywhere. Your pieces must be loaded, primed, always. Your knives and hatchets must be sharp. You must be ready to fight at any moment. Understand?"

The men nodded solemnly. In a firm voice Bacon then reported the proceedings of the afternoon and announced the appointment of company commanders. Each name was cheered. At the end when he declared that Joseph Ingram would be his chief lieutenant there was a veritable roar.

Bacon checked the demonstration with his upraised hand. "We must march against the savages," he said, his voice rising. "We need a picked band, not a mob. Major Ingram will drill you until you drop, exhausted. Your captains will lead you over ground so rough you will cry for mercy. For weeks, perhaps months, you may never see your wives and families. If there is faltering, falter now. We do not want—cannot use—a single weakling. This band must be like Gideon's company—afraid of nothing, willing to challenge the devil in his pit."

There were more cheers. Men began to crowd toward Bacon.

Lance Clayborne was drafted as adjutant. Until late that night he worked on the muster roll.

A resolute band it was, made up only of experienced borderers. Some were in rags and some in leather, sunburned, inured to the chill January wind, expert with musket and with ax, keen of sight and strong of wind, survivors of many dangers, scarred from wounds. Some bore brands on their palms.

Tireless, Bacon spoke personally with every one of them, tested each in the fire of his eyes, called out their names. It was past midnight before the work was done. As the last man departed to his station Bacon looked out among the flickering fires in the meadow. The men had built temporary shelters of pine boughs to protect them from the cold. The dogs had stopped howling.

Half to himself the young man said, "If God will be my judge, I have no fears." He put his hand on Lance Clayborne's shoulder. "As for Berkeley . . . I do not know."

"He is growing old," Lance said.

"You've known him long?" Bacon inquired.

"Yes," Lance replied. "Once he was an Indian fighter. He has crushed a dozen tribes, but now he thinks of beaverskins. He has a handsome wife."

Bacon pondered a moment and replied, "I understand. But it's not wealth alone he seeks. He wants security and peace, and now that he is too old to fight for it he lives on hope. He believes this wave of Indians will pass." Bacon paused. "Perhaps we could buy peace, but only at the price of several hundred families. This is too great a price. It will cost us much less to fight."

"Yes," Lance said. "I'm sure it will cost us less. As for the Governor, he is the lesser of two dangers now."

Bacon's teeth were set. His eyes stared at the wall as though he saw far into the future. He shrugged his shoulders, straightened up and spoke, "I'll be the leader until this borderland once more finds full security. I speak not as a member of the Council but as a freeborn English citizen."

Lance Clayborne ever afterward was amazed at the speed with which Bacon, one of the youngest men in that growing horde of fugitives at Merchants Hope, brought order out of wild confusion. Bacon selected as his group leaders men who shared his determination. Some were former servants; many were farmers; only a few were gentlemen, who in the desperate need decided to share Bacon's fortunes in spite of the Governor's wrath.

Joseph Ingram, veteran of many a forest expedition, was drillmaster. Ned Peo was given a scouting force with orders to take the field before sunset and picket the riverbank and trails to westward. A militia sergeant named John Pygott was made commander of the Henrico group. Matt Bentley, a firebrand from Surry, Thomas Goodrich and Matthew Watts—men who had distinguished themselves in the Potomac campaign—also were given companies. Edward Jones, of Gloucester, was named quartermaster.

Within a week the camp at Jordan's Point was fortified securely with upright palisades. Huts were built within the wall to supplement the plantation buildings. Food supplies were gathered for the refugees. Women and children were sent downriver to the eastern plantations. Available ammunition was redistributed and hay gathered for the horses. These were busy days. On two occasions Lance rode north and checked the picket lines.

In camp, with Peo on outpost duty, Lance received word from the Potomac that more than one hundred families of Indians had crossed on the ice. Bacon strengthened the line of scouts. Five days later there was a sharp fight above the James River falls. The savages retired, moved upriver. Peo's scouts dogged their trail. Back at Merchants Hope Joseph Ingram relentlessly drilled the band. No militia force before had ever had such rigid training. The rough men loved the big man's challenge of their strength.

Messages had begun to come from the Governor at Jamestown now, but none was addressed to Bacon. William Byrd was asked to report on the gathering of farmers at Merchants Hope.

Byrd visited Bacon with the Governor's message and asked ruefully, "What shall I tell him?"

Bacon shrugged and did not reply.

Crews also received a message from the Governor asking if the fort at Shoccoes was in order. Crews answered that Colonel Hill, who commanded the Henrico garrison, had been strengthened with a force of volunteers.

It was three weeks before a dispatch came to Bacon from the

Governor. Bacon knew the contents. He realized that it would be a direct order to disperse the force at his command; therefore, he left it unopened on the table, went out and told his trumpeter to sound assembly. Two hours later with his picked band he moved camp westward to the headwaters of the Appomattox River. On the same day word came that the Indians had crossed the upper James and were moving south.

Bacon summoned his commanders and laid his plan before them. "It's my intention," he declared, "to strike straight for the Susquehannocks' main band and harass it until it leaves Virginia. The Indians may sweep the country clear of game. We cannot carry much forage for our horses or food for many days; therefore, we must make a dash for them and end this campaign quickly. We cannot have fainthearted men. Send the weaklings back to Jordan's Point. We move at daybreak. Any questions?"

The troop commanders cheered.

That night Bacon summoned Lance Clayborne and asked him many questions about the Occaneechees. Lance explained that they were merchant Indians, defenders of an island in the Roanoke River who used their stronghold as a trading post. They were allies rather than tributaries of the Virginia Council, Lance explained. He reported that many beaverskins were there, a full half-year's catch awaiting Berkeley's pack train.

"Could the Susquehannocks raid that island?" Bacon asked.

Lance shook his head. "I think not. MacFarlane has been at work among those Indians. They have a mighty fort. A large Shawnee war party tried to take it four years ago without success. The Cherokees raided from the south and also failed."

"You say they are traders?" Bacon asked. "Have they supplies of grain?"

"Perhaps they have," Lance answered. "They have a herd of cattle."

Bacon snuffed the candle beside him on the table, breathed upon his chilled fingers and suddenly changed the subject. "I am thinking," he said, "of sending you to Jamestown, Lance."

Lance Clayborne stiffened in astonishment.

"I'm thinking of sending you back because . . . because——"

"Because of what, sir?"

Bacon was silent for a moment, then looked up. "Your father, Lance, will ride with Chicheley. I had word from Lawrence and Drummond today. They say that the Governor is sending Chicheley west with all his horsemen to arrest me. It would not do to have you with me if this occurs. I may have to face them over musket barrels."

Lance laughed nervously. "Nonsense, sir. Those eastern men would never fight against us. In fact, if we start out tomorrow, they could never find us. I have seen Chicheley's squadron. It couldn't march a week without a bargeload of forage. Boats could never follow the trail we are taking tomorrow. We are going far above the head of navigation on the rivers."

"You have no anxieties about the part you are playing in this expedition, Lance?"

"None whatever, sir."

"You may be dubbed a rebel by His Excellency. Byrd and Crews have stayed behind to find out how the wind blows before they fight. It might be better if you did so too."

"And leave you in this wilderness?"

"Yes."

"If that is an order, Master Bacon, I refuse to heed it," Lance said. "If you eject me from your column I shall follow it alone!"

Bacon took the young man by the shoulders and embraced him silently.

14

THAT day a sailor sought Lance out at Bacon's headquarters. When Lance heard the man's voice, which was as shrill as a whistle, he ran out of the cabin and greeted him joyfully.

It was Nicholas Jump, an old friend of the *Saucy Mary's* voyage from England years before. In his canvas breeches and his tarry-jacket, Nick stood between two sentinels as nervous as a crow. For several seconds he stared, amazed at the size of the boy whom he had not seen for eleven years.

Lance dragged him into the cottage, pushed him down onto a bench beside the fireplace, ordered up a mug of wine. Mumbling to himself, Nick warmed his hands. He stole a quick glance at the tall, leather-clad young man who beamed at him.

"You old pirate, you!" Lance cried. "What good wind brought you back into Virginia?"

"Humm," said the lean little man. "I don't know if it's you or not. Blast me, but you're furred like a forest cat!" Nick looked around him suspiciously.

Lance nodded to the ranger who had brought his visitor up from the landing. The man left the room.

The old sailor's hand sought Lance Clayborne's knee and patted it affectionately. "I'm glad the banshees didn't git you, boy." He sighed. "I've been fearful at times, fearful. Cap'n Carver told me you'd grown up, but I didn't know for sure. . . . I don't like these woods." Nick fumbled among the inner pockets of his coat and brought out a letter wrapped in oiled parchment.

"Your father sent it," he announced. "You better read it. He was mighty angry, was Sir Mathew. Blast me, if I ever saw a man so mad. He's at Jamestown with Sir William's horsemen."

"They are marching here?"

Nick Jump scratched his chin. "They say they are, my lad, but . . ."

"They're not ready?"

"That's it—not ready. Being as the Chickahominy River is in flood and it's so cold, I'd say that the handsome young gentlemen are not exactly willing either. It's been wetter and colder than Ayrshire."

Lance smiled. "Do they speak of coming upriver by boat?"

"Lord, no, sir. They're no craft to carry their mounts. They'll have to ride. They'd be lost without their ponies." Jump's head bobbed up. "Hadn't you better read that letter, sir?"

Lance tore open the message. He read:

Dear Son,

I take my quill in hand to advise that Alan Walker, master of Gull Cove, has rejected the petition I advanced in yr behalf for the hand of his daughter, Mistress Easter. A pox on the purse-proud blackguard.

His Excell'cy informs us that we soon will march against the savages, so I may join you at the freshes of the river as soon as the weather breaks.

There is no news from Barbadoes.

The dun cow calved three days ago.

Yr obt servant,

Mathew Clayborne, Knt.

Lance reread the letter. Nick Jump, his eyes on the young man's face, rose to go. Lance did not notice. The old sailor reached out, patted his shoulder and left the room.

For many minutes Lance sat motionless before the hickory fire, the letter in his hand. At last he banged his fist on the bench. Why had he launched this comedy of errors? Why had he not ended the masquerade before it reached a pass like this? Why had he not written letters? A grown man he was, yet he behaved like a child.

Even while his self-esteem smarted around the region of his heart Lance realized that he could not blame the girl. Her imagination had been fettered and her dreams fixed in a groove so far removed from her normal daily life that she could not have seen through the deception.

He had deceived himself as well as Easter Walker. He was in fact two men, each as different from the other as east from west—as England from Virginia. Lance Clayborne, in baldric and brocaded vest, was a roystering English popinjay, the ex-page out of Whitehall. Usack—the leather-clad, bearded night owl—was a Virginian out of a mysterious new land.

She loved the Virginian.

While Lance sat brooding helplessly Nathaniel Bacon came into the room and walked up to the hearth, beating his hands together and stamping the mud from his boots.

Lance rose, then sat down again.

"How, now?" Bacon inquired. "Bad news?"

The young man did not reply but held out the letter.

Bacon read it slowly, frowned and put a hand on Lance's shoulder. At his touch the boy began to laugh. He rocked slowly upon the bench, laughing as harshly as a pirate at a feast.

Bacon shook him firmly. "What does this mean?" he asked, handing back the letter.

Lance flung the paper in the fire.

"Do you wish to go home?" Bacon asked.

"No."

"Then . . ."

Lance held up his clenched fists. "I want to march with you tomorrow," he declared. "I want to go to the end of the earth and then jump off." He laughed wildly. "Behold, sir, the most consummate fool who ever bungled his affairs beyond hope of any foreseeable solution!"

Bacon sat down and asked questions. Then he also began to chuckle.

VII

Battle on the Roanoke

THE force in Bacon's camp now was a formidable, trained band. The strong men had been drilled like Ironsides. The weaklings had been left behind at Jordan's Point. Bacon, on the advice of Ingram, used both Indian and English tactics. The men could stand and deliver fire like Swiss guardsmen, but on occasion they could scatter and skirmish from tree to tree like barbarian warriors. A skillful hunter was assigned to each squad, and for each squad a cook was trained. Helmets and armor, possessed by some of the new arrivals in the colony, were left behind; but the men were supplied with knives and hatchets, and each had a serviceable piece with extra flints and twenty rounds of powder and ball.

At dawn the column moved out, heading southwestward toward the country that had been abandoned by the Appomattox tribes.

The buds were thickening on the trees. Overhead a tremendous flock of geese winged northward noisily—another sign of spring. Ten miles out Ned Peo on a shaggy horse met the column and reported that his men had found the Susquehannocks turning southward ten leagues away. He proposed that Bacon move to intercept them. "I believe that they are planning to cross the Roanoke River at the Occaneechee Island ford," he declared.

Lance rode ahead with Peo to rejoin the advance party. That night they camped with twenty scouts in an abandoned Indian town.

Peo was in high good humor. He vowed that never before had such an army marched into the Indian country. "That Bacon, that Bacon!" the frontiersman exclaimed. "Where did he learn his soldiering?"

Lance smiled and said, "Perhaps it's well he knows but little formal soldiering. Like most of us he learned his lessons up in Maryland last fall."

"We'll escape another Bloody Run this time," said Peo. "That was a disgraceful fight. We had Indian allies then. Totopotomoy of the Pamunkeys had a hundred warriors with us. The western Indians cut them up and killed the werowance before we could get up to save them."

"The savages will never break this force," Lance said. "We would never fire all of our muskets in one volley."

"There are too many horses," Peo said. "We'll never find the grass to feed them."

Lance smiled. "We brought the horses to feed us," he explained. "When they wear out we eat them, for as you know there is not game enough for a column of this size."

"Yes, the Indians have swept the country clean for fifty miles."

Lance pulled his cloak around him and drew closer to the fire. The little camp was in a ravine, the fire was shielded by the overhanging banks. Peo rose and went out to inspect his picket line. Lance put more dry wood on the fire, loosened the laces of his moccasins and relaxed. Perhaps a short campaign against the Indians, then Berkeley's wrath.

The men in Bacon's force joked at the prospect, but it was no joke. The Governor had iron in his nature. He hated the new spirit that was rising in the border counties. Moreover, he had allies on the border—the fur traders, the beaver merchants. Doubtless Tam Mac-Farlane kept the old man well informed of Bacon's every movement. Bacon was one leader in rebellion on whom the Governor could put his finger. Bacon was the head of one snake that Berkeley could scotch in his campaign against sedition. The colony would see an eventful spring.

Before daylight the scouts were up. Within an hour Bacon's column had passed the new advance post. The forests became thinner as they reached higher ground, and they made rapid progress now upon an ancient Indian trail and passed along a great ridge south of the Appomattox River watershed. Peo brought friendly Indians into the camp—a dozen frightened half-starved Saponi. The Indians said that a Susquehannock party had scouted their village twenty days before. Many tribes were fleeing toward the mountains.

The next day Bacon hurried southward. His hunters, forming a screen for five miles on either side, found no game. Beyond the deserted Indian settlements along the Nottoway River they intercepted an Occaneechee wampum bearer returning from the north. Bacon handed him rich gifts—a silver chain, a pot of genuine vermilion, white beads, a knife—and let him return with messages of friendship to Rossechy, the Occaneechee chief. This Indian told them that the

Susquehannocks were sending white belts to his fellow tribesmen and asking for hunting rights within the Roanoke Valley.

Bacon, anxious to cross the next river, pressed on to the Meherrin before it could be swelled by rain. Their weather luck held out. The column forded the second river without accident. The horses were failing and provisions now were running low, but Bacon did not slow the march. Scouts reported seeing smoke to southward. That afternoon they halted at an Occaneechee village while Lance Clayborne parleyed with the headman. Yes, a Susquehannock party of full twenty men had stopped there just a week before, had asked for peace, had traded flint arrow tips for maize and moved westward. Rossechy, the war chief of the Occaneechees, awaited them at his fortified village on the Roanoke island. The white men would be welcome as allies of the Occaneechees. The Susquehannocks were mighty men and dangerous. Even their women were larger than ordinary warriors. The Occaneechees did not trust them.

Bacon moved on five more miles before he camped. He posted double guards and called in his officers. His captains now were leaner by ten pounds a man.

"Tomorrow," Bacon said, "we shall reach the main village of the Occaneechees. I want the men to be on their guard, yet treat these savages as friends. I believe they are inclined to help us against the Susquehannocks."

Joseph Ingram spoke: "Let's clean out the Occaneechees, sir. I hear they have a thousand beaverskins."

There was laughter.

"Aye!" said John Pygott. "Let's make the border safe. We'll send the skins to Governor Berkeley."

Bacon frowned. "What if the beaver already belongs to Berkeley?"

Pygott shrugged. The captains laughed again.

Bacon turned to Lance. "You believe this beaver story?"

Lance nodded. "Yes, sir," he said. "There is beaver fur there, and we will be fortunate if we reach the island before the Governor's messenger. Our scouts must try to intercept every southbound traveler to prevent the traders from turning these savages against us."

Ingram frowned. "You think the Governor would do such a thing?"

"I did not say that," Lance replied. "The Governor might not do it, but the Governor's traders might. I'd trust a pirate sooner than those hairy wolves."

Bacon said, "It will be peace, I believe. If not, we can deal with them. Remember, men, our main objective is the Susquehannock force. We must keep peace with other Indians until we settle with our present enemies. See that your men are comfortable. Be ready to move again at dawn. Dismissed!"

The column reached the Roanoke without adventure. The forest was alive with Occaneechee scouts but they kept far ahead of Bacon's outpost line. But at the riverbank two gay-plumaged barbarians awaited them. With great ceremony Lance escorted them to headquarters where, after a smoke and an exchange of wampum belts, the Indians conveyed the greetings of Rossechy, their chieftain. His village, they said, was on the island three hundred paces away. Would the war chief of the English be good enough to visit him?

Bacon courteously declined. No, but there were gifts for his great king, Rossechy. The white men had come to help his king fight the invading Susquehannocks who even now were on their way with gun and hatchet. The whites would guard the northern riverbank, the Occaneechees could protect the southern line.

Rossechy's ambassadors nodded gravely. They would convey the message. The Susquehannocks had not struck their nation. They had spoken words of peace, but Rossechy well knew that they were foxes who spoke with treachery in their hearts.

◆§ 2

BACON fortified his camp and sent Peo and his scouts with the strongest horses to locate the Susquehannock bands. The men were warned against commerce with the Occaneechee girls who, riding in canoes, hailed them from the stream. The Occaneechee chieftain sent two bushels of wild rice to Bacon, a brace of geese and a buck. While the war chief's messengers were in camp Bacon sent Ingram, Lance Clayborne and two soldiers to the island, ostensibly to trade but actually to examine the defenses there. He also sent patrols far down the river to intercept any messengers that might come in from Jamestown. That night the Occaneechee chieftain told Bacon that the main band of the Susquehannocks was approaching and asked to borrow axes to strengthen the barriers on the island. Bacon lent him axmen and thereby obtained more information about the Occaneechee fort.

Bacon had no illusions about the friendship of this trading tribe. He prepared for battle, anticipating action front and rear, for he knew very well that if the Susquehannocks pressed his forces vigorously, the Occaneechees would join in the attack on the white men.

The settlers of the southern counties knew much about Rossechy. He had grown stronger every year through trade and wily politics. It was told that Spanish Jesuits had lived for years within the island stronghold. They had advised him wisely regarding relations with the Cherokees and Catawbas of Carolina and the Monacans and the mountain tribes in the wilderness to westward. For years Rossechy had been a friend of Berkeley's agent, Tam MacFarlane.

Reports from upriver soon confirmed the news that the Susquehannocks were approaching. Bacon strengthened his patrols and reconnoitered the river crossings. Two days later the Indians advanced eastward toward Occaneechee Island. Bacon decided not to molest them on the river path. He would let them reach the main ford of the Roanoke River. There was open space there. Musketry would be effective.

All day the scouts fell back before the Susquehannock war party. Peo reported that the Indian enemies were lean and ill-fed. Their long march from the Potomac had exhausted their provisions. Game was scarce.

Bacon waited patiently, his men in compact ranks upon the wooded heights north of the island ford.

Rossechy sent a messenger, a half-breed trapper, who announced that the Occaneechees would permit the Susquehannocks to start across the ford before they fell upon them. Bacon nodded in agreement, smiling at the shifty-eyed ambassador with a disarming show of confidence. He did not believe the Occaneechees would attack the northern Indians. If the English moved, Rossechy might join them against the Susquehannocks. If they did not . . .

Lance Clayborne took Bacon on a short scout at dawn the following day. The river trail four hundred yards away was filled with the tall

Pennsylvania tribesmen. As though confident that they could not be successfully assailed the barbarians moved slowly with arrogant disregard for danger. They chanted as they marched into the meadow at the ford.

Lance counted full two hundred warriors and women.

"Is that the band that has terrorized the border?" Bacon asked in wonder.

"Yes," Lance said. "A few Indians can do a world of damage. Look."

Through the tall trees they saw a group of marching children herded by the older squaws. Like their elders, the little ones were thin and famished.

Over on the island, scarcely forty yards from the gathering band of Susquehannocks, the Occaneechees had assembled a little fleet of log canoes.

"The children will be taken over first," Lance predicted. "See! Rossechy, the scoundrel, has made a pact with them as we suspected."

Not an arrow flew across the water, not a voice was lifted. The Occaneechee canoes leaped across the gap of shallow water. Children and women were loaded into the narrow dugouts.

"It is time we advanced," said Bacon, signaling to his captains.

Five minutes later Bacon's line came out from the forest's edge and moved in open order toward the landing. Firmly held in check by their company commanders, the men walked steadily through the brown marsh grass, their muskets ready, their hatchets loosened in their belts.

The swarm of tribesmen at the ford began to flutter like a flock of geese. There were war cries. Savages separated from the huddle on the riverbank and advanced boldly toward the line of militiamen.

More of Bacon's men emerged from the forest. The grim borderers came on in a half ring to shut off chance of escape landward. The Indians wavered. And then the Virginian muskets roared.

A storm of bullets struck the huddle at the riverbank. Lance saw Bloom, the Susquehannock war chief, standing waist deep near the bank, trying to rally and organize a rear guard. The tall savage waved a feather-bedecked war club and shouted his falsetto battle cry repeatedly. None heeded him. Panic had attended the volley of the militiamen. A squad of Henrico men, splashing through the marsh, fired one by one at Bloom. Bullets lashed the water all around him. Bacon's line pushed steadily toward the riverbank.

A hairy borderer pulled his hatchet from his belt and plunged into the water to the left of the line.

Bloom, his eyes on his confused tribesmen, his shrill voice still chanting, paid no attention to the approaching enemy. The big warrior seemed benumbed by the catastrophe that had struck his column. The leather-clad militiaman stopped at a distance of fifteen feet and flung his hatchet. The giant chief went down as though swept into the water by a fierce wind. His body, caught in the current, rolled over and over like a log.

There now were many other rolling bodies.

The disciplined fire of Bacon's soldiers drowned out the screams of the panic-stricken Indians and the death songs of the bolder warriors. The Indians fled—some swimming, others floundering through the rapids. By ones and twos most of them died. Here was revenge for the Potomac fiasco; here was payment in full for a hundred deserted plantations; here was release at last from the bronzed marauders who for months had brought terror to the colony.

The Susquehannock rear guard went down in five minutes. The river seemed full of struggling savages.

Bacon shouted a command to reload.

Company commanders beat back the militiamen who sought to wade after the fugitives. Ahead of the fleeing mass the canoes had reached the island.

Lance heard one of his men cry out in horror. Over there the warriors of Rossechy had gone to work at last. They struck down the Susquehannock children and the squaws.

Around the canoes the water reddened. . . .

◆§ 3

THE VIRGINIANS were gay that night despite the slimness of their rations. Big fires were lighted and songs were sung. There was no wine, but the men had drunk of victory. Here was one campaign that had succeeded.

Bacon made a short speech, praising them for the discipline they had shown, but cautioned them to remain in camp. "There are other savages," he warned.

Lance Clayborne had a feeling of emptiness now that the long expected fight was over. It had been so simple, so brief. The mighty Susquehannocks, for all their vaunted reputation, were but half-starved sheep there in the shallows. When surprised they had thought only of escape. The affair had been a slaughter, an annihilation.

He rose and walked to the edge of the woods and looked over toward Occaneechee Island. Fires were piled high there also. The rattles were clattering and wierd howls echoed from the granite bluffs beyond the river. There were prisoners over there. Susquehannock captives were being roasted at the stake.

Joseph Ingram joined Lance. "We ought to clean out the Occaneechee beggars!" he said.

"Our allies?" Lance remarked sarcastically.

"You'll see what wonderful allies they are tomorrow," Ingram said. "MacFarlane is over there."

"What?"

"He got through by the upper ford this afternoon," Ingram said. "The fighting drew our people downriver, and he got across." Ingram spat. "The Governor has a thousand beaverskins on that island. No wonder Tam came down in person."

"To hell with the Governor's beaverskins!" Lance said. "Aren't we going home? There's only one more day's provisions in the camp. But won't the Occaneechees sell us grain?"

"No," Ingram replied. "They are friends of our brave Governor." He spat.

Lance had a gnawing pain below his heart. One day's food left and a hundred miles of marching to the James. The men were almost as lean as the Susquehanocks. The country had been cleaned of game. The horses? There were only five horses left.

The two men joined Bacon at the big fire. Like Ingram, he was serious. "These men need at least three days of rest," he said. "Unless we can get provisions from the Indian town——"

"We'll take the filthy place," Ingram said.

Bacon shrugged. "The river is too high. They have a fort over there that is stronger than that barricade on the Potomac. Besides, the Occaneechees are Governor Berkeley's friends. It would not do to attack them."

"Nor to starve," Ingram said.

Bacon looked up, his handsome face intent.

"Besides," continued Ingram, "why shouldn't we knock down this robber's roost now that we're here? We'll have to do it sooner or later. These people deal with our enemies. They are our enemies. Rossechy proved it this afternoon. Had the Susquehannocks caught *us* by surprise, the Occaneechee warriors would have joined them, and *we'd* be roasting at the stakes over yonder on the island. Do you think the Susquehannocks would have taken this route if Rossechy hadn't given them an invitation?"

"But aren't the Occaneechees tributary Indians?"

"No!" said Ingram hotly. "They pay no tribute to the Governor. They draw tribute from every tribe for a hundred miles. They are guardians of the river crossing—tollgate keepers, these Occaneechees. They are merchants. They sell the Governor's agents beaverskins for . . ." Ingram stopped.

"For what?" Bacon asked.

"For muskets. Rossechy then farms out the muskets in exchange for more beaver pelts. An Indian with a musket can bring in five times the normal weight of skins. I've seen it happen. It means good business for MacFarlane and other agents of the Governor and wondrous profits for His Excellency."

"It is against the law to trade muskets to the savages," Bacon remarked.

"Yes," said Ingram. "It is against the law to sell them. But Berkeley *lends* them to the chief of the Occaneechees and the headman *lends* them to his hunters."

"And never takes them back?"

Ingram laughed. "Let him try to get them back!"

"I've heard such tales but never gave them credence," Bacon said.

"You'll hear worse tales," Ingram added. "Once Berkeley stood firmly behind the farmers of the colony. Once he was adventurous, a bold, brave spirit. Now he has grown old, short-tempered, greedy and intolerant. He is a traders' man, who worries about his wealth. His fears betrayed us on the Potomac. Giants, indeed! Had Allerton really desired to take that pile of sticks, we could have overrun it any day. Giants! I kick myself to think that once we feared those Susquehannock mongrels!"

Next morning, five miles to westward, Lance Clayborne and a patrol of his Henrico men waited, hidden in a dry watercourse near the river trail. For four hours they remained so still that not even the birds revealed their presence.

At last a canoe touched shore sixty yards away and two men walked up onto the path. One was an Indian with the squirrel-tail headdress of a Pamunkey. The other, a red-bearded brute of a man with a gray cloak, was Tam MacFarlane, the factor. He looked around him cautiously as he hitched his walking pack to a more comfortable position upon his shoulders. He picked up his short-barreled fusil and then, with deliberate balanced steps like a great cat, approached.

Lance was tempted to shoot him down, but this was not the mission to which Bacon had assigned him. The Governor would be angry enough without having his western agent killed. Accordingly Lance stepped onto the trail from the shadow of a cedar and held up his hand. Tam MacFarlane stopped as though a bullet had struck him. He moved to raise his gun, then froze. He had sensed the presence of Lance's patrol.

The Indian turned to flee. Lance checked him with a harsh command. Lance then advanced to stand, weaponless, his hand raised in the sign of peace.

"Why, it's the Clayborne lad!" the Scot exclaimed.

"Yes, Tam," Lance replied. "This is a surprise. What brings you here?"

The factor leaned his stubby fusil against a tree and came forward, hand outstretched.

Lance stopped him with a gesture. "No, Tam," he said. "Stay where you are. There. Halt! And bring your barbarian to heel. He must drop his musket."

The Indian complied. Tam stood with his large hands dangling.

"Now, Tam, we'll have a council," Lance said. "You have not told me what you are doing here in the Occaneechee country."

Tam's eyes narrowed. "And you, my boy? Why should you stop me on the trail?"

Lance shrugged. "My orders are to stop all skulkers who may imperil the safety of our camp."

"A skulker, I?"

"You have avoided us, MacFarlane. You visited the Occaneechee fort but failed to smoke a pipe in Bacon's camp."

MacFarlane bit his mustaches. He expected death. He considered the possibility of sudden flight, but by now the heads of the Henrico militiamen were plainly visible as were the muzzles of eight muskets. He tried to smile. "Listen, lad——"

"You will answer questions first, MacFarlane. What is your business here?"

"I am a trader. . . ."

"Where is your pack train? Why do you travel like a forest runner?"

"Now, Master Clayborne, surely you know that men in my business do not always carry freight. I came to see the Catawba werowance, Rootan——"

"Yet for two days you have visited on the island with Rossechy, the Occaneechee."

The factor's eyes shifted as though he wished to make a flat denial. He raised his hands. In spite of the cool morning drops of perspiration began to form on his forehead. "I paused with the Occaneechees to avoid the Susquehannocks, Master Clayborne. I took refuge there."

"And to avoid General Bacon's column, I suppose?"

"*General* Bacon?" MacFarlane's jaw dropped.

"Aye! General Bacon."

"Is it by his authority you question me?" the trader asked.

"It is by the authority of white men campaigning in a hostile wilderness that I question you," Lance replied. "Why and under whose authority have you ordered the Occaneechees to refuse us grain and close their town to us?"

MacFarlane spread his hands. "I?"

"Yes."

The trader's eyes dropped to Lance's moccasins. He hesitated.

"Shall I order my men to fire, MacFarlane? We can shoot you, and if the Governor protests, we can blame it on the fugitive Susquehannocks. Indeed, we can do more than that. We know some Indian tricks, MacFarlane."

The Scot's face paled.

"The Occaneechees tortured Susquehannock squaws yesterday, MacFarlane. Did you enjoy the sight? The legs of captive Susquehannock warriors were eaten to make the Occaneechees tall. Did you enjoy the feast?"

"Surely, Master Clayborne——"

"Then answer, Tam MacFarlane. Are you a messenger of Sir William Berkeley, the Governor? Did he send you here to set the Occaneechees at our heels?"

MacFarlane did not wish to answer, but Clayborne's expression terrified him. The young man's weather-toughened face seemed as ruthless as an Indian's; his eyes were as hard, as cruel as a panther's. The Scot also realized that Lance knew entirely too much to be deceived by any ordinary falsehood. Accordingly he tried to bluster.

"I am a courier of His Excellency," he said. "As such I am entitled to safe-conduct and assistance from all citizens."

"Your papers, Tam?" Lance asked gently.

"I have an oral commission only, lad. You know that I am Sir William's agent. If he should learn that you have arrested me at musket point . . ."

Lance frowned. "If the people of Virginia should learn that you, a factor under license of the Crown, are raising savages against us——"

"That I deny, Master Clayborne."

"You have forbidden, in the Governor's name, the Occaneechees to provision us. Do you deny that, MacFarlane?"

"That I also deny."

Lance stepped back. "Then, Tam, my men will pin you to that tree for a while and roast your feet."

"No, Master Clayborne. No, No!"

"Answer me fairly then, man."

MacFarlane's eyes rolled beneath his red eyebrows and his big frame trembled. He still expected death, but he dreaded torture more. He knew Lance Clayborne had lived among the Indians. He took a deep breath and almost collapsed with terror.

"Answer the question as you like then, Master Clayborne. Say that I have forbidden, in the Governor's name, the tributary Indians to supply grain for this rebel column of your *General* Bacon."

"Rebel column?"

"The Governor has proclaimed Nathaniel Bacon a traitor to the King."

It now was Lance's turn to be surprised. "How? When?" he demanded.

"The proclamation was written and signed at Jamestown two days before Bacon marched," MacFarlane said.

Lance's hands clenched. He stared furiously into the factor's shifty eyes. "You're lying, Tam."

"No, sir. It is a fact. The Governor told Mistress Bacon, who now is in Jamestown, that he would hang her husband should he escape the Indians."

"You would have me believe such foolishness? You would have me believe the Governor would outlaw three hundred farmers?"

"Only their leader, Master Bacon, has been outlawed. If I am not speaking truth, I hope you'll make blood feud against me and slay me on sight when next we meet."

Lance had accomplished his mission. He had learned more from MacFarlane than he had expected. The action of the Occaneechees in refusing provisions had been explained. The Governor had outlawed this half-starved column that had destroyed the Susquehannocks. Without supplies Bacon's men might die there on the Roanoke. The Governor was mad indeed.

"May I resume my journey, lad?" MacFarlane asked.

"I cannot believe the Governor would permit three hundred border men to starve," Lance said.

MacFarlane, bolder now—much bolder because of the shock he had administered—remarked, "They marched without his order or consent. Officially he knows nothing of this expedition or your *General* Bacon. His Excellency is not responsible for these men. They marched at their own risk and at their own expense. They must save themselves as best they may. The Occaneechees will not attack them. That I can assure you. As for selling them a store of grain, that is a matter that is up to the Indians."

Lance frowned and spoke between his teeth. "What if we take this barbarian village, Tam? Had you thought of that?"

The big Scot smiled. "Take it? Ha! Not even Berkeley himself could take that island fortress, lad. You know that. You were in the Potomac campaign, I believe."

Lance stepped off the path now and with a mocking bow said, "Go on your way, MacFarlane. If you've lied, God help you. As for the Governor's Occaneechees and his beaverskins which, I see, you have been unable to take back with you, I expect they will cost his Indian allies dear. If Rossechy refuses again to sell us food, that refusal will be an act of war."

The news which Lance Clayborne carried back to camp occasioned less surprise than he had anticipated. During his hunt for Mac-Farlane there had been further parleys with the Indians. Rossechy again had put them off with vague promises. And he had hinted that the great white chief at Jamestown had forbidden them to trade with Bacon's men.

Bacon questioned Clayborne about every detail of his talk with MacFarlane. As they finished Bacon smiled triumphantly. "My thanks," he said. "This news is worth a drove of cattle, Lance. The Governor has made issue with the welfare of his people now, an issue that will strengthen us immeasurably if we survive this campaign. He has exposed this column to starvation. He has denounced us as traitors. At last he has made a clear-cut choice—his beaverskins, his Indians—against our lives."

Bacon slapped his gloves against his knee, and then he said, "It is not rebellion to defend one's own home against an enemy. Men do not become traitors in England when they take up arms to beat off raiding pirates or put down Scottish robbers. Neither did we when we pursued the Susquehannocks."

Lance nodded.

Bacon mused on. "In England men have a king and a parliament to protect them from unreasonable deputies. Here we are far—so far—from King and government. If need arises, then, the people must protect themselves. As I recall, Virginians sent one governor home who had betrayed his trust—Governor Harvey. It may be we shall have to send another back."

As though to check the question that had risen in Lance's mind, Bacon continued, "That is not rebellion, my friend. Sir William Berkeley is not Caesar. English law protects us even in this almost endless forest. It guards us not only against the Indians, but against . . . against the Governor."

৩ 4

A DAY passed and there were further parleys with Rossechy without result. Bacon summoned a campfire council of his whole command.

Pointing toward the Occaneechee stronghold, he said, "Over there are hogs and pork, cattle and roast beef, corn and ashcake. Those people will sell us none of it, because they are allies of enemies who callously would let us starve to death in the wilderness. The river is falling and is fordable. There are signs of more fair weather. Tomorrow we attack!"

There was a wild cheer from the thick circle of hairy, hungry men.

Bacon continued: "They told us—our enemies told us—that we could not punish the Susquehannocks. We annihilated them. If there are any among you who believe we cannot wade that little river and knock down that fort, he is badly mistaken. We shall do it tomorrow morning."

There was another wild yell from the circle.

Bacon, Ingram, Lance Clayborne and other rangers, who now knew every square inch of the fortified island, later conferred with the commanders of the ten companies.

It was determined exactly where the attackers would ford the stream, and the bounds were marked with stakes so no man would be endangered by deep water. The boat gun, mounted firmly on a large oak log, was emplaced on a rise to the left of the marked line of departure, well back from the riverbank but within easy range of Rossechy's lodges.

Lance Clayborne then explained in detail the conformation of the island, warning the commanders that the wooded swamp on the western half was impassable, and explaining the bounds of the almost circular log-and-brush fort.

"It looks stronger than the Potomac fort," Lance said. "But its position is not strong because the river is low and because the timber and brush of the barricade have become dry." Lance looked over at Ingram.

"We have the fireballs," Ingram reported.

The fireballs were the simplest of weapons—stones wrapped in a thick layer of the dry, fibrous bark of cedar trees. They would be soaked in lantern oil next morning. Ingram issued to each company commander a quantity of these missiles.

Bacon concluded the conference. "Keep your men together, and keep your powder dry," he said. "Take your time. The Occaneechees have many trade guns, but they cannot shoot straight. Instruct your men to shoot at the bowmen. They are the experienced warriors. The smoke from the burning barricade will blow in our direction until we work around to westward. It will give concealment so we can fire at close range as we reach the island." He paused. "Have you any questions? All right. Good luck!"

The hunting parties that day had brought in only four turkeys, scarcely enough meat to make a thin broth for the command. On the morning of the attack Bacon's band was savagely hungry. As the sun rose out of the forest, the breeze from the Occaneechee town brought them the rich smell of roasting pork.

When the lines had formed Ned Peo waded out to the long shadow of the Indian fort. Pausing in midstream, he hailed Rossechy and asked for a parley. The Indian war chief did not come to the parapet, but a man whose feathers indicated a high rank appeared.

In sonorous Algonquin language Peo delivered Bacon's ultimatum: Six canoeloads of maize, four beeves, and twenty hogs would be delivered immediately or Bacon's force would overcome the village. "We will pay the market price for these provisions," Peo said. "Trade with us, and we will withdraw this day to the north. Refuse, and we must advance."

The Indian at the parapet began to laugh scornfully. A cluster of young warriors joined him, waving weapons and making rude noises.

Peo abruptly turned his back on them. At the riverbank he turned, glanced at the sun and looked significantly at the shadow of the palisade on the river.

Lance Clayborne, ten Henrico scouts and a dozen Stafford borderers, all of whom could load rapidly, were stationed on the riverbank. Their orders were to fire in support of the three lines of troopers that would wade to the island; then Lance and his men were to move to the right flank of the last company.

Suddenly there was a musket shot from the Indians. Peo shouted, lifted his fusil, fired. . . . Thus began the battle that for bloodiness excelled every Indian fight that ever had been waged since Cortez the Spaniard fought Montezuma far to southward.

Bacon's impatient, half-starved troops moved forward, splashing across the shallows, shouting. Five men fell, then two more. The front-rank musketeers ducked their heads against bullets and arrows. Still the lines advanced. From the bluff beyond the island and on the other shore the little culverin roared.

The first line composed of Ingram's New Kent militia, supported by the fire of the Charles City men, closed in upon the Indian fort. Each soldier carried his oil-soaked ball of cedar bark. These they lighted with powder flashes from their musket locks, and approaching closely, they flung the fireballs into the mass of brushwood at the barricade. The Surry company waded across the shallows while the first ranks, standing at intervals to lessen peril from the arrows, carefully reloaded. Smoke from the burning palisade began to rise and blow across the water. It shielded the attackers now.

Ingram's men reached the firm ground of the island beach and with a shout rushed to a patch of alder bushes ten yards from the palisade. Crouching under the shielding billows of smoke, the attackers began to shoot deliberately into the Indian town. Its defenders were now in wild, screaming confusion. Some of the savages fired straight upward in their excitement.

More of Bacon's companies completed the crossing of the river, lengthening the lines. The Surry men began to shoot by volleys, and Bacon's tense face loosened into a proud smile at this evidence of discipline. He stood alone on the beach, his sword in his hand, his boots full of water.

Over on the other bank the little boat cannon was firing steadily. This gun and its small store of shot and powder had caused much labor on the march—had worn out six horses one by one. Now it was paying its obligation in full.

The cannoneers—veterans of Cromwell's army—had the exact range of the canoe landing on the island. Dugouts filled with fleeing savages were being knocked around like jackstraws.

Lance Clayborne led his borderers to the extreme right of the attacking line. At a point that had been abandoned by the Indians they began to pull away the logs and brush of the fort so as to gain entrance to the town.

They were the first men through the barrier and they got over barely ahead of the fire that was at its height. The whole east end of the island seemed to be aflame, and the blaze was spreading, encompassing the whole fort.

Lance made his men lie down behind a long bark lodge until he could view the situation. Rossechy's herd of cattle, bellowing in panic, stampeded to the western side of the village; but most of the Indians were fleeing toward the eastern gate and the canoe landing.

Lance led his men forward almost as far as the council ring of the village before they found targets. By this time there were breaches in burned portions of the barrier. The trousers of the men were wet from fording the river, so they could run through the blazing brush to reach their enemies.

Rossechy with a dozen veteran warriors tried to cover the flight of men, women, and children to the east gate. His men were all bowmen, and for several minutes their arrows whistled among the advancing troops. But assailed in front by a New Kent company, which had fusils loaded and ready, and in flank by Lance and his wild foresters the last organized Indian force melted away in the smoke.

The Occaneechee chieftain, wounded twice by bullets, was dispatched by a bearded giant from the Stafford company who used first the stock of his fusil and then his hatchet.

Angry, half-starved, the attackers went completely mad. Drawing their belt weapons, they slew until their arms were tired.

Nathaniel Bacon, lately a gentle student at Cambridge and a man of peace, was appalled at the wild slaughter. For a time, sword in hand, he tried to check the fury of the battle-drunk militia. It was a hopeless task. Some of those men had served with Cromwell and had sacked castles in their time. They followed the old, unwritten law of arms—no prisoners when a fort resists. Moreover, all these farmers hated Indians. They hated them because of friends who had died, because of homesteads burned and cattle stolen; hated them for long nights spent in fear—hated as they hated wolves.

Lance Clayborne had never viewed such a scene. Children and

women died with the warriors, scotched like litters of snakes. Not an Indian was spared.

Bacon directed Lance and his Henricans to salvage provisions from the village. They found the livestock and a rich store of grain, but they failed to save the Governor's beaverskins. They were burned.

Bacon's men marched homeward with the stride of veterans. In the southern forests a grim brotherhood had grown out of hardship and discipline. No longer were these men slouching farmers. They were soldiers. Proud were they now of their tested captains and their leader. They had conquered.

❦ 5

REPORTS of the foray of Nathaniel Bacon against the arrogant Susquehannocks and Occaneechees caused wild rejoicing throughout the colony. No Virginia expedition ever before had slain so many savages. Loot from the Indian fortress was passed from hand to hand in awe. There were bonfires and much speechmaking at the county courthouses.

Governor Berkeley's proclamation which declared Bacon a rebel was torn down and trampled as soon as it was posted at the Council House in Jamestown. The High Sheriff nailed another copy on the pillory. Again the Governor's seal was profaned.

Complete victories over large parties of warlike Indians never had been common in the colony. The slaughter of three hundred savages was viewed as a military miracle. Who was this Jason, this Hercules of the western forest, this Bacon? In years past William Berkeley had led expeditions to the west, but he never had won a victory such as this. Who was the man who had performed with such brilliance a task which the Governor was supposed to do?

Bacon, the Cambridge barrister, had become the guardian of the public safety. And in gratitude the Governor was trying to outlaw the man! Three cheers for Bacon! Down with the dotard Berkeley!

Berkeley called his Council into session. The sober gentlemen of that body brought bad news. Rejoicing over Bacon's triumph was increasing everywhere. Wild young men were marching to join him for a new campaign to root out the mountain tribes. The Governor was cursed for his inaction. Some demanded his recall.

Councillor Daniel Parke was one of the few who dared talk plainly to the wrathful Governor. Parke adjusted his wig and loosened the collar of his jerkin as he begged leave to speak. Berkeley's bloodshot eyes half closed as the lean planter rose from the group beside the big fireplace.

"Your Excellency, we have a choice of two decisions," Parke declared. "An officer may be sent to arrest Bacon, take command of the western forces and press the Indian war, or Bacon may be commissioned and his expedition given the authority of the Crown."

"We want no war," Berkeley said sullenly.

"War has come."

"Forced on us by a lawless band of western cutthroats!"

"Granted, sir, but the people as a whole endorse the move, sir. They say a new Assembly would provide funds for the expedition."

"A new Assembly?"

Parke's lean face paled somewhat. "Yes, sir. Whatever course you take there must be a new Assembly. The sooner the election is proclaimed, the better for public peace and order."

Berkeley's fists clenched. He controlled himself with difficulty.

Colonel Philip Ludwell shrugged his shoulders. "I see no harm in that, sir," said Ludwell. "Give them an election. Let a new Assembly come here and howl awhile. Let the mob then count the cost of a war and help us with the balance sheets."

There was a murmur of approval.

Councillor Bacon now found the courage to speak. "My young cousin is no rebel, sir. Before the month is out he'll be here in Jamestown asking forgiveness for his hasty actions. I guarantee you his integrity and his adherence to the laws. The Indians slew his overseer, sir, and so he heeded unwise counsel. I pray you . . ."

Berkeley paid no attention to the sputtering old man. He turned to Ludwell and said, "You think that an election would appease the border farmers?"

"Yes, sir," Ludwell answered.

"Good day, gentlemen." The Governor departed, followed by Secretary Spencer.

Sir William Berkeley was growing old, but his spirit still burned brightly. In accepting the advice of his Council regarding the need for an Assembly he had swallowed a bitter pill but with good grace. That was sound political policy. But there was another pill that he did not intend to take—young Bacon's challenge to his authority. This was a personal matter which he did not mention to the Council.

As no other man in the colony, Sir William Berkeley realized how far removed Virginia was from England. He also knew full well the difference between the untamed settlers of the western world and the disciplined burghers across the ocean. Not only were the Virginians wild, but they were naturally rebellious. Among them were the dregs from the gutters of London, Plymouth, Liverpool, Glasgow, Dublin. They were desperate, masterless wanderers sent to the plantations because of political crimes—and worse. They needed a strong hand.

The Council was timid, but not he. It was dangerous to compromise with rebels. It was a sign of weakness; it lent fuel to sedition.

Young Bacon was a turbulent newcomer. Only that could be said in mitigation of his grave offense. As it was the sooner he was hanged, or otherwise disposed of, the better. A man who could arouse the scum along the border could be a source of endless difficulty.

Sir William, seated alone in his study at the Council House, rang for Kemp, his personal secretary. Then for several minutes, as the plump and worried scrivener stood awaiting his instructions, the Governor pondered. It was time to act, to summon every resource to meet this dangerous situation. If Bacon died, rebellion would die. If Bacon won his independent war against the Indians, then hell itself might be unloosed.

"Kemp!" the Governor called.

"Yes, sir," said Kemp.

"Oh, I say! I did not see you. Kemp, I must have ships."

"Yes, Your Excellency."

"I must have ships. With ships on the rivers I need not fear a thousand forest rebels."

"Yes, Your Excellency."

"I want you to notify Eveling, Knox and Smart that martial law prevails, that they will not sail without a signed permit from me—no merchant sailor shall."

Kemp made notes on his slate.

"I want Ned Bell to take his sloop and go south to Albemarle, find Forke and bring Forke's ships here. You understand?"

"Oh, yes, Your Excellency."

"They must be here in six weeks with powder, ball, meat, and fully manned."

"I have it written, sir."

"And no ships freshly arrived shall leave until I give them clearance."

"Yes, Your Excellency."

"Go, and send for Arthur Ward."

Ward, the Governor's steward, was an ancient, toothless mummy of a man who had been Berkeley's shadow since 1656. Like Kemp, he had been a bonded servant in his youth. He now was prosperous. His fortune was linked with his ex-master's, his mind enslaved by Berkeley's will; yet he was wise and sly and candid with Sir William.

"You have some news, my friend?" the Governor asked.

The old man nodded, fumbled for a stool, sat down. He perched there like a shriveled bird awhile, half mumbled to himself, then found words and said, "A horseman, sir, from upper Henrico says Bacon's band is encamped on the Appomattox River, seventy miles from here."

"It has not dispersed?"

"Bacon is watching the western tribes, the Monocans, now, sir."

"Who is the messenger? Is he the Clayborne boy?"

"Oh, no, sir. He is Israel Figg, an ironmonger from upriver, who brought the news."

Berkeley struck his fist upon his knee. "Where is the Clayborne boy? He brings clearer, fuller reports."

"I do not know, sir. He has not been seen for several weeks."

Berkeley was silent, thoughtful. He started to speak several times but stopped. At last he looked up and stared into the sharp little eyes of his steward and asked, "Was Clayborne with Bacon's expedition, Ward?"

"I do not know, sir. His father says he is at the Henrico planting, swears he never would associate with a rebel."

"I want that boy, Ward. He knows every river, creek and trail between here and the salt marshes in the farther mountains. I want him. I need him."

"Yes, Your Excellency." The old man cleared his throat. "What, Ward?"

"I was thinking, sir. You have sent for Forke and now you send for the Clayborne lad. . . ."

"Yes, and if Forke harms the boy, I shall hang him. I need them both, Ward, and many another good man. The situation is serious. The colony is rotten with sedition. Bland has tried to get letters to the King behind my back. MacFarlane is a gutless coward. Chicheley is an hysterical ass. Most of Washington's force has deserted him. I need men who know the west. I need Clayborne. He can travel faster than a Seneca."

Ward looked up slyly. "My information, sir, is that the boy, like Bacon, is rebellious. He is not like his father, sir. He runs among Indians. He does not value wealth or social position."

Berkeley beat his fist upon his knee. "I know all that, my friend. Also, Lady Berkeley has informed me that our wild ranger is, like most young men, entangled in a love affair. It is Alan Walker's daughter, Ward. I understand that she can handle him."

Ward whistled wonderingly. "You think of everything, sir," he said.

◄§ 6

AT GULL COVE the green spears of Easter Walker's English daffodils were four inches high. From the woods the fragrance of buds came on a wave of warm wind. Beyond the house the waters of the cove were quiet. The ducks and geese had gone northward. The gulls were out to sea, following the pirate ships that roamed outside the capes.

Easter Walker, seated on the stile in the cedar lane west of the sprawling manor, came out of a daydream for a moment, remembering her Aunt Lucy's advice. It was not proper to rest one's cheek against the knuckles of one's fist. It might make the face misshapen. Faugh!

Again she leaned her cheek on her fist and stared through the hazy cedars toward the west. Perhaps it was not proper either to be there on the stile. She might become flat from sitting there so often.

Once it had not been safe to be so close to the forest because of the Indians. Aunt Lucy could remember when the Indians came in 1644. She was almost as old as the colony itself. She remembered when Opechancanough was killed and when Governor Berkeley was the handsomest cavalier in all the world.

No man ever had loved Aunt Lucy. Women who had been loved showed it in their faces no matter how old they might be. And she, Easter Walker? No one had thought her beautiful until . . . until. . . . She sighed.

Since that day on Archer's Hope wharf the house had been filled with suitors.

John Lee, Arthur Allen, Tom Hansford and Robert Miller, all had visited Gull Cove that winter. With spring there might be others, too. Wealthy girls were not plentiful, and pretty ones were rare.

In a single season she had lost all her tomboyish ways, had ceased to be a child and had become an alluring woman. She now noticed the difference every time she drew a pail of water from the shallow garden well.

As Aunt Lucy said, it was time she married. Had she been a fool, in fact, ever to have come back to Virginia; she who could have had a place in court thanks to her late mother's relatives? With her dowry she might have caught at least a landed baronet.

Aunt Lucy did not know about the westerner, Usack. Nobody knew. People had forgotten her adventure on the wharf. She had told no one about what followed—the visits from the man in leather, the young man with arms like hickory beams and eyes that glowed and a voice that indicated better breeding than even John Lee's.

Lee lived far to northward, and he had a house of brick, her father said. Hansford would be wealthy in a dozen years, perhaps. Clayborne. . . . She was puzzled there. Of all her suitors, why should that rakehell youth have been the first to petition formally for her hand? What could have happened to that brawling favorite of tavern women, that ruffler whom her father called Knight of the Ebon Wig? And where was he? Why had he not presented his prayer in person? Why had he sent his vinegary old father to Gull Cove on his behalf?

She vaguely recalled Lance Clayborne the child, but she remembered little about Lance the young man. He did wear a lovely wig. It was the envy of everyone from the Governor down. She remembered how it had caught the candlelight during the party at Green Spring. She remembered also the long sword he wore that night. No fashionable bauble that. Always, they said, he wore a murderous military-styled rapier.

Easter Walker sighed. It was a pity she had not given Lance Clayborne a more careful inspection. She would have to examine all men more closely now. At a time when she might least expect it they might send petitions to her father.

Married to Lance Clayborne? She shivered. Clayborne, the old knight, had been almost insulting in his proud, confident approach to her father. He seemed to think she would be greatly honored by the alliance. It would be better to remain unwed, perhaps, than marry a youth as grim as Lance.

Why did not the lad present himself in person? He was on an important errand, said Sir Mathew. When would he return? In good time. No one could exactly tell. An errand? Another journey in search of vengeance, perhaps another visit to the bay plantations in search of the mysterious family enemy, Jesús Forke.

She had done nothing to attract Lance Clayborne. The proposal undoubtedly was an idea of the young man's father. The elder Clayborne wished his son to breed a family and settle down, so he had picked a likely maid for him. Had she accepted, doubtless the tough old knight would have to break the news to Lance and issue a command such as: *Go now, son, and marry Alan Walker's daughter.*

Alan Walker's daughter? Who is she?

A pretty pullet at Gull Cove. Go now, like a good boy, and become a married man.

Ha! Easter had listened through the door that afternoon when Sir Mathew came over for a final interview with her father. The old knight was as formal as a second in a duel.

He rode away straight as a bodkin. With his lean, long legs and his well-conditioned soldier's body, he reminded her of someone for a moment that afternoon; and, though he wore a long sword, he did not remind her of Lance Clayborne.

Where was that strange young man, Usack, who even in the flesh seemed like a disturbing dream? There was fighting on the border. Was he there fighting? Indians once more were flowing southward. Messengers had come, crying for assistance, and with them fugitives from the western farms. There was talk of an uprising among the bordermen and of an illegal expedition against the savages.

Nathaniel Bacon, a gentleman and the cousin of the elderly Councillor, had been proclaimed a rebel by the Governor. Governor Berkeley had been cruel to young Bacon's wife. He had told her that her husband would be hanged. This had caused much talk against Sir William among the women of near-by plantations.

Where was Usack? Could he have encountered danger out there among the savages? An Indian could never harm Usack. He was too strong, too wary. He would return.

Beyond the lane the sun was setting. Easter drew her shawl about her shoulders and started to walk toward the house. A fool she was to sit there on the stile so frequently. What if that young man in leather knew her innermost female thoughts and caught her thinking them? He might go away and never call again.

Always she had acted shamelessly toward him. The gilt of custom had dropped from her after that first visit. He seemed to be a part of her that, after wandering for many years, had returned to find a haven in her heart. All other men—even her father—were ordinary men. Usack was more than that.

She stopped beside the well. Why should she go to the house? She did not want to go. There always was a possibility that he might return. So, quickly she retraced her steps and once more sat down on the stile.

Dusk had fallen.

Now she had a strange sensation, a feeling of certainty that he was near. She was almost afraid to look up or to move. The tips of her breasts grew hard and hot.

Aunt Lucy soon would call for her and scold her for staying out in the night air. Let her scold. The twilight deepened. It was very still among the cedars, and there were shadows that looked like . . .

She jumped to her feet with a happy cry and ran toward the deepest of the shadows.

Usack!

For some minutes they did not speak. They flowed together like two streams. There was tumult, a whirling surge of dizzying sensation. His arms were more marvelously comforting than those of which she had so often dreamed. The sharp tang of the woods pierced her senses. Her whole body seemed to melt.

Usack!

Words were useless. It was many minutes before they could converse at all. Then his deep voice thrilled her just as his touch had done. She was a fawn, a little dove, and many other soft and lovely things. He had longed for her throughout long marches and dark nights, through snow and rain and sunshine—every moment.

"Where have you been?" she murmured.

"Beyond the foothills . . . very far this time."

"It's been so long, Usack!"

"Too long, sweet."

"Please, never leave me again, dearest." She could feel his shoulders tighten. She clung to him desperately. "Never leave me, dearest."

"Every moment away from you is wasted," he declared.

"Then——"

He seated her beside him on the stile and held her hands against his cheeks as he explained. "I have been with Bacon, sweetest. There is more work to be done—a little more—and I'll return and we——"

"You have been with Bacon? The rebel, Bacon?"

He laughed gently. "Yes, with young Bacon. He is not a rebel."

"The Governor said——"

"The Governor will change his mind when Bacon comes to Jamestown. He is on his way now to make peace with His Excellency."

"But Sir William told Eliza Bacon he would hang her husband!"

"That was when he was in one of his blind rages. Besides, Bacon will be elected burgess from Henrico. He will have immunity and Berkeley must forgive him."

"Are you . . . a rebel, Usack?"

"I—?" he laughed again—"I a rebel?"

He told her of the campaign to the south, of Bacon's brilliance as a leader of the border farmers, of the ambush which destroyed the Susquehannocks, of the terrible assault on the Occaneechee fort.

"They speak more harshly of Berkeley on the frontier than Berkeley ever spoke of Bacon," he said. "Men become frantic when exposed to danger from the savages. They say many unkind things about the Governor."

"I was afraid you would never come. It has been months and months." She touched him as though to make sure he was really at her side.

"And you—" he said—"have you been safe and well?"

She tossed her head. "Yes, and since you were here I've had many suitors. I even have had an offer of marriage."

This silenced him for several long breaths.

She touched his cheek. "You are angry, Usack?"

He did not reply.

"It was the notorious Clayborne boy, Usack," she said. "And I refused."

She spoke quickly now in an effort to break down his silence. "I could never marry him," she said. "He is a tavern brawler, Usack. He is fierce and dangerous, a fugitive from half the magistrates of the colony. He makes a good appearance; he dresses well, I know. His wigs are envied even by Sir William, but surely you do not think I—— I hardly know him, Usack. I have seen him but once since my return from England. I . . ."

Still the leather-clad young man was quiet. He seemed to have sunk into complete immobility, like a sullen Indian.

She said, "It was presumptuous effrontery for Sir Mathew to present such a petition. I am sure it was all Sir Mathew's idea. He wants the boy to settle down and cease his lawlessness."

Usack finally spoke. "You must remember that I know Lance Clayborne," he said. "I saw him with John Washington during the Potomac fight. I saw him in both Roanoke River fights. He, too, marched with Bacon. He no longer is a boy. . . ."

Easter Walker drew away.

It seemed now as though a barrier of ice had fallen down between them. For the first time she realized that this leather-stockinged figure in the lane was a man, not a romantic figment of dreams.

There was a strange note in his voice that sent chills through her, that utterly destroyed the softness of the night. He was a human being, not a hero of her imagination—a man who moved among other men, a man perhaps as hard and insensitive as Lance Clayborne. A name had destroyed all the magic of their meeting. He released her hands.

"Lance Clayborne has been my comrade," he said. "He has been my friend, my confidant, my evil genius."

She shuddered.

"Aye, a ruffian, and a brawler, and a dandy, too."

"Why do you say such things, Usack! Why do you speak so of . . . of Lance Clayborne?"

For a moment he was silent. She could hear him breathing heavily. From the house Aunt Lucy called. Easter did not answer.

"Because I must speak of him!" he said. "I . . . well . . . must speak of him before I go back to the border. I must speak of him because *I am Lance Clayborne!*"

She remained still there in the twilight, staring at him.

He moved toward her, his body tall and straight as a pine tree, the long fringes of his leather leggings aflutter in the warm wind from the south.

She drew back in terror.

He tried to speak again. Beneath his breath he cursed his clumsy words. Then as she turned his pride rose up and silenced him.

She ran away, up the pathway toward the house.

He did not follow her.

⊷§ 7

LANCE found his father on the green at Clayborne Castle. He was seated in a great oak chair, lean, booted legs asprawl, spurs anchored in the grassy sod.

The rugged old knight rose as Lance dismounted. They embraced gravely, and when Caesar, properly instructed, had led Lance's horse away the boy sat down wearily at his father's feet and began to chew a blade of grass.

"Whence this time, lad?"

"I've been to Rocky Ridge and beyond, sir."

"The western plantation?"

"Peo is still there. He has married Dickon Potts's widow. Only one Negro has run away."

"Peo is clearing the place?"

"Yes. Some work is being done, but the plantings will be small. The border still is in a ferment."

"I thought your friend, that Bacon boy, had put the Indians down."

Lance sighed. "The Indians may be down. That lesson we taught them on the Roanoke will be long remembered. But the men now wish to finish Indian troubles for all time, to drive all of them beyond the mountains. They wish to wipe out even the Pamunkey villages. The farmers in the west have lost a crop anyway, and so they want to end their fighting now."

"Are they rebellious?"

"Rebellious? I hardly know, sir. Restless, yes. If the Governor would go to the border, he would find loyalty enough. But if he leaves those westerners there untended, with rumors dancing among them like peppercorns in a kettle of broth, they'll nurse many ugly grievances, and some will court the hangman. In any event his fur trade has ended for a while."

Sir Mathew's sharp eyes darted toward his son. "We have rumors, too, my lad," he said. "Some who have overheard the recent babblings of our worthy Governor say he is displeased with you. It is whispered that you, like Bacon, are a rebel."

Lance's lips curved ruefully. "You, also, say that, Father?"

"So I am all the more concerned," his father continued, with teasing irony, "that you settle yourself and become a husband soon—a settled citizen with hostages at home for good behavior."

Lance frowned. "I'm anxious to hear first-hand reports about your meeting with Easter Walker's father," he said.

Sir Mathew sank his spurs more deeply into the sod and placed his long fingers together. "I did not see the lady, Lance. I addressed her father. The fat old slug was flattered, of course. He excused himself and went into the house, presumably to discuss the matter with the girl. He came out full of apology and told me as politely as he could that your addresses to his daughter would not be welcome, that she never would wed my son. I asked him if she were pledged to another, and he swore she was not. She was too young to consider marriage, said he."

Lance stared sightlessly into the grass between his boots for a while, then looked up with a wry smile.

"It is my fault, Father. I have been a thrice-compounded fool, but somehow I must have that lovely . . . kitten."

"Why, lad?"

"Have you ever seen her, sir?"

The old knight smiled. "Yes, boy, I saw her not long ago at Jamestown. It will be a fast, uncertain and, perhaps, a merry chase. The maid has, I'd say, a pride as rigid as a barge mast. She has other suitors?"

"Hansford and——"

"Hansford is Drummond's friend. The Governor likes him even less than you. Well, let the devil take the hindmost then."

VIII

A Long-Remembered Spring

ৠ 1

IT WAS A long-remembered spring. A great comet appeared one night like a blazing omen of woe. There was a flight of wood pigeons such as never had been known in all America before. The rustling swarm of birds blotted out the sun by day, and by night they broke great limbs from the trees as they roosted.

Restlessness afflicted the whole colony. Seventy-one border farms had been abandoned to the wandering savages. War parties from the west stabbed and burned and fled back into the forest. Settlements not exposed to Indians were overrun with wolves and robbers. On the coast piracy increased. Idle men gathered at the taverns and drank too much Henrico wine. Tax collectors were beaten.

For all that, the southwest wind grew warmer day by day, the trees took on their bright mantles as usual, and in the sky—mindless of the comet—the clouds piled up like snowy mountains.

News came to Jamestown often from the border, and most of it was fearful. Sir Henry Chicheley with the Governor's best trained band traveled four marches westward to get news of Bacon's force which, rumor said, might soon descend upon the east like an army of lawless Highland Scots. Chicheley's expedition, its march blocked by flooded streams, returned—horses half-starved, men grumbling and officers disgusted at their wild-goose chase. Bacon was not at Jordan's Point. No one knew where his men were camped.

Governor Berkeley posted a proclamation. All men were warned that if they took up arms without authority of the King's commission they would be hanged.

As fast as the papers were displayed malcontents tore them from the pillory posts and tavern doors. Other signs appeared. The phrase "Long Live Bacon!" was chalked upon the walls of the Council House and upon other places in Jamestown. Rudely printed lampoons were found on the benches of the Council Chamber.

The proud officers of the colony fretted. The revenues were falling sharply. There was talk of a refusal to plant tobacco until the head tax was abated. Women besieged the parish ministers and demanded that the ordinaries be forbidden to sell strong drink, because too many men were falling into drunkenness. Citizens railed at the Council and the burgesses, called for an audit of the public accounts, decried the high license fees and the system of tax farming which enriched the Governor's favored few and drained the pockets of the poor, called for purges of the landbooks to clear uncertain titles and demanded better surveys of headright property.

Not even the election calmed the clamor. The sheriffs trembled as they took the votes and were careful for once to make a proper tally. In Charles City, Surry and Henrico there were disturbances so riotous that the officers feared for their lives. In several counties former servants were chosen to the House. In Henrico, Nathaniel Bacon and Colonel Crews were picked by acclamation.

The Governor fumed. When advised by certain of his Councillors to relax his rigorous policy toward the growing Baconian faction he banged the table and vowed that compromise would feed rebellion until it became unmanageable.

Even Daniel Parke became discouraged. He went to Lawrence, the innkeeper, and told him to get word to Bacon that he alone could relieve the tension.

"Tell that rash radical to write to the Governor," he advised. "Tell him to help us make a salve for Sir William's pride. Bacon is a Cambridge man. He should be able to write a conciliatory letter. If he does nothing now, I fear that, despite his station, the Governor will hang him."

Lawrence thoughtfully puffed his pipe. "Why do you think that I can get word to Bacon?" he inquired.

Parke frowned. "If you can't, who in God's name can?" he roared.

Lawrence laughed. "Perhaps I shall try," he said.

Lawrence sat for a long time after Daniel Parke's departure. The shrewd innkeeper trusted few at Jamestown and Daniel Parke as little as anyone. It disturbed him that Parke, a member of the Governor's Council, knew so well his friendship with members of the border faction. If Parke knew, all knew, including Berkeley.

Still the man talked sense. It was plain that Bacon was no rebel. It was plain, indeed, that there were no rebels on the border unless it were treason to slay invading savages. Certainly it was not treason for farmers to disagree with fur traders or for English yeomen to ask that their assembly redress grievances. That was the reason why the Assembly had been created in 1619. Bacon should be informed of the tempest at Jamestown, so he could end the silly talk of treason.

Lawrence leaned back in his chair and stared at his broad boot toes. There were too many feuds without this. Berkeley's senile vanity and greed made life troublesome enough without foolish gossip about a rebellion of border folk.

Who could take a message to Bacon? Who could even find Bacon in the wilderness south of Jordan's Point? None of Byrd's men were in town. The trapper who had come downriver two days before was a Rappahannock man who would not be going westward for a month. Who else? There was the Clayborne boy. If anyone could find Bacon's band, it would be that wolf cub.

≈§ 2

LANCE CLAYBORNE welcomed the assignment. He was sadly out of temper now that the door at Gull Cove was closed to him. In vain he had haunted the place day after day. The owl cry in the lane was not effective. The gates were closed.

Mistress Easter Walker was indisposed, could see no one. Mistress Walker was not at home. Mistress Walker was visiting down the Peninsula.

He sent a present, a box of the rarest Cathayan tea. It was returned with only the barest measure of politeness. Letters he dispatched—more than a dozen—all came back unopened.

Sir Mathew chuckled at the young man's discomfiture, and Lance joined in the cruel mirth to keep his seething brain in balance.

No one gave him comfort save Henrietta Hart. That wise, dark woman of the lonely tavern did not laugh at him.

"It is a sickness," she said. "It saps a man until at last, when the maid relents, he is so weak he cannot raise a finger." She tossed her head and smiled bitterly. "Do I not know, lad? Women in love glow like a forge fire, but men—ha!—men become gloomy, gloomy."

She fetched him a mug of her rich Canary wine. And when he was warmed and relaxed, he remembered that she was his mistress, that she was a beautiful woman.

"You are glowing like a forge fire, Henrietta," he said with a smile.

"I am happy that you have noticed it," she replied. "I love you also, Lance."

"*Also,* Henrietta? What do you mean?"

The dark woman sniffed. "Think you the Walker girl does not love you, boy? You are foolish to be miserable. She loves you, damn her!"

Lance looked skeptically at his boot toes.

Henrietta took his face in her hands. "God, boy! How you have moved back my clock! But you need not love Henrietta, my dear. When you despair just get drunk with Henrietta."

She laughed, not bitterly this time, and he, warmed by friendship and by wine, pulled her head against his shoulder and kissed her clumsily on the temple.

"Oh!" she sighed. "Oh, Lance, I should tell you about that girl—about all young girls. I should, but I cannot."

"Why, Henrietta?"

"You'd not believe me. You'd think of me as a jealous cat. And perhaps I am. Never mind. Just remember that your adoring mistress gives you delight without tears, and enjoys you without any thought of the unpromised future."

She wriggled in his arms, and Lance, instead of releasing her, picked her up.

"Can we go upstairs?" he asked.

"Always, Lance," said Henrietta.

Lawrence's message reached Lance Clayborne at Henrietta's tavern. It braced him smartly. Here was action. Yet during the winding voyage upriver in one of Captain Byrd's ten-oared barges, Lance Clayborne suffered pangs with every stroke that drew him westward.

Henrietta had soothed him. She had quieted his unruly body; she had talked sound sense out of deep experience. But even that wise woman had admitted that girls could be insanely impulsive in love, that there was no telling what an angry snip might do.

Suppose Easter decided to wed some other man—John Lee or Tom

Hansford? Or suppose she took ship and again returned to London? And what if impersonal fate intervened? She might contract a lowland fever and die while he was gone.

What a fool he was! He should have told her at that first meeting in the lane exactly who he was. Her pride, her tenderest emotions had been exposed by that unhappy masquerade. Perhaps she would never reconcile Lance Clayborne with the romantic woodland knight she had saved from drowning and had learned to love.

Faugh! To hell with love! It was agony.

Bacon would welcome him. He could be useful out there on the border. Few could beat the Indians at their own games and read a trail, kill deer with but a single bullet. Bacon needed officers who could awe the wild men in his ranks—outfight them, outswear them and, when food was scarce, jolly them into further effort.

It was no time for women anyway. All the western tribes had taken up the war club. Tributary Indians had fled to join the wild Monacans. Terrified by the slaughter of the Occaneechees the barbarians no longer trusted any white man anywhere. Pipisko had led his band deeper into the mountains.

Lance Clayborne took a deep draft of air and stretched his legs. The forest soon would loosen his knotted muscles. Perhaps it might untie some of the bands which bound his heart.

The boat moved rapidly upriver under the arms of the Negro rowers. Now it was passing Harmony Spit where David Broome, his former tutor, lived. David Broome. He too had suffered many a love pang once. Ann Short, the governess, led him a merry chase indeed, before she married him and made him a sober parson. What were they doing now? Ann Short was a fat busybody; Broome a shortsighted hoeman on his glebe save on Sabbath days when he would deliver interminable sermons.

Must he, Lance Clayborne, become a hoeman, too, the subject of unreasonable female will? Must he, to obtain relief from that ache which squeezed his heart, become as one of Peo's tame deer and beg for kindness from a woman? By the shackles of the Prophet Daniel no! He'd keep his freedom, and be damned to her!

But all his oaths of resolutions did not help him. Waking and sleeping he felt soft hands on his cheek, heard her sweet voice. Nothing could drive her lovely image from his mind.

⋙ 3

IT WAS perhaps a good thing that Lance did not hear the conversation between Arthur Ward, the Governor's personal secretary, and Easter Walker. Ward had a good ear for gossip and he found out at Middle Plantation from Dame Drummond all there was to know about the Clayborne boy's romance with Alan Walker's daughter. He then visited Gull Cove and talked to Easter. When he mentioned Launcelot Clayborne's name she flared up like an explosion of gunpowder. She was so violent, in fact, that the ancient Ward, wise in humanity, realized at once that the maiden was badly smitten with an arrow from Eros.

"He is a faithless mountebank!" she cried. "He never will come here again. I never shall see him again as long as I live!"

"He has tried to repair this . . . er . . . misunderstanding?" Ward inquired.

"Yes, but if he lives to be a Methuselah he never will repair it!" she answered.

Ward did not carry on the discussion other than to remark as he picked up his hat: "The Governor was worried, Mistress Walker, for fear he may have to hang the boy."

She turned pale.

"He has been with Bacon, you see," Ward continued slyly. "We wish to save him from that man's insane folly. But never mind."

Ward took his departure without saying more. He would see her later when she was calmer.

Lance Clayborne's affair with the Walker maid also concerned Lady Frances Berkeley. She discussed it tête-à-tête with Colonel Philip Ludwell.

"Have you also been paying court to the Walker girl?" Dame Berkeley asked.

He raised his square shoulders. "Not I, my dear. I have my hands full here, you see."

He was holding her skein of yarn while her graceful fingers worked it into a ball. She did this very slowly. She enjoyed his impatience at having his hands imprisoned.

"Lance Clayborne has made a fool of her," she said. "This means, of course, that she will marry him eventually. A woman always marries the man who makes a fool of her. It is in a way a method of revenge."

"You have made a fool of me," said Ludwell. "What does that mean, Frances?"

"Hush," she said. "Must you eternally make love? I am glad you do not visit Gull Cove now. You would say the same things there you say to me. It is a habit with you."

He frowned. "Yes, a bad habit that has cost me a fortune in bribe money among your servants, my sweet. But His Excellency does not seem to mind. He is glad enough to have his jewel admired. Doubtless he is pleased, too, at the cruel way you use me. Often he gives me a look of pity."

"Stop this foolishness, Philip, and tell me about the Clayborne boy."

Ludwell sighed. "His mother doubtless was a beauty," he said slowly. "The boy is handsome and has charm, his father none. The lad's mother probably was highly intelligent, too, because Sir Mathew is as stodgy as a cannon wheel. Her name was Latimer—one of the Latimers of Kent. She died of the plague the year before they came to Virginia. They are not related to the other Virginia Claibornes— they sign their name differently. Sir Mathew was a nobody when King Charles knighted him for some service or other at Colchester, or another of those battles with Cromwell."

"I don't mean the family history, Philip. I wish to know about the boy. Sir William thinks highly of him and is afraid he is falling under the influence of Bacon and the border rebels."

"The boy? Oh! Well, from what I hear he is quite a buck. There is a man named Gary on the Eastern Shore who had a fight with him last spring. Gary is supposed to be quite handy with the Italian-style rapier, but Clayborne beat him in a brawl at Kickotan—thrust him through both hams after two passes."

"What else?"

"I don't know much more about the lad. They say he has been out on explorations several times and knows some of the Indian dialects. He keeps his eyes open, too. He told me once that except for the Monacans all the Virginia Indians talk the Algonquin tongue. Also he told me there are enough wild cattle west of the mountains to support quite a considerable population if anyone dared live out there. The Indians kill the beasts by chasing them over cliffs, he says."

"But what does the Clayborne boy look like, Philip? Have I met him?"

"Oh, I don't know. He's a tall, mysterious kind of chap. I suppose a woman would call him handsome, but he is sunburned almost black, and he walks like a panther. Moore Fauntleroy had a wrestling match with him at the Charles City fair a year or so ago, and Clayborne made a monkey out of him. Moore said the boy's arms were tougher than hickory beams. Old Henry Chicheley knows the boy. Chicheley is quite a close friend of Sir Mathew, you know. The boy has been experimenting with some of Henry's Peruvian roots, I hear. They are called potatoes, and they are not bad. They are much better tasting than tuckahoe or acorn meal."

Lady Frances finished her ball of wool, only to have her hands imprisoned in turn. Ludwell kissed them and kissed her.

They both had been affected by their thoughts of the reckless Lance Clayborne and his romance with the lovely Walker girl. The years slipped from Frances Berkeley's normally rigid shoulders, and she became a soft, yielding woman.

Ludwell recalled her epigram of a few minutes previous: a woman always marries the man who makes a fool of her. He kissed her deeply. His left hand partly clutched, partly caressed the hollows at the small of her back. She quivered and with a little cry drew back. Then she was close again, his head in her arms, his lips against the softness of her breast.

The second floor servants had finished their work for the day and had gone to their quarters. The door was locked.

"Frances?"

"Oh, Philip!"

∽§ 4

LANCE found Bacon at a small camp above the rapids of the Appomattox River. Two hundred of his volunteers were under arms.

A sentinel escorted Lance through the gate of the new palisade to the headquarters lodge where he was received with great delight. Bacon seemed years older. His face was thinner, his eyes deep sunken and very bright. His body had been thinned by exercise, but he seemed to be in the best of spirits.

"How now, my leather-clad Romeo?" he said to Lance. "You are ready for a new campaign?"

Lance smiled as cheerfully as he could and reached into his pouch for Richard Lawrence's letter. "I am a messenger," he said.

Bacon read the letter carefully, then flung it onto the table and rose to his feet.

"This land is filled with madness," he declared. "All the forest Indians now are aroused. They are in war paint from here to Massachusetts Bay, and the Governor talks of rebels! Can't he see that the savages are at the root of all this discontent? Can't he see that his river forts are useless, that but for these men of mine the Monacans and God knows what other wild tribes would now be at the gates of Jamestown?"

Bacon looked keenly at Lance. "Could you tell him that, my friend?"

Lance stared at the pine-fringed horizon thoughtfully and said, "I have told him that. Many have told him that. He will not listen. Personal fear and greed, it seems, now guide him. Lawrence has hopes, but only because Berkeley is afraid. The Governor, he thinks, fears your power."

"Who am I to frighten the Governor? I, a simple farmer? It is senseless!" Bacon once more scanned Lawrence's letter. "This Lawrence is a sly one, Lance," he said. "He argues as smoothly as a Scottish merchant, and then, to clinch the matter, he vows that my friends at Jamestown are in peril and I must save them. Ha! As though I did not have my hands full of Indians!"

Lance did not smile.

Bacon scanned the young man's face in surprise. "Is Lawrence really serious?"

"Yes," Lance said. "He means what he says. You will not be safe in Jamestown either even though you have been elected a burgess from Henrico."

"Not safe?"

"You must remember the fears of an old, bad-tempered, frightened man, sir. Berkeley has never forgotten that the citizens of Virginia sent Governor Harvey home to England in disgrace, nor the terrors of Cromwell's dictatorship. Nor has he forgiven the Crown for dealing too leniently with the murderers of Charles I. He is bitterly jealous of your influence and popularity."

Bacon's lips turned down skeptically. "Jealous? Jealous of my popularity? Ha! Cromwell excited him once, so now he sees a rebel under every bush. Where is the real Berkeley? Where is the stout Berkeley of whom I heard so much in England, the Berkeley who defied Cromwell and awed a bloody English Parliament? Where is Berkeley, the champion who so often rode against hostile Indian villages? Where is the gallant Berkeley whom every Virginian once loved? He has gone, and in his place there is an old, decrepit, greedy, demon-ridden hulk."

Bacon's hand tightened on his sword hilt until the brier-scratched leather scabbard tilted upward. "Look you, Lance Clayborne, so you can bear witness. If that tyrant at Jamestown does not heed the border's call for aid, if he persists in his refusal to sanction our expeditions into the woods, I cannot promise to hold these men in check. He must be warned that this uprising on the border against the Indians really can become a revolution."

Bacon pointed through the window of the lodge. "Look, you!" he said.

A line of grim young recruits stood on the fresh, new grass. Before them was a scarred, helmeted sergeant. At his command the men drew ramrod, tore cartridge, loaded firelocks and rammed home the charges in unison. The drill seemed perfect, but the sergeant growled and snatched a musket from the nearest man and gave another demonstration.

"Look!" Bacon repeated. "Once those Virginians out there were children of the Governor, helpless toddlers dependent on him for guidance, livelihood and protection in a wild and terrifying country. Now what do you see? They are grown men, resolute, spirited, self-sufficient and able to make their way even on this war-ridden border. The Governor needs only to recognize their manhood to live with them in peace, but what does he do? He calls them rebels!"

Bacon's sword scabbard tilted up once more until his cloak resembled the ruffled tail feathers of a fighting cock. "Rebels! Rebels because we are fighting the Indians! Rebels because we have kept the savages from sneaking past his useless forts! Rebels because we value human skin as well as beaver pelts! Does he think that these men fear his manifestos? Virginia has a charter from the Crown—Virginians have all the rights of English citizens. Has proconsul Berkeley forgotten that?"

⋘ 5

LANCE CLAYBORNE started back to Jamestown almost with reluctance. There was less heartache for him there on the border amid the comradeship of Bacon's garrison.

A letter from Bacon to the Governor was borne by Colonel Crews. It was Clayborne's mission to take less formal word to Lawrence and Drummond.

Rebel or no rebel, Bacon was determined to occupy his seat as a burgess from Henrico in the June Assembly, but he did not raise the issue in his communication to Sir William. He respectfully maintained that his command had violated no law by marching against the savages, that he would be ready at any time to follow the orders of the Governor in pressing the Indian war. He defended himself from charges that he had been in any manner disloyal to colony or Crown. There was no plea for forgiveness, because, with a lawyer's reasoning, he had made it plain that there was nothing to forgive. Bacon did discreetly recognize the Governor's resentment but waved it aside with the assurance that he was and forever expected to be Berkeley's most humble and obedient servant.

Bacon's word to Drummond and Lawrence was more straightforward. It was his intention, he revealed, to meet them secretly at Drummond's home in Jamestown two days before the Assembly. Here he would receive the latest news and plan his course in the light of fresh events.

At Jamestown there was a growing restlessness. Lawrence's Inn was so well filled that Lance had to lodge in a chamber with a sea captain who smelled of opium and snored with sounds like those of a feeding hog.

He held his conference with Drummond and Lawrence after darkness on the quay behind the tavern. Lance told them of Bacon's band and answered questions until his throat was dry and he was half drunk with the liquor required to wet it. He was disturbed at the tension of these sober burghers.

"He sent us nothing in writing?" Drummond asked.

"Nothing," Lance answered. "He told me to tell you what I saw and nothing more. He has written to Berkeley by Crews."

Lawrence looked at Drummond and exclaimed, "He has written Berkeley!"

The Scot nodded somberly, turned to Lance and asked, "Why did he send his letter by Crews? Why not by you?"

Lance replied, "Crews is his colleague in the House of Burgesses. It was more appropriate to send it by him."

"Bacon evidently feared the Governor might learn that Lance was a messenger of *ours*," Lawrence said.

"That's it, I think," said Drummond. "Listen, lad. Say nothing of this mission you have so shrewdly performed for us. Say nothing of Bacon's attitude or of his plans. Go home, and wait word from us and Bacon. He will need you in his new campaign. The colony will need you."

But Lance found next day that he could not go home immediately. Before Lance had downed his breakfast old Arthur Ward, the Governor's steward, had delivered a summons from His Excellency.

Sir William received Lance in the east room of the Council House. The old man's eyes were very bright, his face smeared with unguents, his ruffled, linen shirt awry; but he greeted the young man with good humor.

"You forest-running rascal, you!" he cried, his hand on Lance's shoulder. "How goes it in the west? The wits of most westerners seem to be muddled. What of yours?"

"Mine, Excellency? I am young. I have no wits."

The Governor laughed. "Sometimes I believe it, lad. From the tales I hear of you, you're as daft as John the Baptist."

Lance chose his words as carefully as he could. He told of the abandoned plantings and of the panic that still prevailed in spite of the defeat of the invading Susquehannocks. He spoke boldly of Bacon.

"My good neighbor, the younger Bacon, sir, has the only mobile band beyond the forts," Lance declared.

Berkeley's hot eyes narrowed.

Lance continued. "He will not be surprised by the Indians, sir, you may count on that. He has terrified the southern tribes, and now even the fierce barbarians to the west are afraid. They will not attack his outposts. His scouts must go twenty miles to make contact with the Monacans."

"His camp is fortified?"

"Only by watchful scouts, sir. The bordermen will not trust ramparts."

Berkeley's face, in spite of an attempt at self-control, now became red. He clenched and unclenched his hands repeatedly beneath his lacy cuff. Lance was shocked at the sudden change. Twice the old man started to speak, only to turn away and wrestle with his emotion. Berkeley did not wish to disclose anger, that was plain. He was suspicious, yet politic; angry, but not at the young man whom he was trying to examine.

"What of Colonel Hill of my Henrico garrison?" the Governor asked suddenly. "I have ordered him to bring the younger Bacon back to Jamestown to answer charges of insubordination."

"Bacon, sir?"

"Yes, Bacon. Why has he not arrested Bacon?"

"I do not know, Your Excellency. I did not see Colonel Hill. Why, sir, are you seeking Bacon?"

Berkeley was pale. "Do you presume to question me?"

"Pardon, Excellency."

The Governor, suddenly angered, thrust out a warning finger. "Listen to me, young man! I am not to be fooled. You know why Bacon is sought by my officers. Furthermore, my bright young forest runner, I know your part in the sedition that threatens to tear this colony apart. Go tell your father he is foolish to let you run abroad like a wild colt!"

It was Lance's turn now to become angry, but he did not speak.

Berkeley continued: "Heed, my boy! This is no ordinary party controversy. The General Court will find that it is rebellion, nothing else. Do you know the word? Rebellion! High treason, sir! As Governor I am responsible for the policies of state, and I am answerable only to the Council and my King. While I am Governor no border ruffian will fix our policies. I'll use the gallows. I'll use it here as well as in the west!"

If the Governor had expected to make Lance flinch, he failed. The young man listened with full respect though he was troubled to control his anger. Berkeley breathed deeply twice, not without effort, and assumed a milder tone.

"Harsh words, you say? Yes, and chosen advisedly," continued the Governor. "You are wise beyond your years, Master Clayborne. You have the fine qualities of your father and your uncle—and more. In men like you lie all the hopes of this Virginia of ours. You would not have it torn apart by strife, I know. We fear the savages, yes; but what are the Indians? Childlike barbarians—no less, no more. Have you not hunted with them? You know their traits. They must be punished. They will be punished. But all the resources of the Crown cannot do the things that Bacon tries to do. Thrust the tribes beyond the mountains? It's absurd. We might as well try pushing our Chesapeake Bay into the ocean. Bacon's talk is greater than his abilities, and the adulation of a border mob has filled his brain with delusions. As for you, I know you are not a fool. Your father rode with Rupert. I shall count on you to help us heal the wounds of discord in this unhappy situation."

Lance wished to reply. He wished to tell Berkeley that the lesson Bacon had given the Indians on the Roanoke River would make it simple for any organized column to push the Monacans beyond the mountains. He wished to tell Berkeley that so far as Indian warfare was concerned Bacon possessed genius beyond all men who ever had entered the wilderness. But the young man knew that talk from him would be futile. Berkeley long since had passed the age at which he could heed or even listen to advice. The old man spoke with the conviction of one who was certain that he knew the situation and every possible solution.

He placed a firm hand on Lance's shoulder. "You have done well, young man, but henceforth you will stay east of Shoccoes until directed otherwise by me. Bacon is coming here, and we will settle this affair. You will stay in the east, my boy. This is a command."

Lance bowed respectfully and took his leave.

⚜ 6

WHEN Lance told his father about the Governor's command Sir Mathew was delighted. He had been gravely concerned about his son's association with the rebellious border leaders. Not for a moment had he doubted Lance's loyalty to the Governor or the Crown. Such doubt would be unthinkable for the aging Cavalier. But he was concerned about the young man's reputation. Lance had been too much in the west. He had lost contact with the strong and gentle easterners who might advance him in favor and in knowledge of public affairs. No credit was to be won in small border skirmishes. Brent and Mason, Washington and Allerton, all were discredited men because of the failure of their efforts in the west. As for Bacon, the man had marched without orders, without authority. He was a fool hothead whose reports could not be credited.

Sir Mathew explained to Lance that the leaders of all the eastern counties were gossiping like magpies. The small farmers would control the next Assembly; that was certain. The Council and the traders would have to await another season. Every crackpot in the colony was speaking from a stump, but things would quiet down in time. Why? Because—thanks be to God!—there was no religion in the row, no Cromwell; there were some ancient firebrand Covenanters, but no Covenant. At least the dissidents were satisfied with the Church of England.

But Lance was disturbed. There was too much talk of Cromwell. It might breed a Cromwell. There was too much talk of rebellion, of the gallows. If Berkeley began to hang those border men, if he imprisoned Bacon as he threatened, there would be violence. If Berkeley touched a hair of Bacon's head, the border men would march, and, in blind rage, they might sack the eastern settlements. The wildest Scots could be no worse than they.

He told his father about the Occaneechee town. For a while the old soldier's eyes lighted up. Then he waved his hand as though to say, *You call that affair a battle!*

"That Bacon, sir, is full of genius," Lance said.

Sir Mathew chuckled. "You think he is a soldier, Son?"

"I've seen him in two campaigns, Father."

"Campaigns! You believe those things to be campaigns! You call three hundred men an army! *General* Bacon. Ha!"

Lance forebore to argue with the veteran of Marston Moor and Naseby, but he wondered if any regiment of King Charles's men could march on foot four hundred miles, living the while upon lean horse-meat and woodchucks, dug from their winter burrows, and then assault a fortified island with but a single cannon. Bloody Run in 1656 had been a bloody defeat for the English. There was no such leadership or resolution when Jamestown was stripped of its shipping by the Dutch ten years before. Allerton had failed in Maryland. Such affairs did not match the European struggles, but men had marched and died.

His father spoke of wagon trains, of cavalry control, of artillery fire and musketry. If he could but see an Indian fight! If he could but measure the effect of such a feat as Bacon's! Three hundred Indians had died, more than had lost their lives in warfare since Virginia's first colony was established. There might be other marches, yes, but no Indian force in Virginia would ever try to stand again and fight.

"You have become a man of importance, my son," Sir Mathew said. "Your work as a courier attracted much favorable attention."

Warmed by his father's more cheerful mood and by a mug of spiced Madeira, Lance felt better. Sir Mathew had evidently no fear of rebellion, although he realized that the small farmers would control the forthcoming Assembly. Lance did not contradict his father, but he did not share Sir Mathew's optimism. He had seen Bacon's command in the hills of the Appomattox valley. He had heard Berkeley mention the gallows. Again he reflected that if Bacon were hanged, hell itself would be let loose.

Lance knew the spirit of the border, but there was one thing that Lance did not know—his own role in Governor Berkeley's schemes.

During the following week, an acquaintance here, another there, questioned him casually about Nathaniel Bacon's camp, about Byrd's flight downriver from Shoccoes to Windmill Point, about MacFarlane and various other agents of the Governor in the west. Lance told them what he knew. For the first time in his life Lance was sought out by the elders of the colony much to the amusement of his cynical old father. They told him that he would win promotion to a captaincy in time; that he would soon become, perhaps, a collector of the port; that he was a young man of promise in the colony.

"What do they want?" Sir Mathew asked. "I think you have some secrets, boy. Have you become a politician as well as a soldier?"

Lance wondered, waited.

The elder Bacon came to Clayborne Castle; so did Daniel Parke of the Council. They seemed to be casual visitors, but all examined Lance as though he were a man of large influence. Lawrence and Drummond also came, and others of the anti-Berkeley faction came. They spoke of no rewards except those of loyalty and friendship to the border band. They candidly placed great value on Lance's services in the recent past and asked him to help prevent a further breach between the Governor and Bacon.

Lance meanwhile fretted more about his own affairs than those of Berkeley. He could not forget the Walker girl. She haunted him at work, in bed and in the hunting field. One day he would think of her as a haughty queen and on another as a hot savage girl begging him for love. He asked news of her from every visitor. They said that she was visiting Lady Berkeley at Green Spring, that she was lovelier perhaps than any woman in the colony including Lady Berkeley. Perhaps, indeed! They said that she had many suitors now. They watched Lance's face for signs of love sickness.

Then, one day a Negro hostler at the farm by the ferry told Sir Mathew's servant, Cato, that Mistress Easter had returned to Gull Cove. And Simeon Jones from Sturgeon Creek provided further news: The young lady had rejected Hansford's suit. She was sad and moody.

Simeon Jones—who was brother-in-law to Arthur Ward, the Governor's secretary—was quite a gossip. He chattered like a magpie for an hour, telling them of his mother's fever and his father's gout, of Parson Broome's last sermon on Saint Paul—a sermon which had caused much talk because Broome called the saint a busybody and a meddler with mysteries he could not understand.

Lance smiled. Of late Saint Paul had been a pet hate of his former tutor, but the young man was in no need for Broome's theology.

"Is Edward Walker's warehouse done?" Lance asked.

"Oh, yes," said Simeon. "He expects to come to see you soon. He wants your smith to make him hinges for his barn. His sister wants to see you too."

Lance looked up. "Who told you that?"

"He did."

"She told him that she wished to see me?"

"Oh, no, but she was there, and she did not contradict her brother." Simeon Jones rode off well filled with wine.

Lance began to dream better dreams.

ஃ 7

NEXT time he made the owl call at Gull Cove there was an answer. A great barrier stood between them; but she was there by the stile, twisting her kerchief, biting her full lips, still and proud and frightened.

It was not a forest ranger who greeted her, but a nervous young man in polished boots and a velvet cloak. For a long while there was silence there in the dusk of the spring day.

"I received your message," he said at last.

"I sent you no message."

"I received a message."

"I do not understand."

"Let us forget it then. You are here to see me. I have come here before, many times, and in vain."

"My father . . . my father ordered me to meet you."

This threw him back upon his heels.

"I never would see you of my own accord, Lance Clayborne!" she cried. "I hate you, hate you!" She turned as though to run away.

He took her hand, checked her. Then quickly he loosed his hold on her. There was another silence. A whippoorwill began to whistle in the forest near by.

"I don't care why you came," he said at last. "That is the truth whatever says my pride. I love you. Perhaps my pride will hate me because I've said it, but it's true. I love you. You have filled my heart for months. I cannot keep your image out of my mind. If I have been a fool, I'm sorry. If you really hate me, I shall hate myself forever."

Lance did not know the tempest that was tearing her, and it was well he did not. In her warm presence he forgot entirely what she had told him, nor could he concern himself with reason. He pleaded like a hungry child there in the twilight. At last when he came to her side and took her hand it was very cold.

"I do not love you," she declared, "and you . . . in time will learn to hate me."

"Hate you?"

"Yes."

A faint noise caused him to start. He turned, his eyes searching the shadows.

She spoke now in a whisper as she said, "Pay no attention. Let us go farther down the lane."

He followed her, puzzled.

When she stopped she whispered again, "Now do not raise your voice." She moved close to him as though in an embrace. With a nervous, half-frightened laugh, she explained. "I am a Delilah tonight, Lance Clayborne. Please listen so that you . . . so you will not be harmed."

He moved as if to lower his hand to his sword.

She checked him firmly. "No, please! Listen. My father has ordered me to see you, to permit you to visit me at home, here. He thinks that you are . . . that you are one of the worst of Master Bacon's rebels and——"

She had to hold him firmly by his muscular forearms lest he pull away. The effort broke her sentence, and she paused. She now breathed like a frightened fawn.

He said in a low voice, "I am beginning to understand. The Governor issued orders and your father——"

"Yes," she whispered.

"And you despise me?"

"I? Why . . . why, yes. You——"

"You despise yourself, too, I suppose?" He was standing very straight.

There was a long pause.

"Yes," she said.

"I am permitted to visit you in order that your father and you may execute the Governor's will?"

"Please. . . . Did I not tell you that you'd hate me? I am a fool, a worse fool than you, Lance Clayborne. But they told me that you would be arrested, perhaps hanged, if I did not see you and . . . and . . . Are you a rebel?"

Clayborne squared his shoulders. "If I am not a rebel now, Saint Peter will write down my name in his book as the most patient fool that ever knocked on the gate of Heaven!"

She said hurriedly: "I know none of the wherefores of all the politics, but there is deadly danger, Lance. And though I do not love you any more I do not want you dancing from a gallows. My father is frightened. The whole country is in a turmoil. That old man, the Governor, is as deadly as a timber snake. Even Frances Berkeley says so—with pride. Frightened men are dangerous, Lance. Tell me that you're not a rebel. Please. So I can tell them truly that you're not."

He tilted her face upward. "Tell them this, my lovely Easter," he said bitterly. "Tell them that I am a Virginian. Tell them that it was only through the lips of a girl that any man in this colony would dare to hint that I am a traitor to my King. Tell them that. This, too, my dainty sweet—who is subtle now in spite of her youth—say to your worthy, frightened father: that if the Governor were not thrice my age and afflicted with so many creaking bones, I'd call him out and cut his throat for this!"

It was her turn now to anger. "You speak now like a tavern bully!"

"With all sincerity," he said.

"I was not told to be candid with you, Lance Clayborne. In being so I betrayed my father's plan——"

"Sir William Berkeley's plan——"

"Hush! Do not use that name even in a whisper. I tell you he is dangerous. He is not the man he once was. He is to be feared, I say!"

"You would not have been so candid, my dear, had you, with your keen intelligence, suspected me of treason." Shock and pain had cleared his mind somewhat. Still whispering to the trembling girl, he continued. "I came here as an anxious lover. I find myself the victim of a politician's plot. If I had been kicked into Haskins' bog, I would not feel so cheap. Never mind. I've played the fool before, and perhaps I'll wear the cap and bells again. They are on some occasions, I think, becoming to a youth. You ask me if I am a traitor to the Crown. I say no a thousand times. But if you'd ask me if I were Nathaniel Bacon's friend, I would say yes ten thousand times. Tell them that, Mistress Easter. Be sure to tell them that!"

He moved to draw away from her, but her strong fingers held him. "I'll tell them nothing—ever—to your harm," she said.

He took a deep breath. "Gentle beauty!" he mocked. "My angel of the lane! My heroine here to wrestle with the devil for my soul and for Berkeley's beaverskins! I'd like to throttle you. I'd like to thrust you down the very muzzle of your father's arquebus. I see it there beyond the cedar bush. It is shaking. He thinks I have his daughter in my arms. He thinks I speak of love. Perhaps he is afraid that I shall make a traitor out of you." Her head was bowed again.

"I'll never wish you harm," she said. "You mocked me, Lance. You made me into a silly fool with that cruel deception of yours. You made me hate myself, made *me* feel like Haskins' bog. You did! But I shall never wish you harm. I have hated you, because I have despised myself. I have hated you, because you cheapened me, dragged me to the level of a dirty savage woman. I've hated you, Lance Clayborne! I've hated you until my mouth seemed full of gall and my very soul crawled on the earth. But whatever you are or in your anger believe please know that I shall never wish you harm. God made you as you are, and someday maybe He will give me back my self-respect."

Suddenly she pulled away from him and, hurrying as fleetly as a frightened animal, disappeared in the direction of the house. Lance moved as if to follow, stopped and went back slowly into the forest.

৺§ 8

As LANCE rode home that night the owls and whippoorwills made sport of him. He tried fiercely to purge his mind, his very life, of Easter Walker. At every trial he failed. He attempted to think of other things—his thoughtful mistress, Henrietta Hart; politics, the black omens hanging over every family in the colony; travel, a long postponed voyage to England which his father had recommended; Bacon's war against the western tribes. It was a hopeless effort. Nature had planted a woman in his brain, and hell itself could not remove her.

Let some other suitor take her and good riddance. The Virginia woods were full of women. England, France and Italy were full of women. He would wander afar and take them as they came. She would be sorry, for she never now would see the Henrico lodge which in his dreams he had built for her. She would wed a fat, old money-lover like her father and live a dullard's life. He groaned aloud until his pony shivered nervously.

But in spite of his mood his body somehow felt relief. At least he had seen the maid who had been haunting him for months. He had seen her, touched her, talked to her. There had been something in the contact which made him feel a better, stronger man. He was surprised at this.

Lance remained awhile, chafing, at Clayborne Castle. His father asked him to train two colts to the saddle, and this he did with calmness and skill; but the task did not quiet his spirit.

Tradesmen came from Jamestown and Kickotan with more news of the factions in the eastern settlements. Bacon, it seemed, had many supporters in the east. The entire anti-Council party had embraced the cause of the bordermen. If Bacon came to the Assembly, he would be arrested, said Jacob Capp, the peddler. Perhaps he would be hanged, for the Governor was old and fearful and very angry indeed. McNair, the tinker from Edinburgh, did not agree with Capp. He argued that Sir William would not dare do violence to a gentleman of Bacon's standing; that he would, instead, treat him with guileful kindness and seat him once more on the Council bench.

"Bacon would oppose some of the Governor's measures as a member of the House of Burgesses," the Scot insisted. "In the upper branch of the government, the Council, he would be harmless, for he would be outvoted."

At church in Jamestown the following Sunday gossip held more interest for churchgoers than the sermon. Men gathered in sober groups at the edge of the churchyard, and many of them did not join the ladies in the pews after the opening hymn. The wildest reports were rife. Bacon would attend the Assembly with a band of bravos at his back and write an entire new book of laws. . . . Bacon was bankrupt and desperate, so Berkeley might buy him off. . . . The Gloucester men would form an army to subdue the borderers. . . . No, there was sedition in Gloucester as well as New Kent and Henrico. . . . The King would soon send troops to back the Governor's authority. . . .

Lance listened to the chatter in high disgust for a while and then repaired to the church where, in spite of himself, his eyes strayed constantly to the Walker pew. The girl was there, still as a statue, her lovely face pale, intent and, he thought, somewhat fearful, though he could not be certain at first because of the lacy bonnet that shadowed her features.

Once she turned and looked at him so that he saw her eyes. They shocked him. Gone was the pert mischief, gone the anger. There seemed to be a message in her eyes for him, an urgent command to caution, a plea for understanding. Edward Walker, her brother, stared sullenly toward the pulpit. Her father, as was his wont, dozed and nodded beneath the shower of soothing words from the parson. "Let not your hearts be troubled. . . ."

Lance shook a fly from his sleeve, dropped his Psalter, picked it up and squirmed on the hard bench. He noticed that Dame Drummond was watching him disapprovingly from her place to his right. Then that sharp-faced lady glanced toward Easter Walker before she turned toward the droning minister.

Once more the girl looked squarely at him. He searched for some sign of personal interest. Her concern, he noticed, was not far from intimate. Her eyes now were saying plainly, *I wish to see you. I must see you.* Impulse told him to scorn her; but deep within him he rejoiced, and finally he surrendered.

When the long service ended he was in the aisle, bowing and making small talk with drowsy Alan Walker, asking Edward about his Orinoco plants; but he saw no one except the graceful girl in blue and white.

"Your father—" she said—"is he well?"

"Yes, and engaged today in drilling some of Sir Henry's new militia," answered Lance.

"But it is the Sabbath. . . ."

"Yes, but Sabbath or no Sabbath he is drilling horse recruits."

They passed slowly through the chattering crowd about the door.

"Tell him my father will call at Clayborne Castle during the afternoon," she said.

"And you?"

"Not I. I shall be at home."

"At home . . . to me?"

She seemed to hesitate. Her arm beside him trembled slightly. "Yes."

He helped her mount her sorrel pony and held his great hat carefully to keep it from frightening the nervous little beast. She did not look back as she rode away. Some dark affair was heavy on her mind.

Why did Alan Walker proclaim a pending visit? Why was she chosen to give him warning of that visit to his father?

There on the porch at Gull Cove, sitting ill at ease beside her as she talked, Lance for once felt very young and almost helpless. She was coldly matter-of-fact.

"My father," she announced, "is reopening the matter which your father presented to him last autumn. Your father, you will recall, suggested an alliance between our families. It was rejected then. My father has changed his mind."

"You mean——"

"I mean exactly that," she said almost impatiently.

He swallowed a tremendous lump that had arisen in his throat. "You have consented?"

"No!" she cried. "He speaks for himself and not for me."

"But, but——"

"I'll die first," she said. "I summoned you so I could explain the craven circumstance, so there would be no misunderstanding."

Bewildered, Lance breathed deeply, looked at her as if she had stabbed him and was turning the blade back and forth inside his heart. Her words were less shocking than the calm manner of her speaking.

But then her words flowed rapidly as she recognized his pain and pitied him. "You must realize, Lance, that you and I have fallen into the middle of events we do not understand. You have become an important figure in public affairs. It is because of your knowledge of the west, your friendship with Master Bacon, your skill at arms, your station, that we are exposed to this intrigue. The Governor wants you for his own. He is wooing your loyalty because, I am sure, he doubts it. As for me, I am just a tool—one of many. I have not been consulted."

He said nothing. He sat still, slapping his gloves against the scabbard that lay across his knees.

"I'll explain it all to you, Lance, because you must help me. You understand? You are no man to take a woman as a mere commodity—as a bribe of politics—against her will and judgment. Perhaps I know you better than you think. I was not blind there in the lane. Your woodland garb and manners excited my senses, but they did not blind me."

Still he did not speak.

Easter Walker sighed. "I suppose now, I have talked too much as usual. . . ." She touched her hair.

At last he found his voice, and with it a wry, somewhat sardonic smile. "My father," he said slowly, "will not be pleased. Perhaps he will be polite when he is approached on . . . on this subject which you mentioned. It may be, though, that he will be very rude. Would you forgive him?"

"Oh . . . oh, yes."

"Even if he told your father to be gone in . . . er . . . a soldier's language?"

Taken aback, she nodded. Her fluttery loss of poise gave him courage. He calmly took her hand and held it as though it were a bit of porcelain.

"Listen to me, Easter Walker," he said. "I care little about these antics of our elders, this effort to make us pawns of Berkeley. Things that are said of me are true. I am a friend of Bacon and of those wild men at the freshes of the river. I am familiar with the forest paths, with some of the Indian dialects and customs. At times, too, I have diced in the taverns and have done violence to certain bullies. But since those days last September when I met a maid at Archer's Hope landing, I'm sure that I have changed. . . ."

Her fingers quivered.

"Yes, I have changed, for I no longer think of hunting trips beyond the blue mountains." He paused. His gauntlets fell unnoticed from his knee. "I shall never think of you as a commodity," he continued.

"You are the companion of my thoughts, a part of me no matter what you do or say. The silly masquerade that hurt your feelings has only deepened mine."

She withdrew her hand. He made no motion to recover it. He sat as though dazed, staring out into the grove.

"You trouble me," she said.

"Not I. Your pride has troubled you, perhaps." He shrugged. "Oh, mind me not, my dear. I merely think aloud at times. It is a habit of those who wander in the forest alone. You would have many trials if you married me. I would sit beside the fire and say nothing until you took a poker to my head. At other times I would drench you with a passion that would make you giddy as a loon in August, and then you would wish that you were twenty women. I would tell the children Indian tales instead of soothing nursery rhymes. They would not fear the forest or any man or animal or ghost. . . ."

"You talk like——"

"Go on and say so."

"Like Usack," she said.

"Of course. I am making love to you as best I may. You do not like my boots. You believe that I am foppish in a London wig and awkward with an ordinary velvet cloak. Be that as it may, I am Usack, too, and I love you."

"I wonder. . . ."

He smiled in spite of the angry harshness in her voice. "You must credit me for trying to make it easier for you," he chided. "As the Indians say, my tongue is straight. There is no serpent's fork in it. I am willing to play the Governor's game in one respect: I shall be happy to take the lovely bait he offers me, if she will have it so."

"I am afraid," she sighed.

"Of me?"

"Oh, no. You do not seem to realize that the Governor speaks of hanging you, that for a while we must pretend."

He laughed.

"I mean it. He thinks you are inclined to be a traitor. He only wishes to reclaim your loyalty."

"You, too, think I am a rebel?"

"I only know that I could never change you. . . ."

"Already you have changed me," he said. "I am not pretending."

"I mean that——"

"That you could not be a rebel; that you think you are English rather than Virginian? I am doubtful on that score. I have not preached sedition to you, darling. I have been making love to you, not talking politics. I have not been pretending," he repeated.

She did not move nor did he touch again her still hand there beside him. Her face was pale as though some inner wave of terror was afflicting her. At last she spoke.

"I cannot argue either love or politics," she said. "I am bewildered. Like you, I have changed. I am not the same girl whom a boy named Usack came to see out there in the lane. Not long ago I was carefree, and now, even as you sit there and speak softly of love, I think only of gibbets and of cold terror. My father was a seaman once. He has words that shock and hurt. He told me things that I have not dared to speak to you. He said flatly that you will be hanged unless I marry you. Your father likewise may be branded as a traitor."

Lance sat up straight. "He told you that?"

"Yes, and more. I say it for fear that you might hear it first from others and wish to recall your words about . . . our marriage. Can you understand?"

The point of his chin was white with anger. For a while he was silent, struggling with himself to keep hot words from bursting free— hot words aimed inward at himself.

Thrice fool he was to be sitting here, playing the greedy Governor's game by speaking love to this befuddled girl! His lean muscles quivered. Through the red anger he heard her voice again.

"No man could desire a maid who had saved him from a hangman," she said. "No maid with spirit can be threatened into wedlock. I am bewildered, Lance Clayborne. You must go away and let me think for a while. You must believe me when I tell you again that this politics is grim and serious and deadly, too. I do not want you hanged."

In the midst of her uncertainty and under the influence of her voice he regained his self-possession. He tried to smile. He cleared his throat and after a long pause said quietly, "I had a tutor once who tried to teach me logic. I think he failed, for this discussion puzzles me as well as you. You say now that I shall be hanged unless I marry you. You say you do not wish me hanged. You called me here presumably to save my life. Yet when I—forgetting parents, politics, pride and everything except the girl beside me—agree to this proposal, offer you my hand, my life, my love, you hesitate. Must I then go and meet the Sheriff and my doom?"

"This is not the time for irony," she said. "I cannot make you see this . . . this terror. The Governor must believe that we . . . that we . . . still love each other."

He stood up, hand on his sword, and stared across the meadow to the forest wall. "You'd have me shiver at the mouthings of a senile tyrant? You'd have me be afraid of angry gossip?"

"No, but I would have you understand my fears. A woman, Lance, has feelings different from a man. We stay at home and think of things we dare not talk about to men. Not often do we dream as once I did with Usack in the lane. We plan much oftener than we dream— plan for terror, pain, illness and anxiety."

"You are planning now?"

"Yes."

"You want your lover hanged?" he asked bitterly.

"Of course not."

"So you will marry me tomorrow?"

"Of course not!"

"Why not?"

"If I did, you would hate me all your life and mine. You would have to add a noose to the Clayborne arms."

"But I have agreed to take the Governor's lovely bait, to pledge away my bachelor liberty. I repeat, do you mean that you do not care whether I am hanged or not?"

"No, silly fool!"

"So then it means that you are confident that you can make me behave without marrying me?"

She said nothing to this.

He pounded his hands together thoughtfully for a moment. "Very well, Easter Walker. We shall see what we shall see. My pride tells me to tell you and your dotard Governor and your anxious father to go to hell. My heart tells me that I should not become angry because you are, like me, a wild Virginian. My heart has assured me, Easter, that you did not call me here to change my mind, but to hear me vow a dozen times that I love you."

She blushed furiously.

He did not permit her to say anything, and unaccountably he became angry. "I do love you!" he said sharply. "I am sorry for it. I wish I had never gone to Archer's Hope. I wish I had never seen you. Somehow I hope to break this spell that has reduced me to half a man. Damn the Governor and his gallows! Damn your uncertainties, and damn your father's cattle business!"

He bowed. "You may say to your father that I agree with him in one respect, my dear," he said in parting. "You do not know your own mind!"

Lance's mount that day was an Arabian mare. Any of the Clayborne horses would have headed directly back to Council Point when the young man wheeled away from the hitch rack. But the Arabian, for some reason which Lance never was able to understand, took the eastern trail to Henrietta Hart's tavern.

For a time Lance did not realize where he was going. Then he burst into laughter.

ஃ 9

IF YOUNG people of the colony were bewildered by hurrying events that spring, their elders were in scarcely better case. Even Sir William Berkeley wavered. When all his efforts to arrest Nathaniel Bacon on the frontier failed he heeded the advice of Daniel Parke and other sober Councillors and decided to permit the young man to take his seat in the Assembly. Informal word to this effect was sent to Bacon, but when Bacon sailed downriver in his sloop and signaled for permission to make a landing at the quay a cannon shot was the reply. Bacon withdrew to an anchorage out of range and that night sent a boat ashore to Lawrence's. Lawrence counseled caution because it was apparent that Sir William had changed his mind again.

Next day Bacon's boat, beating upriver, ran afoul of the guardship. He and his men were made prisoners.

Jamestown was crowded with members of the new Assembly, and the Governor observed that many of them wore their swords that day and cheered the culprit, Bacon, when he was brought into the Council

House. Some spectators had fusils as well as swords, though soberer heads were working mightily to quiet the more unruly ones.

It was then that Sir William played his cards in a fashion that reminded members of his frightened Council of a younger, wiser Berkeley. Confronting the sullenly defiant young barrister-at-arms, the Governor said with simulated joviality, "Behold, the greatest rebel that ever was in Virginia!"

Bacon bowed respectfully and kept his peace. His straight figure in the plain dress of a lawyer offered great contrast to the elegance of the Governor's costume. Except for his sharp and bitter eyes Bacon resembled a bashful boy who had been haled before his tutor for a caning.

The Governor paused and, not without sarcasm, said gently, "Master Bacon, have you forgot to be a gentleman?"

Bacon answered, "No, may it please Your Honor."

"Then I'll take your parole," the Governor said.

The young man bowed and answered, "My thanks, Your Honor."

There was a great twittering in the crowd when Bacon came out and, grim of chin and downcast of eyes, repaired to the residence of his cousin for refreshment.

His men remained in irons and he under parole, so it was difficult for him to dissimulate his anger or to free himself of suspicion of the Governor's game.

No one heard the talk that day between Bacon the elder and his fiery relative. For hours they talked. The old man wrestled mightily for his kinsman's soul—told him again that he would be heir to the second-largest fortune in Virginia, that Sir William never meant him harm but only discipline, that the Indian troubles would be settled to every farmer's satisfaction.

Meanwhile there was other talk elsewhere in Jamestown. The new burgesses were there from all the colony, and some were wearing leather garments proudly as a token of their service on the Roanoke with Bacon. Much ale was drunk. The Governor would have the young man tried by the General Court. . . . No, no. He was too sensible for that. Burgesses were never tried during sessions of the House. . . . Sir William would not have the man indicted. He would forgive him with a flourish and restore him to the Council once again. The Council? Yes, on the Council young Bacon would be outvoted.

In the House of Burgesses this might not be the case. A majority of the House might vote with Bacon.

Parke, Ludlow, Ballard and other conservative Councillors kept their peace. The temper of the wild, new members of the House of Burgesses alarmed them.

Lance Clayborne hurried to Jamestown when word came of Bacon's arrest and found the young man in his cousin's courtyard alone, weary and filled with pent-up, rueful rage.

But Bacon greeted his friend with great delight. "I'm glad to see you, Lance!" he said. "You are a sane breeze in the doldrums of this sweating bedlam of a village. You have your sword, too, so you aren't under arrest."

Lance pulled at his laced collar and sat down on the bench beside the well. "What are they doing to you, General?" he asked.

"General! Thanks, my boy. A general, indeed! But we shall see. I am a punished schoolboy now, a contrite prisoner in the custody of my worthy relative. Tomorrow I shall be hauled before the Governor and given a lecture. After that who knows?"

Bacon laid a heavy hand on Lance Clayborne's knee and mused, half to himself. "I can hardly believe it," he said. "I saw rebellion in the public square today—men's hands grow white upon their sword hilts. It is hard to believe. I am not a rebel, boy, but this thing perhaps has gone too far. There are ugliness and terror out in the streets. I believe they would fight Sir William's guards, if the Governor laid a hand on me. I had never dreamed it would go so far as this. Lawrence told me. Drummond told me. Whaley, Hansford, Bland and Carver told me. But I didn't believe them. Why can't we fight Indians with peace among ourselves? Why must a war on Indians turn English swords to English throats? Who talks of rebellion except the Governor?"

Lance had no explanation. In simple friendship he was content to sit there and wordlessly sustain his friend.

Bacon paced the narrow brick walk between the myrtle bushes, wiping perspiration from his forehead with a damp wad of a handkerchief. At last he stopped and stared down at the well-muscled lad. "Why are you here?" Bacon asked. "Don't you realize that you too, in this madness, may be arrested? Yes, you are Virginia itself, my lad. You are the embodiment of this strange dominion. You are

America. You are the New World. You are violent and hopeful. You are young, uncertain of yourself, but you are strong, more strong than kings and governors suspect, and you will outlive all this whimsical tyranny to which we are now exposed. You are not an Englishman, Lance Clayborne, you are a Virginian. What is a Virginian? I hardly know." Bacon sat down and put his chin in his hands.

"There's justice at Jamestown, I'm sure," Lance said.

Bacon laughed. "You too tilt up your sword when you mention justice. Good. Perhaps it is wise to remember that justice has a sword. Never mind. I'll act the play tomorrow as my worthy people here have written it. I shall formally beg forgiveness for a crime the Governor believes I have committed. It is a crime I have disavowed. It will not hurt me to bow and beg forgiveness. The Governor will grant it with ostentatious generosity, but he will hate and fear me as before. Meanwhile, out yonder on the border, the Indians will shake their turtle-shell rattles in another war dance. That noise cannot be heard at Jamestown."

A Negro brought them ale and maize cakes.

"My cousin Nat is over at the Governor's house," Bacon continued. "The play will be rehearsed awhile. Poor Cousin Nat. He worries more of me than of his money. If I'll behave, he'll leave me all his money. . . . Here, drink. They cool it in the well. Where will you stay tonight?"

"Here if I can be of help," Lance said.

Bacon laughed. "Not here, my lad. Keep your hot head level. I am in good hands. If need be, I shall leave this stinking village and get back to my camp. It would not do to have you in irons. You can be too useful otherwise. I trust your father is well?"

"Yes, sir."

"Please give him my regards, and tell him that I am not a rioter."

"Already I have told him that."

Lance took his leave with some misgiving.

᎒§ 10

ON THE following day there was calm in the capital of the colony, but underneath were rage and fear. In a little ceremony in the Council House Berkeley gave full pardon to young Bacon. Hairy border burgesses watched and ground their teeth.

"God forgive you! I forgive you!" declared the Governor dramatically.

Colonel William Cole of the Council then remarked, "And all that were with him?"

"Yes, and all that were with him," replied the Governor. The growling in the Chamber became less pronounced at this.

Bacon was duly seated in the Council, much to the discontent of those who desired his voice among the House of Burgesses, the larger branch of the Assembly.

For a time during that tense day there was hope that harmony might be restored. The Governor anticipated the wishes of the House and sent in a message urging that they consider first the Indian war. It happened then that the first deliberation of the session was on Indian affairs. Here again the Governor played shrewd politics. The border party wanted the forts abolished and a mobile army authorized with Bacon as its general. The Berkeley faction nodded an ingratiating assent but insisted on a hearing of the case.

Yes, the forts were useless but what of their paid garrisons? Surely they should be incorporated in any frontier army. What of the friendly Indians? Were they to be slaughtered with the others? What of Sir Henry Chicheley? He was the ranking officer of the Crown and Berkeley's lieutenant. Should he serve under a radical barrister?

The new burgesses fretted and waited, in vain, for a chance to vote. The wise heads of the Governor's faction postponed action on the issues and talked of law and rules of procedure.

Sir Mathew Clayborne laughed at his son's impatience. "What would you have?" he asked. "Do you think the old Governor will surrender his prerogatives? Not at this session. Perhaps you will have to wait until the King sends us another governor."

"Wait until the Indians reach Clayborne Castle?" Lance replied.

Sir Mathew shrugged. "The Governor thinks the Indians have had enough. If he delays, perhaps . . . perhaps . . ."

"Yes," said Lance. "His beaver trade will not be ruined."

"What would you do," Sir Mathew said, "if you were Berkeley? Would you permit a gang of border thieves in leather breeks to order you about? I doubt if you would be gracious enough to compromise as he is doing. Let us not bother, Son. The old man knows precisely what to do. He will let the hotheads cool. He will organize a mobile force. In time the Indians will be quieted."

There was a knock on the door, and the servant, Cicero, announced a visitor, Alan Walker. Lance looked wryly at his puzzled father.

"Know you aught of this, my boy?" Sir Mathew asked.

Lance smiled somewhat bitterly and said, "Please keep your temper, Father, if you can. Remember that I want the maid!" He took his leave and fled the house.

Sir Mathew was as patient as a priest while Alan Walker sputtered his appeal. The fat old man was terrified. There had been a grave mistake, he said. There had been a change of mind. His daughter would be honored to become Lance Clayborne's bride. There had been a senseless lovers' quarrel, but the thing had been repaired. "Ha, Ha! You know, sir, how such quarrels come about!" said Walker.

Sir Mathew ground his teeth together. His fingers itched to grasp the lacy collar of the Gull Cove magistrate and throw him out of doors, but he abstained. This waddling, purse-proud cattle trader! This hanger-on of moneygrubbing Councillors! This ex-sailor with splayed feet, with stubby hands that never held a sword!

But Sir Mathew listened silently. Lance had said, *I want the maid*.

Alan Walker struggled on. "They quarreled, but I did not know of this when I was here before. The quarrel has run its silly course by now. I'm sure, sir, that she loves your boy, will have no other gallant no matter what we elders say. She has refused other suitors."

"She sent you here?" Sir Mathew asked.

Now Alan Walker stammered hard. He dared not say she had. "You see, Sir Mathew, I have interviewed the child and learned her h-heart."

"She sent you here?"

"I c-cannot say it, s-sir!"

"Then why this visit?"

Alan Walker's face was dewed with sweat. He tried in vain to shift his ground, to change the subject.

At last Sir Mathew got the truth. "So the Governor desires this match?"

"Indeed . . ."

"It is His Excellency's will?"

Walker bowed his head reluctantly.

"I see——" Sir Mathew pondered with ironic calm—"I see."

"She is devoted to your son, Sir Mathew! P-please be assured of that. Have you not heard him speak of her? Indeed——"

"Be silent, man!" Sir Mathew's rage had risen now in spite of his efforts at self-control. "You need not primp with me!" Then he asked, "Why come you here in groveling deference to Berkeley's demand? Do you think I give three groats for what *he* wants? Good God! If Lance is of a mind to marry your daughter, he will do it when it pleases him—and her—and both no doubt will join me in declaring that Sir William Berkeley be damned!"

Walker rose and fumbled for his hat. "My thanks, Sir Mathew!" he mumbled in great relief.

IX

Gallows Fruit

◦§ 1

THE new burgesses from the border knew less of state-craft than of Indians. At every turn in Jamestown they were outwitted by a minority of the Governor's men who never met an issue squarely.

In arguing Bacon's cause Crews described the campaign on the Roanoke River, and with rugged, stammering eloquence he told of the well-trained, little band of volunteers that now held the western savages at bay along the upper James.

In rebuttal the wily merchant members prompted Chicheley to ask Crews military questions. Sir Henry, rich with lore of European camps, loaded the debate with ponderous complexities. How many pounds of meat and maize per man? How much ammunition was needed for a ten-week expedition? Had Bacon considered cutting a wagon road? How did outpost parties handle problems of security? What of pike drill for those who could not be furnished better arms? What of cannon and entrenching tools? Could an army operating west of the freshes depend on supply by boat?

Crews replied that Bacon's band knew how to march and fight and use pack horses, that its hunters filled its commissary with meat.

"We have been talking not of a band but of an army," Sir Henry Chicheley replied.

"We do not need an army," Crews insisted. "We need a tough, small band that can move rapidly."

Sir Henry shrugged in supercilious disbelief.

Crews declared that the victory on the Roanoke had shaken the Indians throughout the colony, that but little force was needed to end the war. "They can evade all but a speedy band of woodsmen," he declared. "They must be pursued by small companies of fusiliers who will burn their villages, give them no rest day or night, harry them beyond the mountains."

Sir Henry presented estimates which indicated that ten thousand savages lurked between the falls and the nearest mountains. Crews listed the Indian towns and their warriors to show that there were fewer than a thousand scattered barbarians under arms.

The argument got nowhere, but as the days passed rumors flew like witches through the town. Bacon and all his party became heartsick and then angry and then impatient.

While men dallied in the Council Chamber and the House the savages were raiding on the border. While the western men clumsily assembled their arguments in the House of Burgesses Bacon, in the Council Chamber, likewise encountered dismaying obstacles.

To the unctuous and fatherly advice of the elder gentry, Bacon gave due respect; but his words, even when spoken calmly, enraged Parke the aristocrat and Beverley the ambitious.

"You speak rebellion!" roared Parke.

Bacon smiled. "Has this august Council come to such a pass that one cannot advocate the cause of simple public safety without being accused of rebellion?" Bacon asked.

When Parke subsided, sputtering, Bacon made another short speech. "Gentlemen, I'm a barrister, not a rioter. It happens that I live out in the forest and that there I have encountered problems foreign to you people here—problems that make the ownership of property, the possession of good reputation, yes, even the favors of a royal prince, matters of little importance. Out there, gentlemen, life itself, not property, is the stake. Do you really believe that we fight because of a cantankerous turbulence of spirit? Can you think that the men out there are all fur-chasing savages? I tell you the yeomen of the western marches are freedom-loving planters like yourselves. They have fought for life, not policy.

"Where did this trouble start, I ask? Here at Jamestown? No. It started when the savages began to kill our people out on the border. If discontent has spread since to the east, are we to blame? I know nothing of this stuff you call rebellion. Our sin has rested only on the preservation of our lives, and that the Governor graciously has forgiven.

"We ask only that an expedition which already exists be maintained in the field by proper legislative action. The trained band in the west wants no special favors. Its needs are simple. Given the simplest means it will accomplish its mission before midsummer and break the power of the savages for all time.

"You talk of armies. We require no army. You talk of mustering the militia again. We need no general muster. We have volunteers enough. You talk of vast supplies, of fleets, of pack trains, of cannon. That is utter foolishness. Give us a small measure of powder, shot and maize, and in two months we will give you a complete victory."

The Council sat in doleful indecision. They shared the Governor's fears of Bacon's band, but they would not admit it. They remembered Cromwell, too. In their dreams they saw hairy borderers marching eastward, plundering farms. They feared the new voters in the House of Burgesses across the hall. What of their privileges as members of the Council? Would the Bacon party take away the tax exemption of the Councillors and abolish monopolies and fees? Would they change the courts? Would they send petitions to the King?

Stubbornly the men of Berkeley's faction delayed action. Guilefully they let Bacon talk and talk. Outside on the village square Chicheley's new militia drilled, but the Council did nothing.

Bacon avoided the hotheads of the town. With a lawyer's patience he worked hard, but at last he realized that here he was defeated.

At the next Sabbath recess he asked the Governor for permission to visit his wife at Curle's Neck. The other Councillors had obtained leaves of absence, so the Governor approved the paper as a matter of routine. Within the hour Berkeley regretted his action and ordered the High Sheriff to stop Bacon. The Sheriff did not find him on the road, nor any trace of him.

The guardship was dispatched upriver with so much sail it almost tore out the mast. But Bacon was not on the river. Bacon had taken to the forest.

∻§ 2

SUCH is the contrariness of politics that Bacon's absence caused more difficulty than his presence ever had. At Lawrence's and in every tavern new rumors hatched like baby harpies. It was reported that Bacon had fled because his death had been plotted by the Governor, and this tale was given credence by the new anxieties of Berkeley's party. They admitted his arrest was sought.

More troopers galloped westward. Bacon was not at Curle's. Other secretive emissaries crossed the river and stole swiftly through the Surry forests toward Bacon's hidden camps.

The fever of dissension heightened. Farmers shook their callused fists and vowed that Berkeley had torn up the charter, defied the law, nullified the very purpose of the Assembly. A majority favored the reforms and prosecution of the Indian war. But Berkeley seemed determined to defeat the will of that majority.

Lance Clayborne remained at home. His father had a siege of gout which kept him in his chair, so Lance's aid was needed with the planting. There would be none on the western farm that year, for the Indians had raided almost to the Chickahominy. They were Monacans, tall, raw-meat-eating hunters from the foothills. In former days the tributary tribes had kept these raiders back; but now the friendly Indians were huddled in the swamps, bewildered by dark reports that the white men soon would wage a war among themselves.

Sir Mathew could not take calmly all the talk of civil war. He had seen such a war in England. He cursed both factions with military eloquence. "Madmen!" he roared. "Both Berkeley and Bacon are mad!"

Lance paced the hearth as restless as a bear. "Granted, Father. Meanwhile the Monacans have reached Kendall's. A small war party took four hogs there Thursday."

"Confound this foot! Have you issued extra ammunition to our hands?"

"Yes, Father."

Lance looked out the window. A thunderstorm was rolling downriver, and the sun, already low, was half obscured by outriding clouds. In the courtyard the trees, with their leaves fresh green, were very still.

"Confound this foot! Hold me, my lad, and I shall try again."

Lance turned to his father and helped him rise. Gingerly the old man put down his foot, stood firmly once, and then again.

"It's free of pain!" Sir Mathew cried triumphantly. "Look, lad." Throwing off the woolen wrappings, he pointed to his great toe. The swelling had subsided. "And now my boot. This talk of war has healed me."

Free now to visit Jamestown, Lance rode downriver to obtain news. At the ferry and at Thrift's ordinary near Green Spring there was news enough. The land was in a turmoil, for Bacon had returned to Jamestown! Bacon had returned to Jamestown with two hundred of his Indian fighters to demand a commission to make war upon the Indians!

Every peddler and every gossip along the way had tales to tell of this adventure. A thousand men had tried to join Bacon's column on the march. Women had thrust roses into the muzzles of his muskets. What of Sir Henry Chicheley's companies of guards? His force had melted away, and some of his men had cheered Bacon's column!

Early that morning Bacon's company, with drums beating "Parley," had moved to the Council House. Sir William Berkeley came out. His wattles were as red as any turkey cock's. He stood before the company of leather-stockinged Indian fighters.

"Here, here!" he cried and opened the front of his coat. " 'Fore God, a fair mark. Shoot!"

Bacon saluted and replied, "No, may it please Your Honor. It is not our intention to injure a hair of your head, nor any man's. We are come for a commission to save our lives from Indians, a commission which you have promised us so often. Now we shall have it before we go."

Sturdily the men stood in formation. A patrol was detached to watch the rear entrance of the building.

The Governor turned. Bacon followed him to the door, hand on his sword, eyes on the windows which by now were filled with the anxious faces of Councillors and burgesses.

Bacon said in a clear, cold voice, "You will sign my commission, sir, and I shall go and leave this town in peace."

Berkeley swore beneath his breath, whirled as though to draw his sword, then hesitated. "By God, you will, sir!" Bacon declared.

All morning the company remained in formation, muskets cocked. The burgesses did not have to act. They had no power to grant commissions from the Crown. The Council trembled. The Governor finally signed the papers.

Larger and larger grew the mob of spectators. From miles around they came.

The presence of Bacon's band desperately frightened the Governor's supporters and emboldened the liberal faction in the Assembly. Bills that for weeks had moldered in the hopper were snatched out and passed with hardly a dissenting vote because of Bacon's influence.

The crowds on the streets at Jamestown were strangely quiet that afternoon. It seemed as though the show of force had sobered everyone.

Rebellion! It was nothing else. Berkeley had been an obstruction through his diplomacy and guile. Bacon had swept away all obstacles with force.

There was a sentinel at Lawrence's. The inn had been taken over by the border company. Lance returned the soldier's salute and turned away.

At Dame Gaylord's tavern Lance blundered into a host of chattering women, wives of burgesses and officials. They asked him questions which he was too heartsick to answer, and then they tittered at his bewilderment.

"That Clayborne boy, is he a rebel, too?" one of the women asked.

Lance himself did not know. There was war against the Indians. He would fight the Indians. But this threat against the laws, this blow against the Crown . . . No wonder now that Berkeley had been fearful. He, better than some of Bacon's closest friends, had read that young man's mind, had understood the revolution that was brewing in the border counties. Lance tried to clear his mind with ale but did not succeed.

Dame Ballard, with a clucking coterie, descended on the table to talk about his father's gouty toe and poultry and of Eliza Bacon's baby. They thought that Bacon's soldiers were as romantic as Scottish bandits.

The ladies seemed amused at something, and while Lance stammered pleasantries as best he could Dame Ballard peeped over her shoulder at the stairs.

Thereupon Lance forgot all war and politics because a girl had appeared from the upper landing. For a moment Easter Walker glared with imperious displeasure at the little group. Then, as boldly as a mother hen, she drew Lance out onto the terrace.

"What are you doing here?" she asked.

He did not reply for a while. He stood and looked at her, and, vastly pleased by what he saw, he permitted his mind to stray while she peppered him with questions.

"Answer me!" she cried.

"I think you are very lovely," he said. "I am glad you came to town and yet—"

"You came with that rebel band?"

"—you should be at home. There are rude soldiers here."

"Soldiers! Rabble!"

"Not rabble now, my lovely. I have seen them in action more than once."

"You came with Bacon?"

He shrugged, and slowly shook his head. "Oh, no. All this is strange to me, but it seems as though this happened weeks ago. I am somewhat relieved, except for finding you and these other ladies here. These men are soldiers, yes. But they are almost as savage as the Indians. You all should be at home."

His eyes grew clearer now, and he observed that she was much disturbed and very angry though not with him. Several times she tried to speak; then she paused, fearing that tears might come. She tossed her hair back proudly, and when she looked away he gently tried to take her hand. She jerked away as though his touch were vile.

"They . . . they have . . ." Once more she tossed her head.

"They have done what?"

"Threatened my father with arrest!" she said.

He looked down at her, amazed.

"They say that he has profited too greatly from his stores of powdered meat. They say his contracts with the Crown have been outside the law. They have arrested others, too, and they have called the General Court. And now they are writing new laws which the House of Burgesses will pass before the week is out."

"Where is your father?"

She dashed her tears away. "He is at Councillor Parke's. Those rebels served him with a writ an hour ago."

"He was not imprisoned?"

"No."

He smiled wryly. "This *is* rebellion, isn't it? Your father!"

She frowned. "This is no joking matter."

He sobered instantly. "I know, my dear, it is not. But justice will be done, I'm sure of that. And justice or no justice, I am Bacon's friend as well as yours, and Bacon will not oppress your father no matter how much the mob may shout. You'll see." He moved to touch her, but she withdrew as though he were some frightful giant.

"I am afraid," she said. "My brain is full of bumblebees. I do not know you, Lance. To me you are an utter stranger. You have a different manner in this English garb. I don't know what it is. I——"

He laughed.

Usack would not have laughed, she thought.

He said, "If I had known you would be here, my sweet, I would have worn forest clothes, you may be sure. I'll wear them day and night henceforth. Then will you wed me and go west?"

"I'll never, never wed you, Lance."

"You will be sorry when I'm hanged," he teased.

"You should not joke of either marriage or the noose," she said.

"Which shall it be? Have you interceded with Sir William?"

She started to shake her head; then she paused and looked away. Slowly color came and flamed across her throat, cheeks and forehead. "You have no right to ask me that," she said.

"I have at least a minor interest in the matter," he replied. "As I've said before I much prefer the parson's matrimonial halter to any that the Governor's hangmen can provide. I still can overlook the politics. I see the girl and nothing, nothing else."

"I would not want a dog to hang."

He laughed. "I thank you, darling, for your pity." Then suddenly he became serious. He took her hand. "You have not fooled me, sweet, for all the rose dust in my eyes. I've hurt you and I'm sorry. I'll make you love me somehow. You love Usack. You hate Clayborne, the man who will hang unless you marry him. I don't know which man I am. I want to marry you of course, but now, like you, I am confused. Perhaps I am a rebel. Perhaps you'd never change me. If I'm to hang it would be best, I suppose, to hang as a bachelor."

She shuddered at his joke and failed to see the bitterness therein.

As his farewell he said, "I love you. I shall be only half alive until I hang, or until I see you again."

She said nothing.

🙦 3

SIR MATHEW, back from his ride around the fields, found Lance sitting on the grass beneath a walnut tree with misery in his eyes.

"What now, my forest lion?" asked his father. "Have you brought bad news from Jamestown?"

Lance told him of the lawlessness that came with Bacon's band, of the Assembly's bold moves against the Council, of the Governor's order that he stay at home.

Sir Mathew shook his white head impatiently. "O Tempora!" he sighed. "Damme, boy, I wish old Berkeley and young Bacon were both in hell! They've brewed a pot of pepper stew for fair!"

"The issue is an Indian war."

"Yes, and now there are many other issues. My foremen all are wild Baconians. Even Gale will ride with him. And Peo too—your Peo—is one of Bacon's roundheads. Messengers have come with every hour to stir our plantation men into furious talk and idleness. By God! We've got to watch the crop. We can't have Bacon making bandits of our men!"

"The Indians can make all of us wanderers," said Lance.

Sir Mathew grunted with disgust. "Indians! Faugh! The savages are down for good. For that I give your wild friend full credit. He treated them so roughly on the Roanoke that they'll never rise again. You know that as well as I. Bacon may march this time against the Monacan confederacy, but the Monacans will not stand and fight him. They'll flee beyond the mountains. The Indian issue has been succeeded by another far more dangerous. It is Berkeley or Bacon now."

"Yes," Lance said slowly. "I'm afraid it is Berkeley or Bacon."

"The King must settle this."

"I hope he can."

Sir Mathew reflectively poked holes in a mole burrow with his walking staff. "How would you like to visit London, boy?"

"I? To London?"

"Yes, you. Someone must take these matters to Whitehall, so why not you?" Sir Mathew avoided his son's eyes and stared out over the wide reach of the river.

Lance watched his father's face closely for a moment before he spoke. "Not I, sir."

"And why not? His Majesty will remember you and surely the Queen will. You were her darling baby once. Remember? She strapped you to a board to keep your bones straight. And she tried to make you a papist."

Lance frowned, paying no attention to his father's humor.

The old man spoke again. "You know Bacon, you are one of Berkeley's couriers, you are the son of an old Cavalier who fought at Naseby. Who could be a better ambassador of peace?"

"You think," said Lance, "you really think, that there will be fighting here . . . among Virginians?"

"I said no such thing."

"You think so, Father. You would send me away at such a time to . . . to save me—to save me from choosing my part in what may be a civil war?"

"Now, now! You're saying things I did not say, my boy. If you settle this affair in London there can be no trouble. If you do not go, there may be serious consequences. What, now?"

"No," said Lance with emphasis. "If there is trouble, I want to be here with you."

"You would go with Bacon's rabble," Sir Mathew said bitterly.

"Not against the King, sir."

The old knight poked more holes in the mole burrow at his feet. At last he said, "You do not think so now. But what will happen, pray? Can Bacon oppose a royal deputy without opposing royal power? Berkeley already has sent for ships and soldiers. But if you should see the King and tell him of the Navigation Acts, the Indian war, the beaver trade, and the troubles of our farmers, he could settle this trouble without recourse to ships and soldiers. Don't you see?"

"The Governor would never commission me as a courier to the King. He talks of hanging me and half the colony."

"The King would heed the message you bring from Virginia. He would give it more weight than any sent him by Berkeley, or his stuffy Council, or any of Bacon's faction. You have a full right to make the voyage to England. And I know King Charles, my boy. He would be glad to see you and so would Her Majesty, the Queen."

Lance squirmed, ill at ease. He had been taken by surprise. He could give no answer to his father. Here was a mission worthy of an earl—one that would take all the wits he had, one that might save Virginia from civil war.

He looked up at his father and said, "But, Father, why give such a task to me when you could do it better?"

"A long voyage would kill me, son. Moreover, you know the facts,

I do not. You know Bacon, I do not. You know Berkeley and his coterie. I am but a muddleheaded farmer who must stay here and watch our property." Sir Mathew sighed. "I'd like nothing better than to get another glimpse of the moors of Kent before I die. But this cannot be." He clenched his gnarled hands. "And—God help me!—I would be intemperate of words in my message to the King. We have an Eden here, my boy, a land too fair for factions such as now are tearing it apart. I despise the very name of Bacon; and for Berkeley and his coterie, I have even less respect. I would speak my mind and make matters worse, and in my ignorance of these Virginians I would confuse instead of help the King. You must go. There is a merchant sailor, Christopher Eveling, at Lower Norfolk. He has two ships each June. He is shipping cypress lumber to Plymouth."

That night Lance and his father burned many candles while they made plans.

4

LANCE had no intention of informing Easter Walker of his mission; but his resolution failed when he called at Gull Cove Plantation to say farewell.

She was aloof and cold. Her hand gave no response at all when she received him. She treated him as a casual acquaintance entitled to formal hospitality and nothing more. They spoke of the weather and of other minor matters for a while—of Lady Berkeley's new coach and of the latest, incredibly large flight of wild pigeons from the south.

He said, "I have obeyed you, Mistress Easter."

At this she shrugged. "I do not remember giving you injunctions," she replied.

"Then I have obeyed the Governor. I have remained at home. But I am puzzled. I hear His Excellency has gone to Gloucester. Is that true?"

She nodded and said somewhat bitterly, "Perhaps he is no longer Governor."

"Does he think so?"

"The new and unshaved Assembly is in full control. It is levying troops, my father says. It is impressing horses and supplies. But you know this. You are in the confidence of these rebels."

"Not I, my sweet. I am but a farmer boy these days."

"There is talk that Bacon intends to make you a captain."

"I have not heard of that," he said, surprised.

"You are on his list of men to be commissioned and so are others, some of whom have never had commissions from the Crown—men who have been only common soldiers."

"Did the Governor sign them?"

"Under duress."

Lance smiled. "He says that?"

"Oh, no. But now there is talk of nullifying all of Bacon's laws. Such headstrong procedure cannot be permitted. What has happened in the Indian war? Why does he not march? Why do his ruffians stay in Jamestown?"

Lance said nothing for a while. He leaned back in the stiff porch chair until it creaked and looked over the black pines toward the retreating sun. In the distance a calving cow was bellowing. Hounds bayed in the meadow near the creek where Edward Walker was hunting. In London he would miss such sounds, Lance thought. In London he would miss this lovely, exasperating girl. Much could happen during a voyage like that.

Suddenly he said, "I came to bid you farewell for a time. I must go away."

She looked over at him curiously. "You are going west in spite of the Governor's command?"

"He did not forbid a . . . voyage."

"A voyage?" She was startled.

"Yes, my dear, a voyage. For weeks and months you will not be bothered by my presence."

"You are going to London?"

"Yes, to London."

She stood, her hands upon her breast, her great eyes staring at him fearfully. "But . . . but——"

"I go to London with a message from my father to the King. Sir Mathew wearies of this foolishness at Jamestown. He wants King Charles to settle it."

"But why send *you* away?"

"You care?"

"I . . . there are pirates, Usack. There's peril on the sea."

"But you cared nothing about pirates, sweet, when you made the voyage. I'll return."

"I know, but . . ." She stamped her foot. "You men with your affairs! It makes me tired. Why should you go away? Why should you go to London?"

He smiled. "My father says that it may save my neck and many others. You would not have me hanged?"

Her eyes opened wide. There was a pause. "Perhaps, then, it is well for you to go," she said.

⊸§ 5

SIR MATHEW's forecast of events proved sound throughout the preparations for Lance's eastern voyage. Disorders flourished, and, in spite of the discipline in Bacon's camp, they all were blamed on the western militiamen. Rude mobs at Jamestown threw mud at the public hangman, and on one occasion they stoned the Governor's coach. Members of the Council began to employ personal bodyguards.

One day the Governor and all of his suite took a ship and disappeared. It was discovered that he had gone to Gloucester and there had tried to raise a trained band to drive Bacon's westerners out of Jamestown.

Bacon moved his command to Middle Plantation so he might watch both the York and the James rivers.

The Governor's effort to raise troops failed. From Gloucester he went across Chesapeake Bay to the Accomack peninsula. His Council joined him there at Arlington Plantation, the seat of Colonel Custis. He commissioned Custis a major general in order to win the loyalty of the Accomack and Northampton militia.

Rumors were flying like vampire bats by now. The Governor was going to England. No, he was too bold a man to run away from Bacon and his band. But the Governor had sent messengers to the King. Two thousand soldiers were coming from England to enforce Berkeley's decrees and to dissolve the unruly House of Burgesses. Was it rebellion? Was the House of Burgesses, the parliament of Virginia, in revolt against a Governor; or was it the opposite, the Governor in revolt against the Virginia parliament? If there was rebellion who was the rebel, Berkeley or Bacon?

Sir Henry Chicheley, the Lieutenant Governor, on his way from Middlesex to join Sir William, was arrested and held under parole in Bacon's camp. The guardship *Rebecca* was in Bacon's hands under the command of the popular William Carver, who had been once the Governor's High Sheriff. Berkeley had other ships, some stronger in guns than the *Rebecca*. Bacon was sending messages to the Governor, demanding in the name of the House of Burgesses that Berkeley return to his post in the Council Chamber at Jamestown.

⊸§ 6

SIR MATHEW insisted that Lance take the sloop to join Eveling's ship off Lower Norfolk. A barge voyage would never do now that the summer storms blew nearly every afternoon. The boy departed, confident that he would return before the snows. His father stood on the path above the wharf until the sloop was far out in the river. Twice Sir Mathew waved with his walnut staff.

A southwest breeze promised Lance an early arrival at his destination, but, in spite of his spanking progress down the broad channel of the James, Lance was restless. Already his thoughts were wandering in distant London.

The Negro, Cato, coiled the deck lines, sluiced muddy footprints from the counter, adjusted the spare sail over the baggage on the deck. Lance paid no attention to the servant's mumbled chantey.

What should he tell the King? The truth and nothing else, his father had said. What was the truth? There was an old and frightened Governor, a man who had been made proud and greedy by an unwise marriage to a young, ambitious widow. There was a stubborn, radical Cambridge lawyer with a host of bitter followers. Tell him that? Tell His Majesty of the beaverskins, of the license fees and levies which had made Berkeley's favorites rich? Tell him of an Assembly long delayed, of cruel punishment of the poor, of land-grabbing and of bribes? Or tell him instead of reckless bordermen who cared little for law and little more for life itself? Should he appeal to royal fairness or to royal dread of force?

It might be well, perhaps, to tell the king much about Virginia's great promise as a daughter of the Crown. Here was Britain's hope for an empire greater than that of Spain. This colony of Virginia was larger than England. It was fairer and richer too, because of its population of sturdy yeomen. What of the wilderness? Lance could tell him much about its mysteries. There the soil was richer than gold. On the clean land beyond the tidal flow there was no fever. Great cities would be built to house the wealth from the land. . . .

The little sloop flew past Jamestown like a seabound gull, and Lance gazed idly toward the almost barren wharves. Here there could never be a city amid the foul swamps and fouler dwelling places, Lance thought.

Cato put the helm to starboard past Hog Island, watching the course of a two-master that had come into view beyond South Point. The Negro grunted curiously, for the schooner had four guns in sight and a dozen men or more upon her cluttered deck.

Lance wondered also at this vessel which was a stranger to the river; but when Cato changed course again to give the other craft more leeway Lance took the tiller and corrected him.

"You know that schooner, Cato?"

"No, sah!"

"Is it Kendall's?"

"No, sah."

"Keep on this course."

The Negro frowned and obeyed.

And Lance too soon felt on his neck rising hackles of anxiety. The other vessel changed course, took on sail and bore swiftly across the reach to intercept them. Could that weather-stained craft be one of Berkeley's guardships? If so, why was its captain curious? Any of the Governor's men could identify the Clayborne sloop. What did the fellow want?

Steadily the schooner came. The men aboard her watched the sloop with more than ordinary interest. Lance swore beneath his breath. Arrest? Was Berkeley arresting him? Would the old fool do *that*?

The crew of the two-master now moved quickly, purposefully, acting on sharp command. A match was lighted. Lance saw it smoking near the forward starboard gun. The man waved the match staff toward the sloop. The sailor near the wheel cupped his hands and shouted, "Heave to!"

Lance flushed angrily.

"Heave to, sir!" The voice was louder now.

The man with the linstock waved it around his head to keep the spark alight.

Lance nodded to Cato. The Negro brought the sloop around until the sails flapped, empty; and then they waited.

"In the Governor's name!" the seaman on the schooner shouted.

For a moment Lance recklessly considered flight. With an effort he controlled his rage. "Who is the master of that tub?" he called.

There was no reply. The helmsman skillfully brought the schooner alongside to windward. A man tossed Cato a line.

Lance went aboard, staring at the hard-faced men before him. "The master!" he cried. "Where is the master who stops travelers here?"

He heard a voice behind him now say, "A warrant, sir, a royal warrant signed by His Excellency, William Berkeley."

Lance turned and stared.

At the companion rail stood a red-cloaked figure in a beaver hat, a figure with a heavy, graying beard, a man whose bow was foxlike. His head moved, but his eyes—red, crafty eyes—stayed still.

Impetuously Lance started to speak but stopped and stood silently in stunned amazement.

"Captain Forke, sir, at your service." The bandy-legged figure bobbed a cautious, watchful bow.

"Forke!"

"Aye, sir. Well met!" The man shrugged in deprecation and spread his jeweled hands. "I had no choice. I do His Excellency's bidding."

Lance's hand was on his sword, but some instinct kept him sane. Three armed sailors were within two paces of him. The bearded man who faced him wore a pistol at his side. Forke possibly would like to have him fight. That paper in Forke's belt actually might be the Governor's warrant.

Forke spoke again. "Well met!" said he. "I see you are the younger Clayborne."

Lance said nothing. He had faced death before, but nothing in his experience had been so grim as the unctuous figure there before him.

Forke was sinisterly debonair as he bowed again. "Pray join me in the cabin, sir," he said. The request was half a query, as though the man expected Lance to draw his sword.

The prisoner had no such thought. His senses had recovered quickly from the surprise and now were keen. Sailors on either side of him bore fusils which were freshly primed and cocked. Another sailor at the poop-deck rail had an arquebus which was almost as heavy as a boat swivel. Forke wore a pistol in his sash. It was defensive armament, protection against the Clayborne temper, Lance decided. They did not mean to kill—yet. When Lance entered the cabin and faced his ancient enemy, Jesús Forke, his eyes became completely blank, as though he were playing a game of cards.

Forke stared a moment, studying the youth with interest. Lance's handsome face resembled that of Walter Clayborne, the man whom he had killed years before. Lance's body was Sir Mathew's—a lean and mighty soldier's frame. But the boy's legs were longer, not bowed from riding, and his face reflected a more alert intelligence and fewer passions.

"You'll have a seat?" Forke said.

Lance relaxed on a bench, holding his tongue in check.

Forke smoothed the warrant before him on the table, fingered the ribbon of the seal, reversed it so that Lance might read the charge. The clerk had written with a flourish the words, *On Suspicion of High Treason.*

Lance smiled derisively and said, "High treason! Who accuses me?"

"It says, 'on information.' "

"Whose information?"

Forke shrugged. "I am but an agent, sir. These are troubled times. I was there at Arlington landing on the Eastern Shore. I had my two-master there, and so I was deputized to serve the paper. That is all. It was with great regret I had to act against you."

Despite himself, Lance winced. "You fled back to Carolina?"

"I . . . fled? I think you do not understand."

"I understand."

A shadow of malignant annoyance passed over Forke's reddened eyes, but in a moment a bland smile replaced it. "We shall not argue, sir. You and your father chose me for an enemy. It was not my doing.

But that's beside the point. You and I must go across the bay to Arlington Plantation where you will answer to the Governor. Then I shall go my way, and perhaps you will return to yours."

"Perhaps?"

"Perhaps. Now to business. This is a legal arrest, Master Clayborne. May I have your parole?"

"Yes."

"And that of your servingman?"

Out on the deck there was a scuffling sound, followed by a mighty splash. A man thrust his head into the cabin. "The black man, sir. Shall we shoot?"

Forke cursed and went out. Lance followed. Cato was swimming strongly with the ebb tide, his head bobbing thirty yards alee. The sailor on the poop had a fusil ready.

"Fire!" Forke commanded.

It seemed as though Cato heard the command. As the bullet sped toward him his head went under water like an otter's. Nor could those on shipboard see him for a while. There were scattered pistol shots and curses, but by now Cato was out of range. He was deep in the grassy shallows of the Surry shore. No boat could follow him.

Lance breathed a sigh. He must play for time and for opportunity. The Governor had learned about his trip. The Governor would tolerate no messages to the King except his own. Suspicion of high treason! Was it high treason, then, to visit London?

Lance abandoned thought of argument with Forke. That would accomplish nothing. Beneath lowered lids Lance watched him and said nothing. Here was the enemy of his house, the man whose villainy had filled his boyhood with hate, the assassin of his uncle. This long-faced seaman, this foppish scoundrel with a Spanish given name, this beach rat from the Indies who had been dignified by Berkeley beyond his worth!

Lance was motionless in spite of his itching sword arm. He remained as stolid as a captive Indian while Forke fluttered about the roundhouse like a fowl.

"We shall go to Arlington," said Forke. "His Excellency and the General Court are there. I hear that Bacon and his band have marched—"

Lance did not reply.

"—westward against the Indians," Forke continued. "Friendly as well as hostile tribes are fleeing from his path. His band is making war on the Indians of every tribe including the tributary tribes."

He handed Lance a pipe and struck a spark to light it. His prisoner accepted with a nod.

"Late yesterday," Forke said, "the Governor recaptured the *Rebecca*, his guardship. Bacon sent Carver and Bland to arrest the Governor. Sir William again has turned the tables."

The prisoner said nothing.

"Carver, captain of the *Rebecca*, has been sentenced to the gallows by a court-martial. He will hang today, I think. Others, too, will hang."

Lance made no sign. Forke studied him curiously. It was obvious that this elegantly clad young man was building schemes. Why was he as quiet as a heathen image? Was he frightened, stunned? There was no evidence on his handsome face. Was he impatient or angry? Of course . . . and yet . . .

In numbers of years Lance Clayborne still was but a boy. In fact, however, he was much more, for his very presence made cold spots come between his adversary's shoulder blades. Berkeley, no doubt, would hang this buck. If he were not hanged, some other convenience of fate must be arranged. This silent boy was dangerous, far more so than his stupid soldier-father.

Lance, behind his masklike expression, meanwhile was calculating time and space. Cato had landed on the Surry shore, a full forty miles from Clayborne Castle. The Negro would waste no time. He would find a canoe at dark and make his way upriver with the tide. Sir Mathew then would ride to Jamestown, seek news and aid of those who there remained, would learn that Berkeley had moved to Arlington in Northampton County across the bay. Then the old man would find a sloop and go to Arlington as quickly as he could. Within two days, at most, he would be knocking at the Governor's door and asking why his son had been arrested.

Sir William would not hang both Claybornes; that was certain. Even if the Governor were insane enough to murder Bland and Carver, he would hesitate to execute a friend of Charles II. Lance reasoned that he was now a hostage and that later he might be killed by some obscure arrangement. But for Berkeley to kill his father would be far too hazardous a move.

Forke still moved restlessly about the cabin. The vessel was creaking under heavy sail. "Since I have your parole," Forke said, "you may have the freedom of the deck."

Lance nodded.

"As I said, we shall go to Arlington to see the Governor."

"Very well."

Lance had no more words with his captor.

The ship's sails were patched and stained; most of its cordage was spliced in many places. There was a shot scar on the deck abaft the foremast and several unsanded blots on the deck. The vessel stank of excrement and sweat, as though it lately had had slaves aboard. Four guns were mounted to a side—guns of varied patterns.

Most of the men were surly beasts who dropped their eyes as Lance approached. Like a pirate craft, the vessel was overmanned. Lance watched the wooded shore awhile. The shock of the encounter with his enemy had chilled him past help from the warm breeze; but as he stood on deck his tightened heart relaxed, and his lungs began to breath away his fearful humor. Now was no time for haste or rage or foolish talk. Death might be his companion on this little voyage.

But he was still alive. Forke had not cut his throat immediately. Perhaps Forke did have orders from the Governor. Perhaps he would reach Arlington Plantation. Lance smiled grimly. The course was east—downriver—and the quartermaster held the middle of the stream where the flooding tide was strongest. It was plain that the steersman was unfamiliar with these waters.

To the west a towering cloud was gathering, and the northeast wind was fresh. As Lance approached the steersman nodded toward the thunderhead. "We'll have a blow, sir," the sailor said.

"Yes," said Lance.

The helmsman had the accent of Cornwall, and he was garrulous. That northeast breeze could mean a week of rain, and it was troublesome. They would make two knots perhaps on the starboard tack; then they would come about beyond the sand bar which marked the entrance of a creek. What was the creek? There was no chart. Oyster Creek? Oh, yes. The gentleman knew these waters well? Confound these shores with all their sunken cypress trees. Did His Honor know that sandspit where the fish were jumping?

Lance knew the spit. He nodded and his eyes turned toward the clearer water to the north. The quartermaster followed the direction of Lance's eyes and changed his course three points, heading the vessel toward clearer water. As they passed the creek mouth Lance stared southward; and once more the quartermaster slightly changed his course, conforming to the young man's line of sight. Lance knew the channel well, and the sailor sensed this knowledge. Without conscious directions from his passenger, the man had used him as the pilot.

The channel angled sharply from the mouth of Oyster Creek. It was wide enough for half a navy if one knew the way; but if one held too long upon the starboard tack . . . Lance said nothing. By now perhaps old Cato had a boat. He would waste no time. The wind and tide would help him up the stream. If this voyage Lance was on could be delayed a bit . . . Lance glanced at a mighty wall of rain that now swept from the thundercloud behind them. It was a scant league off, he judged. Gusts shook the vessel, but the sails still bellied steadily on the starboard tack.

The steersman watched Lance's eyes as they again looked at the channel water ahead. At least the steersman believed that Lance was watching the channel.

The river now was very wide and this meant shoals. Mud boiled in the vessel's wake. Lance half smiled. Again the nervous steersman followed the young man's steady eyes, and then he shifted course. This time as Lance had planned disaster struck. There was a jolt, a sharp report as the mainsheet snapped and a billowing cloud of canvas tumbled to the deck. The vessel shuddered to a crashing, grating stop—fast aground.

The helmsman swore. Forke's voice rose in an angry scream. Men hurried to the bits.

Lance looked ruefully at the confusion and shrugged his shoulders. Six men could bear witness that he had spoken not a word; yet his eyes had grounded the vessel as deftly as if he had been the helmsman. So far, so good. Four hours at least would pass before the tide would float it off the buried cypress branches. Four hours' delay would help. By then the storm and darkness would be upon them.

292 The Forest Cavalier

Lance pulled his cloak around him. The Cornishman looked up at him with comical reproach.

It was late afternoon of the following day, amid the murk of a northeast storm, when Forke's battered ship and the captured Clayborne sloop anchored off Plantation Creek beside a silent vessel whose swaying lanterns were alight.

Forke, his red finery bedraggled by the driving rain, tried to conceal a heightening nervousness as the boat brought them across a shallow bar and up to a landing which was half hidden by great pine trees. A sailor-sentinel at the wharf gave them a reluctant salute as they landed.

They proceeded along a sandy trail for a hundred yards to a clearing. Here Forke paused and looked for a moment at the lad beside him. Lance had seen the gibbet. Near the edge of the wood, with scud whipping past its skeletal uprights, the scaffold stood. Its dead fruit was swaying and twisting in the mist.

"Carver," said Forke. "And soon there will be others."

Lance Clayborne's soul was hot with rage, but not a flicker of emotion rewarded his tormentor. The young man looked upon the gibbet calmly and shook the water from his hat.

"A good seaman, that Carver," Forke said. "As you no doubt recall, he brought you to Virginia in '65."

As Forke chattered Lance fought for self-control. He marveled that Berkeley could have dared to commit an atrocity like this. Carver, the captain whose gallantry in the Dutch war had been so conspicuous and who had been named High Sheriff after that, hanging like a felon because he was a friend of Bacon! It was monstrous! Unbelievable! Lance looked closely and identified the empurpled face of his dead friend.

"A firm hand and the scaffold," Forke was saying. "The day for compromise has ended. Berkeley has decided not to tolerate sedition. All the ringleaders will hang."

Lance furiously suppressed the anger and fear which should have come. Berkeley, that senile fool! That woman-ridden ass! That doddering old blunderer now had stooped to murder! It was hard to believe, but here was the awful evidence. It was a good thing that his voyage had been deferred. The King would act without petition when he heard of this!

Forke was in a better humor as they proceeded to the group of plantation buildings beyond the clearing. He continued talking. "Carver came to invite the Governor into . . . er . . . custody at the Jamestown gaol," said Forke. "Carver and Bland were too polite, and so they lost their ship *Rebecca* to Captain Latimer and his lads. Too bad! His Excellency will return, but to the palace, not to the gaol."

Lance made no reply.

The sentinels who were guarding the plantation house halted them; then they let them pass into the mosquito-ridden gloom of the hall-way. In the main room was Berkeley, a field sword on his lap, drying his boots before a little fire.

"This is Forke, Your Excellency," one of Berkeley's men announced.

"Aye, Forke! Come in."

"And with me is the Clayborne lad," answered Forke.

"Clayborne?" the Governor said, staring and frowning. "Ah, yes. The Clayborne lad. Come in. I'm glad to see you, Clayborne. Very, very glad to see you!"

Lance bowed. The rain water from his hat traced a rivulet along the puncheon floor. "At your service, sir," Lance said.

"Indeed!" The Governor sought to stare him down, with scant success. Without insolence Lance blankly returned Sir William's stabbing glance. Berkeley slapped a mosquito, which had bored through his breeches at the knee, and said, "You were arrested, Clayborne, because you disobeyed me."

"I'm sorry, sir. I misunderstood. My orders were not to go west. I was upon the river, sir, and sailing eastward."

"Aye, too far eastward. Who gave you warrant to depart this colony?"

"Do gentlemen require permission, sir, to go out on the river?"

"They require port clearance before they take a voyage to England."

"Clearance had been arranged with Captain Eveling, sir. The law is plain." Lance had decided in cold blood to protest. It was expected of him. To do otherwise would arouse suspicion.

"With Your Excellency's permission," Lance continued without pause, "I must object to this arrest. The warrant shown me by this deputy of yours alleged that I had committed some act of high treason. I am guilty of no such offense. I am guilty of no breach of law, no breach of trust, no breach of peace. I demand to be released at once."

The Governor pursed his lips and, with an ironic wink at Captain Forke, replied, "So you do?"

"I do."

"Then you have not heard of the rebellion?"

"Rebellion, sir?"

"Just so. There now is martial law throughout this colony, and I am the commander, the deputy of the Crown. You have your sword, and so I presume Forke has your parole. You will remain here under arrest until your case is settled by a court."

"What case, Your Excellency?"

Berkeley smiled sourly. "You ask me that, my boy? You know your heart, and yet you ask me that? Do you take me for a fool? Damn these mosquitoes!" He slapped his knee.

That night, seated on his maize-husk bed, Lance reflected bitterly on the ways of womankind and on his plight. He had Easter Walker to thank for this. She doubtless had told Frances Berkeley of his father's plan to send a message to the King. Perdition! She had not only betrayed him into the hands of the jealous Governor but also into those of his family's bitterest enemy.

Sweet maid! If he lived a thousand years, he never again would trust a woman. Should he escape a place beside William Carver on Berkeley's gibbet, he would go west, and he would go alone. He would leave the stinking eastern plantations forever.

Carver, hanging like a thief! If Carver deserved death, then many another would die by the Governor's hand. That would mean rebellion indeed. Men would fight to stop this anarchy.

⟨§ 7

ALL night the rain beat down on the shingled roof above his cot. He was aroused by every creak in the loose timbers of the house. Outside he could hear guards and horses. In the distance were sounds from the anchorage—the rattle of a block, the sound of oars.

His enemy, Jesús Forke, had been afraid to cut his throat. Cato had escaped to inform his father about this imprisonment. There was hope.

For a week Lance was an unwilling and all but unnoticed guest at Berkeley's busy armed camp at Arlington Plantation. Forke's two-master disappeared. The pirate had been sent up the James in search of Tam MacFarlane. Lance breathed somewhat easier in the absence of his enemy.

Others in Berkeley's entourage—friends of former days—were courteous to him. Thomas Ludwell, Colonel Philip Ludwell's brother, was there. He was sardonic, certain of himself—as always—and undaunted by the excitement and confusion. Peter Knight, who had been in command at Berkeley's Rappahannock fort, was captain of the Governor's guard. Noll Wiggins, of Nansemond, was there also, as was Robert Beverley. Beverley teased him, calling him a truant; and so did Wiggins, a hairy farmer whom Lance had known since his first year at Clayborne Castle.

It was significant that none referred to the gibbet and its burden. They had not actively opposed the murder of Carver, and they were not well informed of the confused situation precipitated by the Governor's abandonment of his capital. These men behaved like the courtiers of a tyrant.

Lance learned that Bacon, prior to his march westward, had sent Carver and Bland to the Eastern Shore for a parley with the Governor. Bland had remained on board the vessel while Carver undertook the mission of ambassador. There had been a dinner at Arlington that night. Sir William had never been more slyly gracious. Carver had taken too much wine and had believed too much. The next day Bland, who was on the *Rebecca* in the bay, believing Carver had made peace, let down his guard and lost his ship to Berkeley's seamen.

Slowly Lance was able to piece together other bits of news. Bacon had sought to delay the sailing of Christopher Eveling's vessel, the ship on which Lance's passage had been booked. This had failed. Eveling had sailed with Berkeley's letter to the King but with no word of Bacon's cause. The Governor alone would report the situation to the King. The King would never question Eveling or any lesser man. He would read the Governor's dispatches and accept them as the truth.

The generous treatment accorded Lance relieved some of the young man's fears of Forke. It was clear that to most of the gentlemen at Arlington Forke now was of little consequence. The Governor needed ships and men and so had called this seaman from the south. A pirate? Most coastal merchantmen were suspect anyway. In times like these a ship was worth its weight in treasure, even if its color locker contained red flags. They understood that Forke had been of service to the Governor in the past. Some remembered vaguely the captain's previous residence in Jamestown and recalled his feud with Mathew Clayborne. What of that?

But Lance realized full well the menace of the pirate captain's presence in the colony. Each day he spent at Arlington increased his danger from this man. It was time for him to go, if go he could.

Lance went up to his bedchamber. His baggage had been searched inside and out. Even the linings had been probed. He smiled. Little they found, he knew, for there was not a word of Bacon in his papers, not a hint of any disturbance in the colony. He took off his silken breeches and changed to a suit of heavy woolen stuff. Into his pockets he put a sailor's folding knife, his flint and steel and tinder, a needle and finally a small pistol. Then buckling on his sword, he left the room.

He sought out the Governor. His Excellency was engaged. A ship was being loaded for a voyage back to Jamestown. Along with two other smaller vessels the entire party was returning soon to the capital. Bacon's band had marched westward. It no longer threatened Jamestown. There was much to be done. The Governor had no time for him.

Lance went to Captain Peter Knight, who was foot-drilling troopers in the pasture. Knight could not see him. Philip Ludwell? Colonel Ludwell was not engaged. Lance found him at the stables supervising the mending of a broken saddle fork.

As Lance approached Ludwell looked around him as though he feared eavesdroppers. He then nodded a signal for Lance to accompany him over to the well house. There they sat for a time exchanging inconsequential family news. Ludwell had arrived the night before from Kickotan on the mainland. With Captain Latimer, he had helped in the capture of Bland and the guardship a week before. Ludwell was now Berkeley's most trusted officer among the members of the Council.

"How now, boy?" Ludwell said at last. "Do you go with us to Jamestown?"

"I do not know, sir. I am a prisoner."

"A prisoner?" Ludwell was thoughtful for a moment, and then he said in a low voice, "I saw your father yesterday at Kickotan."

Lance said nothing.

"He sought passage to this plantation. I advised him to return to Clayborne Castle."

There was another pause. Ludwell took off his large, feathered hat and wiped his brow. "Sir Mathew is very angry," Ludwell continued. "It is best he not come here. I assured him of your safety, lad, and told him that in time you would be freed."

"I am accused of treason," Lance remarked.

"On warrant only, boy. No indictment has been drawn."

Lance started to inquire if Carver had been indicted, but he held his peace.

"No indictment will be drawn," Ludwell continued.

Lance said slowly, "You understand, sir, that the sailor who arrested me is a blood enemy of my house?"

Ludwell waved his hand. "Oh, yes, I understand. He asked the privilege of intercepting you. The Governor warned him not to harm a single hair, and he obeyed. He did not even take your sword."

"Yet the Governor hanged Carver!"

Ludwell shrugged. "Carver was accused of mutiny, my boy, and given summary treatment. No gentleman would be treated so. Carver was a rude sea captain. The law must govern."

"Military law?"

"Civil law must govern cases such as yours." For a while Ludwell was silent.

"I then request a hearing now," said Lance. "You are a magistrate under civil law. Or if military law must govern, I appeal to you as an officer, a colonel of the Crown. Let's have it over so I can return; or, if you will, so I can hang with Carver in the pines."

Ludwell shuddered. "I shall see Sir William about your case," he said.

"Now?"

"Now. Before Captain Forke returns."

"My thanks, sir."

"If Forke should hang a gentleman . . ." Ludwell rose, put on his hat and frowned. "Listen, Master Clayborne, listen well. This is a grievous situation. This madness must be checked somehow. If we should hang another man, we may have much trouble. Besides, Sir Henry Chicheley is a prisoner of Bacon."

"Indeed?" Lance closely watched Ludwell's face. Then he said, "Sir, if you can see His Excellency, pray tell him this: At noon I shall surrender my parole. If he desires to hold me in arrest, he must confine me as he did Bland and all the others from the guardship."

Ludwell was shocked.

"Tell him that," Lance said. "Tell him that I must be given hearing or must be locked up! There is a quorum of the General Court in camp. I have counted the Councillors."

Ludwell moved with heavy steps up the path to the plantation house.

Lance looked at the sun. It was scarce two hours until noon. He walked across the clearing and looked over toward the creek. The Clayborne sloop still lay tied to the pier. In the distance, in deeper water, was a larger vessel which he did not recognize. Towboats and a pinnace were alongside the larger craft; and from the pinnace a horse, kicking in a clumsy cordage sling, was being hoisted to the ship. Evidently the Governor's party was planning to return to Jamestown very soon.

Lance examined the little sloop carefully. The mainsail was in place along the boom. And in the waist a man was drowsing beneath a tarpaulin. A guard, no doubt. If they released him, he would take the sloop; and if forbidden this, he would go by land far up the peninsula to Carrick's and there hire passage across the bay. He must not stay at Arlington until Forke returned.

The minutes dragged. Lance returned to the house, but Ludwell did not appear. He asked the sentinel to summon him. The guard politely refused. More minutes passed. Captain Knight rode up and dismounted at the hitching rack.

Lance saluted him and said, "Sir, I request to be placed in custody."

Knight stared, astonished. "You what?"

"I ask to be locked up, sir. It is noon. I hereby surrender my parole. Unless I am confined, I shall go home."

The officer laughed nervously. "You want me to clap you in one of our makeshift dungeons?"

"Yes," Lance said. "The Governor has sent word he cannot see me; so I hereby give notice to you, as his deputy."

Knight did not know what to do. He understood clearly enough that Lance Clayborne had displeased the Governor, but he knew of no serious offense committed by the boy. And, after all, he was the son of Mathew Clayborne, once Master of the Horse for Charles II.

Lance pressed on. "I have informed Colonel Ludwell also, sir. I shall go home unless I am placed in custody. I shall break arrest at noon unless I am given hearing on the charge that is lodged against me."

"But damme, boy, why be so impatient? The Governor needs your sword—needs you. We return to Jamestown to fight Bacon and his robber band. Why, strike me blue!"

Ludwell now came out. His face reflected his uncertainty.

Lance approached him and looked up at the sun. "The decision, sir?"

"Faugh! There is none! The Governor will not order your release."

Lance said slowly, "Then I demand to be locked up."

"He will not have it so."

"Then I give notice here and now that I shall go. I withdraw parole."

"There then is nothing else for me to do but confine you, sir," said Captain Knight. "This is a deuced nuisance."

Lance did not reply except to unbuckle his belt and tender his sword. Knight, still grumbling, took the rapier reluctantly and ushered Lance into the house.

He did not notice his prisoner's careful study of the premises. Lance memorized the angles of the hall, the location of every piece of furniture, the peg upon which Knight hung the sword belt. He even counted the stairs and landings as they proceeded to the only empty chamber in the house, a room beneath the angles of the heavy roof.

Here he found himself imprisoned. Outside the door a trooper, with a sad-looking mustache and many lines of care upon his brow, was placed on guard.

Lance was relieved, for his inexperienced gaolers did not search his person. His pistol was hidden in his sash, and in his pocket was his clasp knife and his flint and steel.

He surveyed the room with care. The shingled roof was supported by thick cedar beams. The windows beside the chimneys at each end were narrow slits too small to allow the passage of a healthy fox's body. The only light in the room came through these slits which had been covered with oiled strips of hairless cowhide. It was obvious that the place had been used for a prison previously. There were no loose boards, no movable thing with which to strike a guard or force an exit through the roof. The room was almost as barren as the inside of a hogshead. In one corner was a gourd of water and a wooden platter.

Lance had made his plan. There was no time to waste. He picked up the platter and put it in the middle of the floor. He cut some shavings from the nearest beam and piled them in the platter, and on the shavings he placed an old rat's nest he found in the angle of the chimney. He tore the parchment from the window slits. Then, stooping over his pile of refuse, he struck a spark and blew it into a flame.

The little fire in the platter burned slowly, but in three minutes it filled the room with heavy smoke. Lance lay down and breathed the clear air near the floor. If this plan did not work, he would try another; but he had high hopes. Outside they would see the smoke escaping through the window slits, or possibly his guard would smell the fumes. They would unlock the door to keep the house from burning down. When the door was opened . . .

Lance cocked his pistol and waited.

There was an outcry. The house shook as heavy boots ran up the stairs. Outside the door were voices shouting: "Ahoy, what is that smoke from?"

The prisoner did not answer. The guard banged on the door. Still there was no answer from within.

Lance heard the sounds of hurrying feet, more shouts and a command. As the key rasped in the lock Lance pulled up to a crouch.

When the door swung open he stood up with the pistol in his hand. The guard, dismayed, stepped back in a cloud of smoke. Lance shifted his weapon to his left hand. He grabbed the *quillon* of the soldier's sword and jerked it from his hand. There was another dragoon standing agog in the hallway. This other man recovered sooner than the first, and as Lance dashed forward to the landing he blocked the way.

Lance started to shoot the man; then he changed his mind and received a clumsy thrust upon his blade. Thereafter, as more footsteps banged upon the stairs, he feinted once as though to use the blade's edge and pinked the fellow in the upper right forearm. As his foe leaped back Lance ran past him and down the stairs.

He did not have to fight again immediately. There was a downy-chinned young officer below him with a bucket of water in his hand. When he saw the prisoner rushing down on him, the man tried to turn and fell. Lance went past him to the second landing, two steps at a time. It seemed now as if all the people in the house were on the lower staircase. He did not pause but dived upon the press.

"Fire! Fire!" he roared as though he were a panic-smitten fugitive. The terrifying cry had its effect. The excited throng on the stairs and in the hall below milled backward.

Outside was Captain Peter Knight. Unlike the excited horde within the hall this officer was suspicious of the sudden turmoil. His sword was out. He crossed the courtyard and blocked the path.

Lance did not want to kill this man or any man of Berkeley's company there. But time was short and the whole area was strewn with enemies. It took six lightninglike passes to disable Knight; and then as Lance fled toward the landing an officer, Colonel Edward Hill, ran out from the well house. Here was a tougher adversary.

"You must surrender, boy!" he roared.

Lance again thought of his pistol. It would free him in a trice, but he decided not to shoot. He parried several thrusts until he had the sun behind his back. Hill was not so furious in his attack now. He tried to turn but found Lance's point two inches from his face. He tried to parry, but with the glaring sun in his eyes he lost his nerve.

Lance struck him with his hilt and flung him backward, stunned into inglorious helplessness. As Lance ran down toward the wharf his head was clear. He had played a simple game. He had almost completely surprised his captors. Barely a hundred seconds had elapsed since he had left the smoking room.

Beyond the trees, hard by the gibbet on which Carver hung, he slowed his pace. He then proceeded calmly to the wharfside and his sloop.

The sailor who was guarding it was half asleep. The distant hubbub at the house was just arousing him. Without parley Lance seized the man by the belt and flung him overboard. While the startled seaman sputtered in the muddy shallows Lance flung the line loose and shoved off into the tide. From the shore there were some musket shots fired and many shouts as he hauled up the sail, but he was free. The bullets missed by many yards. Within ten minutes he was out of range.

Lance made westward for the York's mouth, taking full advantage of the northeast wind. There would be pursuit, he knew, if Forke returned. It was wise to stay clear of the James lest he meet the guardship. It would be best to clear the bay as soon as he could. Only in the river's shoals could he escape the larger vessel.

৺§ 8

THE die was cast. Carver's swinging corpse had made of Lance a rebel.

He would join Bacon now. Devil take the consequences! Come what might he would have no more traffic with a senile murderer or any of his menial party. He could not make his voyage to London, but he could take the field with Bacon.

Early that night, Lance brought his sloop into a creek eight miles north of Kickotan and concealed it among the cypresses.

By daybreak, ragged from a hurried journey through the forest on a stolen horse, he was at the tavern of Henrietta Hart. At Henrietta's Lance rested, found food, forest garments and a fresh mount. Leaving his sword and pistol, he selected a fusil, ammunition and a hatchet.

The woman and her gypsy brood were excited by the news. So Berkeley would return to Jamestown after all? So Forke was with him now. That pirate from the south?

Henrietta's handsome face was grim. Yes, she would get a message to Sir Mathew. He was not, she said, at Clayborne Castle. His company of militia had been mustered against the Indians on orders from the Council. The Indians were raiding far to eastward. Sir Mathew was in the field somewhere with Brent. And where was Brent? Brent's command had marched with Bacon, but now it was in Middlesex.

Lance was puzzled. At Arlington the Governor was at war with Bacon. In James City County the Governor's staunch retainer, Brent, was sharing in the Indian war!

Where, asked Henrietta, could Captain Forke be found?

Lance guessed it would be off Jamestown.

Henrietta's lips became as thin as sheets of parchment.

"Why, pray, is your throat uncut?" she asked.

Lance could not explain. His medicine was strong. The Governor's uncertainty perhaps had saved his life. But all that mattered little now. He was free and armed. He would not be taken by surprise again. He would find his enemy before Forke found Sir Mathew.

Next day Lance rode away alone to Middlesex to locate his father. Sir Mathew did not know that Forke was in Virginia. It would not do to have that murderer surprise him.

The trail to Middlesex was marred by war as well as harsh weather. He passed the rotting, wolf-torn carcass of a horse. Gear had been abandoned by the marching levies, and there were signs that Bacon's men had gained much loot from the Indian villages. Gourds of maize and packs of rabbit pelts and various stone weapons had been thrown aside. Reading the signs on the muddy loam, Lance marveled at the small size of Bacon's column. Hardly two hundred men accompanied him on his countermarch to Jamestown. Berkeley had brought three times this number back from Accomack and Northampton.

In Dragon Swamp Lance found dead Indians. They were prisoners who had faltered on the march. Some borderer had rapped them on the head. They were Pamunkey warriors, friends of Berkeley. Beyond Dragon Run Lance saw signs that made his heart beat rapidly awhile—the footprints of a Monacan war party.

But a mile beyond there was a further story written on the forest floor. White men, probably scouts for Brent, had waylaid the Monacans. Scattered Indian corpses had fed the wolves and vultures. These

Indian raiders had not lived to dance in triumph in their village. Laden with spoil, sluggish with stolen food, they had been careless once too often on the homeward trail.

≈§ 9

THUS Lance Clayborne became an outlaw at a time when more than half the population of Virginia shared that estate.

A colony which at best had been but loosely tied together had collapsed in chaos.

On the rivers men steered wide of the boats of others. Horsemen pulled off the trail when they saw another man approach. They did not know whether even their children were their friends. Troopers of both factions looted abandoned homes of grain, utensils and blankets. Women were mistreated, and children were lost in the marshes. Friendly Indians were murdered, until every Indian became a foe of Berkeley as well as of Bacon.

Lance found his father ill with ague at Rosegill House in Middlesex. The news of Forke's return he told with caution. He was afraid the shock might have a bad effect, but the old knight took it like a soldier.

"He is with Berkeley?" Sir Mathew said.

"Yes," answered Lance.

"You have seen him?"

Lance told of his adventure on the river, of his stay at Arlington and his escape.

Sir Mathew tried to rise but failed. He sank back on his pillow, wet with perspiration. Then, regaining his breath, he cursed with such a wealth of epithet that Lance stood back in admiration. "That rat spawn of the Indies!" cried Sir Mathew. "That outcast bastard of a Spanish jennet! That cringing lackey of a senile fool! That whining sneak assassin! That . . ."

When the old man paused to catch his breath Lance said, "Come, now! We are agreed on all of that!"

Sir Mathew voiced his opinion of William Berkeley in language almost as eloquent.

Then, between deep breaths and draughts of barley water, his father told him of Cato's return, of sundry messages to Berkeley and of a letter from the Governor. "He assured me of your safety, so I marched with Brent," Sir Mathew said, sighing. "Damn these woods!" he shouted. "I lost Maria, that Arabian mare. She couldn't live on leaves and bark. I never saw a savage, by gad! I never saw an enemy! And here I am as full of fever as a kettle!"

The old man nearly climbed out of his bed when Lance announced that he was joining Bacon.

"Horns of Beelzebub, boy! Are you mad!"

"No, Father. It is a long-considered decision!"

"You're joking!"

"No, sir. It is Berkeley who is the rebel, Father, not Bacon."

"But you are a gentleman!"

Lance shrugged. "I wonder."

"You'll be hanged!"

"I shall not be hanged," Lance said.

X

Civil War

⌐§ 1

On the following day when Lance reached the Pamunkey trail, fifteen miles west of Jamestown, he waylaid a traveler, Michael Goode. He learned from Goode that Bacon's column had countermarched to Jamestown and was confronting Berkeley's Eastern Shore militia there. It was civil war, said Goode. Bacon was besieging the Governor's expeditionary column. His force had taken tools— axes, hoes and spades—from Joseph Barber's farm and had built a trench across the neck of the little peninsula. They were mounting guns with which to fire into the town. Berkeley's ships were tossing shot into the woods at Bacon's men.

Grimly Lance rode toward Jamestown. He did not stop at Clayborne Castle. When he reached the neck he found that Goode's report had been accurate.

Bacon's hard frontiersmen, alert, determined and filled with bitter anger, were there behind their field fortifications. Scarce half a mile away, Berkeley held the town, but he was being confined firmly under siege by Bacon's force.

A sentinel took Lance to headquarters in the Barber house. Shortly thereafter Bacon arrived. The young commander was soaked, splashed with mud and so weary that for a moment he did not recognize Lance Clayborne.

They sat down together by the kitchen fire. Lance sensed the many changes that had been wrought by the hardships of recent weeks. Bacon had lost flesh. His face was pinched, his eyes were yellowed, his nervous hands were clawlike. But his eyes were as bright as ever.

He laughed when Lance reported his recent misadventures. Then, when wine was brought, he summarized the situation. "We have him pinned down," Bacon said. "We'll knock Jamestown down around his ears unless he behaves himself and permits us to finish our campaign against the Indians."

"There are women there," Lance said.

"I know. But he has shipping. We are giving him time to send the women out. Except . . ."

"Yes?"

"I think that Berkeley will strike our line at dawn. He is insane. We fight the savages. But he attacks our rear and cuts off our supplies." Bacon's thin fists were clenched. "We shall chase him out of Jamestown. We must burn the stinking place to keep him from returning to it. Then we'll finish our fight against the Indians."

"How many men has he?" Lance asked.

"Six hundred. But I have my veterans here." Bacon's voice was rich with pride. "These men!" he said. "I've never seen their like. With them I could batter down the gates of hell and march on through from pit to pit. You should have seen them on the march through Iron Gate three weeks ago. It rained. They did not care. Brent's column straggled so I sent him back. My boys went on into the valley villages. The savages would not fight. Next time we'll pass the second ridge of mountains where the rivers flow southwest. We shall go as far as the salt marshes. Out there is grass which will sustain our ponies and shaggy buffalo which we can use for food." Bacon rubbed his eyes and touched his visitor upon the knee. "This land!" he cried. "Virginia is an empire!"

"I know."

"It is worth all this strife into which we have been thrown. It's vast beyond all dreams. The black soil along the western streams is twenty feet deep. The grass is high enough to hide a horse. The oaks are thicker than this house and higher than a castle tower. There are beaver enough to make a hat for every prince and princess in the world and every duke and earl besides. That much I saw in spite of the rains."

Young Bacon now frowned bitterly. "This Berkeley!" he said. "This aged ass who is our Governor! What a fool! He doesn't know. He has one foot in England still, although there is a continent within his reach, and his other foot is in the grave. He talks rebellion while we think only of peace. He threatens us with ropes while out beyond the falls is land in which a million families could live without dependence on the King or fear of all the powers of Europe. Let him send for troops. We'll make happy farmers of the King's dragoons."

Bacon raised the candle and pointed to a crude map upon the wall. "We have him imprisoned on the Jamestown neck," he continued. "He has too many men to feed. He must attack or send his militia back across the bay."

"Will they try to storm your line?"

Bacon laughed. "I hope they will. My western boys despise those pirate fishermen from across the bay. See—here, out off the shallows, is the Governor's largest ship. He hopes to drive us back with her guns, but they reach only to this point where we are sheltered by the trench. We will have a gun in range of her tomorrow, and he will have to pull her back. Let him assault our line if he dares."

Lance rested fitfully that night amid the excitement of the camp. Some Henricans patrolled the swampy field in front of Bacon's works and made more noise than fifty demons. They filled some small gourds with powder, sneaked close to the enemy lines and flung the gourds into the campfires of the Governor's nervous pickets. At times they shouted raucous insults at the militia in the village. Once they drove a herd of half-wild horses into Berkeley's lines and caused the Governor's men to start firing. The westerners in Bacon's force were gay as well as fierce. They enjoyed thoroughly the midnight terrors which they inflicted on their enemies.

There were women in the town. Lance shivered at the thought of them and wondered at the whereabouts of Easter Walker.

At dawn Lance found Joseph Ingram at the redoubt astride the road. The westerner was alert and eager. Ingram had a sailor's glass and was peering through the half-light at some sentinels in the town.

"They are afraid, I think," Ingram said. "They do not want to fight us. See. An officer beats them with his sword!" He laughed.

Lance asked about the women in the town.

"We'll see," said Ingram. "We have heard from them. They do not like this business. They have nagged His Excellency the whole night through because he is plunging the colony into civil war. Dame Drummond came into our lines awhile ago. She vows she'll stop this affair if she has to stand on the parapet. I say, look now!"

The dawn had chased away the mist, and the men had begun to assemble in the tobacco field beyond the swamp. One broke from the formation and ran toward the causeway and Bacon's lines.

"Don't shoot!" commanded Ingram. "Bring the man to me."

The deserter was a wild-eyed fisherman. For several minutes he was dumb. He said that the Eastern Shore militia intended to attack.

Ingram gave the man a mug of ale and showed him his array of tough defenders. "We hate to shoot you boys," Ingram said. "Go back and tell your comrades what you have seen. Tell them we shall drop a dozen at first fire and kill the rest in the ditch with hatchets. See?" Ingram displayed the Indian weapon at his belt.

The trembling fisherman went back across the neck, fearing now the bullets of his friends. No one fired at him. He joined the mob that had gathered in a meadow west of the tobacco field.

"What a war!" Ingram exclaimed. "Look. We have other visitors."

Berkeley's force was moving now, advancing toward the causeway. Bacon's men began to yell defiantly.

The officers of the attacking force waved their swords. Lance looked for Berkeley. The old man was in the center of the line, his plumed hat on his sword tip. He limped forward, gallantly shouting encouragement to his nervous men.

Lance checked the priming of his weapon. He could shoot the Governor if he chose, but he looked for other targets. There were Philip Ludwell, Daniel Parke, Edward Hill and an officer from Accomack whose name he did not know. The officers were bold enough but not their men. As the bullets of Bacon's force began to whistle the attack became very slow. Two men went down. But Lance held his fire.

The guns of the ship opened up. Shot crashed into the woods to the right of Ingram's trench. Bacon was over there. They heard his men yell and shoot their culverin.

Lance fired at an Accomack sailor. His shot fell short. He cursed and rammed another cartridge home.

The attack suddenly halted. The men from across the bay were arguing with their officers. They had lost all stomach for the fight. Berkeley had been pulled back from his exposed position. The two wounded men were dragged away.

Ingram's borderers were on the parapet, anxious to assail the mob. He roared commands. Stand firm. They must not leave the trench. He had to manhandle half a dozen fierce Henricans to keep them from charging across the causeway. Out on the river the ship which had retired to deeper, safer water was splashed by the shot from Bacon's small cannon in the woods.

Lance put a twig into his ash-dry mouth and lowered his fusil. So this was Berkeley's battle! Ha! There had been no fight worthy of the name. Bacon had won with moral force, almost unaided by his weapons.

Over in the meadow Berkeley's officers tried once more to marshal his reluctant militia. Again they formed ranks. This time Bacon did not fire a shot. He brought ten Indian prisoners to the parapet and displayed them. Berkeley's men looked at the captive warriors, remembered Bacon's war against the savages and refused to fight. The Governor was helpless.

Many in the Governor's militia now tried to desert, but Bacon drove them back. Berkeley had recruited them. Let him feed them. Only the women were invited to Bacon's camp. They straggled in all day. Among them were the hungry wives of some of Berkeley's Councillors. Madame Bray and Madame Ballard stood upon the parapet and screamed out orders to the other women in the town. So many more came. Bacon fed them and gave them safe-conduct to their home plantations.

Lance watched and waited anxiously, but Easter Walker did not come. Madame Nathaniel Bacon, wife of the elder Bacon, gave him news of her. Easter was with Frances Berkeley on a ship off Kickotan. The Governor had tried to send them both across the bay to Arlington, but they would not go.

Bacon did not assault Jamestown, but he gave every indication that he would. He built two extra causeways across the swampy ground to his left and mounted more boat culverins. Large shot was scarce so he fired the cannon blank to frighten them. His men, hiding in the woods like Indians, rattled bullets off the housetops.

ৰ্চ 2

LANCE was asked to patrol far down the riverbank, because Berkeley's boats might land a force to attack them from the rear. Late that afternoon Lance's squad of nine Henrico borderers skirmished briefly with a party of sailors at a landing on Wool Creek, but the seamen retired as quickly as they came.

Lance then moved on toward Henrietta Hart's, wondering if her inn had received attention from the raiders. It had. But the visitors promptly departed as Lance's patrol approached, and took flight downriver in their boat.

Henrietta was in a mood so black that she scarcely had the spirit to give them welcome. Lance found her seated on the porch in the twilight, her black eyes burning as with fever.

"I have never seen you so beautiful," he said with a bow. "Are you drunk?"

Staring out upon the river she breathed deeply, and paid no attention to his joke. She wore her silken dress and had a scarlet warrior flower in her hair. Her cheeks were flushed. Her lips trembled several times before she spoke.

"You interrupted me," she said. "Our . . . our mutual enemy was here awhile. I tried to charm him—successfully, I think."

Lance started. "Forke was here?"

"No less! You frightened him away. He had a watchman who gave the alarm when you approached."

"There was . . . no violence?"

She shrugged. "Oh, no. He came in peace surrounded by eleven men. He paid for his wine. He chucked my chin and called me Retta as he used to do." She spat.

"I marvel that you did not kill him."

"And have his cutthroats rape and slay me and my girls? Oh, no! We took his money, not his life. I bide a better time. He vainly believes that I am still a slave of his. He thinks he is young again. Since the fight at Jamestown he is afraid, too. The Governor owns the river, but Bacon's men own all the land except Northampton, Accomack and Jamestown."

Henrietta clasped her knee and leaned back on her bench. She had perfumed herself with a potent essence and had marked her eyes with willow charcoal. Small wonder she had charmed the captain once again. But as Lance watched her darting eyes, he was reminded of a snake. This woman's hate was rare to see. It seemed to boil beneath her stays.

He told her of events upriver, of how Berkeley's bravoes had decided not to fight at Jamestown.

"I knew it," she declared. "Forke said that Bacon put women on his ramparts."

Lance laughed and told how Dame Ballard and the others had abandoned the beleaguered town.

Lance became as glum as Henrietta when she asked about Easter

Walker. He did not know what to do. He feared that the Governor's wife might take her back to England. He was also afraid that Easter might be held as a hostage for his conduct.

Henrietta laughed at him and ordered her girls to bring him food and wine. "I heard of your adventure," Henrietta said. "She will find you, never fear. No matter if you flee beyond the western range, she will find you."

"But *I* seek *her.*"

"That's unnecessary, boy. Just sit and wait. She will come when she is ready, never fear." Henrietta looked up at him. "You think she will love you if you wear your finery and boots? Or does she hanker still for Indians?"

He bade her hold her tongue, although he got much pleasure from her teasing.

⊷§ 3

THE GOVERNOR sailed back to Arlington with all his troops and thus abandoned the town to Bacon. Bacon thereupon destroyed Jamestown.

Lawrence burned his own tavern. Drummond put the torch to his own mansion. The Council House, wharves and every inn went up in smoke. The records of the colony and essential supplies that Berkeley had left behind were preserved and sent to Middle Plantation.

Bacon was sad, but he saw no other course. He had no garrison and few guns. To leave the town behind him was to leave a base for Berkeley. Henceforth the Governor would have only his ships.

Bacon's army marched north to Tyndalls Point and learned that Berkeley had sent messengers to Brent. Bacon thereupon took his picked men into Gloucester to meet any challenge Brent might offer. He camped at Warner's big plantation near the point. Brent withdrew westward.

The Gloucester men were troublesome at first. There had been no Indian raids in Gloucester and the elders resented Bacon's levy of supplies. They wanted to be neutral. Bacon treated them with firmness. To Councillor Cole and Parson Wading, their spokesmen, he was courteous.

"We are not bandits, gentlemen," Bacon told them, "but we are desperate men whose lives are forfeit if we fail to stand together. The Governor has fled. His militia refused to fight us. We await the King's decision on Berkeley's actions. I am not Governor. I am but the leader of an Indian expedition, an officer with the Crown's commission for this service. Nor am I a rebel. This colony has law. From it not even Berkeley is exempt. He calls me a rebel when it's he who has rebelled. He breaks the law, not I. I am under arms by virtue of a commission which Berkeley signed."

Cole protested that his county had no quarrel over power. "We will be neutral in this disturbance," he declared.

Bacon rose, hand on his sword, and cried, "Then I say, damn your craven neutrality! Stay neutral if you can!"

As Cole and Wading started to leave a Gloucester militiaman touched Bacon's sleeve. "Our Councillor, Colonel Cole, was talking for the horse, not for the foot," he said. "The common men in Gloucester are for your cause."

"I've been talking to the men, not to their steeds!" cried Bacon fretfully. "I hope you'll make the horses understand!"

Out in the meadow Parson Wading was reporting the failure of his meeting with Bacon to a group of Gloucester men. For a while Bacon watched him from the porch. The preacher finally waved his arms in rage and roared: "This anti-Christ wants all of us to join him in rebellion!"

Bacon walked over, elbowed through the group, faced the angry orator and bowed respectfully. "You curse us, sir?" Bacon asked. "You cry perdition on our cause?"

"Yes, I do!" the irate minister replied.

Bacon's thin face lighted with amused mischief. "Here in the camp of David you preach the cause of Saul?"

There was laughter in the crowd. The parson for a moment had no answer.

"You are no Samuel," Bacon chided. "So perhaps you are a warrior? No? Then pray go home. We have a place only for warriors here. Go home and prove to Saul that David does not use the rope, that Bacon did not hang you!"

The minister lost heart for further speech. He took his leave.

ᵉˢ 4

EASTER WALKER learned from Colonel Philip Ludwell of Lance Clayborne's escape from Arlington. Ludwell stopped at Gull Cove to order fifty kegs of pickled beef for the Governor's ships. He arrived at night on a ten-oared barge, in not a little anxiety that he might be intercepted by some of the Baconians. He urged Alan Walker to abandon his warehouses and come to Arlington, but the old man could not bear the thought of surrendering his property.

This failing, Ludwell communicated to Easter Walker an invitation to visit Lady Berkeley on the Eastern Shore. The girl shook her head. Ludwell noticed that she was distressed—Frances Berkeley being quite a gossip—and he soon ended her suspense.

"The young man fought half the camp," Ludwell said. "He fought Peter Knight and winged him. He knocked two of Ed Hill's front teeth down his throat. He crippled a dragoon and half drowned a sailor. And got off in a shower of musket balls."

"Was he wounded?"

"Oh, no. The Clayborne luck stayed with him throughout. Where did he go? Have you seen him?"

Ludwell looked very closely at the girl. He suspected that even if she had she would never admit it. But the candor of her denial convinced him that she had not seen him and the sadness in her eyes was a clear indication that she wished she had.

"You are sure he was not wounded by the . . . er . . . shower of musket balls?" Easter repeated.

"Certain. I saw him setting a sail that two ordinary men could hardly handle on a calm day. He was not wounded."

Easter wanted to talk about Lance Clayborne. It was plain that Ludwell admired the lad exceedingly. She wanted to hear everything he could tell her. Did he know why Lance had wanted to escape from Arlington? What had been his motive?

Ludwell gallantly guessed that she herself was the motive; but she waved this aside and asked more questions.

"It may have been because of Forke," Ludwell finally said. "Forke, you know, is that sea merchant from Carolina who is an enemy of the Claybornes, and he had joined His Excellency. Perhaps the Clayborne boy feared Forke's influence with the Governor."

"Lance fears no one, Colonel," Easter said coldly.

"I beg your pardon, my lady," replied Ludwell. "And come to think on it, Mistress Easter, I agree with you."

"Then what?"

"Perhaps he wished to see his father, to warn him that the family enemy had returned to the colony."

"That sounds more reasonable," Easter said. "Oh, I wish you men would cease this foolishness!"

At that moment Lance Clayborne was in Bacon's camp in York County, and he had no intention whatever of seeing Easter Walker again as long as he lived. He believed that she had betrayed to the Governor his plan to make the voyage to London. It was agony to think of the girl now. But his duties as Bacon's adjutant kept him busy, otherwise he might, in sheer pain, have indulged his natural bent toward recklessness and gone west.

Most of the Gloucester men took Bacon's oath, and soon the men of Middlesex did likewise. The whole mainland of Virginia had joined the cause. It was Berkeley now who was the rebel—Berkeley exiled at Arlington. Messengers were sent to Carolina and to Maryland with the news.

Bacon did not man the border forts. Instead he sent three mobile companies westward under Ingram to patrol the uplands and harass any Indian war parties that might try to cross the fall line of the rivers. A campaign across the mountains must await the news from England.

Berkeley had asked the King for troops. This had caused laughter in the camp on the York. What could European soldiers do here in Virginia? Rebuild Jamestown? They would require many ships to supply the place. Attack borderers in the forest? Bacon's woodland warriors grinned and slapped their leathern breeches. No army in the world could live on their trail.

Suppose five hundred troopers were sent for the Governor's use? A hundred would be dead of fever in three weeks. Full fifty more would die of flux. The others doubtless would be weak for months and hungry, too, when all their ships' supplies were gone. They would not dare march out into the woods against the foresters of Henrico.

Bacon took no part in such speculations. Berkeley's ships were raiding river farms for grain and stock, so garrisons were posted. Bacon also feared the clutch of famine. He guarded the stores his men collected and moved them upriver to West's Point, a natural fortress. There were letters to be written, laws to enforce, fears to be allayed.

All the while attention must be given to his idle army on the York, his little band of wild men from the border. These men went to church bare-breeked, mixed willow bark with their tobacco, ate pig kidneys raw and tried to drink up all the wine left in the colony. A strong arm was required to handle them.

Lance Clayborne found himself busy, passing Bacon's mandates to the scattered garrisons and soothing the wrath and fears of sundry farmers of the neighborhood. The general's compliments to Goodman Smythe, but the general was not a judge. If someone shot the good man's cow a magistrate should be sought, not General Bacon. The general's regrets to Goodman Arnold. Loss of his daughter's virtue was unfortunate indeed. Let her name the man and he would see what could be done. No, the general was not Governor of the colony. No, the general was not a Tartar bandit either. No, the general could not come to dinner on the twelfth. Yes, the general was grateful for the pound of Jesuit bark. Its bitter tea would help his fever. . . .

Rumors caused a vast amount of correspondence and brought an unending stream of anxious visitors. Some were spies of Berkeley, but Bacon received them courteously. He had not hanged his captive, Sir Henry Chicheley. The only execution in his camp had been inflicted on a wretched rapist for whom no man could speak a word of mercy. Bacon had burned no farms. He usurped no powers beyond the bounds of his permission. The Governor took comfort in but a single circumstance: Bacon's health was failing rapidly.

Fever or no fever, Bacon took but little rest. He was in the saddle for the large part of every day. At times he lost his voice and had to whisper his instructions. His handsome face was almost fleshless now. Warnings about his health went unheeded. There was so much to do.

Lance Clayborne's arm was sore from unaccustomed penmanship. His eyes began to ache from reading by candlelight. Free from ague, Lance failed to notice for a time the ravages of the illness of his friend. Neither wine nor fever affected Bacon's fervid spirit. He ever was the calm commander, always the sober counselor and good-humored comrade.

If there were fears, he never showed them; but he asked Lance many questions about the King. At this Lance said he had been very young at Court; thus he remembered little. Bacon pressed him further nonetheless. The King had been a fugitive for years. Did he not have sympathy for men of resolution? Perhaps he had, but Charles had also lived in spoiled luxury in France. Yes, he showed mercy after he had been restored, but his nobles had shown none. At Whitehall Berkeley had a brother—a proud and narrow-minded man from all reports.

Bacon shrugged. What was rebellion? Could a great mass of people be rebels? Could fifty thousand colonists be outlaws?

Lance shook his head.

"I am a rebel," Bacon said. "A rope can hang me, but not the people with me. Cromwell was a rebel, but not the people with him. Revolution never is one man's perversity. Had I not been chosen, they would have found some other leader. Revolution is a tide that rises to protect our freedom. Berkeley thinks this movement in Virginia is a tide of terror and disgrace. I say it is a tide of glory!" Bacon snuffed the candle with ague-shaken fingers. "A tide of glory!" he repeated. "The people in these scattered Virginian glades are realists. They know that common law was made for common men by common men, not by barons or governors or kings. The people value their right to make their local laws, because they know that without such local laws they all would have died long since in this vast wooded wilderness. None of us were rebels there at Merchants Hope Plantation. Our sole purpose was to drive back the Indians. It was our right to guard our lives. . . ."

Bacon sank down onto the bench and stared at the candle.

"We expected aid from Berkeley," he continued. "The Governor failed to perform his duty, failed to guard us from a common enemy. He violated the fundamental law of the colony. Therefore, the common men have taken back the power their laws gave to their Governor. It matters not to them that Berkeley is a royal deputy. They would not fear him if he were the deputy of hell!" Bacon flung out his hands. "Someday I hope to see the King and tell him this. Unless he knows, he may lose an empire, Lance. Virginians have no awe of a scepter that is a thousand leagues from here."

Bacon sighed and passed a hand across his eyes; then he said, "I wish that I could live another year. The King will have this matter settled, then. He will send us a Governor with common sense. He will find a policy to fit these wild plantations."

"You'll live for many years," Lance said.

Rising, steadying his fever-weakened frame against the table, Bacon answered, "I fear otherwise. Oh, Lance, I envy you your strength! The future does not bother you, nor do lice, nor does ague, nor any hardship. You are alert and hopeful, free of mind and self-sufficient. You have no knowledge of the meaning of rebellion, for rebellion is a part of you. Not of me. I have a tender Kentish skin, a Cambridge brain all filled with liberal foolishness, a conscience painful as a pope's. Yes, I envy you. You are a Virginian. You got your schooling in the woods and swamps. You learned humanity upon the banks of forest streams and freedom in the pagan villages of Indians. You never had, nor will you ever have, respect for precedent. An ocean flows between Virginia and precedent."

This was Lance Clayborne's last talk with Nathaniel Bacon. Fever burned Nathaniel Bacon down, sent him staggering to his shuck pallet in the main room of Pate's house. The calm voice lost its tone and became the babble of delirium. The faces of the sentinels became grim and their manners curt as they turned away anxious visitors.

Lance gave the sick man strong infusions of Peruvian bark, but the frail body could not retain the medicine. Bacon's life flickered for two days like a sputtering candle. Chills shook him and the fever flared, subsided, and flared again. Gaunt captains, themselves feverish, stood silently beside the cot until the end.

The news of Bacon's death swept into the camp like a storm of ice in summer. The little army could not believe it.

Then the drums were beaten upside down and four hundred weeping men filed past the bier. Bacon . . . dead!

They buried his body in the deepest waters of the York at night. The makeshift coffin was weighted with fifty pounds of shot lest Berkeley find the body. Even after the burial it was hard to think of Bacon dead.

The little army on the spit began to melt away. Lawrence came and called a council. Drummond harangued the regiment. Another chieftain must be chosen. Bacon's cause must live. Bacon's memory must live. Nevertheless the band began to scatter. They were Bacon's men—not Lawrence's, not Drummond's. The border men wanted to go and find Ingram in Henrico. He was one of their kind.

Lance Clayborne rode westward toward Ingram's camp. His heart was sick. Ingram must come east at once, for he alone could hold the frontiersmen in ranks. He alone could stand against the Governor's senile wrath and protect Bacon's friends from Berkeley's hangmen. . . . Ingram, Bacon's sturdy drillmaster; Ingram, the veteran with the steady, fearless eyes; Ingram, the blind worshiper of Bacon; Ingram, a sword arm—but little else. Ingram knew nothing of politics. He was a fighter only. He had no use for Lawrence or for Drummond or for anyone except Bacon. All depended now on Ingram.

Lance's pony dropped dead eleven miles from Shoccoes. He borrowed a hunter's mule and reached the landing in the middle of the night. He aroused Byrd's men, got another horse and pressed on. At noon the following day he encountered Ingram's scouts and was led into the hidden camp.

Ingram chewed a straw and stared unseeingly into the trees for many minutes. At last he rose and slapped his gloves against his boots. "Yes, I'll be going east," he said. "I'm not a Bacon, but I'll look out somehow for the boys."

Lance slept far into the following day. Meanwhile Ingram had assembled scattered outposts and was ready to break camp. He left a small band of horsemen to block the westward trail and moved the others eastward to the falls.

"I shall stop at West's Point," he said. "I shall go no farther. All who want protection from old Berkeley can find it there."

Lance suggested that they ride on to Tyndalls in Gloucester, but Ingram was firm.

"I'll have to feed my men by hunting, so I cannot go as far as Gloucester," he said. "I'm no Bacon. The farmers won't bring supplies to *me*. . . . Where is the Governor?"

Lance did not know.

"He will be on the warpath once again. He will come back across the bay."

"Yes, he'll take up the hatchet again," said Lance.

Berkeley wasted little time. Three days after Bacon's death one of the Governor's ships was in the York. Before Ingram could get in touch with Bacon's eastern garrisons, before all the commanders had the news of Bacon's death, an active civil war had flamed again.

A detachment at Read's Plantation was overwhelmed. One by one, Bacon's scattered stations fell. Winter was approaching. Food needed to maintain strong garrisons was lacking. The Governor subdued these posts by parley or by force.

Ingram fortified West's Point as he had promised and made it a haven for all fugitives who had taken the Baconian oath. Berkeley issued manifestoes. The Governor erected a fine new gallows at his camp and threatened death to every man who did not make submission promptly. Ingram replied that he was fighting Indians, not Englishmen. The Governor sent word that Ingram's commission would be revoked. Ingram did not reply to this.

Berkeley's forces regained possession of Green Spring and the Allen house in Surry. He occupied the ruins of Jamestown and stationed Beverly at Middle Plantation with a well-mounted squadron. But he did not dare approach the sullen camp at West's Point.

Lawrence disappeared. Drummond was arrested along with many others of Bacon's party who had not fled to Ingram's camp.

అర్ 5

LANCE CLAYBORNE remained but briefly at West's Point. He then rode eastward in search of news. He feared particularly for his father's safety from the pirate, Forke.

All New Kent seethed with rumors. Many Indian war parties were raiding to eastward. A force of King Charles's troops was on its way from England to suppress the border men. The eastern levies already had been defeated in detail. A proclamation of the Governor had remained three days upon the New Kent courthouse door. No one this time dared to tear it down.

Lance read the list of "rebels." His name was on the roll. He smiled grimly and rode on, huddled in his cloak. The list contained the names of some of the stoutest and the bravest men in Virginia— outlaws because they had fought Indians or voted for the Baconian laws against the Governor's wishes.

Lance held his fusil on the pommel of his saddle as he rode. He was ruined perhaps, but he was determined that he would not become a prisoner of the Governor's men. Ingram had warned him harshly of the rope and had begged him to remain at West's Point. Bacon's realistic second-in-command had no illusions and no hope in anything save force. But Lance decided he must go.

He avoided every plantation along the trail and moved as warily as a wolf as he approached the Charles City settlement. Whenever his horse's ears came up he pulled off the trail to let some other traveler pass.

The Governor's men would watch the paths to Clayborne Castle. Doubtless, too, they would expect him soon to seek out Easter Walker. Berkeley's minions had discovered many ways to bait a trap. The prisons were full. Captain Forke was at the old man's elbow. The fate of Carver was to be the fate of many now. Sir Mathew? Here was no Baconian; yet Sir Mathew also need fear.

His father's peril was the impelling motive for Lance's decision to return. Outlaw or not, he must keep watch on Jesús Forke.

Peo had preceded him from Ingram's camp. He would have news by now. Peo would meet him at Lightfoot's landing with another horse.

Lance pressed on watchfully. If they would make him into a wolf, so be it. He would not flee far. Berkeley's friends would have to watch their cattle closely too. He sighed and stretched the saddle cramps from his long legs. Away with dreams awhile. Here were realities.

He was an outlaw whatever might be the justice of his cause. The satrap, Berkeley, was in the saddle, and there he would remain until King Charles could resolve this madness. Lance had no doubt that the King would do it. Charles himself had been an outlaw once. Lance found Peo at the rendezvous. The lean forester was delighted and relieved to find his master safe. But all the news was unfavorable. Berkeley had reduced one Baconian post after another. Without Bacon the eastern farmers were being herded like meek cattle. The public hangman was very busy.

✎§ 6

SIR MATHEW CLAYBORNE wearily thrust aside his bowl of wine and water, cursing because it did not warm his aching joints. Even the hickory fire, although it heated the hall almost to suffocation, did not warm him, nor did the wolfhound at his feet.

Another winter was approaching, a hungry winter for the rich as well as the poor. Kendall had been stripped and so had Walker, Allen, Tate and many others—stripped to feed militiamen and rebels. All ships were overdue. Some had turned about at the river's mouth and sailed up the bay to Maryland. Some had been stopped by the pirates who now flourished in many a hidden inlet.

Clayborne Castle had escaped the general pillaging, for Bacon's men respected the property of Lance Clayborne's father. . . .

Sir Mathew pulled his shawl around his shoulders and stared bleakly at the fire. He had never understood rebellion. Cromwell he had hated and had never understood, and now these wild Virginians offered an even greater mystery.

Damn this wilderness! What had happened to his boy? Lance was a gentleman. He was industrious and sober, fair, respectful to his elders and the Church of England. He was no bully for all his strength and skill with weapons. He was no puling beau in spite of his grace of form and handsomeness of face.

But something in this land had altered Lance. The boy had grown apart. He had forgotten London and the King. He had made new memories of his own. Virginia memories. Damn Virginia! They should not have left Whitehall! The stinking fogs of London were better than the breezes of this miasmic province.

Sir Mathew had seen England burn from Berwick to Lands End; then he had witnessed its return to sanity. He had seen men die in vain for their King, for liberty, religion and pride and live—likewise in vain—for hope and for revenge. But this insensate struggle in Virginia was for something new. Even the men who followed Berkeley had refused to fight unless their foes were Indians. Berkeley's defense of Jamestown had been a farce.

Where were the roots, what was the genesis of this rebellion? There had been no Buckingham, no bishop-hating nobles, no Laud, no Strafford, and, in fact, no Cromwell. Bacon was a fool, but certainly he was no sermon-shouting Roundhead. There was a parliament of sorts, the House of Burgesses, and a King of sorts, the Governor. What else? There were no Puritans, no renegade noblemen who feared that their lands would go back to the Pope, no siege of La Rochelle and no murdered Huguenots, no dispute about the King's divinity. Sir Mathew shivered.

But there had been much talk of English liberties. He remembered other talk like this. The Ironsides had shouted "Liberty!" at Naseby, he recalled, and they had fought like jinn from hell. He had faced a snub-nosed yokel on that field, a farmer boy who shouted with a Yorkshire accent but listened constantly for his captain's commands. The troop leader called, and, like an automaton, the yokel disengaged and backed his charger free. Then two others—red-faced Roundheads—joined the yokel and they came at Sir Mathew with relentless power. Discipline had made those farmer boys invincible—discipline and prayers for English liberty.

The old knight reached for his wine bowl and looked up in surprise. His son was standing on the hearth, an elbow on the mantel, smiling down at him.

Sir Mathew roared an oath and started to his feet.

Lance touched his shoulder and said, "Keep your seat, sir. I am not a ghost."

"Then where in . . . ?"

The boy was in his forest dress, hairy and unkempt, but cheerful enough.

"How did you get here, Lance? How did you pass the guards?" Sir Mathew asked.

Lance gestured. "I am half Indian now, perhaps. Never mind. It is good to find you well. You were grumbling and swearing to yourself like olden times."

"You have no business here, Lance! Your name went on the hangman's list last week!"

"I know, and proud I am to be in honest company."

"I have not seen Sir William. If you are caught——"

"I'll not be caught. You see—" Lance squared his shoulders— "they will look for me upriver. They never would seek me here where I am almost on the doorstep of the Green Spring gaol. I have a score to settle, Father. This done I shall go back to the woods and guard my skin with great care. Don't fear for me. I shall not be surprised as Hansford was."

"You are hungry? Let me up to fetch that scoundrel, Cato."

"I've seen him, Father. I shall banquet in good time. You have a cautious outpost. It took two hours and all my skill to get past undetected. None know that I am here except my friends, your hounds and Cato."

"The news, son. What is happening upriver?"

Lance spread his restless fingers. "The rebellion has ended."

"Thank God for that!"

"The westerners will keep on fighting but only in defense of their lives. The easterners who were with Bacon have laid down their arms in frenzied panic. The Governor will hang more of them, no doubt. With western men who keep their arms he'll make peace in time, so he can get his beaverskins."

"But the King's commissioners are coming soon!"

"Perhaps they will stop the hangings. At any rate they will not bother Ingram and the border force. If all the troops of the New Model army landed here they'd never catch the western hunters. They will be rebels for a hundred years unless the Governor pardons them. I hope you will tell him as much."

Sir Mathew frowned. "This will not do!"

"We'll form an empire in the valley lands, a tribe of Tartars. In time the Governor will offer peace . . . and tribute, too, no doubt. Lady Berkeley cannot buy her laces unless the beaver fur starts to flow again. I shall be happier there than in any feverish river settlement. There is meat enough and Indian corn and foxgrape wine."

"What of the Walker girl?"

"Yes, what of her?" Lance said bitterly.

"She is at Gull Cove."

"So I have heard."

"You will not go there?"

Lance shook his head. "No, Father. There are other places to go. There is a man to meet, you know, a certain sailor."

Sir Mathew sighed. "Yes, I had almost forgotten that."

⋙ 7

THERE were certain compensations in an outlaw's life, Lance decided. He need not stop at taverns, nor visit tiresome friends. Since all men now were enemies there was no need to waste his time in table talk, or shave his chin each day, or wear a clumsy sash and sword.

He was freer than a wolf and, like a wolf, a slayer of tame pigs and straying fowls, a thief without conscience and, should the need arise, a highwayman. He slept each night in some deep patch of woods, enjoyed the rest as a wild thing would, and rejoiced in his strength of body and his skill in evading nosy hounds and men.

He prowled constantly and eavesdropped to hear the talk of the burghers of Middle Plantation. Berkeley's court was at Kickotan. The Governor was at the Halley house and with him were Lady Berkeley and her ladies. The men of Berkeley's company were scattered among the other homes. Some nervous Councillors still slept on the guardship.

There was grim talk. The trials continued. Many were condemned, among them Crews and Farlow. Other staunch Baconians—one was Edmund Cheeseman—had died in prison.

Lance walked the streets of Kickotan at night unrecognized. The watch avoided men in buckskin after dark. Most such men were drunk and dangerous.

Captain Forke had gone upriver on a mission for the Governor. The tavern chatterers said that he sought Lawrence, whom, of all, the Governor most wanted hanged. Lawrence had disappeared.

Lance followed Forke by the southern trail. It would not do to wait while the pirate was cruising near his father's house. At some landing where the ale was strong Forke would stop someday. . . .

The nights now were frosty. The trees had shed their leaves. The moon of harvest waned, and winter moved remorselessly across rebellion-wracked plantations. Lance's bag of food was light, but he had no time to poach or hunt. For two days he dined on toasted hominy and dried grapes from his pouch.

The cold and his half-empty stomach made his senses very keen; so no one saw him on that hasty journey. His property was forfeit now—all except his fusil and his hatchet and his knife—but he was free. His property was gone, but he had health and strength. There was room for outlaws in Virginia. There would always be room in the vast uplands to the west.

He could join Pipisko who was now beyond the mountains near the diamond cave. Pipisko still had his traps and a year's supply of powder. Peo had heard from him. The tribe had lost its iron kettles on its move westward, but it had found wild cattle along the river that flowed northward. There was ample food. Pipisko had taken Miskee into his lodge. She knew how to salt a stew.

Lance stretched his arms. There might be no mutton and no puddings for him for quite a while, but his teeth were as strong as any Indian's. And in good time King Charles would send another Governor . . . and peace.

Lance increased his vigilance as he approached the settlements on the James. The scattered landings on the northern shore had been the haunts of Jesús Forke. Here he had traded in smuggled pirate merchandise. Near ruined Jamestown was Henrietta Hart. Forke, surrounded by his crew, had shown no fear of Henrietta. He had greeted her as a charming reminder of his younger days.

She, at least, would have some news of Forke, and then the hunt would start again, thought Lance. The hunt . . . His heart thumped hard as it always had done when he thought of Forke. The search for Jesús Forke had been a part of him for many years. In his dreams he had slain the man a hundred times. He had shot him, had throttled him, had cut his throat in numerous ways and each time as remorselessly as a public executioner. The villain's life was forfeit. He was a murderer. There could be no peace of mind in the Clayborne family until he died.

Lance scouted Henrietta's tavern carefully that night. The woman's furry wolfhound who was a friend made no alarm. Lance counted seven seamen in Henrietta's public room and two girls. All the men were drunk. They talked too loudly and laughed too often. The girls were tired. One sat, head down on the table, with a bearded sailor's arm around her waist. The other girl held a tray containing mugs of wine which soon were snatched away. She came to rest upon an outthrust knee. They yelled for her to sing.

Henrietta was not in the public room. Lance, holding the wolf-hound by the collar, walked around the house and approached the rear door.

A woman was leaning against the lintel staring at the moon. "Hector!" she called.

"I have Hector," said Lance as he released the hound.

"You!"

"At your service."

"What are you doing here?"

Lance leaned his fusil against a post and sat down at her feet, caressing the rugged beast beside him.

"I haven't seen you for a long, long while," Henrietta said.

"Is *he* here?"

She waved a hand. "Oh, yes. You'll find him upstairs in the Turkish room, asleep. I half expected that you would come in search of him."

"You mean it? He is really here?"

She laughed bitterly. "Look and see."

As Lance climbed quickly to his feet she put her hands against his chest. "Stop now! And make no noise. I spoke in jest. I'll not have you waking up my . . . friend. Sit down."

Lance resumed his place on the lintel stone, and Henrietta sat down beside him, whispering, "You should not come here at this time, you handsome panther. Those men in there are hunting you."

"I am a hunter, too."

"I know, and so, perhaps, am I." Henrietta spat an oath so bitter that he frowned in awe. "Stay with Hector here until I fetch you food."

He waited.

If Forke were here, his quest was ended. Henrietta doubtless lied. Who could sleep in such a pandemonium? Even if the man were here, the matter would take thought. If he should kill his enemy in Henrietta's house, then she and all her girls would hang. That would not do. Besides, he could not kill a sleeping man.

Lance cursed his problem while he cursed his foe. Here were revenge and justice at his hand. Here was the culmination of an earnest aim in life. His fingers played on his hatchet blade and loosened his knife in its fringed sheath of squirrelskin. But he was no bedroom assassin.

He heard a sound within the door and stepped into the shadows. It was Henrietta returning with a loaf and a hock of boiled ham. She placed the platter on the step; then she went back for ale.

Lance dined in the half-dark of the courtyard and tried to think. There might never be so good an opportunity again. He would wake the man, give him a choice of weapons and then cut his throat. But again came the thought: what of Henrietta and her wenches? If he slew Forke within that house, the Governor would execute them as surely as the night was dark. They might be burned to death by the public executioner. He must not endanger Henrietta and her brood.

Henrietta joined him beneath the shadow of the chestnut tree near the door. Her presence calmed him. She had been a trollop; yet she had been a selfless friend throughout all his years in Virginia. She had been his tutor in the earthy ways of women, as his tender mistress. She had given balance to his spirit by stripping from it the fears of sin and hell and human nature.

"I must kill our mutual friend," Lance said at last.

She touched his arm. "You are an Indian tonight, you handsome fool, but I cannot let you cut his throat in bed. You would hate yourself when you became an Englishman again."

"My father would be safe."

"I know, but hold yourself in check, my rooster. Did your father send you here?"

"Oh, no. I came east because I feared that Forke was on his way to Council Point to harm my father. I doubt if Captain Forke would find the murder of my father such a simple task; but the man is dangerous. Besides he hunts also for me. He is one of the Governor's hangmen. Is he really here? You are not teasing me?"

"He is really here. I've never told you false tales, my buck. The greasy beast is here! He treated me as if I were a tart from Drury Lane. So swollen is he in his pride and pocketbook he thinks that

I've forgotten what he did to me. The fool shows less of caution than an ox. Almighty God! He thinks I have forgotten!" She hissed another stream of bitter oaths.

At last she paused, but only to begin again in whispers which dripped with malice. "He's less a villain than a nauseous worm!" she said. "He has killed but only as a sneaking weasel kills. He never steals like an honest pirate but like a pickpocket. To him his second nature is a lie. He has a vulture's soul and the habits of a water viper from the swamp. He reeks of evil like a wolf who has fed on carrion. My God! You do not know a tenth of what this scoundrel is. His evil is as deep as hell itself!"

She continued breathlessly. "He was a pimp of Berkeley for years. He and his greediness helped to breed rebellion in Virginia. He murdered Walter Clayborne, the finest gentleman who ever lived." She touched his shoulders with her nervous fists.

"Oh, Lance! All women loved your uncle just as they love you. He was a salty blade, who saw no sin or guilt in any human soul. I would have rotted like a hulk except for him. I have resolved to ruin his murderer, and so I shall. I had a plan, but now I have a better plan."

For a while she whispered rapidly. Lance must not go inside. No one must see him there. She would scream and rouse the household. She would scream and Forke would come. There would be a fight in the darkness of the courtyard, an ordinary tavern brawl.

Lance for a moment did not understand.

She gave him a little time to find his wits; then she screamed. She screamed until the chestnut trees seemed to sway under the storm of sound. "Help, robbers, thieves! Help!" Henrietta cried. "I am being raped and slain! Help! Help!"

There was a clatter in the house and bearlike roars. Benches were overturned. The door flung open wide. A girl fetched a lantern, but in the rush it was knocked out of her hand. Lance tripped a cursing sailor and watched Henrietta. Still she screamed as if her lungs were full of furies. She ran into the courtyard like a terror-stricken animal.

Then, framed by the doorway, Jesús Forke appeared. He had a cutlass in one hand, and a cloak was wrapped around his left arm. In the dim glow of the moon his face was pale and wary. He darted after Henrietta. Lance followed.

Henrietta collapsed on the flagstones in a realistic swoon and Forke ran to her. Behind him staggered four half-tipsy sailors who in the gloom mistook each other for their enemies and began to fight among themselves. Lastly came Henrietta's girls, each squalling fearfully.

Lance backed beneath the chestnut tree. No one saw him for a while. He moved to take his fusil but decided that it best be left beside the tree trunk. Instead he drew his hatchet. Forke, with naked cutlass in hand, now was leaning over Henrietta. As Lance watched the man drew back as though a snake had stung him.

"You bitch!" Forke cried. "And so you'd knife me?"

Lance had to move like lightning to save the woman. Even then Forke's stroke was half completed before he caught the man's arm. Henrietta wriggled free. The drunken sailors now joined the fray.

Lance had been in other rough-and-tumble skirmishes. He had wrestled with Indians whose naked bodies had been oiled and had fought with men who had tried to thumb out his eyeballs and to paralyze him with kicks. He had learned the hatchet strokes of Pipisko the Wary. This night—for a crowded minute—he needed all his lore of violence.

He wrenched free from Forke, drew back and, crouching with his knife-hand on the ground, received the onset of one sailor and flung him off; then, with a hatchet stroke above the heel, he hamstrung another. The stricken man roared furiously and fell.

Forke meanwhile gained a clearance for a cutlass blow at Lance; but the young man, eyes accustomed to the half-light in the courtyard, used another attacker as a shield and side-stepped. The cutlass blade fell on the seaman's shoulder and the man went down. Lance now tried to close with Forke and again found himself beset about the legs by a man who smelled of musk and sweat, a large bewhiskered brute who called to Forke in Spanish. Lance struck, lost his footing and tumbled down among a mass of skirts from which shrill and angry screams were flowing. The girls had joined in the melee. Molly, an Irish girl, was belaboring a fallen sailor with a copper pot. The dog was barking furiously.

Rolling free from beneath a laurel bush, Lance gained his feet and turned toward Forke again. The battleground suddenly had become quiet except for muffled moans. Four men were down. Another was crashing away through the underbrush. Lance started to pursue, believing for a moment that it was Forke. Then he noticed Henrietta standing over a writhing figure near the door.

Lance moved up warily and looked at the wounded man. A poniard was buried in Forke's body near the buckle of his belt. He jerked at the hilt with trembling, weakening fingers for a while; then he died.

Henrietta went to Lance's side. "Go," she whispered. "Go quickly, and go far."

Before he could gain control of his labored breathing she had thrust his fusil into his hand and was hurrying him away.

Deep voices were calling from the ship off shore, demanding news of the disturbance. A cloud across the moon threw the courtyard into a deep shadow. The hound began to howl. Lance, dazed and puzzled, left the scene as Henrietta had commanded.

It was an hour before he realized how she had managed this event. Her reasoning had been direct and simple. Forke had many enemies. One such enemy had come by midnight, knife in hand, and frightened her. Forke, with his companions, had engaged the midnight visitor. Who was this executioner? All the witnesses were drunk. They had fought a violent shadow in the gloom. A jeweled poniard had been used on Forke, a Frenchman's weapon, a trinket no Virginian would touch. Someone had thrown the knife. That was not a Virginian's trick. Therefore, some foreign enemy would be suspected. No one would dream that the Clayborne boy had been the midnight visitor or that Henrietta Hart had thrown the blade.

Lance marveled. Henrietta had accomplished all her purposes. Her enemy was dead. Her friend was free. She would never be accused, for no eyes except Lance's had ever seen the French blade in Henrietta's stocking.

When dawn arrived the young man found himself twelve miles from the tavern in a vine-tangled thicket. He, exhausted, could sleep now in peace. His father's life and property were safe. The bandy-legged pirate who had dogged their lives was dead. It had not happened as Lance had wished, but Forke had suffered a most appropriate fate. A woman's knife had ended him, a woman's poniard.

XI

The American

❦ 1

CHAOS now prevailed throughout Virginia. The Monacans' confederacy of western Indians had taken full advantage of the situation. War parties filtered through Ingram's line and assailed the eastern farms.

Lance was amazed that so much happened and so quickly. Monacan war parties were moving eastward. Had they reached Gull Cove or Clayborne Castle?

He was cool and rested now. The tingling rain refreshed his sunburned skin and cleared his brain. He was a forest man again.

There was much evidence of death on the trail. Barnaby's ordinary, east of Middle Plantation, had been burned. Welche's plantation farther on was barred as though to withstand a siege, and there was not a hog, or horse, or fowl in sight. He passed old camping grounds of Bacon's soldiers.

Middle Plantation he avoided, but he found a tame pony in Queen's Creek swamp; and rigging a rawhide bridle, he mounted. Beyond the creek, to his amazement, there were fresh hatchet marks of western Indians. A party of seven, he observed, now shared the northern trail with him. He blew out the damp pan of his fusil, wiped it, renewed his priming and shielded the lock with his hand.

Now as he rode, cautiously watching his pony's ears as well as the trail ahead, he wondered anxiously if Gull Cove had been attacked. It was like the Monacans—this dash into the fat and helpless country to the east. They probably had a young war chief who lusted after power and glory. The chief had struck at exactly the right moment while the whites were quarreling among themselves. The raiders were busy among plantations that had not felt a hostile foot for thirty years. The Monacans were poor except for their allies. They mustered less than two hundred warriors. But boldly led, these meat-eating men were as dangerous as Susquehannocks.

Lance saw wolf tracks now, and after a few minutes his pony snorted and shied. Off the trail beneath a clump of cedars was a broken foot peddler's pack. He dismounted and found the peddler's

337

corpse. The wolves had not yet touched it, but the savages had beheaded the man and had cut out the heart and liver.

Lance pressed onward. The war party was scarcely an hour ahead and still moving on toward Gull Cove. Undetected, he would have to pass these Indians somehow. His ill-fed horse was flagging now, but Lance pressed five miles more out of the beast before deciding to go ahead on foot. He unbridled and freed the pony.

The Monacans, he saw, were careless. Perhaps they had found some rum among the peddler's wares. Judging by their trace, he noted that they were heavily laden with their spoils.

At the next ridge Lance, running steadily, closed up on them, and a few minutes later he sighted an Indian among the pines. The man was dressed in the peddler's hat, and he was carrying a large bundle bound in yellow cloth.

Lance made the most of his opportunity to delay the war party. Moving noiselessly down the trail's slot among the dripping trees, he slowed his pace; then he stopped. When Lance cocked his fusil the Indian dropped his bundle and, turning swiftly, jerked at his belt for his war hatchet.

Lance's shot stopped a savage whoop. Quickly, Lance then advanced past the squirming body and side-stepped into a clump of Judas bushes north of the trail.

There was a deathlike silence. Minutes passed before the other Indians reacted to this surprise blow from the rear. Without attempting to conceal his trail or to reload, Lance silently moved past them and, re-entering the trail four hundred yards ahead of the Indian party, sped toward Gull Cove. He estimated that his attack would give him a lead of at least thirty minutes and that, even then, the war party would follow him with great caution. He paused finally only to reload and resumed his journey at a steady trot.

When he reached the wagon road near Gull Cove he was three miles ahead of his pursuers. A few minutes later he had forgotten these enemies in his horror at a new discovery. Gull Cove plantation had been raided! The house and stables were smoking ruins and flames still hissed among the shattered rafters. Frantic horses were huddled in a corner of the pasture lot.

Lance stopped. Far over near the slave quarters he saw a wolf retreat slowly into the cedars. This meant no men—no live men—were near. He approached quickly. His heart pounded until it seemed that his blood was blurring his eyes. Two dead Negroes were lying in the herb garden. They had been struck down by arrows. Their bodies had been stripped and mutilated.

Easter Walker? The women? For minutes he found no sign. Rain had partly obscured the tracks of the raiders. Finally in the muck by the well he found the marks of a small slipper and the tracks of not less than eleven Monacan moccasins.

Lance Clayborne became a savage now. He remembered little of what happened during the next several hours.

From the scattered, discarded loot from the stables he found a bridle. He caught Edward Walker's chestnut mare. A moment later he headed westward at a run. Instinct, rather than conscious planning, guided him up the obscure, rain-sodden trail.

The Indians had avoided the big trace along the ridge of the peninsula. The war party also kept away from the banks of the York on which white men's boats would be moving. They took a trackless course through the thick jungle and swamps between the main ridge and the York.

Lance realized he might not surprise these warriors. They would expect pursuit. Accompanied by women prisoners, they would be followed by every white patrol which cut their trail. If pressed too closely, the Indians would kill their captives.

At the next creek Lance was near enough to read the trail's rain-soaked signs. There were two women, Easter and another. No men captives were with them. There were twelve Indians, all of them laden with spoils. They were not hurrying, but they were cautious. They had a flanking party out near the main trail, and a rear detachment of four men was a mile or more behind the main body.

Sometime on the trail ahead, well before darkness, they would stop at a point of rendezvous so that other scattered bands could rejoin them. Among these would be the band Lance had attacked. They would tell the main body about their loss. This party, too, would have read his trail and would realize that at least one man was following the Gull Cove raiders. If they rejoined, the captives might be killed.

Within two miles of the band Lance pulled his mare to a halt and began to make a trail which would confuse the band behind him. On a sapling he cut four notches, a death sign. Then with a pile of sticks and pine tags he built a medicine cairn and tied above it, with a strip of dogwood bark, a lock of his own hair. Around and around these symbols he walked his horse until the place was well trampled. The Indians would stop at this. They would marvel and make magic before passing such a mystery. Fearful and overcautious after what had happened earlier, they perhaps would not reach the rendezvous that night.

❧ 2

EASTER WALKER was in a daze of terror and fatigue. The Indians had loaded her with incongruous burdens. One warrior made her pack two hams across her shoulders. For another she carried her father's silver-mounted fowling piece and three horns of powder. When she stumbled they struck her viciously.

The captive Negress, Nola, was in a worse condition. Her shoes were gone, and she could hardly walk. They had relieved Nola of her bundles, but she was flagging at every step. She was not so strong as Easter, and the horror of that day had weakened every fiber of her body.

The Indians had attacked in midmorn while the servingmen were about their early chores. There had been no warning whatever; but Alan Walker had escaped the attack and so had Easter's Aunt Lucy, because they had been visiting over at Queen's Creek Plantation. The Indians apparently had not intended to kill the Negro menservants, but when the Negroes attempted to run away Indian boys struck them down with arrows.

Squaws were of value. Smallpox had taken away many Monacan women; so Easter and the Negress were led away. Easter's fear weakened her at first, but in time pain brought her back to sanity. Thereafter she thanked God for her firm muscles and husbanded her strength as best she could. Her dress was torn off above the knees. Her stockings were in shreds. In the swamps a leech had attached itself to her ankle, and to the amusement of the Indians she had screamed; but she was beyond such minor irritations now. If she and Nola could survive, if they could live a few hours or perhaps a day, they might be rescued.

Where was Berkeley's militia? Where was Brent? Where were the men who had marched away to fight these savages? And where was Lance Clayborne, who knew the Indians so well? By now, she believed, he was on his way to London. But hope would not die! Other women had survived capture by the savages. So would she.

The chieftain of this band had an otter cloak like the one Usack had worn. The Indian had laughing eyes. He had enjoyed his coup deep in the eastern settlements. He carried Edward Walker's saw and hammer at his belt and a Dutch musketoon that had belonged to her grandfather. An older Indian had shown him how to load it. Around the savage's head was a strip torn from a Turkish rug. Raindrops gathered like beads on his oily body. Once he kicked her from behind to hurry her progress. She reacted without thinking. She dropped her burden and struck out fiercely at his broad, paint-smeared face. This pleased him. He made another Indian take the hams, and he walked behind her for a while, his right hand twisted in her hair.

Ahead, the slave woman cried out again. The older Indian had grown impatient. Easter heard the crunch of the blow, and it was over. As she passed the mud-covered, huddled form it seemed anything but human. An Indian stooped to take the scarf from around the Negro woman's neck. Now Easter's rage began to give her extra strength. She forgot the soreness of her legs and the aches between her shoulders as she wondered how she might kill these beasts around her. Six hours of captivity had made of her a thing almost as wild as any Indian.

The savages rested more often as the shadows lengthened and looked backward as though expecting others to rejoin them. As they moved farther from the settlement they became more joyous over their achievement. A stout boy danced ahead, re-enacting in triumphant pantomine the murder of a Negro slave. He fitted an imaginary arrow to his bow, aimed, then looked and aimed again and sprang forward with his club. Easter had seen white boys play games like that. Another youth began a chant in cadence to his toed-in march, but the war chief ended that by a growled command. It was not safe to sing on that path.

Two men grew ill from gorging chunks of ham. They stopped and gagged while the others laughed at their discomfort. The chieftain would not let them pause for long.

⊸§ 3

LANCE CLAYBORNE was within a mile of the war party by sundown. He had read from the soft sod every detail of the march. The news was good. Their leader was not half so wary as the situation warranted. He did not know he was being pursued. Furthermore, the Indian was tired and so were two other older tribesmen. Two who had eaten raw ham were sick. The others were loaded down with loot.

Lance sweated as he thought of Easter Walker. But she had her shoes. No Indian could wear her little shoes. She was not so heavily burdened now. Her steps were firm. Only the young warriors were as strong as she; and they, no doubt, would welcome rest at dusk. All the savages were thin. They had marched with little food and rest for many days during this raid. And they could not stop to feast for many more days to come.

Lance brewed many plans. If he should attack outright, they would brain the girl at once. If he should wait until the rearward party joined the band when dawn came, there would be alarm; and they might kill their remaining captive. He must act this night and soon.

How? He knew of many ways. The Chiskiacks had played such games in the moon of ripening corn. Pipisko had not feared the owl ghost, and Usack the heron could fly at night. None of the Monacans belonged to owl or heron clans. Mountain Indians were afraid to fight in darkness. These tired Monacans, no doubt, would sleep like denned bears until the sun awakened them.

The Indian band halted on high ground beyond another swamp at dusk. The Indians made camp quietly in the dripping forest. There was no fire. The chieftain handed Easter a lump of sugared maple sap to eat. Bound to a small tree by a thong around her middle, she slept for hours in a pile of wet pine tags.

At last, the coma of exhaustion ended, she was awakened by the pain of her aching muscles. Almost at once she sensed a strange presence near her. The forest seemed as dark as the inside of a grave. She could not see the sky nor the great pine beside her head. She heard the dripping rain and the breathing of a sleeping savage. In her hand she still held the lump of maple gum. She tasted it and the sweetish stuff helped to awaken her.

Again she sensed an alert presence. Her flesh became chilled; then something gently touched the torn hem of her dress. She waited, scarcely breathing, hearing not a sound. There was no other movement for several minutes. Then a firm hand was clamped across her mouth and another held her firmly by her shoulders. There was a faint whisper and the hold relaxed. Her bonds were cut and hands kneaded her chilled legs back to life. Now she recognized a voice, a voice so low she wondered if she dreamed it.

It told her not to move. It was an English voice. Usack's voice! At last the whispering stopped. There were many quiet minutes. At his command she then took off her sodden outer dress without a sound and left it by the tree. He thrust the end of a long stick in her hands and bade her hold it and crawl after him. Guided by the stick, which she clutched so fiercely that she hurt her hand, she moved an inch ... and another inch.

It took them an hour to proceed a bare fifty yards from the Indian bivouac. They had heard a rustle from her guards as they crawled. A savage had reached over, felt her—now empty—skirt and, reassured, had gone back to sleep.

Clear of the ring of sleeping savages Lance helped her to her feet. Then he led her through the blackness for many minutes before he spoke. "You'd make a bonny squaw," he said.

It was then only that she wept. He held her on his shoulders until she cried away a thousand terrors.

"Usack!" she murmured.

After a while as the dripping sky became gray with dawn they resumed their flight. He led her to a flooded creek bed, and they waded many minutes to conceal their tracks.

She laughed awhile nearly in hysterics. "I am naked, Lance!" she cried.

"And you are alive. Thank God!" he said. "There is a clearing on the river near this place, and if the Indians have not found it, there is a cabin."

᷍§ 4

IN THE half-light of dawn they arrived at the cabin, and with a gourd of water Lance concealed their tracks up from the creek. He found some old deerskins among the loft poles, then he made her a bed and she collapsed.

When she awoke she found him sound asleep beside her on the puncheon floor. For a while she did not move, afraid she would awaken him. He slept as peacefully as a kitten. His face was boyish in spite of the terrifying arches of his brows. His thin beard formed a graceful pattern on his chin. His skin was a rich brown color. She started to touch his arm; then she hesitated.

He had no shirt. His leggings were in shreds. His hair was tied with a strip of harness leather. At the fingers of his right hand was his knife hilt. On the other side of his belt, hung in a loop, was a small French hatchet. One side of the blade was brightly polished from its contact with his body.

She was in no better condition. Her shift was in ribbons below her waist, her hair a tangled mat of burrs, her skin a maze of brier scratches. Moving gently to keep from rousing him, she struggled to her feet. Her muscles ached cruelly, but she felt triumphant. She was more alive now than she had been in all her life before.

Her home had been destroyed and with it all security. She was deep in the wilderness without food or clothing. She was in danger of death; yet she was unafraid.

The drip, drip of water through the roof continued. Still her heart was singing. She turned. Lance Clayborne's eyes were open, watching. She blushed as he smiled up at her. "I'm sorry about my clothes," she said.

He said, "You are cold. Wait. I shall build a fire." He was on his feet in an instant.

She watched him, fascinated. He sharpened a splinter and with it

plugged the touchhole of his fusil. Then he pulled a strip of cedar
bark from one of the cabin's uprights and shredded it into a fluffy
ball. This he dusted with some priming powder and placed on the
edge of the pan of his gun. He snapped the lock. There was a flash,
and the ball of bark began to glow. In a moment he had blown it
into a flame, and a tiny fire was growing on the hearth.

"There is no danger from the Indians now, so we can have a fire,"
he said. "I scouted them at daybreak. They have passed on westward.
Fearful of their lives now, they have dropped much of their booty."
He pointed to the corner. "There is a sack of flour and some salt."

She helped him gather wood and clumps of grass with which to
patch the roof. After a while, when the fire was burning well, he
took his fusil and went out into the clearing. Almost before she
realized that she was alone she heard a shot. He returned with a
young wild turkey.

For two hours then they both were very busy. She prepared the
game bird while he cleaned the cabin and patched the roof. This
done he cut a deerskin into a long strip and mended the bunk in the
corner.

"You'll need another sleep," he said. "We are many miles from
... from ..." He stopped.

She did not reply. The turkey was roasting and the cakes were
baking on the coals.

"We need more meat. Otherwise we are fortunate," Lance observed.

"I thought of you," she said. "I thought of you and then remembered that you probably were on the ocean, on your way to London."

He frowned. "But you saw to it that I was not on the ocean," he
said. "You told Berkeley, and he saw to it that I did not sail."

She was appalled. "What do you mean?"

He shrugged his shoulders. "It is well I did not make the voyage.
Had I gone to England, you would be a squaw by now."

"I don't know what you mean, Usack!"

"Lie down," he commanded. "You'll need another sleep before I
can get you out of here."

Bewildered she sank back on the bunk in tears. "I did not mention
your voyage to a soul, Usack! You must believe me. What has happened to you!"

He did not answer her. He gathered more wood and made the half-ruined cabin bright and dry. He cleared away the cobwebs and the nests of wood mice and swept the place with a damp broom of dogwood brush. Outside the storm continued without pause.

He would have to find a boat to get her back to the plantations and find someone to care for her. Who? Every farmstead in miles had been alarmed by the Indian incursion or by the lawless bandits who prowled the trails. The whole land was in chaos. No place was safe. He alone was left to feed her and to guard her.

Easter was asleep again. He placed more faggots on the fire and went to the door. Outside the rain poured down. The high grass of the clearing had been beaten flat. Beyond, in the mist, every wavelet of the river was being knocked level by the pelting sheets of rain. Along the shore a fat black bear was fishing. As Lance watched the beast struck the water with his paw and leaped backward, gingerly nosing a struggling crab that had been flung out onto the sand. The bear touched his quarry and leaped again.

Lance picked up his fusil and from the door took careful aim. Even as he prepared to fire he remembered the sleeping girl. If he fired from there, it would awaken her. He loosened his knife and hatchet then and, shielding the pan of his fusil from the rain, went out and closed the door. He had difficulty with the bear. The beast survived his shot, and when Lance closed in the animal turned in pain and rage to defend himself.

Lance laid aside his gun and cautiously approached with his hatchet ready. The beast struck out too soon. Lance, watching his footing in the wet sand, dodged and with his hatchet landed a blow. The animal rolled backward with a roar, but was up as the man approached to strike again. The claws seemed to miss Lance's body by a fraction of an inch; but always they missed. At last the stunned beast rolled into the water and as he floundered Lance's hatchet reached the brain.

As he disentangled himself Lance started in surprise. There on the beach was Easter. She had caught up a club and had come to join the fight.

"You!" he cried.

"Are you hurt?"

He frowned scornfully. "Hurt? Why should I be hurt?"

As he dragged his heavy quarry from the water's edge, she helped him as best she could, flinging back her wet hair from her face. She was mindless now of her nakedness.

When they had pulled the carcass above the tidemark she caught her breath and scolded him with fury. "You are a fool, Usack!" she cried.

He was amazed. To him this was an ordinary hunt. He had killed bear like this before. The animal was meat and fat and clothing. They needed these things. He ordered Easter to return to shelter.

She refused. As he skinned the animal, she assisted, scolding him the while. "You should have shot him, not fought him like a savage."

"I shot him and in the rain there was no chance to reload for further shots."

"Suppose that he had hurt you?"

"Me? I am no feeble child. How could he injure me?"

"I was afraid."

"I'm sorry. Please go into the cabin. Take my gun and dry it carefully." This time she obeyed.

❧ 5

THE bear gave them some busy hours. Preparing and drying the skin was rough work, but the girl seemed to enjoy it. Here was subsistence and a warming cloak. The fat strong flesh they roasted by their big fire, and the feast gave them new strength. Later they dried strips of the loin for future use and cured the hide after the Indian's fashion. As the tough pelt dried before the fire Lance softened it with the crushed brains and liver of the beast and broke the fiber by dragging it repeatedly across a rafter overhead.

Never had Easter Walker done such labor before. Her shoulders ached, her hands grew sore; but no thought of protest came into her mind. It seemed the natural thing to share the toil, to help this boy— this man—who was so confident and competent here in the wilderness. He was unhurried and painstaking. Often he bade her pause and rest or to go more slowly.

"There is no need for haste," he said. "You must regain your strength, so I may find you a place of safety." He shook his head in puzzlement and continued. "The north bank of the York has been abandoned since the raid, I think. I have seen the smoke of several fires. That Indian, your captor, was a brave and skillful man."

"A savage murderer!" she cried.

"Yes, a warrior fighting the savage type of war. We have no cause for too much sorrow. We are safe. Here is meat and shelter, and I have ten charges for my gun."

She stole a glance at him. He was at work on the pelt with his knife, removing bits of fat and flesh, patiently and carefully thinning the heavier portions. His muscles played smoothly beneath the brown, weathered skin of his bare shoulders. He did not waste a motion. Often, as smoothly as an animal, he rose to unbolt the door and glance watchfully out over the river and the clearing.

He turned to her. "There may be another day of rain. All the creeks are in flood." He refastened the heavy door and turned to mend the fire. "I'm glad we found this house unburned," he said. "It was Dick Potts's cottage years ago. He built it well, thank God!" He told her of Dick Potts's death at Curle's Neck. "It made Bacon very angry. After that he joined the company at Merchants Hope and agreed to be its leader."

"Always you speak of Bacon."

"Yes. He was a man with qualities of greatness—the one man I have known with such."

"A rebel!"

He looked up at her in sour scorn. "Yes, a rebel!" he retorted. "Who wouldn't be a rebel among these eastern plantations, these pest-holes inhabited by vile men and treacherous women!"

She looked at him coldly and said, "Had I been guilty of what you say I did, I would not blame you for hating me."

"I'm done with the damned eastern plantations!" he said.

"And with me?"

"Yes. I am done with you!" He looked like a savage as he stared back at her.

"You think I told Berkeley of your contemplated voyage?"

"I know you did."

"You are a fool, Usack! I did not even tell my father or my brother."

"So I was arrested!"

His bitterness was so violent that it almost sickened him, but slowly a faint comprehension began to pierce the red fog of his mind. His father had engaged his passage with Christopher Eveling well in advance. Berkeley had stopped Eveling's voyage and had held the ship in the reach below Jamestown. Eveling could have told Berkeley about the plan to visit London. . . .

He continued his work on the bearskin. It was a large bear, one of the largest he had ever seen east of the mountains. The woman would need a cloak. The . . . She still stared down at him.

"I am sorry I am a burden," she said.

"I'm not sorry I am a rebel!" he retorted. "Go out on the shore and scream. Maybe one of Berkeley's pirates will come and save you."

She said nothing for a while. Then she said, "Am I in danger, Usack?"

"You are," he said. "You are camping with a hairy Virginian with whom no decent person is safe. You are in the company of a western outlaw who is proud of his condition!"

Her use of his Indian name began to reduce his anger. She spoke his name in a way that tore at his heart.

"Then I am an outlaw, too, Usack. I'll go with you. We'll find horses, and I'll go with you . . . out to the west."

He looked up, surprised.

"I mean it, Usack. I don't know what has caused all the confusion in the plantations, but I know about myself now. I want to go where you go. I'll cook your meat and . . ." She tossed her hair back and turned away, but not until he noticed that her face and neck had flamed with color.

"You don't know what you're saying," he replied.

"Why not?"

He turned aside and whetted his knife for a while upon a hearthstone. Again she blushed. This time because of his indifference. She must bathe and find a comb somewhere and other means to make herself attractive. The soiled fragments of her shift did not cover her.

"You must go out for a while, a little while," she said. "Not far."

Lance rose, but still he did not look at her. For hours he had struggled with himself. Her blushes had not helped. For all her raggedness she was beautiful—too beautiful. He tightened his belt and picked up his pouch, fusil and powder horn.

"I'll remain in hailing distance," said Lance. "Cry out when I can return."

He went out into the rain. The driving drops refreshed him and washed away his rage. He went beyond the clearing and into the dripping forest. A squirrel nagged at him awhile, but otherwise the woods were quiet. He found a dry spot under a vine-hung oak and waited.

The girl was rested now and well. He had feared fever. But he would have to take her back to the plantations without delay. Where should he take her? Every farm for many miles had been abandoned with Berkeley's flight to the Eastern Shore. Robbers and savages prowled everywhere. Clayborne Castle would not do. There were no women there now. Drummond's? Dame Drummond was a bold, resourceful soul; but she probably had fled to the coast by now. There was no safety anywhere except in hiding or at the point of a musket. Keep the girl with him on his trip west? It was unthinkable. He would have difficulties enough alone. Besides . . .

A handsome creature she was in spite of her scratches. Now that she had recovered from her weariness she had made that rat-gnawed cabin glow. She was like an Indian in one respect. His rage had made her more gentle. He should treat her like a squaw. She probably would enjoy it. No. He would have to remember somehow that he had once been an English gentleman. She might hate him all her life if he became unchivalrous and weak.

To his left he heard a rustle in the underbrush and sundry gruntings. It was a wandering family of hogs. In a moment, remembering his dependence on wild meat and the somewhat strong taste of bear, he moved upwind and stalked the porkers. In time a half-grown pig came close enough. Lance rose to his knees, disengaged his hatchet and, carefully estimating the distance, flung the weapon. The pig went down. Sweet meat, this was, and better far than bear. So let it rain another day. They would have another banquet.

After he had dressed the pig and hung it above the spring branch she called him. As he approached the door she told him to wait and asked the loan of his knife. A bare and graceful arm was thrust out from the door to take it.

He went down to the riverbank and impatiently waited. He wished to see her once again and quickly. He had been away from her less than an hour and he was lonely. Queer it was, this yearning. It had never been so acute before. He hated her; yet he also desired her. Would it always be like this? Would he want her with him constantly?

Easter had located a treasure, a bit of ancient Osnaburg cloth which had been used to chink the window frame. From it she unravelled several yards of thread, and with this and bits of the bearskin she had made a wonderful garment. There were no scissors or needles, but the knife did very well; and the bearskin now was pliable enough . . .

She called Lance in and laughed as he looked at her with amazement from the doorway. She had controlled her hair and banded her forehead with a white strip torn from her shift. But a half vest of bearskin, and a short kilt of the same material were the startling items of her new wardrobe. He started, confused. She was lovely, lovelier than any picture he had dreamed of on lonely nights. Her eyes, her skin, her hair—all seemed to glow with vigorous life. Behind her the fire brightened the little hut. Stunned, he stood dripping at the doorstep like a lout.

"Come in, foolish one!" she cried. "You will catch your death of ague!"

He laid aside his gun and rubbed his eyes. She took his hand and pulled him to the fire. "You like my skirt?" she asked.

He did not answer. He wanted to take her in his arms, and she expected something of the sort; but he was afraid. She was close to him. Her smooth bare shoulder touched him. Her hair had a wild fragrance.

He rubbed his eyes. "We must go," he said.

She did not reply. She sensed his indecision and enjoyed it. He did not really want to go. Besides, the water in the creeks and swamps was very high, and it still was raining. They had food and warmth and shelter.

"We must go," he said again.

"Why must we go?"

"Because a devil shares this cabin with us," he said.

She laughed. "Is that another of your foolish forest superstitions?"

He took her hand. "Oh no. The devil's here." He struck his chest. "I want you, and——"

"Then why is a devil in your heart?"

"I am a man."

"My man?"

"Of course!"

"And not a devil?"

"A devil, too."

"I am not afraid."

He took a deep breath and shrugged his shoulders nervously. "You have cause to be," he growled. "Here we are all warm, well fed, alone together and far off the trail."

"So?"

"We are not . . ." He hesitated.

"Wed you mean?"

"Yes."

She looked into the fire. "No, we are not wed." She looked up with pert daring in her eyes. "Faugh! My Usack dreams of parsons!"

Fiercely now he struggled with himself. He moved back from the fire and clasped his hands across his knees. The devil whispered that the pair who had built that hut had never had a parson mumble over them. This girl was not afraid. Why was he? There were few ministers. Most of them had fled with Berkeley. But this maid was not a squaw. She was helpless and in his care.

He groaned. She was teasing him. She was siding with the devil in this fight. She was like a doe during the moon of falling leaves. She had become as coquettish and as sly as a vixen ready for a den. He turned his eyes away. She kissed him behind the ear.

"Stop!" he commanded.

She pouted and kissed him again. The devil departed for a while. Strangely her lips brought an angry calm. His strong, long-fingered hands made white marks on her shoulders.

"Stop!" he repeated. "You are mad! I should not have fed you bear meat."

She laughed. "You are a fool, dear Usack," she said huskily.

"Do not touch me!"

"Why not?"

"It is unseemly."

"I want to kiss you."

He climbed to his feet with a fierce oath. "Stop, I say!"

For a while he busied himself with the cleaning of his fusil. This done, he repaired a broken stool, straightened a bent fire iron and played at other chores.

She sat, eyes on the yellow driftwood coals, talking softly, as if in a dream. "I feel as if I'm in a freshly made world," she said. "Storms once were gloomy, but this storm is full of joyous rain. It has imprisoned us in a cell full of happiness. I should be sorrowful, but I am glad despite your silly talk of devils. I thought I was an English girl. I'm not. I'm a rebel, too, Usack. I am a barbarous Virginian!"

He flashed a sharp glance at her. "Here, take this stool," he commanded.

"I'd rather stay here as I am."

He took her by the shoulders and placed her on the stool beside the chimney corner.

"Do you hate me for wanting you?" she asked.

He did not reply.

"No, you do not," she said. "You've known it all along, but there is European blood still in you. It has filled your mind with phantoms, ghosts of ancient custom. This stool is a symbol. You fear me when I sit among those deerskins on the floor. Now that I'm on a stool I am once more a proper maiden." She kicked the stool aside, and once more sat on the floor.

He emptied his hunter's pouch on the window shelf and began to chip at a blunted gun flint with the back of his knife blade. He tried not to look at her. He should go out. He should walk over to the ridge trail and seek out news. He should escape this hut which had become a place of torture. But he could not. The creeks were high. There were no travelers. It would be cowardly besides. Damn this girl! She was as wild as a widowed Chiskiack!

He breathed deeply and began to overhaul his stock of bullets. The mold had left ridges upon a few of the lead balls. With care he trimmed them with his knife and smoothed them against a chimney stone.

She seemed to read his mind. "Am I as pretty as your Indian girls?"

"Of course."

"You'd rather have me than an Indian girl?"

"Of course."

"I am a better cook."

"I know."

"I can beat flax and spin and weave it, too, just as I spin and weave Scotch wool and cotton. Someday I'll make some linen shirts for you. Then maybe you will love me."

"Perhaps I love you now," he groaned.

"I'm afraid you do not. You think I am a shameless wench. Perhaps I am. Perhaps I do not care."

He cursed the need that dried his throat and dizzied him. What could he do? Womanlike, she might soon grow angry with him. The devil began to whisper. The world would never blame him. And were not his shoulders wide enough and strong enough to take all censure for this situation? Gossips would swear he had forced her anyway. Old wives would chatter and take delicious, vicarious pleasure in the maiden's plight.

Besides, an act of God had thrown them into this rainy Eden. The fates had told him to escape in time to save her from the Indian war party. God, not the devil, had provided them abundantly with food, and fire and shelter. God, not the devil, had planted those human senses in his heart. Paradise was built before there was a parson on the earth. He flung his flints and bullets back into the pouch, put fresh fuel on the fire and sat down beside her at the hearth.

Now she would have none of him. When he sought to take her hand she jerked away and called him a fool. Her mood had changed completely. He recoiled in anxious wonderment and stared at her.

"Go whittle on your bullets!" she said.

"I have finished them," he replied.

"You'd rather chip flints than make love to me."

"That's not so."

"It is."

"It's not."

"Go away, I say. There is a broken bench to mend. Besides you promised to make me a smaller table."

"There is plenty of time for that."

"I want it now."

He now was in no mood for building furniture. He stroked her arm. She pulled away. He complimented her upon her bearskin vest. She frowned. He chafed until his forehead was bedewed with perspiration. She would not let him touch her.

When he rose to cut fresh pegs for the broken bench she was displeased. She did not really want him to work on the bench. Unaccountably, she began to weep. He knelt to comfort her, only to have her bite him on the arm and push him furiously aside. At this he looked so utterly ridiculous that she forgot her grief and laughed at him. His fingers now itched for a stick with which to humble her, but when she tossed back her hair he realized that she was not an Indian.

"You are so fierce!" she cried.

He was too angry to reply.

"Poor boy, you want to beat me?"

Her arms went around his neck and all his anger melted in two breaths. They kissed until the cabin seemed to whirl end over end, and all the world seemed to turn red; but in a moment she began to fight him like a wildcat. He had to free her.

"You should be ashamed!" she said.

"A plague on you!" he answered hotly.

"You . . . you—!"

"Yes, I did, and you know why, and . . ."

She sat breathlessly awhile, her head upon her knees, her face covered by her great wave of hair. "You're not a gentleman," she said.

"Nor you a lady," he replied.

There was silence for a while. It was broken by her laughter, and once more she was in his arms. This time he was as proper as a vicar at a funeral, and she liked it not at all. She pouted.

"You love me not," Easter said.

"I love you enough to beat you senseless," he said.

"Oh, maybe. But you wouldn't."

"This is no time, no place for coquetry," he said. "You have no right to torture me. I'll not stand it any longer."

He caught up his belt and buckled it. She ran after him and tried to hold him. He thrust her away and went out into the rain. In the coolness of the storm his mind began to work again.

The wind was whipping spray along the shore. He cleared his eyes of it and straightened his shoulders. A rivulet of water ran down his feverish body.

◄§ 6

HE RETURNED to the cottage in a mood that puzzled the girl. She had fixed her hair aright and was lying curled up on the bunk as though she were asleep, a vision out of Heaven. He pretended not to notice. There were fresh cakes on the hearth, and a bit of pork was browning on the spit. He grunted approval as he warmed his hands, but he did not look at her.

Easter sighed, and several times she squirmed in irritation. He did not move. She reached out, touched his hair and asked why he did not eat. He would not reply. She battered him with words—called him a lout, an ass and an ill-mannered brute. This made him smile; so she took his hand and held it against her cheek awhile.

"You want to beat me?" she asked.

He did not reply.

"I thought you'd gone out to cut a hickory switch."

He shook his head.

"I wish you had. I shouldn't treat you as I've done. I love you, Usack. You can switch me if you wish."

Still he did not move.

"I am cold, Usack."

He put some wood upon the fire and resumed his place on the floor.

"I did not mean more fire, you clumsy dolt!" she cried.

He shrugged, and for a time she sulked. Then, disturbed, she sat up, leaned over and peered down at his now stony face. There was no answering smile.

She kissed him, pulled him to her and curled up close beside him. The light was fading. In the corner it was dark save for an occasional flicker from the fire.

"I am cold, Usack," she sighed as he surrendered.

❧ 7

NEXT day the storm had passed but not the flood. The creek was far out of its banks, and the low ground was impassable. They were glad. Dick Potts's old cottage was now a place of lovely magic. Outside a wild dominion was at civil war. Friends were dying upon a tyrant's scaffold. Savages roamed among once prosperous plantings. Pirates cruised along the coast and up the rivers. But Lance and Easter forgot such things while they loved and dreamed and planned.

They built a house with charcoal lines on the hearth and furnished it and peopled it with children and with favorite servants. She insisted that there be a place for books as well as racks for weapons and for tools. They would send to France for mirrors and to Smyrna for rich carpets. There would be Scotch wool for blankets and linen from the low countries for napery. She inventoried every pot and pan and pound of feathers left her by her mother. He itemized every bit of iron and saddlery and leather they would need.

To both it seemed as though they would never have their fill of love. It was as if they had discovered something new about the force that makes a boy and girl become a family and welds families into mighty nations. For Virginia was to be a mighty nation. No governor for long could resist its laws, no savages could deny the power of planter pioneers. This land was paradise unlimited.

Easter said that she would like to stay forever in their magic hut and so did Lance. But there were many things to do. He must find a place of safety for her. Perhaps there was security for her at David Broome's. She could wait there for his return. Then there would be a wedding to satisfy the gossips of the colony.

When an empty log canoe came drifting past Lance swam out and brought it to the creek. Next day they poled their craft southward through the flooded bottoms toward the main trail. They came to the upper reaches of the creek near Kendall's western quarter. Here they found three frightened slaves and horses for their journey over to Broome's. The Indians had not raided the populous north bank of the James, which was a good thing for peace-loving David Broome.

Lance blew some music on the gate horn, a bugle call of Rupert's which Broome recognized. The bars were off the door when they rode up to the house.

⋖§ 8

ANN SHORT, Broome's wife, was horrified at Easter's bearskin costume, and she soon corrected it with a voluminous one-piece dress. Broome, his nearsighted eyes alight with pleasure, clucked like a turkey cock and opened his best pipe of Madeira. There were sturgeon steak and roasted venison for dinner, and there was much talk.

It was small wonder that David Broome was a fat and happy man. Ann Short's herb sauces and her cakes were richly tasty wonders. She trotted to and from her kettles like a busy hen, keeping the table laden with a steaming feast. Ann kept her eyes on Easter Walker, marveling at her loveliness, and envying the light within her eyes.

There must be a wedding and that quickly, Ann thought. Lance Clayborne was an outlaw, but there must be a wedding at once, somehow. Ann Broome was horrified at their sojourn in the cottage on the York. They must never tell a living soul of *that*. Easter's reputation would be ruined!

David was ready early the next day with his book; but when he asked Ann if he should awaken their guests, she demurred. The poor children were weary. Besides she must clean and decorate the common rooms so it would be a proper wedding.

It was nearly noon before the big chamber was in order. The sun was casting its shortest shadow before Lance and Easter were ready for the merry ceremony.

The servants, dressed in their Sunday garments, came in from the field to watch. David had on his best broadcloth. Lance had cleaned the mud from his buckskins and had brushed his hair. Easter, in a dress of Ann's that had been reduced in size by sundry pins and stitches, looked like a mischievous blond angel. She did not share Ann's distress at having the wedding in a house instead of a church. She pretended, to Ann's horror, that she cared little for weddings anyway.

"But thuppose——" said Ann who was having some difficulty with her speech because her mouth was full of pins as she made a final adjustment to Easter's gown.

"Nonsense!" said Easter. "We are hoping, not supposing!"

At last they all gathered before the big hearth. Seven candles were lighted, and the chamber was bedecked with cedar greenery. But as David Broome picked up his prayer book to face the laughing couple there was an outcry from the servant who was at the window.

Horsemen were in the stable yard. Colonel Edward Hill with a patrol of Chicheley's dragoons were paying them a visit.

Lance Clayborne kissed Easter with passionate deliberation and whispered that she was to remain at Broome's until Byrd's next boat. Thereafter he himself took up his weapons and slipped away. He went westward at great speed while Hill's troopers flung pistol shots into the forest at his heels.

◆§ 9

SIR MATHEW CLAYBORNE'S visit to the Governor at Green Spring caused talk for many weeks. By that time Drummond had been hanged and many others doomed by Berkeley's court-martial.

The blunt old soldier did not fawn on Sir William as his Councillors were wont to do. He bowed as stiffly as a stallion as he faced the angry Governor.

Sir William looked up from his papers and remarked, "I suppose you come with a petition?"

Sir Mathew overlooked the Governor's sneer as he replied, "I do not, sir."

"What then, Clayborne?"

"A warning."

The Governor frowned. "You come here breathing threats, Sir Mathew?"

"A warning, I said, not a threat."

Sir William frowned again. Lines of weariness marked his aging face. For a moment he was hesitant, uncertain. Sir Mathew Clayborne was no churl to be dismissed without an audience. He had been a good soldier and a power at court. True, his son was outlawed for good cause, and yet . . .

Sir Mathew followed up his bold attack. "These bloody assizes must end," he said. "Too many men are being hanged."

The Governor interrupted. "Is this a lecture, Clayborne?"

"A warning." Stubbornly the old knight had his say as he continued. "I am not here to ask you mercy for my son. I am here to caution you against this spate of fury in the colony. This morning you hanged Bland. Hansford is also doomed and many more. A thousand men or more will hate the Crown and you for this. From that thousand who will not fear, but hate—I say, will hate—may rise another Bacon."

Berkeley's sneer returned. "They would hate the Crown, you say?"

"Yes, the Crown!" Sir Mathew roared. "Think you I care for else? Let them hate you! I care not. Your life, like mine, is nearly ended. But I would not have them hate the Crown. Charles Stuart is my friend. Think you I want this great dominion snatched away from him? Virginia must not become another Ireland, nor must it ever be a colony of Spain or France. I warn you, sir, this murderous course of yours must end!"

Lights of rage began to flicker in the Governor's nearsighted eyes. "Mind your tongue!" he cried.

"If you will mind your actions, sir!"

"Silence!"

Sir Mathew bowed and stared in grim obedience for a while.

At last Sir William spoke with quavering anger. "God's boots, I believe you are a rebel too!"

"To that, I say, sir, mind *your* tongue!"

"You threaten?"

"Is it a threat to recognize an insult, sir?"

"Mind your tongue!"

For a moment they were two old men in violent quarrel. Sir William called Sir Mathew a breeked shrew. Sir Mathew called the Governor a power-blinded ass. The Governor waved his cane. Sir Mathew touched his sword hilt. Then, at last, in sheer exhaustion they began to talk sanely again.

"I'll have no rebellious remarks from you!" the Governor said.

"There'll be no mutiny from me. I've had my say as a free-born Englishman and with your permission, I shall leave this place."

Sir William hesitated to dismiss him now. There was a pause. "What of your son?" the Governor inquired.

"I have lost my son."

"What? He is dead?"

Sir Mathew wrinkled his brow. "He is not dead, but I have lost him, as you know. This senseless tempest you aroused has made an outlaw of the boy. He is on your hangman's list."

"He is a rebel."

"I shall not be an accuser of my son."

"He was with Bacon."

"I know naught of his relationship with Bacon. But I do know full six hundred men who were under arms with Bacon. Do you expect to slay them all?"

Sir William did not answer for a while. At last he said, "I'll hang every officer who had a part of Bacon's cabal. There will be no lily-livered mercy, I assure you."

"Then reap the whirlwind as you will," Sir Mathew said. "I have done my duty in this affair. I have warned you honestly. You are a deputy of Charles. Each throat you cut you are supposed to cut by royal warrant, not for personal revenge. Remember, Berkeley, you must account for all of this!" Sir Mathew turned his back and left the chamber.

Beverley and Parke and others who from the anteroom had heard this angry colloquy said nothing for a while. The Governor was very thoughtful afterward.

Sir Mathew was about to mount and ride away when a Negro boy approached him. Mistress Walker wished to see him at the well house for a moment. Walker? Walker? She was the maid whom Lance was courting, Alan Walker's pretty daughter.

The old knight smoothed his laced cuffs and strode over to the rendezvous. The child was lovely! No silly chit at all! She was as graceful as a Russian hound. He swept her a bow that almost broke the aging hinges of his back.

She had a finger on her lips. "I must hurry, sir, because no one must see us. Is Lance well?"

"I hope so, child. I do not know."

"You spoke to the Governor?"

Sir Mathew frowned and started to reply; then he stopped.

Easter sighed. "I see. I, too, have done my best without success thus far. Pray tell Lance, sir . . ." She paused and looked around. "Pray tell him he must stay with Ingram. He must not come east."

"You mean my boy is being trapped?"

She curled her lip in bitter contempt. "The Governor is insane. He used my name to procure Hansford's arrest. He must not hang your boy, my boy. I am a virtual prisoner."

"The fool! That thrice-damned senile fool!"

The girl was gone. Sir Mathew stamped back to his horse and, muttering furiously, rode away.

ᵉᔮ 10

INGRAM could not save the easterners who hugged their farms until the Governor's men arrived, but he could hold his lines on the York.

To messengers from Green Spring he was firm. "Let Sir William Berkeley take us if he can, or grant every man who is with me full amnesty," Ingram declared.

Many messengers arrived. Rebellion had been crushed, a dozen men executed, the property of a hundred forfeited. The prisons were full and new pillories were being built.

Ingram stood firm. He kept his camp in order and alert. No boat approached without an ample warning being given by foresters in fast canoes. No man came near by land who was not covered by the fusils of Ingram's scouts.

Some of the farmers at West's Point were in despair, but not the western men. These borderers knew enough of trail and wilderness to feel safe. Not even a mighty army could dislodge them from their forest.

Berkeley's ships which approached West's Point were grounded on the mud flats many hours, and did not dare unloose a single cannon shot. The Governor sent some horsemen through New Kent, but Ingram's canoemen captured the forage boats which were to meet Berkeley's men at Pamunkey landing; so the Governor's cavalry withdrew and half the starving horses had to be abandoned.

The Council urged a treaty. If peace were not effected soon, gangs of hairy bordermen would raid the eastern settlements. It was too costly to wage war on wild hunters. Besides, the flow of fur had stopped. There were no beaverskins, no deerskins, no winter cargoes from the west. The ships lay idle while the merchants raged.

The colony was awakening from rebellion like a man arising after too much ale. Heads ached and bitter words flew back and forth. Children sickened, food was scarce, the gibbets creaked with stinking burdens. The York was dragged in search of Bacon's corpse, so that it too, like Oliver Cromwell's, might be hanged in chains. They did not find it.

Lance escaped the Sheriff of James City County by the narrowest of margins. Green Spring was guarded like a medieval keep, and every effort to see Easter Walker failed. In Surry he was forced to flee a posse which had lain in wait for many days at Allen's house.

The trap was well concealed, but Lance sniffed danger and backed away. For ten hours a pack of wolfhounds was on his trail. This angered him and so he circled and harassed the men who followed until they believed ghosts were in the swamp. Then he went west again.

✒§ 11

LADY FRANCES BERKELEY was delighted with Easter Walker. The girl had manners and charm. She knew London like a Spanish spy, she was a bonny gossip and she accorded Lady Frances all the flattering courtesies due a Governor's lady.

The girl had been rather persistent in trying to save the life of the rebel Hansford, but one could not blame her for that. Hansford had been a beau of hers. Lady Frances had tried to help Hansford, too, but it had been to no avail. Sir William flew into one of his tantrums. Pleading in vain for a soldier's death by shooting, Hansford was hanged.

Easter Walker thereupon had asked leave to depart from the Governor's household. When this was refused by His Excellency she said nothing. She had said nothing beyond the barest formalities to His Excellency since. Lady Frances preferred not to notice the fire behind Easter Walker's eyes after Hansford's execution. It was unpleasant, and the Governor's lady wished to overlook ugly things. There were too many rebellious spirits in the colony already, too much hate and disrespect, too much fear.

Among the comforts of Green Spring it was difficult to realize the hardships that of late they had experienced. Those ships! The food from dirty kegs, hard sailors' biscuit, rats and other vermin. For months the Governor's party had moved about like fugitives. The rebels had threatened to make Lady Frances wear canvas clothing, and they almost had succeeded. But all this was ended now. The archrebel, Bacon, was dead and the rebellion with him. Soon Jamestown would be rebuilt. Only Ingram's band remained.

Ingram's band. Berkeley was worried about Ingram there at West's Point. Ingram's best men were westerners. Ingram had horses and grain with which to feed them, grain he had stolen from the eastern plantations. He would be raiding all winter. Not even Green Spring would be safe against the rebel horsemen. A regiment of good troops could not take Ingram's fast-moving foresters.

Sir William sent Philip Ludwell to subdue Ingram. Ludwell's men refused to fight the borderers. Sir William sent many messengers upriver to parley with the stubborn lout, and Ingram would not see them. Ingram's women needed blankets, his men needed cloaks and trousers, for it was growing cold; but he was holding his lines. His men shouted bitterly at Berkeley's couriers: "Where is Carver? What did you do with Carver? Where is Hansford? Where is Bland?"

Lady Frances laid aside her knitting bag. She was a practical woman. William Berkeley had promised her great fortune, and they had almost attained it when this disaster had overwhelmed them. He might live five years longer and make a measure of recovery. He might if this blight on the whole colony could be repaired without delay.

Five years—surely no longer than that could the old man live.
Then if Green Spring were not burned meanwhile by Ingram or some
other border outlaw, and if the Indians could be held in check, she
again would be a widow; and this time free to marry a man of vigor,
Philip Ludwell. She had been wife to two Governors—Samuel
Stephens, one of Lord Culpeper's deputies who had not survived the
Carolina fevers, and Berkeley of Virginia. She might make Ludwell
also a royal governor.

It was time to end the senseless civil war. Berkeley once more was
in the saddle, and she must see that he was not thrown out of it again.
But the fighting and the raiding must end. Lady Frances went upstairs.

Easter was in her chamber. She rose respectfully as Frances Berkeley entered and laid aside the book she had been reading. The girl
had grown more mature since her return from the wilderness. There
was sadness about her lips and a new depth to the dark eyes which
shone in such lovely contrast to her corn-silk hair. She would be good
bait for any man.

"Have you seen the new ship, Easter?" Frances Berkeley asked. She
pointed out of the window toward the river. "It is the *Concord*."

Easter nodded.

"Captain Grantham is in command. He is coming here at noon to
pay his respects to the Governor. Isn't he your Captain Grantham,
Easter?"

"Yes, Lady Berkeley," said Easter. "He brought me back from
London."

"I remember that. And I have an idea, child. Isn't your young
man, Launcelot Clayborne, with Joseph Ingram?" She lowered her
voice.

Easter Walker listened incredulously to Frances Berkeley's plan.
At last, with a thoughtful glance at the distant ship, she agreed to
talk to Captain Grantham. Frances Berkeley, almost dancing with
delight, pulled the bell cord for a servant.

She asked the butler if Sir William was in his room, and then she
told him to announce her. After a few fluttery minutes at Easter
Walker's mirror and a merry wave of her hand to the girl, she went
down to the west-wing chamber.

Sir William had been resting on a long French chair, but he was on his feet as she entered. The war had thinned his frame and his face so that he seemed younger, but his hands trembled.

"Yes, Frances? You wanted me? I was on my way to you," said Berkeley.

"Sit down, sit down, my dear," she said, and with a quick little kiss she settled him again on his couch. Then after tucking the robe about his feet she chattered idly for a moment about the sauce that was to spice a dish of eels that would be served for supper. Sir William could not think of food. Many papers were on the floor beside his couch, dispatches from the garrisons on the York.

Frances idly touched them with the toe of her slipper. "News, my dear?"

"Good news," he said. "But——"

"What?"

"There is no way to capture Ingram's band."

"Ingram? Oh, yes. The bandit at West's Point."

Sir William gestured toward the papers beside him. "I have had word from Ludwell. He has made no progress against West's Point. His men will not fight Ingram's borderers, and Ingram will not move. Ingram has a strong position out of cannon range from the river, and his forces are surrounded by swamps and shallow water and deep woods. He has grain for his horses; so his cavalry column under Wakelett can raid far and wide. He has more grain than we have and more horses. You are right, my dear. Ingram is no rebel. He is a bandit."

She touched his knee and smiled. "Had you thought, William, that . . . well . . . bandits can be bought?"

The old man sat up suddenly. "Why, Frances!"

"Aye, dearest. Where is your logic? Bandits can be bought. As sure as sunset Ingram can be bought."

Sir William straightened his wig and moved to rise as if completely invigorated by his wife's idea.

She thrust him back. "Now wait. Let us think about this business," Frances said. "Let us consider a plan."

They talked for many minutes in low tones. She told him of the great merchant ship, the *Concord*, and of Captain Grantham. She reminded him of his lovely guest and hostage, Easter Walker, and of Lance Clayborne, Easter's lover, who was now with Ingram. Ingram had women and children in his camp. He needed woolens for the winter. There were woolens aboard the *Concord,* woolens brought to Virginia to be exchanged for skins and tobacco and lumber. Ingram had skins. He could not refuse to parley if the right persons reached him with a sound bargain.

"Leave it to me, my dear," she said. "Easter Walker can find her beau; then Lance Clayborne can talk to Ingram."

৺§ 12

JOSEPH INGRAM'S camp, while not a place of joy, was well administered. The Indian fighters were housed in half-buried huts of logs along the fringes of the forest overlooking the reaches of the York. Drills were held each dawn and sunset, and a careful watch was kept.

Ingram was content to play a waiting game. He enjoyed a number of advantages. His scouts had interrupted all trade flowing from the western forests. He had captured or impounded enough fur to pay a prince's ransom. With Wakelett's troopers he had raided all the grist mills of three counties. Powder and shot were scarce, but so was the Governor's ammunition. Ingram still had enough ammunition to keep hunters busy among the salt licks of the Rappahannock Valley.

The rebellion was at an end, but Ingram was capable of resisting the heaviest and most ingenious of attacks. Foot troops only—foot troops skilled in woodland fighting—could reach him, and the Governor had no such troops willing to fight.

Ingram's policy was simple. He resisted only to defend his life and the lives of Bacon's friends who had come to him for protection. Unlike Bacon, he made no speeches, wrote no laws and published not a single manifesto. But he held his captains strictly to the mark. Some eastern farmers urged that he defend all of the plantations which had declared for Bacon. This he refused to do, because he realized the limitations of his force.

"All who want protection must join me at West's Point," Ingram insisted. "I cannot guard the whole colony against our rebellious Governor."

Most of those whom Berkeley had hanged were Baconians who could or would not heed this invitation. Some valued their homes above their lives and in the white heat of the Governor's triumph lost them both.

One blustery day a pair of boatmen brought to Lance Clayborne's hut a shriveled little sailor. The man trembled with terror as well as with the cold, but when his eyes became accustomed to the semidarkness of the room, they brightened at what they saw. At that moment recognition also dawned on Lance.

"Nick Jump!" Lance cried. The young man rose from the table with a cry of pleasure and embraced the little man.

"The same, Your Honor, and—thank God!—these robbers here have brought me to you!"

Lance helped his guest remove spray-wetted outer garments; then he warmed him a mug of sack.

Jump explained in his shrill piping voice that he now was quartermaster of the *Concord*, a three-master, under Captain Grantham; that the *Concord* was not far off and aboard her was a . . . a lady.

Lance's heart began to pound. With scant patience, he wrung the seaman's icy hands.

"It's Mistress Easter Walker, sir," Nick Jump answered. "She says she knows you will come. She will vouch for your safety on the captain's ship, and so will I, sir."

Lance desired to go at once, but Ingram, when Lance asked leave, demurred.

"It is just another trap," Ingram growled. "You must not go."

Lance insisted that Nick Jump would never betray him, not even for a ton of Berkeley's gold. Nick stood by the fire, his old eyes wet with tears due to the cold, as he protested shrilly against this doubt of his integrity.

"Heed you, sir!" the little sailor said to Ingram. "Captain Grantham is no more a friend of Berkeley than of you. Two nights ago a man named Lawrence was aboard the *Concord*. Lawrence has a thousand pounds on his head, but my captain would not turn him over to the Governor's men."

"Lawrence?"

"Yes. He wanted Grantham to help you fight the Governor's party."

"Is Lawrence coming here?"

"I think not, sir. He said that he was going north into Maryland."

Ingram glared hard at the old sailor. "So your Captain Grantham then declared for Berkeley?"

"He declared for no one, sir. He said that Berkeley is as crazy as ever Bacon was and that he'd take sides with neither party. Furthermore, he said he'd end this senseless civil war so he could sell his woolens, salt, beef, biscuits, nails and copperware."

Ingram shook his head in doubt; so Lance explained that Easter Walker was aboard.

Ingram frowned. "You wish to take the Governor's lovely bait?"

Lance replied, "If she betrays me, I'd place no value on my life. But she will not betray me."

"I did not say she would, Lance. I said she may be the Governor's bait and this unknowingly. Without realizing it, she baited the trap for Hansford, I hear."

Ingram was obdurate, though he realized that if an honest overture for peace were due it would come through one of the idle merchant captains.

Lance argued desperately. At last, with many strict conditions, Ingram granted his consent.

Next day Lance Clayborne rode southwest while Nick Jump went back to Captain Grantham on the *Concord*. When Nick Jump returned aboard he took to Easter Walker a message for her ears alone. To Captain Grantham he reported that the rebels were suspicious and wanted further time.

The captain stamped his feet and blew on frost-reddened fingers. He would wait. There was nothing else to do. He would wait until the rebels froze to death.

Then Easter summoned Grantham. She wished to go ashore around the point. She pointed to the southern shore. She wished to see Ingram's adjutant, Captain Clayborne, at a cottage there. She must go with Nick Jump as her only companion. There was no other way. Ingram would not consent to other terms.

The captain roared a hundred nays. Easter would not give an inch. He declared that he'd be hanged as high as Haman and with justice if harm should come to her. He swore he would weigh anchor, drop back downriver and return her to the Governor's house. He said that Ingram was behaving like a treacherous scoundrel, and . . .

Easter smiled and tapped her toe on the cabin deck and looked wide-eyed through him and beyond him. "Don't be foolish, Tom Grantham," she said. "Why did you fetch me with you anyway? You knew that Ingram would be shy. He has refused to parley before. You brought me here to meet an emissary of the rebel leader. That I intend to do if Jump will row me round the point. You are here to stop a foolish war, and you cannot do it with your cannon. So lower the dory for me, please. I shall get an extra cloak, and if I should not return at once, don't be alarmed. Just wait and see what happens."

Grantham shivered as the dory left the ship; and he waited. There was no explaining these Virginia girls. They were as bold as any lion. They were as stubborn as a Turkish jennet.

Lance Clayborne waited too on the doorstep of Richard Potts's cabin. The fire was burning brightly, and the place was tightly chinked and warm; and this time it was stocked with Christian food. He saw the dory turn the point and held back a strong desire to swim out to meet it. Even so, he waded knee-deep in the icy water to receive her in his arms. He bore her, scolding mightily, up to the cottage and the fire.

There they talked about each other rather than the fate of Berkeley and Ingram—talked until Nick Jump was sound asleep—and then made love until they were warm and dizzy. They would ride to Parson Broome that very day, and he would marry them. They never would be apart again. To hell with politics! Then they remembered why they were there, and they talked awhile of politics.

She told him that Frances Berkeley was determined to have peace and had asked Sir William to commission Captain Grantham as negotiator. The grumbling Governor was willing to accept the terms which were agreed upon, Easter reported.

"What does Grantham wish me to tell Ingram?" Lance asked.

She smiled. "He wishes you to tell Ingram that the Governor will propose amnesty for all on Ingram's rolls; that all men including Ingram are to be paid as soldiers for the time they have been under arms. Further, he will suggest that those who wish to do so may enroll for long-term service against the Indians. All others can go home at once."

Lance was amazed. "Berkeley has agreed to that?" he asked.

"He has agreed," she said.

"Well, I'll be . . ." He looked at her. "Did you do this?"

"With Lady Berkeley's aid."

He stared in thoughtful wonder at her face. "I can forgive you now for living in Berkeley's household! Tell Grantham I am sure the West's Point garrison will take these terms. I must go at once to Ingram."

She clung to him. "At once?"

"I must tell Ingram."

"But must you go at once, my darling? Nick yonder is sound asleep and . . ."

⚜ 13

THEY were aroused by a rude knock on the door. "In the King's name!" said a sharp voice outside.

Lance turned to Easter Walker and asked, "Who is this man beyond the door?"

"I don't know," the girl answered. "Is it you, Captain Grantham?" she called out.

"In the King's name!" the shrill voice demanded again.

Lance drew his sword and unlatched the door.

An officer in a fur-lined cloak stood, sword in hand, at the door. It was not the shipmaster, Grantham. It was Colonel Edward Hill.

"I arrest you in His Majesty's name," Hill said. Touching then a paper in his belt, he added, "The warrant charges treason, Master Clayborne."

Lance lowered his point as though he had been shocked suddenly into exhaustion. He sat down heavily at the table in the center of the room. Hill's two fusiliers, weapons ready, watched him closely.

Colonel Hill now bowed to Easter Walker. "Your pardon, please, Mistress Walker——"

The girl interrupted. "You must listen to me, Colonel. You cannot arrest this man. He is an emissary from Joseph Ingram. I am here to parley with him."

Hill bowed to conceal a smirk of amusement. He had heard the gossip about Lance Clayborne and Easter Walker. He said, "You, Mistress Walker, say that you parley with this man in the Governor's name?"

This threw her into confusion. Actually her mission, a tentative parley, was not officially authorized by Berkeley. It was a scheme of Lady Berkeley. And Easter had been pledged to secrecy by the Governor's wife.

"Surely, my lady, you, a gentlewoman, could not have been empowered to make a compact with a band of rebels!"

Lance then spoke in despairing exasperation. "She tells the truth, sir. I am an informal emissary from Joseph Ingram, commander of the insurgent garrison at West's Point. Mistress Walker came to this meeting place from the ship *Concord* which is anchored in the deep water upstream from here. She was escorted here by the quartermaster of the *Concord*." He waved toward Nick Jump.

It was plain that Colonel Hill gave no credence whatever to Lance's statement.

"If you detain me, Colonel Hill," Lance added, "this unhappy insurrection may last another year or perhaps two years or longer." The young man, although he continued to show signs of exasperation, spoke in a conversational tone.

"Wait, Colonel!" Easter Walker said. "I'll send Nick Jump for Captain Grantham. He will confirm our story. You can see his ship from the beach. He——"

Nick Jump rose and went with Easter Walker to the door. He had recognized in Lance's eyes the flash of command.

Hill stood aside, his eyes on the prisoner. "I do not know your Captain Grantham, Master Clayborne, although I have heard of him," Hill said. "You must come with me. Perhaps the Governor will see you and hear your story."

Nick Jump stopped beyond the door and looked over his shoulder at Lance Clayborne.

"Go, Nick," Lance said to him. "Take Mistress Walker back to the ship. And heed this, Nick. Tell Captain Grantham to drop downstream and anchor off Pate's wharf in Gloucester tomorrow night. Do you understand? Pate's wharf in Gloucester."

Nick nodded and hurried after the girl.

Lance sighed and for a moment his apparently benumbed fingers relaxed on his sword hilt. But he never had been more alert.

Hill was foolish not to have had him pinioned immediately. The Governor's officer was off guard, and Hill had with him only two stupid troopers. Hill was puzzled. Lance Clayborne's delivery of a categorical command to Nick Jump for Captain Grantham made him wonder. Grantham had the largest merchant ship in the Virginia trade.

It was then that Lance, watching the uncertainty in Hill's eyes, exploded into action. He shouted, and in the same instant he upended the table. Both of Colonel Hill's fusiliers fired. Their balls harmlessly struck the oak table top. The room was filled with smoke. Lance hit one trooper with his hilt and stepped past him to the door as the man fell backward.

Lance was outside when he parried Colonel Hill's first astonished lunge. Lance could have killed the officer then, but he was content to hold him at the door.

By now Nick Jump and Easter Walker had launched their small boat. The little sailor was pulling out into the upstream tide.

"I must go, Colonel Hill," said Lance, parrying another furious lunge. "I must return to Ingram."

Hill was trying to hold him in play until his musketeers could reload. But one man was down from Lance's blow. The other, coughing in the smoke, had dropped his ramrod and was fumbling for it on the floor.

Lance moved in close to his adversary and circle-parried Hill's lunge in *quarte*. In the next instant Hill disengaged and tried a head cut. It was the opening Lance had been seeking. Leaning forward, he locked hilts and the colonel's sword was torn from his hand and flung a dozen yards. The young man then gave the Governor's dismayed officer a quick salute and left the scene.

He rode into West's Point that night on Colonel Hill's horse.

∽§ 14

LANCE said nothing to Ingram about his misadventure with Hill at the rendezvous, but he said much about Lady Berkeley's peace plan.

"You must go to Pate's," he said.

"And walk into a trap," Ingram growled.

"A trap? Wakelett is camped at Pate's and no land force could move him."

Ingram continued to grumble nevertheless. Gun or sword in hand Joseph Ingram feared no man. But in a parley he always felt at a loss.

Lance continued: "The terms they are proposing are almost incredible, sir. Your men not only will be pardoned, they will be paid for every day they were in arms against the Indians, for every day they were with Bacon here in the east and for every day they have drilled here at West's Point."[22]

Ingram's mouth flew open for a moment; then snapped shut again. "And my reward, no doubt, will be a rope?" he asked.

Lance smiled. "For you they propose a token punishment only. You will be disqualified from holding public office. Otherwise you will have complete immunity."

Ingram laughed. And at last he agreed to go to Pate's on the morrow.

Grantham, ashore at Pate's plantation, repeated the extraordinarily liberal terms, and Ingram accepted them.

Two days later Berkeley confirmed the peace pact in a written document.

∽§ 15

THE rebellion of 1676 ended prosperity in Virginia for that season and several more. But the Governor's unexpected concession to Ingram's stubborn band quieted the ferment of hate and uncertainty. Farmers tightened their belts and went back to work. The bordermen returned to their pillaged cabins and killed meat for the winter.

Lance was with Ingram at Pate's. He hoped to find Easter Walker there on Grantham's ship, but she had departed on one of the Governor's sloops to tell Lady Berkeley about the parley. So Lance crossed the York at Tyndalls Point, found a horse at the Courthouse and rode southward.

Wary because the peace pact had not yet gained official sanction, he came to Green Spring in the nighttime. Servants whom he knew told him that Mistress Walker had come and gone. Lance rode then to the Gull Cove settlement and roused Ed Walker from his bed. Easter had not come back to Gull Cove. Mud-spattered, almost asleep in the saddle, Lance reached Clayborne Castle before dawn. There was no news there.

He ate the first food he had had in fifteen hours and went to sleep. And despite his weariness he dreamed. First he dreamed of perils, and when Cato came in to build up the fire he started up and almost stabbed the old Negro. Then, deep in his feather bed again, he dreamed of more pleasant things. All the Indians had been tamed, and he was in his great brick house at Shoccoes attending a rich plantation. A wife was at a flax wheel by the fire, singing in time to the clicking treadle, her long fingers busy. A baby was in the trundle bed—a stout-limbed son. Peo was standing in the doorway, two wild turkeys over his shoulder. . . .

Lance awoke with a whoop which brought the servants hurriedly to the room. The sun was high. Cato brought a tray with maize cakes and milk, and he brought news of Easter Walker. She had gone up the James the night before in one of the Green Spring barges. Where? Lance knew.

Four hours later he rode into the stable yard of David Broome's glebe. She ran to meet him, and she fitted into his arms as though she had been there always.

"I knew you would come here very soon," she sighed. "This is the place appointed for our wedding, sweet. Do you remember?"

He could say nothing as he returned her kisses.

David Broome came out to rub down the lathered horse. His long face was happier than Lance had ever seen it. Ann Short trotted out and shooed them into the house lest they catch cold in the brisk December wind. Beside the great fire in the common room they caught their breaths.

"This place is near the border, Lance," said Easter. "I wanted you out here far from the Governor's men. No one knows I'm here. So no one will know you're here. See?"

"But I'm on Ingram's rolls," he explained. "I have full pardon under the agreement. We can honeymoon in one of Clayborne Castle's feather beds——"

Ann Short dropped her skillet at the hearth, and Easter turned pinker than the blaze. The parson and his wife insisted that they have a proper wedding in the Chickahominy log church.

This took irksome days of preparation. Meanwhile Sir Mathew returned from Chicheley's camp near Jamestown and had the east rooms at Clayborne Castle readied for the bride and groom.

Lance and Easter waited with scant patience, but they agreed on many necessary plans. Peo already was upriver with a team of Sir Mathew's skillful Welshmen. They would have their house by summertime.

The new home was theme for many a happy argument. Lance insisted that it be a fortress. Easter wanted more. She would have a kitchen separate from the living quarters and connected to the house by what she called a work porch. There must be fruit trees and a flower garden and a bower—and a colony of Gull Cove bees.

It was only when they spoke of politics that Lance was grim. The colony soon would be rid of Berkeley. The Governor had decided to go to London and render an accounting to King Charles.

"He will not return," predicted Easter Walker. "We'll have Chicheley for our Governor for a while. He is a peace-minded man. He will hang no one. Bacon was kind to him."

"Chicheley!" sniffed Lance.

Easter put a soft hand over his lips. "Now, Lance. You no longer are a rebel, remember?"

"I am afraid I always shall be a rebel, sweet," he answered.

⋙ 16

THE wedding was a quiet one, but Roger Kendall and other neighbors came, and so did Ingram and Gregory Wakelett, who had commanded Bacon's cavalry. There also were William Byrd and the Ludwells from Berkeley's late party and many ladies. The merriment was enhanced by the reunion of the recent enemies who formerly had been friends. The guests drank three tubs of Madeira punch and ate half a dozen hams; and for the first time dancing livened David Broome's parsonage.

Lance and Easter stole away in Sir Mathew's sloop in midafternoon. Cato was at the wheel of the sloop, and there was a fair wind to Clayborne Castle.

"We're wed!" cried Lance, gathering his bride within the folds of his great blue-velvet cloak.

"This should be an otter mantle," said Easter.

He chuckled. "You would be reminded of your passion for a naked forester?" he chided.

"You'll always be a forester," she said. "You'll never be a proper Englishman, Lance Clayborne."

He laughed. "And you?" he asked. "You're not English either, sweet."

"I am not European either, Lance. We are Virginians—Americans."

THE END